LOVE IN A FALLEN CITY
and Other Stories

EILEEN CHANG

Translated by
KAREN S. KINGSBURY
and
EILEEN CHANG

PENGUIN BOOKS

PENGUIN CLASSICS

Published by the Penguin Group
Penguin Books Ltd, 80 Strand, London WC2R ORL, England
Penguin Group (USA) Inc., 375 Hudson Street, New York, New York 10014, USA
Penguin Group (Canada), 90 Eglinton Avenue East, Suite 700, Toronto, Ontario, Canada M4P 2Y3
(a division of Pearson Penguin Canada Inc.)
Penguin Ireland, 25 St Stephen's Green, Dublin 2, Ireland (a division of Penguin Books Ltd)
Penguin Group (Australia), 250 Camberwell Road, Camberwell, Victoria 3124, Australia
(a division of Pearson Australia Group Pty Ltd)
Penguin Books India Pvt Ltd, 11 Community Centre, Panchsheel Park,
New Delhi – 110 017, India
Penguin Group (NZ), 67 Apollo Drive, Rosedale, North Shore 0632, New Zealand
(a division of Pearson New Zealand Ltd)
Penguin Books (South Africa) (Pty) Ltd, 24 Sturdee Avenue, Rosebank, Johannesburg 2196,
South Africa

Penguin Books Ltd, Registered Offices: 80 Strand, London WC2R ORL, England

www.penguin.com

This translation first published in the USA by New York Review 2007
Published in Penguin Modern Classics 2007

015

Printed and bound in Great Britain by Clays Ltd, Elcograf S.p.A.

978-0-141-18936-9

Translator's dedication

For C. T. Hsia

CONTENTS

CONTENTS

INTRODUCTION

EILEEN Chang was born in 1920 into a China wracked with instability. The new Republic of China, under the nationalist leadership of Sun Yat-sen, had just deposed the last Confucian dynasty in 1911. But while the Qing dynasty had ruled for nearly three hundred years (and Confucian-style governments for two millennia), the Republican government was to be deposed in less than forty years—pushed off the mainland, onto the island of Taiwan, by the Communist revolution. In 1920, however, the chief threat to the fledgling Republic came not from the Communists but from regional warlords who resisted the authority of the central government. Starting in the late 1930s, there was also the steady encroachment of the invading Japanese.

In its first years, the Chinese Republic was marked internally by a New Culture Movement that promoted modern (and more or less Western) forms of patriotism, science, and individual rights, including women's rights. A year and a half before Eileen Chang's birth, the movement had taken to the streets: in the pivotal May Fourth demonstrations, outraged students protested the Western powers' high-handed treatment of China at the close of WWI (Japan's occupation of Germany's colonial territories in China was sanctioned, and foreigners' imperial privileges in China were preserved). Then the protests widened into a broad critique of various domestic ills. Many intellectuals felt that China's military weakness was at root a cultural problem: effective reform would have to be directed at basic habits and thinking.

These huge changes were emancipatory for broad swathes of Chinese society, and excruciating to others. This can be seen from Eileen Chang's family story. Her family belonged to the late-Qing elite and had once been quite wealthy and powerful. Her paternal great-grandfather was Li Hongchang, the nineteenth-century statesman who had played a leading role in the Qing dynasty's drive to modernize, after the humiliating defeat it had suffered in the Opium Wars. For his descendants, Li was the equivalent of a famous and effective prime minister, not too far back in the family tree. Chang's father, however, was an entirely different sort of aristocrat: he smoked opium, kept a fawning concubine, and, when his temper flared, beat up the members of his own family, especially the women. This happened with fair regularity, since his wife and his sister, Eileen's maiden aunt, were daring and independent in the New Woman mode: they traveled to Europe and remained there for several years, leaving Eileen and her younger brother behind in the care of the family patriarch. Nonetheless, by the late 1920s, Chang's mother had rejoined her family and was living with them in a Western-style house in Shanghai. Her husband overdosed on morphine, and went to a hospital to recover his health, leaving her free to manage the household and supervise her children's education. "This was basically the only time in my life when I enjoyed the lifestyle of a Westernized young lady," Chang wrote in her memoirs.[1] There were lessons in art, music, and English. And when the girl was enrolled in school, her mother simply transcribed her English name into Chinese

1. In addition to the memoir-essays in *Liuyan* (*Written on Water*), (Taipei: Huangguan, 1968), which are the main source for details of Chang's early life, this introduction draws on memoirs by Hu Lancheng and Ke Ling, and also on critical studies by Fu Lei and C. T. Hsia. Readers interested in further analysis of Chang's place in modern Chinese culture may wish to consult Rey Chow's *Woman and Chinese Modernity* (University of Minnesota Press, 1991) and Leo Ou-fan Lee's *Shanghai Modern* (Harvard University Press, 1999).

—yielding a Chinese given name with a slightly foreign and (according to the writer herself) pleasantly awkward feel. But after her father returned from his hospital stay, the conflicts between the self-possessed, Westward-leaning mother and the self-destructive, reactionary father proved irreconcilable: they divorced in 1930.

Chang's family world was now ostensibly split in two—father's dark, smoky lair; mother's bright, modern apartment—but for a sensitive teenager this was not a simple split. Her father's nostalgic "afternoon" world was subtly appealing, while her mother's brisk coolness could be altogether alienating. Still, at the age of eighteen, Chang fled her father's house and sought refuge with her mother. She was making her escape after a six-month ordeal: she'd been brutally beaten by her father for impertinent behavior toward her stepmother (who indulged her father's habits), then confined to her room for half a year. Chang contracted dysentery, and her father denied her medical treatment. In the throes of her illness, she suffered lurid hallucinations.

In 1939, some eighteen months after she'd escaped from her father's house, Chang enrolled in the University of Hong Kong as a student of English literature. She had hoped to go to London, but wartime conditions made that impossible. War broke in on her studies anyway: the Japanese invaded Hong Kong in December 1941, at the same time that they attacked Pearl Harbor, and the university was shut down before she could complete her degree. Chang returned to Shanghai, to the bright little apartment in which her aunt and mother lived. She'd been writing for some years, for school publications and the like; now she started publishing for pay in Shanghai's newspapers and magazines, first in English and then, quite spectacularly, in Chinese. Shanghai then—as now—was the main cultural competitor to Beijing, and a huge gateway for new, imported ideas, especially in the realm of popular and middle-class entertainment. During the Japanese occupation, however, the more intellectually ambitious writers either left the city or simply refrained from publication. Chang stepped into that silence like a diva entering the limelight. The public response was passionate —fulsomely so, the sober critic Fu Lei complained, before going on to write a lengthy and careful consideration of all Chang's work to date, clearly the response of one serious writer to another. She had already published a dozen stories in as many months, five of them ninety-page novellas, along with a steady stream of short, scintillating essays. The stories were eventually collected in *Romances* (1944; revised edition in 1947) and the essays in *Written on Water* (1945).

Hu Lancheng, another influential man of letters, was so impressed by Chang's work (especially "Sealed Off," her modernist slice-of-life anti-romance) that he looked her up, swept her off her feet, and became her husband. It was a secret marriage, however, witnessed only by two friends, because Hu Lancheng had served in the puppet government installed by the Japanese, and the political situation was very delicate. After the Japanese were defeated, Hu Lancheng was indeed branded as a traitor, and Chang too was viewed with suspicion, even though their pact had dissolved in less than three years due to his sexual and emotional infidelities.

Hu Lancheng aside, Chang's response to the outburst of public adulation was one of cool bemusement. She was a consummate performer, appearing in startling new outfits that she designed herself, alternately cajoling and flattering her readers, and turning out page after page of hauntingly precise, achingly beautiful fiction. She offered wry, disturbing insights into various moral and mental conundrums, insights that were partly based on Freudian ideas, but probably were more deeply influenced by Chinese habits of thinking about human motives and manners—a subject about which she learned much from traditional drama and fiction. That grounding in older art was an essential part of her stylistic brilliance: Chang's great achievement was to meld the language and conventions of Qing-dynasty vernacular fiction with the ironic, worldly stance of Edwardian British writers (there are several direct nods to H. G. Wells, and many echoes of Asian travelers like Somerset Maugham and Stella Benson), then project her stories by means of a visual imagination that had absorbed many scenes and techniques from the Hollywood films of her day. The result was a rich, flexible, marvelously apt medium for exploring middle-class mentalities, both traditional and contemporary, in modern Shanghai. Chang's worldly form of the sublime was achieved, we may say, by viewing her father's world from her mother's perspective, but with an artist's compassionate detachment.

But Chang's moment of fame was brief. In Japanese-occupied Shanghai, she had stayed out of trouble with the authorities, and gained success with the public, by focusing on current manners and mores, avoiding any mention of the war or politics. Surrounded by danger—she knew at least one editor who was detained in an infamous prison, until Hu Lancheng intervened and obtained his release—she masqueraded as a light, unserious writer. Following the Japanese defeat, this stance made her vulnerable, especially to criticism from the socialist left. In any case, given Chang's family background, it is unlikely that any stance of hers could have rendered her innocuous in the Communist Party's eyes. She was too clearly a product of the privileged elite, even if now she had no financial resources beyond her meager earnings as a writer. The pressures in Shanghai grew, and in 1952, Chang fled to Hong Kong, where eventually she accepted a job as a translator and fiction writer for the United States Information Service. Propaganda was not her preferred form of literature, but she managed to write a pair of nuanced and complex "anti-Communist" novels: *The Rice Sprout Song* and *Naked Earth*. In 1955, she was awarded entry into the United States.

Chang was thirty-two when she left her beloved Shanghai for the last time. For the following three decades, she was a banned writer in her homeland, though still much loved by loyal readers in Hong Kong, Taiwan, and the overseas Chinese communities. She tried, with little success, to break into the English-language fiction market, most notably with *The Rouge of the North*, a reworked version of her celebrated novella "The Golden Cangue." But the cultural and linguistic gaps were too wide to cross. As C. T. Hsia, one of her earliest and most perceptive advocates, remarked (in *A History of Modern Chinese Fiction*), mid-century American readers' views of China were greatly influenced by writers like Pearl S. Buck, which left them unprepared for Chang's melancholy incisiveness and insider's perspective.

Shortly after arriving in the United States, Chang met and married a minor American playwright and novelist, Ferdinand Reyher, and the two of them traveled from one temporary residence to another. Reyher died in 1967, and over the next three decades Chang retreated into deepening seclusion, but never stopped writing. Working mostly through her Taiwan publisher, she kept turning out essays, translations, film scripts, and, less frequently, new fiction.

During the last years of her life, while Chang was shunning visitors and even old friends, a "Chang craze" was starting to build not just in Taiwan and Hong Kong but in the liberalizing People's Republic of China, too. The news of her death—alone in a scantily furnished Los Angeles apartment, in September of 1995—was a major media event, and prompted a flood of reappraisals, adaptations, and biographical speculations. It was as if Chinese readers were trying to make up for the decades of neglect that Chang had suffered since the 1940s. The "craze" continues throughout the Chinese-speaking world, and Eileen Chang's place in the pantheon of modern writers is now firmly assured. If American readers are just now beginning to hear of this literary star who lived half of her life in deep obscurity, we can easily attribute this fact to Chang's own shyness, and to the political circumstances of her career.

———

The four novellas that form the core of this collection are the most sustained and widely acclaimed efforts in Chang's first volume of fiction, *Chuanqi*. (I've followed the usual translation, "Romances," but the title could easily be rendered instead as "Legends," very much in the sense of "urban legends"). Many readers feel this is the point at which Chang's talent shone most brightly; it is at any rate the period for which she has become a cultural icon. The choice of shorter works was not so simple, as there are many of great interest. In the end I chose two, "Jasmine Tea" and "Sealed Off," that seem to me to make transitions between, and serve as complements to, the novellas. Two other important stories, "Traces of Love" and "Steamed Osamanthus Flower," could have come after "Red Rose, White Rose," both logically and chronologically, but fortunately they have already been published in *Traces of Love and Other Stories*, edited by Eva Hung.

Dr. Hung was the first editor of my Chang translations during her tenure as editor of *Renditions*, the Chinese University of Hong Kong's translation magazine. I am grateful for her early guidance through that infinite number of small difficulties that are the art and essence of translation, and hope that she will approve of the changes I have made to "Love in a Fallen City" since she first published it. Fortunately—and thanks to C. T. Hsia—we have here Chang's own fine translation of "The Golden Cangue" to help us hear how the author herself thought it should appear in English. If the reader finds that the timbre of that story is different from that in my translations, in ways that go beyond dialect difference (British or Hong Kong versus

American English), this probably is because I've pushed hard at commonplace idioms and metaphors, trying to find lively equivalents instead of letting them dissolve unobtrusively, as could well happen in a skilled Chinese reader's mind. My excuse for this is that my Taiwanese students have often told me that Chang's Chinese is not easy for them to understand—they belong, after all, to the full-fledged multimedia age, while Chang grew up in a world that was still deeply focused on books and writing. It seems to me that if Chang is tantalizing but tough for young Chinese readers today, a translator ought to err on the side of "over-translation," even though Chang herself (perhaps because translation was not her favorite mode of writing) rendered "The Golden Cangue" in fairly plain, understated English.

Another translator whose work has been of great use to me is Carolyn Thompson Brown; her strong, spare version of "Red Rose, White Rose" (which she entitled "Red Rose and White Rose") can be found in her American University dissertation on the novella. Still, my deepest debts are to the many readers whose mindful attention to early drafts helped me improve, step by tiny step: Deirdre Sabina Knight, Kailin Wu, Tam Pak Shan, Joy Chen, Shuchin Lin, Sarah Dettwiler, an anonymous reviewer, and, most of all, Edwin Frank. To none of them, of course, should the remaining errors and infelicities be attributed.

Beyond and between all the details that these readers and I have wrestled with, these translations are but one reader's attempt to articulate at least some part of the psychological and sensory experience that Eileen Chang's fiction has provoked in her mind and, judging from various sources, those of many Chinese readers. Thus, these translations grow out of the central conviction that Chang's melding of Qing and Edwardian, patriarchal and feminist, past and present offers her readers a nuanced, historicized view of their own cultural moment, in all its singularity and repetitiveness. Like the moon and the mirrors which figure so prominently in her work, Chang's stories themselves are a succession of echoes, or the infinite series produced by a three-way mirror, recalling and restoring an ancient, anterior sense of selfhood in the midst of modernist, wartime rupture and dislocation. Even if our times are different now (and I'm not sure that they are), a vision like this is both unsettling and satisfying.

—KAREN S. KINGSBURY

PREFACE TO THE
SECOND PRINTING OF *ROMANCES*

WHEN MY book comes out—I'd long said to myself—I'll go around to all the bookstalls just to have a look. I want that turquoise book-cover that I like so much to open up, in every bookstall, a small window of midnight blue; in that window, people might see the moon, or watch some bit of noisy human activity. I want to ask the bookseller, feigning nonchalance: "So, how are sales? The price is way too high! At such a price, are there really any buyers?"

Ah, indeed—get your fame early in the game! Get it late, and the pleasure's lost its punch. That first time, when two of my compositions got published in the school magazine, I was elated. I read them again and again, beginning to end, each time as if I'd never before seen them. It's not easy now for me to get so excited. I have to hurry: faster, faster, or it'll be too late!

Even if I could wait, our whole era is being pushed onward, is breaking apart already, with greater destruction still coming. Our entire civilization—with all its magnificence, and its insignificance—will someday belong to the past. If the word I use most often is "desolate," it's because I feel, in the back of my mind, this staggering threat.

Here in Shanghai, "Hop-Hop" folk opera is considered quite passé, and so, even though I'd long wanted to see a show, I had trouble finding the right person to ask along. Putting the word out, letting others know I was eager to see this kind of rickety-rackety, low-class stuff, was a bit embarrassing. But recently I found a lady, none of whose relatives would brave the summer heat with her to see Zhu Baoxia, and the two of us went off together.

When the *huqin* player scraped bow on string, the sound was strangely painful: it was a sky-high tune, urgent like the wind, sibilant and sliding. The world was dark and ominous, the universe wide and wild. The wind went screeching through the desert passes, nowhere to stop, nowhere to stay: emptiness itself is chasing me, it wailed. A man in a blue gown beat the rhythm out with strong blows of a big bamboo stick: *kua! kua! kua!* He came out to stage-front, close to the audience, and pushed the singer hard. *Kua! ke-jia! ke-jia!*—the pitiless pounding went on and on.

I was in the second row, jolted till my head was spinning, my eyes glazed over. Bit by bit, the contents of my brain were pounded out, till only the most primitive things remained. In those cold caves of the northwest, people have to live very simply, and even then it's not easy to get by.

Back onstage, human voices struggled hoarsely with the rattle's metallic clatter and the *huqin's* astringent tune. Third Daughter Li was played by a northern girl with a bare, yellow face; no powder, just two long eyebrows painted black. She was headed toward the well, buckets on her shoulder-pole, when the bitter complaint rose up inside her. "Cannot be compared to Third Sister Wang, but even so..." Eyes fixed on the ground, she belted out each word and phrase.

Just as she was drawing water, "astride his steed, a brave young general appeared." It was her son, but, meeting by chance, they didn't recognize each other. Eventually, the young general began to wonder if this "poor peasant" might be his mother, so he asked about her family. "What was your father's name? Who was your mother? Your brother?" She answered all of his questions, stretching "my" into "maah," and knew all the details of even her sister-in-law's life history: Maah brother's wife's from the Zhang family..."

The outside world, for those who live in the yellow-earth caves, is a perpetual dusk of flying sand and rolling rock. Existence, shrunk by the cold, comes down to this: who your father is, who your mother is, your brother, his wife. There isn't much to remember, so memory holds on hard.

Before the main performance, there was a "murdered-her-own-husband" farce. Two great swathes of rouge had been painted down the wanton woman's face. Even the flanks of her nose were rouged, leaving only a thin center-line of nose to be powdered white. This made a high, thin, Grecian-style nose, which did not sit well on a big, broad face; the glistening eyes seemed to grow one to a side, close to the ears, like an animal's. She also had gold teeth, a pair of greasy braids that hung down to her knees, and fat, round, dusky yellow forearms that stuck out from pink jacket-sleeves.

When the ghost of her wronged husband came to lodge his complaint, an official in a sedan-chair was told that "a dust devil is blocking our path." "Male or female?" the official asked. The bailiff took a careful look. "Male." The official gave the order to "follow that dust devil, and make no mistake." They followed the ghost to a fresh grave-site, then seized the young widow they found there. The widow knelt and explained how her husband, one night, suddenly dropped dead. She phrased it a hundred ways, but the official still didn't get it. "Your lordship!" she bellowed, "Where is there a stove-bed with no fire burning? Where is there a chimney-flue with no smoke rising?" The audience cheered wildly.

In the savage wilderness, the woman who comes to power is not, as most people imagine, a wild rose with big, black, burning eyes, stronger than a man, whip in hand, ready to strike at any moment. That's just a fantasy made up by city-folk in need of new stimulation. In the wilderness that is coming, among the shards and rubble, only the painted-lady type from "Hop-Hop" opera, this kind of woman, can carry on with simple ease. Her home is everywhere, in any era, any society.

So I feel an aching sadness. I often think about all of this, perhaps because of H. G. Wells's predictions. It all used to seem far away, and now it seems not far at all. But it is autumn still, water-clear and mirror-bright: I ought be happy.

September 1944

ALOESWOOD INCENSE
The First Brazier

GO AND fetch, will you please, a copper incense brazier, a family heirloom gorgeously encrusted now with moldy green, and light in it some pungent chips of aloeswood. Listen while I tell a Hong Kong tale, from before the war. When your incense has burned out, my story too will be over.

The story starts with Ge Weilong, a very ordinary Shanghai girl, standing on the veranda of a hillside mansion and gazing vacantly at the garden. Although Weilong had lived in Hong Kong for two years now, she was still unfamiliar with this wealthy residential district in the Hong Kong hills: this was her first visit to her aunt's house. The garden itself was little more than a rectangular grass lawn, framed by a low wall of white, swastika-shaped blocks, beyond which lay a stretch of rough hillside. This garden was like a gold-lacquered serving tray lifted high amid the wild hills: one row of carefully pruned evergreens; two beds of fine, well-spaced English roses—the whole arrangement severely perfect, not a hair out of place, as if the tray had been deftly adorned with a lavish painting in the fine-line style. In one corner of the lawn, a small azalea was in flower, its pink petals, touched with yellow, a bright shrimp-pink.

Still, inside that wall, spring was only puttering about. When it flashed into flame, it could leap out, scorching everything. Already, beyond the wall, a roar of wild azaleas was blooming across the hill, the fiery red stomping through brittle grass, blazing down the mountainside.

On the far side of the azaleas lay the deep blue sea, with big white boats bobbing in it.

But these glaring color clashes were not the only reason why the viewer felt such a dizzying sense of unreality. There were contrasts everywhere: all kinds of discordant settings and jumbled periods had been jammed together, making a strange, illusory domain.

The white house in the dip of the hills was smooth and streamlined—geometric like an ultramodern movie theater. The roof, however, was covered with the traditional glazed tiles of emerald green. The windowpanes were also green, their chicken-fat yellow frames trimmed with red; the window grates, with their fancy ironwork, had been sprayed the same chicken-fat yellow. A wide, red brick veranda circled the house, with monumental white stone columns that were nearly thirty feet tall—this went back to the American Old South.

From the veranda, glass doors opened onto a living room. The furniture and the arrangement were basically Western, touched up with some unexceptionable Chinese bric-a-brac. An ivory bodhisattva stood on the mantel of the fireplace, along with snuff bottles made of emerald-green jade; a small screen with a bamboo motif curved around the sofa. These Oriental touches had been put there, it was clear, for the benefit of foreigners. The English come from so far to see China—one has to give them something of China to see. But this was China as Westerners imagine it: exquisite, illogical, very entertaining.

Weilong glanced at her reflection in the glass doors—she too was a touch of typically colonial Oriental color. She wore the special uniform of Nanying Secondary School: a dark blue starched cotton tunic that reached to her knees, over narrow trousers, all in the late Qing style. Decking out coeds in the manner of Boxer-era courtesans—that was only one of the ways that the Hong Kong of the day tried to please European and American tourists. But Weilong, like any girl, sought to be stylish, and she wore a small knitted vest on top of the tunic. Under that little vest, the tunic stretched down a long way— the effect, in the end, was unclassifiable.

Facing the glass doors, Weilong straightened her collar and smoothed her hair. She had a small, round face, bland but pretty, a "powder-puff face" that would be considered old-fashioned nowadays. Her eyes were long and lovely; the fine creases over the lids swept out almost to her hairline. Her nose was delicate and thin, her little mouth plump and round. Her face may have been somewhat lacking in expression, but vacuousness of that sort does impart the gentle sincerity that one associates with Old China. Once she'd been quite dissatisfied with her white skin; she'd wanted a tan, to match the new ideal of healthy beauty. But when she got to Hong Kong she found that the Cantonese beauties generally had olive complexions. Scarcity pushes value up: at Nanying Secondary, her white skin had earned her an untold number of admirers. One time some-body made a wisecrack, saying that if girls from Canton and Hunan, with their deep-set eyes and high cheeks, were sweet-and-sour pork bones, then Shanghai girls were flour-dipped pork dim sum—an "ill-bred remark" that popped into her mind just as she was appraising her looks. Weilong frowned, turned around, and leaned back against the glass door.

Her aunt's housemaids seemed full of mischief—the sweet-and-sour type. They were jaunty, clopping back and forth on the veranda in wooden clogs. Just then, one of them called out sweetly: "Glance, who's that in the living room?"

"I think it's someone from Young Mistress's family."

Judging from her voice, Glance was the one who'd poured tea for Weilong—a long face and a water-snake waist, and though she wore a braid down her back like the others, her bangs fell loosely forward. Something was bothering Weilong. Who was this "Young Mistress"? Weilong had never heard anything about her aunt having a son, so how could there be a daughter-in-law? Could it be Aunt Liang herself? Weilong's father had had a terrible row with his sister when she became third concubine to Liang Liteng, a Cantonese tycoon; ever since then, the family had severed relations with Aunt Liang. All that had happened before Weilong was born, but she knew that her aunt was two years older than her father, and had to be over fifty now. How could she still be a "Young Mistress"? Could this maid be a longtime retainer who'd served her aunt for many years, and had grown used to calling her that? Weilong was mulling this over, when she heard Glance's voice again.

"It's not often that our Young Mistress gets up so early!"

"It's Thirteenth Young Master from the Qiao family, that little devil, said he'd take her to Tsim Sha Tsui for a swim!"

Glance let out a little gasp. "In that case, I don't know when she'll be back."

"Naturally. After they've gone swimming they'll go to the Lido Hotel for dinner, then go dancing. This morning, before daybreak, she had me pack up evening wear and dress shoes to change into later."

Glance tittered. "That Qiao fellow! He's enough to make a person sick! I thought Young Mistress had given up on him. How can someone as smart as she is still be in his grip?"

"Hush! Hush!" the other one said. "Don't prattle on, there's someone inside."

"Tell her to go," Glance said. "Asking people to wait around for nothing isn't very nice."

"Who cares? You said she's a relative of Young Mistress, so she's probably come for a handout. We can't offer that much hospitality!"

Glance was silent for quite some time. Then, in an undertone, she said, "Better send her off. The Russian piano tuner is coming soon."

As soon as she heard this, the other girl started to laugh. "Oh," she said, clapping her hands, "you want to commandeer this room so that you and that Alexander Alexandrei can fool around! Here I was wondering why you were suddenly so pious and good, not wanting our guest to wait around for nothing. *Now* I know why!"

Glance chased after the other girl and struck her; a scuffle broke out. "Gentlemen use words, only scoundrels use their fists!" the other girl shrieked.

"True enough," Glance yelled back, "but only a hussy kicks! Hussy! Tarty toes! You do have tarty toes!"

Just then, a darling little wooden clog, with a painted spray of golden plum blossoms on a bright red background, skimmed through the air and smacked Weilong right in the knee; she had to bend over and rub the spot, it hurt so much. When she looked up, a winsome little dark-skinned maid had come bouncing into the room, knees and elbows lifted high; the girl skipped up to the clog, slipped it on, then turned and strode away, entirely ignoring Weilong.

Weilong couldn't help but be angry. Then she remembered "The King of Hell is a gentleman, but the little devils are pests" and "When you go under another's roof, how can you avoid bowing?" That was the rub, when you had a favor to ask. Still, judging from the looks of things, there wasn't much hope today—why hang around, inviting this sort of treatment? But, she thought, here I've climbed all the way up this mountain, after telling a lie so I could get out of school—how can I get another day off tomorrow? Besides, who knows if my aunt will be home tomorrow. And I can't simply phone up and make an appointment—not for something like this!

She hesitated. May as well leave, she decided at last. Going through the glass doors, she found Glance leaning sideways against a stone column, the bottoms of her trousers rolled up so she could pound on her calf with her fist; there was still a red mark where she'd been kicked. The dark-skinned girl peeked out from the end of the veranda, then ran off quickly.

"Glint, don't run away!" Glance called out. "I'm going to pay you back!"

Glint laughed from a distance. "What makes you think I have time to tangle with you? You want to slap and kick, well, wait till that Russian fellow comes—he'll be happy to slap and kick with you!"

Glance muttered under her breath, calling Glint a slippery-tongued scamp, but still she had to laugh. Then she looked around and saw Weilong. "You're not leaving, are you?" she asked.

Weilong smiled and nodded. "I have to go now, I'll come again another time. Could you see me to the gate?"

They cut across the lawn, taking a shortcut to a little green-painted iron gate. In Hong Kong, to escape the damp, rich people build their houses high off the ground, on stone foundations of some thirty or forty feet; from the gate, a winding flight of steps led down to the road. Glance was just opening the latch when a car horn sounded from below. Glint popped out of nowhere. Elbowing her way past Glance and Weilong, she clattered down the stairs, shouting all the while, "Young Mistress is back! Young Mistress is back!"

Glance shrugged and smirked. "Such a little thing, is it really worth flinging yourself around, just to get first prize? We're all mere servants, but I can't get used to the way some people degrade themselves!" She turned and went back in.

Weilong was left alone at the iron gate, staring blankly. Glint's crazy haste had jangled her nerves. The car door opened and a small, slender woman in Western clothes stepped out. She was dressed all in black, with a green veil hanging from her black straw hat. Pinned to the veil, an emerald spider the size of a fingernail flashed in the sunlight and climbed up her cheek. When it gleamed it looked like a trembling teardrop that was just about to fall; when it darkened it looked like a green mole. The veil, several feet long, was wrapped around her shoulders like a scarf, and it floated and fluttered about her. The driver couldn't be seen clearly, but he seemed to be a young man. He leaned his head out to say good-bye, but the woman stiffened her neck and headed up the stairs.

Glint had already rushed in with a greeting, her face wreathed in smiles: "Won't Thirteenth Master Qiao come up to have a glass of beer?"

"Who has time to waste on his little games?"

Hearing this, Glint quickly put her smiles away. She took the woman's small rattan suitcase. "You must be tired!" she said softly. "Coming back so early!"

The woman turned and found that the car was leaving. She spat hard at the ground. "Go on then, and don't come back! We're finished!"

Realizing that her mistress was in a fury, Glint kept quiet now. The woman glared at her, consumed by her own thoughts, not deigning to disclose her complaint to the girl. Then, with a bitter snort, she snapped out of it. "Listen to this, Glint. He begs me to go to the beach early in the morning—a pretext, as it turns out. He wants a date with Mary Zhao, but those Cantonese are straitlaced and he thought her father wouldn't allow it. If someone older were there to keep an eye on things then the Zhao family's precious jewel would be protected by a safety charm. That was his little scheme—how very kind of him to let me in on it too!"

Glint stamped and sighed, cursing Qiao.

The woman paid no attention. She paused to catch her breath before continuing: "This certainly isn't the first time I've taken the lid off somebody's little secret. So, Mr. Qiao, you don't explain what's going on, you think you can make a fool of me. Well, I've seen plenty of men, and anyone who's got his eye on me can't be eyeing someone else too. Go ahead, sing that love scene from the opera about lovers meeting secretly in the rear garden—but I'm not playing the nurse! When I go to a banquet, I'm not the second-class guest! Qiao, you little half-breed, your father may have bootlicked till the British gave him a garter, but your mother's a Portuguese whore from who knows where, a poker-chip girl from the Macao casinos. You monkey-chops, brazen as the sky is wide, gamboling about like a devil, and right in my face!" She yanked the veil around behind her hat and headed up the stairs, ticking off his offenses as she went.

Now Weilong could see her face. She really was an older woman. There was a green-blue tinge to her white skin, and she wore purple-black lipstick, the "mulberry red" that was the latest thing from Paris. Weilong recognized those deceptively drowsy eyes; in her father's photo album, there was a family portrait, yellow with age, that showed those very eyes. A beauty may age, but her eyes do not. Weilong grew flustered: she felt her cheeks getting hot. She heard Glint, who was still following her aunt, say, "Qiao is quite a rascal, but he can't pull one over on you. You didn't really go with him to pick up Miss Zhao, did you?"

At this, the woman's eyebrows flew upward, and her face quivered. "Do you actually think I'm such an idiot? When he raised the idea, there in the car, I said, 'Fine, let's go pick her up, but three's a crowd, so you'd better get someone else to come along too.' He said fine, but he wanted to pick up Miss Zhao first, and then invite another person—of course, he didn't want Mr. Zhao seeing two couples and getting suspicious. So I said, 'How about no fuss at all, just simple, like leading a goat: we can invite Mr. Zhao, won't that be nice? I can't swim, and he can't either, so we'll lie on the sand and sunbathe side by side.' He was quiet for a long time, but at last he said, 'Forget it! It'll be simpler if the two of us go on our own.' 'Oh,' I said, 'what's the matter?' He just drove on, not saying a word. I waited till we were almost to Tsim Sha Tsui, and then said I felt faint in the heat. He was riled up, but I made him drive me all the way back. He was worn out, covered with sweat, but when he wanted to stop for a soda, I wouldn't let him—I did feel a bit better then!"

"Terrific!" said Glint, clapping her hands. "Young Mistress fixed him, that's for sure! There's only one thing—I assume he's no longer invited to tomorrow's party, but should we invite someone else in his place? Awaiting your orders, ma'am."

Cocking her head to one side, Aunt Liang thought it over. "Who to invite? Those British officers only come for the drinks—they haven't got any self-control, and just get soused. Oh, that's right! Help me remember—that army lieutenant, he shouldn't be let in again. He got drunk and chased Glance all over. No manners at all!"

Glint agreed, smiling.

"Has Sir Cheng Qiao telephoned?"

Glint shook her head. "I can't understand it. Before, when Master was still with us, the Qiao men, young and old, would phone up every day, full of schemes and ideas, causing all sorts of trouble for Young Mistress and scaring the servants to death—we were so afraid that Master would find out. But now that Young Mistress's friends can come in through the front door, they're suddenly too high and mighty!"

"What's so hard to understand? It's just their thievish way! It has to be sneaky, or else it's no fun!"

"When Young Mistress gets married again, and to the right man, they'll feel it, that's for sure!"

"Bah! Talking foolishness again. Let me tell you—" But then she stopped, having reached the top of the stairs and found, at the iron gate, an unknown face.

"Aunt," said Weilong, stepping forward bravely.

Madame Liang thrust her chin out and squinted at Weilong.

"Aunt," Weilong explained, "I'm the daughter of Ge Yukun."

"Is Ge Yukun dead?" her aunt snapped.

"My father, I'm happy to say, is quite well."

"Does he know that you have come to see me?"

Weilong didn't answer right away.

"Please leave at once," said Madame Liang. "If he hears of this, he'll be very upset! This is no place for you, you'll only sully your good name!"

Weilong responded as pleasantly as she could. "Of course Aunt is angry—here we've been in Hong Kong a long time, and haven't come to pay our respects. It's all our fault!"

"Oh, so you've come today just to pay your respects! I guess I'm too suspicious, thinking that no one climbs a jeweled staircase without reason, and that there must be something you want from me. As I've said before, when Ge Yukun reaches his end, I'll be good and buy him a coffin. But while he's still alive, he's not getting a penny!"

Madame Liang thrust deep and hard. Weilong was too soft and young, it was too much for her. She'd put on a big, broad smile; now the smile was frozen stiff.

Glint couldn't bear seeing Weilong paralyzed with embarrassment. "She's not said anything yet—why does Young Mistress think she's here to borrow money? Of course, as the old saying goes, 'Bit by a snake, scared by a rope, three years later.' Let me explain, Miss Ge. Here in this house we get distant relatives and former neighbors streaming in all year round, asking for so many favors that Young Mistress is now thoroughly alarmed. Don't be angry, Miss. You've come a long way to see your aunt—you two should have a nice chat before you go. Come inside and sit for a while. Let our Young Mistress rest up a bit. I'll call you when she feels better."

"So here you are, slave, making polite excuses!" Madame said coolly. "Stop meddling! Must be quite some tip you got from her!"

"What!" Glint protested. "As if I'd never seen money before! Judging from the looks of this young lady, she's not a big spender—I doubt she's got enough to buy me!"

Glint's intercession had been well-intentioned, but this last sentiment was hard for Weilong to take. Still wearing her forced smile, she flushed and then grew pale. Her feelings were in a tumult.

Leaning over, Glint whispered in Madame Liang's ear: "Young Mistress, you always forget. Dr. Feng at the beauty salon told you not to frown; you'll get wrinkles around your eyes."

When Madame Liang heard this, she smoothed her face into a pleasant expression.

"Standing in the hot sun like this," Glint went on, "you'll get freckles if you don't watch out!" With that, she talked Madame Liang into entering the house.

Weilong stood dazed and alone in the sun. Her cheeks were burning, but the two tears that rolled down her face were cold, chilling her to the bone. Wiping her face with the back of her hand, she walked slowly, unwillingly, through the passageway and into the living room, where she sat down. "Aunt doesn't have a very good reputation," she said to herself. "I always thought it was because people will gossip maliciously about a widow, especially since Liang Liteng was one of Hong Kong's wealthiest men and he left Aunt, who was his favorite, a lot of money, not to mention the property. Of course there would be plenty of people too jealous to say anything good about her. But now it looks as if all their talk is true! Here I am wading into muddy waters, and for a girl there's no way to get clean again, not even if she throws herself into the Yellow River. I should give up, and try to think of something else. But I've put up with so much already—and now it's all for nothing!" When she thought back over everything, she felt heartsick again.

The Ges were only a middle-class family, but Weilong had always been pampered—she'd never faced such a fierce attack before. Naturally she was quite hurt. From another room, she could just make out the sound of a loud argument going on, then the slam of a door, and someone sobbing bitterly. A junior maid came into the living room to clear away the empty teacup; another girl in evident distress followed behind. She tugged at the first girl's sleeve. "Who made Young Mistress so angry?" she asked.

"Glance is the one who's in trouble," said the other, with a smile. "Why are *you* so upset?"

"How did it get found out?"

"I'm not sure," the first girl said. "She invited Sir Cheng Qiao but he didn't accept. Then she found out that Glance has gone out several times to see him. Of course he'd rather have her go out to him—that way, his time's not wasted on pointless visits here."

Although they spoke in undertones, Weilong caught about half of it. The girls cleared the tea things and went out.

Looking up, Weilong noticed a prickly pear in a blue ceramic dish on top of the piano. It was budding, and the thick blue-green leaves pressed upward on all sides like a nest of green snakes; the red tinge at the tip of the leaves looked like snake tongues. Behind the plant, a curtain shifted: Glint emerged smiling. Weilong shivered. Glint beckoned, and led her into the hallway.

"You arrived at an awkward moment, right after Young Mistress had lost her temper," Glint said gently. "Then, after we came in, and before she had calmed down, an uppity person we've got here broke a house rule. I'm afraid, young miss, that you've been caught in between, and have suffered quite unfairly."

"Oh you needn't say that, good sister! How have I been treated badly? Sometimes older folks take things out on younger ones—why can't she, my own flesh-and-blood aunt, do the same? Even a couple of slaps wouldn't really matter."

"Miss is very perceptive," Glint said.

Weilong was led into a small study decorated entirely in the traditional Chinese style. White walls, a pale green throw rug, a gold-lacquered table, chair cushions of fine crimson silk, and the same fine crimson cloth for the curtains. A person of Weilong's generation rarely saw this kind of rich, old silk, except perhaps on a quilt top. On the floor was a square cloisonné vase, about two feet high and filled with little rustling flowers that looked at first like white lilies. In fact they were the pale flower buds of wild rice, but only someone who'd lived in southern China a long time would know that.

Weilong decided, in light of her many misgivings, simply to make good use of the opportunity: she'd just follow her original plan and ask her aunt for help. The decision was her aunt's to make, and if she refused, it might be for the best anyway.

Now that her mind was made up, Weilong felt much steadier. Looking around, she saw that the decor was simple but tasteful. Madame Liang lay half reclined in a lounge chair, one leg hooked over the armrest and a gold-embroidered high-heeled slipper dangling from her foot, ready to fall off at any moment. She had removed her hat; around the house she wore a parrot-green head wrap. Weilong couldn't help wondering about the color of the hair beneath it, and whether it had been dyed. She stood in front of her aunt, who appeared to take no notice. Her face covered with a banana-leaf fan, Madame Liang seemed to be sleeping.

Weilong wavered, shifting her weight from foot to foot. She was about to leave when her aunt barked, the sound coming out from around her ears: "Sit down!" Nothing more; apparently it was her turn to speak.

Humility was Weilong's only choice. "Aunt," she said, "you're like a Buddha made of solid crystal, reflecting undisguised reality—lying to you would be pointless. Here's the truth: two years ago, when Shanghai was full of rumors of war, our family fled to Hong Kong and I enrolled at Nanying Secondary. But life in Hong Kong is expensive, and my father doesn't have enough to support us. Now that the situation in Shanghai is improving, my parents are thinking about going back. My own idea, though, is that since my studies here are going well, I can graduate next summer. If I go back to Shanghai and start at a new school, I'll lose a year. But if I stay in Hong Kong by myself, it will be hard to pay my living expenses, not to mention the school fees. I've been thinking this through on my own, without saying anything to my parents, because what would be the point, it would only make them worry. I thought about it for a long time, and finally decided to see if Aunt could help."

One of Madame Liang's delicate hands held the banana-leaf fan by the stem. As she twirled it around, thin rays of light shone through the slits in the leaf, spinning across her face. "Miss," she said, "it seems you've thought of everything except my own position in this matter. Even if I wanted to help you, I couldn't. If your father finds out, he'll say I've seduced a girl from a good family and stolen her away. What am I to your family? A willful degenerate who ruined the family honor—refused the man chosen by my brothers, went to Liang as his concubine instead, lost face for a family that was already on the way down. Bah! These declining old families, they're like outhouse bricks, pure petrified stink. You were born too late—you missed all the fuss, and didn't get to hear what your father said to me then!"

"Father's got that stuffy old bookish way of thinking, and he won't change for anyone. He doesn't know how to moderate his speech—no wonder Aunt is angry. But it's been so many years, and you're a generous, fair-minded person—would you bear this grudge even against the younger generation?"

"Yes, I would! I like to chew on this rotten little memory! I won't forget what he said to me then!" She waved the fan, and the yellow rays of sunlight filtered through it onto her face, like tiger whiskers quivering around her mouth.

Weilong tried to placate her aunt. "Aunt hasn't forgotten,

and I won't either. Aunt should give me a chance to make up for my father's mistakes. If you raise me till I'm grown, I'll be your child. I'll make it up to you!"

Madame Liang kept picking and tearing at the slits in the fan. Suddenly Weilong saw that her aunt was treating the fan as if it were someone's face—and that it was *her* face that appeared through the slits. Weilong turned red. Madame Liang let her hand fall, then tapped the fan against her chin. "Do you plan to live at school?" she asked.

"That would be best, I think, after my family's gone. I've inquired, and found that boarders aren't charged much more than the day students."

"It's not a question of expense. If you live with me, there'll be someone around to keep me company, and anyway I have a car so you can get a ride to school every day. It won't be any trouble."

Weilong was stunned. "That would be perfect!" she finally managed to say.

"There's just one thing," her aunt said. "Are you sure that your father won't say anything? I don't want to be blamed for a family breakup."

"If my father opposes this plan in the slightest, I won't be back to trouble you."

Madame Liang laughed. "That's right! You can make up your own lie to tell your father. Just be sure that it's not too flimsy!"

Weilong was in the midst of declaring that she had no intention of lying when Madame Liang cut her off. "Can you play the piano?"

"I took lessons for a few years, but I'm not very good."

"We don't need a concert pianist. Work up a few popular tunes, some songs that everyone likes; the only thing you have to do is play the accompaniment. All the young English ladies can do this, and here in Hong Kong we follow the English ways. I'm sure that your father, with his antique notions of child-rearing, never let you go to parties. He doesn't understand that after you're married, you'll have to know how to mix in society. You can't spend your whole life hiding away. There are things you can learn if you live with me—a lucky break for you, I'd say."

Weilong kept murmuring her agreement. Then Madame Liang said, "If you know how to play tennis, you can be my practice partner."

"I can play."

"Do you have a tennis outfit?"

"Just what the school gives us."

Her aunt groaned. "Oh yes, I know, those long bloomer pants, truly awful. Take my outfit and try it on for size. Tomorrow when the tailor comes, I'll have him make one for you."

She told Glint to bring out a goose-gold knit shirt and some dove-gray shorts. Weilong tried on the outfit. It seemed large. So Glint got a needle and tucked in the waist.

"Your legs are too skinny," said Madame Liang, "but girls are always thin."

Weilong was deep in thought. She wanted to get home and tell her mother and father, to see what they would say. She quickly took her leave, changed her clothes, and went out, carrying a parasol. Of course there was a junior maid to open the gate for her. Glint also came, giving her a proper send-off. "Goodbye, young lady!" she said. It was all very different from the earlier treatment.

Weilong followed the road down the mountain. The sun was already sinking in the west, and reds, purples, and yellows mingled in florid profusion behind the hills, like a picture on a cigar box. The hot sun had baked the banana trees and the palms till they were dry, yellow, and wispy, like tobacco leaves. In the south, the sun sets quickly, and dusk lasts just a moment. The sun had not yet set, but far down the road, where the trees and haze blurred into a smooth greenish black, a crescent moon appeared. Weilong walked toward the east, and as she walked the moon seemed to grow whiter and more translucent. A pale phoenix with a plump white breast had alighted somewhere along the winding road ahead and was nesting in the forking tree branches, or so it seemed. As she walked, the moon appeared to be just beyond her, in the clump of trees around the bend, but when she got there it had gone. Weilong stopped and rested for a bit, feeling slightly dazed. She looked back at her aunt's house, and strangely enough she could still see the yellow and red of the window frames, and the green glass panes reflecting the sea. That splendid white house, covered in green roof tile, bore more than a passing resemblance to an ancient imperial tomb.

Weilong felt like one of those young students in Pu Songling's old ghost stories, the kind who goes up a mountain to see a relative and then, on the homeward journey, looks back at the mansion and finds it has become a grave mound. If the white Liang mansion had turned into a tomb, it wouldn't have surprised her much. She could see that her aunt was a woman of great ability, and had held back the wheel of history. She had preserved, in her own small world, the opulent lifestyle of the late Qing dynasty. Behind her own doors, she was a little Empress Cixi.

As for me, Weilong thought, here I am charging straight into the devil's lair. Whose fault will it be, if I get caught in a trap? Then again, we are, after all, aunt and niece, and she's got to consider appearances. She'll treat me properly, so long as I keep on my best behavior. If others want to talk, let them talk—I'll just concentrate on my studies. Someday, when I meet someone who cares for me, he'll be sure to understand, and won't believe any silly gossip.

When she got back home, she thought it through carefully.

She'd have to invent a story to tell her father, but with her mother she'd be more truthful. That way, she'd have someone in Shanghai to back her up, and there'd be less chance of being found out. With this plan in mind, Weilong told her mother all about going to see Aunt Liang, and how her aunt had agreed to pay her tuition and wanted her to move in. As for what she had gathered about the overall situation at her aunt's house— she said nothing about that.

Weilong's mother wasn't too happy about leaving her daughter alone in Hong Kong, but then neither did she want her studies to be disrupted. All that fuss about the aunt was water under the bridge, old history, practically forgotten. The aunt was a lot older now; and of course the years must have changed her. If she wanted to bury the hatchet and make a generous effort to repair things, by helping her niece continue her studies —well, this was good news indeed. Weilong's mother wanted to go and thank her sister-in-law in person, but Weilong stopped her by saying that Madame Liang was just about to go to the hospital to have her appendix out, and the doctor had ordered complete rest. The sisters-in-law hadn't seen each other in many years; if they got together, there certainly would be a tearful scene, and stirring up the emotions isn't good for someone who's sick. So Mrs. Ge had to give up the plan. To her husband, she said that the headmaster had noticed that Weilong's grades were very good and that he was offering her a scholarship to cover tuition and living costs. Ge Yukun was a man who relied on his social status, with little regard for the niceties; he didn't bother about the formalities the way his wife did. When he heard the news, he praised his daughter offhandedly. But he gave no sign of planning a trip to personally thank the headmaster for working so hard to educate young people.

Mr. and Mrs. Ge were eager to return to Shanghai, so they hurriedly packed their things and gave up the house they'd been renting. One old servant, the cook, who had been with her employers for many years, was returning with them. The maid of all work, Amah Chen, had been hired in Hong Kong, so they paid out her wages and let her go. Weilong went to the boat with her parents to see them off. Night had already fallen. With Amah Chen carrying her suitcase, she set out for Madame Liang's house.

It was a humid spring evening, and the Hong Kong hills are famous for their fog. The white Liang mansion was melting viscously into the white mist, leaving only the greenish gleam of the lamplight shining through square after square of the green windowpanes, like ice cubes in peppermint schnapps. When the fog thickened, the ice cubes dissolved, and the lights went out. The Liang house stood alone on the street; the asphalt road was empty and quiet, but there was a row of parked cars. "I've picked the wrong day to arrive," Weilong thought. "Aunt has guests; she won't have time for me." She went up the flight of steps to the little gate. There she found a palace lantern, a replica of an antique, hanging from its arm of ornamented bronze. When she reached the door, she was surprised to find that it was quiet inside, as if there weren't any guests after all. But then, listening intently, she could make out the light clicking sound of mah-jongg tiles—probably four or five tables.

Big houses in Hong Kong are more densely packed, more modern and compact, than houses in Shanghai, and they make a different impression. Weilong was about to ring the bell when Amah Chen called out from behind, "Miss, be careful, there are dogs!" A pack of dogs started barking just then. Amah Chen was frightened. She was wearing a brand-new tunic of light blue cotton that was stiff with starch. When she got flustered she twisted around inside her clothes, so that the cloth rustled noisily. She wore her hair in a braid, as did Glance and Glint of the Liang household, but the braid was tied murderously tight, like a nine-segment steel whip in a martial arts novel. Weilong suddenly felt that she didn't know Chen, that

25

she'd never taken a good, hard look at her; now she realized that this longtime servant was not at all presentable. "Amah Chen, you should go now," she said. "If you wait any longer, you'll be scared going back down the hill. Here's two dollars for the ride. Leave the suitcase, someone will come to take it." She sent Amah Chen off, and rang the bell.

A junior maid went in and announced her just as the eighth round of mah-jongg was ending and dinner was about to begin. When she heard that her niece had arrived, Madame Liang hesitated for a while. Always careful about financial matters, she was planning to spend quite a lot on this niece, but still felt some uncertainty. Did the girl have potential? Was she worth the investment? Her tuition wasn't very expensive, but it wasn't cheap either. Since the money hadn't gone out yet, the smart thing would be to make use of this opportunity—tell the child to change her clothes and come meet the guests. As the saying goes, "True gold does not fear testing by fire." Then she'd find out right away. The only problem was that tonight's guests had been carefully matched; she'd gone to considerable trouble over the details. If this girl, with her very first trill, did cause a sensation—if the young phoenix sang more thrillingly than the old one—that would lead to all kinds of fuss, and the balance would be upset. If, on the other hand, Weilong wasn't up to the job and things went wrong, well, a blockheaded child in the middle of a party can spoil all the fun.

And there was another angle to consider: too many greedy-eyed people here. Madame Liang glanced at the lean and hungry tiger seated across from her. Of all her paramours, he'd had the greatest staying power. He was Situ Xie, a rich boss from Shantou, the owner of a factory that made ceramic toilets. Although Madame Liang knew a lot of people, she usually preferred Hong Kong's local big shots, members of the gentlemanly class who had ties to officialdom. Nonetheless, she'd been quite taken with this businessman, for he was an expert charmer, with a talent for pleasing the ladies. They'd known each other for a long time now, with Madame Liang always walking in slight fear of him, letting him have his way and keeping herself in check. If twenty years had passed like a single day for Situ Xie and Madame Liang, it was because he understood her all too well, and paid her plenty of attention; besides, although she didn't pick up the tab for him, he didn't have to spend money on her, either. When he wanted to throw a dinner party, he could use her place—it was lovely and the guests were well treated; people could relax and enjoy themselves here. This evening's party was a send-off for Situ Xie himself: soon he would be returning to Shantou to marry a girl. Then again, if he were to take a liking to Weilong he might not go back to Shantou after all—that could get complicated.

Madame Liang quietly summoned Glint. "Go and make my excuses to the Ge girl," she ordered. "Tell her I can't get away right now, but I'll see her in the morning. Ask her if she's had dinner. The blue bedroom will be hers, so take her there."

Glint went off to discharge her duty. She was wearing a lilac-colored fitted tunic over a pair of narrow, kingfisher-blue trousers, her arms folded inside a white vest embroidered with gold thread—a slave-girl costume from the days of *Dream of the Red Chamber*. She wore no powder at all, only a bit of green oil, highlighting the lusciousness of her coppery skin.

As soon as she saw Weilong, Glint rushed forward and took her luggage. "Young Mistress has been anxiously awaiting your arrival, asking every day why you weren't here yet. But tonight, as luck would have it, she has guests."

Then, leaning over to Weilong's ear, she added, "They're all old masters and wives, and Young Mistress is afraid you'll feel awkward and uncomfortable with them, so she's ordered a separate supper for you upstairs."

"Thank you very much," said Weilong, "but I've already eaten."

"Then I'll take you to your room," said Glint. "If you get hungry later on, just ring the bell and order a sandwich. There will be someone in the kitchen all night."

When Weilong went upstairs, the people below sat down for dinner, and radio music drifted upward. Weilong's room, small like a boat, was launched on waves of music. The old wall lamp in its red gauze shade seemed to bob and float, and she felt herself swaying about, exuberant and elated. She opened the pearly net curtains and leaned against the frame of the glass door. There was a narrow balcony and, beyond the metal railing, the mist was drifting by, thick, white, and rolling; it felt like a shipboard view of the sea.

Weilong opened her suitcase, ready to put her things in the drawers, but when she opened the door she found the closet was full of clothes—gleaming, gorgeous clothes. "Whose are these?" she gasped. "Aunt must have forgotten to clear this closet out."

Like the child that she still was, she had to lock the door and try on all the clothes, which fit her perfectly. Suddenly she realized that her aunt had put them there for her. Silks and satins, brocade housedresses, short coats, long coats, beach wraps, nightgowns, bath wear, evening gowns, afternoon cocktail dresses, semiformal dining wear for entertaining guests at home—everything was there. What use would a schoolgirl have for all this? Weilong hurriedly stripped off the dinner dress she'd been trying on and threw it onto the bed. Her knees grew weak and she sat down on the bed, heat surging across her face. "Isn't this just how a bordello buys girls?" she whispered to herself. She sat for a moment, then stood up and put each outfit back onto its hanger. Hanging inside each dress was a little white satin sachet filled with lilac petals; the closet smelled of their sweet scent.

Weilong was leaning into the closet to straighten out the sachets when she heard a woman's laugh downstairs. It was a sweet, slippery laugh, and Weilong couldn't help laughing too. "Glint said the guests were all old masters and wives. Well, there's no telling whether those masters really are old, but as for the wives, they don't sound like old wives—or like young wives either!"

When dinner was finished, the mah-jongg started again, but some of the guests turned on the phonograph and started to dance. Weilong couldn't get to sleep; as soon as she shut her eyes she was trying on clothes, one outfit after another. Woolen things, thick and furry as a perturbing jazz dance; crushed-velvet things, deep and sad as an aria from a Western opera; rich, fine silks, smooth and slippery like "The Blue Danube," coolly enveloping the whole body. She had just fallen into a dazed slumber when the music changed. She woke with a start. The panting thrust of a rumba came from downstairs, and she couldn't help but think of that long electric-purple dress hanging in the closet, and the swish it would make with each dance step. "Why not give it a try?" she murmured softly to everything downstairs. Only her lips moved, without any sound, but still she yanked the blanket up over her head. No one could hear her. "Why not give it a try?" she whispered again. Then, smiling, she fell asleep.

Weilong was used to getting up early, and the next morning she washed her face, combed her hair, and was downstairs at eight o'clock. The mah-jongg games had just broken up; the smoke in the living room was a choking, dizzying haze. Glint was supervising some junior maids as they picked up the snack trays. Madame Liang had taken her shoes off, and now sat cross-legged on the sofa with a cigarette, scolding Glance. Glance leaned on the mah-jongg table, scraping the tiles together and dropping them, with a clank, into a sandal-wood box. Madame Liang wore a head wrap of midnight-blue crepe silk and a pair of dangling diamond earrings that, when they caught the light, seemed to wink and smile. Her face, however, was as hard as iron. Upon seeing Weilong, she nodded and asked, "What time do you go to school? Tell the driver to take you. He's just returned from taking guests home, so he's still up."

"We're still on spring break," Weilong said.

"Oh?" said Madame Liang. "In that case, we could have a nice long chat today, except I'm so terribly tired. Glint, go and get some breakfast for the young lady." And she went on smoking her cigarette, just as if Weilong wasn't there.

Thinking that Weilong's arrival had put a stop to Madame Liang's scolding, Glance took the mah-jongg box and started to walk away. "Stand still!" Madame Liang shouted. Glance stood still, her back to her mistress. "We won't discuss what you were doing with George Qiao before all this," said Madame Liang. "I've told you about this so many times, but you let it go in one ear and out the other! Now I've barred the door to him, and you go sneaking out to look for him. And you think I don't know! You're so cheap, giving in to him like that! A natural-born slave girl, that's what you are!"

Glance was still young and couldn't back down, at least not with Weilong standing there. "Even if I did give in to him," she said sullenly, "he wouldn't want to keep me around. And if I wasn't like a slave girl, he wouldn't even give me the time of day. Why is that? I do not understand!"

Leaping to her feet, Madame Liang slapped Glance full in the face. Glance's feelings boiled over. "Who's been feeding you all this gossip anyway?" she cried out. "Maybe the Qiao family's driver? All the men in the Qiao family, young and old—you've got them all sewed up—probably even their Seventh Daughter-in-law's new baby boy! You haven't overlooked a single one, not even the driver. So hit me, go ahead, hit me! But watch out or I'll tell everything I know!"

Madame Liang sat back down, smiling. "Feel free!" she said. "Go ahead and tell it to the press. This kind of free publicity is always a great bargain for me. I don't have any family elders to report to, I don't have any children or grandchildren. I've got money, I've got friends, so who am I afraid of? But you'd better learn to be more careful. I've been running this place for quite a while now, and I don't plan on letting a servant get the upper hand. Do you think you're irreplaceable?"

Glance turned and cast a glance at Weilong. "There's no question of my being irreplaceable," she said with a bitter smirk. "The replacement has already arrived. Must be a very satisfactory arrangement, one's own flesh and blood, everyone living together so cozily, and 'no water wasted on other folks' fields.'"

"Why do you always drag others in? You make everything dirty, don't you! I was going to have it out with you, but I'm too tired. I haven't got the energy to deal with your carryings on. Get out of here!"

"Then I'll go for good!" Glance declared. "I could spend a lifetime here and never get anywhere!"

"You think you're going to get somewhere? You'll lose the ground under your feet, more likely! You think you can spend a few years here, meet a few big shots, and one of them will help you out. Well, you can forget about that! I've got people at the governor's office: leave my place, and you'll never find another situation in Hong Kong. Who would dare to take you in?"

"Is this little patch of dried tofu they call Hong Kong the only place on earth?"

"You'll never get away! Your parents will marry you off in the countryside."

"My parents—control me like that?" Glance snorted.

"Your mother's no fool. She has half a dozen daughters and wants me to find places for them. She wants me to take care of your little sisters, and of course she's not going to cross me. She'll keep you under control."

Glance was stunned. At first she couldn't grasp what

Madame Liang had said, but after a moment of shocked silence, she burst into tears. Glint rushed up and practically dragged Glance out of the room, shushing her all the while. "It's all because Young Mistress has spoiled you, never keeping you in your place. Try to be more sensible! You know, as soon as Young Mistress feels better, she's sure to give you something toward your dowry."

When Glint and Glance had left the room, a junior maid crept in gingerly, bringing slippers for Madame Liang. "Your bath is ready, ma'am," she murmured. "You've been up a long time. Wouldn't you like to take a nap after your bath?" Madame Liang slid her feet into the slippers, tossed her cigarette into a potted azalea, stood up, and left the room. The azalea was densely packed with flowers, and the cigarette butt fell among them, scorching a petal brown.

Weilong stood alone in the living room until a junior maid came in and called her to breakfast. After breakfast, she went upstairs and stood at the window of her room, gazing vacantly. There was the rectangular grass lawn, neatly trimmed, sprinkled with dew, a bold deep green. With sharp jerky steps, a sparrow was crossing the lawn, only to stop along the way, as if dazed by that continent of stupefying green. Step by jerky step, it started back. Weilong had thought that sparrows only hopped; she had never realized that they could move in long, measured strides, and she watched for a long time. Perhaps it wasn't a sparrow? She was still wondering when two porters passed down the garden path, puffing as they carried a red trunk through the gate. They were followed by a middle-aged woman in a tunic and trousers of black gambiered silk; Glance's mother, apparently. Glance came out too and just stood there. She was waiting, it seemed, for another porter who was still inside. Her eyes were red and swollen from crying, and her powder had turned her face to a light brown. Weilong could only see her in profile, eyes staring straight ahead, face expressionless, a clay mask. After watching for some time, Weilong noticed the slight twitch of a muscle running from cheek to temple. Oh, so that was it: Glance was eating peanuts. Every once in a while a shred of red peanut skin would pop out of the corner of her mouth.

Suddenly Weilong didn't want to watch anymore. She turned and opened the closet door, leaning against it. It was dark inside the closet, and the lilac scent made her dizzy. The air of the faraway past was in there—decorous, languid, heedless of time. In that closet there was no bright, clear morning like the one outside the window, with its flat green grass, mute frightened face, and peanut skins at the corner of the mouth... all that dirty, complicated, unreasonable reality.

Once Weilong had gone into that clothes closet, she stayed for two or three months, and she had lots of opportunities to dress up. A banquet, a tea party, a concert, a mah-jongg party —for her these were little more than occasions for putting on fine clothes. She considered herself fortunate, since Madame Liang merely used her as a signboard to attract the mainstream sort of youth. Her aunt did take her to fancy dance halls a few times, but usually she invited people over to the house. Steeped as they are in the conservative habits of the British upper class, the young ladies of Hong Kong's great families maintain an air of dignified reserve, quite unlike Shanghai's socialites.

Madame Liang was extremely picky about the young men who pursued Weilong, more severe even than the imperial household when it is choosing a royal son-in-law. If the lucky half dozen who were in the running grew excessively ardent in their pursuit, Madame Liang simply took the precious goods off the shelf: none of the suitors would be allowed to go near her niece. Then, when she had permitted one of them to get close, she swooped in with a dexterous display of charm, and recruited him for her own purposes. When a youth paid his addresses to Madame Liang, he was like an old drunk who pretends he doesn't want a drink; in the end, he succumbed, and there he'd be, deep in an affair. Weilong got used to watching this little drama, without caring much about it.

One day, as she was preparing to go out, Weilong urged Glint to do up her hair quickly. Madame Liang had assigned her favorite attendant to wait on Weilong, and Glint had quickly got a very good grasp of Weilong's temperament. Weilong, with no family in Hong Kong to turn to, had found that Glint, though she could be quite cold-hearted, always had warm, wise advice for her. Glint was now her trusted confidante.

"How about the dress first and then the hair?" Glint said now. "Otherwise, you'll muss your hair when you pull the dress over your head."

"Pick out something simple," Weilong said. "The choir is going to practice in the church, and I'm afraid the people there won't approve of fancy clothes."

But Glint went ahead and chose a ginger-yellow crepe cheongsam. "I don't understand," she said. "You're not a Christian, so why join the choir? Your social schedule keeps you busy all day long, and then you study till dawn. These past two weeks you've been working so hard to get ready for your exams that you're positively wasting away! Why are you ruining your health this way?"

Weilong sighed and dipped her chin to let Glint part her hair. "You say I'm studying too much. But you know very well that I go out to parties just to help my aunt and keep her happy. I worked very hard for this chance to study, so now I have to do a good job and get respectable grades."

"I don't mean to rain on your parade, but what is the point of graduating? You're still in secondary school, Hong Kong has only one university, and university graduates can't find work anyway! If they do find a job, it pays fifty or sixty dollars a month, and for that they have to teach in a primary school run by the church and put up with the foreign nuns' bad tempers. It's really not worth it!"

"You think I haven't thought of all that? Still, I have to take what I can get!"

"Now don't get angry at what I'm going to say. I think you should use all these social occasions to look around and find someone who'll be right for you."

Weilong smiled sarcastically. "And who would that be, in my aunt's circle of friends? They're either young men as slippery as dance-hall playboys or the kind of old man who likes to hang around a harem. Or else they're British military men, in which case, if they're lieutenants or above, they don't want to get involved with someone from the yellow race. That's how it is in Hong Kong!"

"Oh, now I get it!" Glint responded with a sudden laugh. "No wonder you joined the choir even though you don't have any free time. They say there are quite a few college students in that group."

"I don't mind if you joke about this with me," Weilong smiled. "But don't go saying anything to Aunt!"

Glint was silent.

"Did you hear me?" Weilong was insistent. "Don't go spreading rumors!"

Glint was startled out of her reverie. "What do you take me for? You think I can't keep quiet about a little thing like this?" She glanced around, then said quietly, "Miss, you'd better be careful. While you've been looking for someone to pick, our Young Mistress, with her sharp eyes and quick fingers, has already picked one out for herself."

Weilong looked up sharply, knocking Glint's hand aside. "Who do you mean?"

"That Lu Somebody in your choir, the one who's good at tennis. He's a college student, isn't he? Oh, now I remember, his name is Lu Zhaolin."

Weilong's face flushed bright red; she bit her lips in silence. Finally, she said, "How do you know that she..."

"Eh! How could I not know? If it weren't for this, she wouldn't have let you join the choir in the first place. She wouldn't let you go off on your own to make friends, not even to sing with a big group of people in the church. That's the rule here. Anyone who wants to see you has to come in through the front door and pay a proper visit. And once they've come in that way, it's easy to manage things. I thought it was strange when she didn't say anything about your joining the choir. Two weeks ago, all she could talk about was holding a garden party and inviting your choir friends, so everyone would have a chance to get acquainted. Then that Lu person went to Manila for a tennis match, and the garden party was put off. As soon as Lu came back, she started talking about it again. As for the real purpose of tomorrow's party, well, of course you've been kept in the dark!"

Weilong ground her teeth. "If he falls for her sweet-talking and goes off with her, then he's not someone who can be trusted. I'll see through his act right away. Probably just as well."

"You're being foolish," Glint said. "Crows will be black, wherever you go; men will always fall for this kind of bait. Don't forget—your Mr. Lu is young, a student, probably inexperienced. If he falls for this, you can hardly blame him. Write him a letter, if you know him well enough. Ask him not to come tomorrow."

"Know him!" Weilong smiled blandly. "We've barely spoken to each other!" She let the matter drop.

The garden party was on the following day. There's a touch of nineteenth-century England in every garden party. In England the skies are hardly ever clear, but when at last the balmy summer days do arrive, the lords and ladies hold these sorts of semiformal parties on their country estates. The ladies wear straw hats with broad floppy brims, corsages of old-fashioned artificial flowers, and elbow-length silk gloves, all very fancy, just as if they were attending a formal court function. Anyone in the county with the least claim to status is sure to attend, and the local minister and his wife show up to bow and scrape. Decked out in their finery, the company paces about the castle grounds and through the rocky ruins, engaging in stiff conversation. Then, after tea, they beg some young ladies to play the piano and sing "The Last Rose of Summer."

Hong Kong garden parties are even better. Hong Kong society copies English custom in every respect, but goes on adding further touches until the original conception is entirely lost. Madame Liang's garden party was garishly swathed in local color. "Good luck" paper lanterns had been planted on five-foot poles all around the lawn; when they were lit at dusk, they glimmered vaguely in the background—a perfect prop for a Hollywood production of *Secrets of the Qing Palace*. Beach umbrellas were stuck at various angles among the lanterns, an incongruously Western touch. Young maids and old amahs, their hair oiled and twisted into long braids, wove through the forest of umbrella poles, proffering cocktails, snacks, and fruit juice on shaky silver trays.

Since Madame Liang was throwing this party for the handsome young men in the choir, the guest list had been carefully scrutinized. Not a single tipsy little British officer was to be seen; the atmosphere was prim and proper. Given the religious nature of the choir, half a dozen Catholic nuns had also been invited. The monks and nuns of Hong Kong are used to attending social events, and they know how to mingle; they have lively, pleasing manners. These nuns, however, were not as brilliant as some, and they spoke only French and Latin. Since Weilong was taking French at school and had picked up a few phrases, Madame Liang dispatched her to entertain them.

Weilong watched helplessly as Lu Zhaolin arrived. Madame Liang, gorgeously attired, took his hand and, blinking in the bright sun, said something Weilong couldn't hear. Lu Zhaolin left his hand in Madame Liang's, but he glanced about, searching for Weilong. Madame Liang's sharp eyes found her first. Madame Liang's gaze slid from Lu Zhaolin to Weilong, then back to Lu Zhaolin. Weilong gave Lu Zhaolin a forced smile. He was a tall, broad-shouldered, dark-skinned youth; when he smiled in return his white teeth flashed in the sun.

Then the wind changed, and started blowing toward Weilong; she could just hear Madame Liang saying, "Poor child! She hardly ever gets a chance to use her French. Let's not bother her while she's having fun." With that, she led him off, and they disappeared into the crowd.

The second time Weilong caught sight of them, they were sitting under a blue-and-white-striped beach umbrella. Madame Liang's elbows were propped on the table; she sipped on a straw and gazed at Lu Zhaolin, who sat across from her. Lu Zhaolin, however, was coolly scanning the crowd. Weilong followed his gaze as he looked around. There was only one person there who made his eyes grow fixed and brilliant. Weilong's heart fizzed sourly, like a carbonated drink after a squirt of lemon. Lu Zhaolin was looking at a mixed-race girl who was no more than fifteen or sixteen years old. The whiteness of her skin was not that of a Chinese; it was a flat white, altogether opaque. A snow-white face with large, pale-green eyes hinting of mischief, jet eyebrows and lashes, and full, luscious, scarlet lips—a face of almost forbidding beauty. This was Zhou Jijie, peerless among the party girls in Hong Kong's younger set. Her genealogy was said to be very complicated; it included, at the minimum, Arab, Negro, Indian, Indonesian, and Portuguese blood, with only a dash of Chinese. Zhou Jijie was quite young, but she had quickly risen to prominence, and her place in Hong Kong's social scene was quite secure. Weilong, by contrast, was a newcomer. A certain amount of enmity was unavoidable, but the two of them got along well enough.

Zhou Jijie could feel Weilong scrutinizing her, so she smiled back, and waved at her to come over. Weilong winked in return, and then, pouting, glanced over at the nuns. The nuns were going on about the preparations they were making for the eightieth birthday of their mother superior. Suddenly a young Vietnamese appeared, speaking fluent French and asking about their recent fund-raising for the orphanage. The nuns were thrilled and started telling him, in great detail, all about a visit they'd received from the governor's wife. Weilong took the opportunity to escape, and went looking for Zhou Jijie.

Zhou Jijie pointed toward her own face. "You should thank me!" she teased.

"Was it you who sent the bodhisattva that saved my life? How extremely kind!"

Just then, a small scuffle broke out at the iron gate. Glint, all smiles, was barring the way to a man who was trying to get in. In the end, however, she couldn't prevent his entry; he strode right into the party. Weilong nudged Zhou Jijie. "Look, look, it's your brother, isn't it? I didn't know you had an older brother."

Jijie glared at her. Then her brow softened and she spoke in a deceptively pleasant manner. "I really don't like hearing that I look like George. If I had a face like his, I'd marry a Muslim straight off, and spend my life behind a veil!"

Weilong suddenly remembered being told that Zhou Jijie and George Qiao had the same mother but different fathers, though the details were of course entirely hush-hush. No wonder Zhou Jijie avoided the topic. Weilong was ashamed to have made such a faux pas, and hurried on to another subject.

But Jijie, after expressing such contempt for George Qiao, was now following his every move. Five minutes hadn't passed before she was stifling a giggle; covering her mouth with her hand, she whispered to Weilong: "Look over there—George is buzzing around in front of your aunt, and the more she ignores him, the more outrageously he flirts. She's just about to lose her temper!"

Weilong looked, but the first thing she noticed was the great change that had come over Lu Zhaolin; he and Madame Liang were now getting on very well indeed—fused together, almost, their eyes beaded on a single string. Weilong and Lu Zhaolin had known each other for a while now, but they had never reached this stage. Weilong choked back anger, and her eyes grew red. "What an idiot!" she cursed under her breath. "What an idiot! Are all men so stupid?"

Meanwhile, George was pacing back and forth in front of Madame Liang, both hands thrust deep into his pockets. He was talking to the surrounding company, but his entire attention was fixed on her, and he kept glancing in her direction. Now people started looking at Madame Liang and Lu Zhaolin. Things got so heated, as the two of them battled it out with eyes and eyebrows, that everyone had to laugh. Madame Liang was the very picture of tolerant magnanimity, but now she felt a bit ill-at-ease. Pushing away her juice glass, she draped her arm over the back of the seat and gave Weilong a little wink. Weilong looked over at George Qiao; her aunt nodded slightly. It was time for Weilong to leave Zhou Jijie and make herself pleasant to George Qiao.

Walking toward him, she held out her hand in greeting. "Are you George Qiao? We haven't been introduced."

They shook hands, after which he put his hands back in his pockets and examined her appearance in great detail, smiling all the while. Weilong was wearing a cheongsam of thin, porcelain-green silk, and when he stared at her with his dark green eyes, her arms grew hot, like hot milk pouring out of a green pitcher—she felt her whole body melting. She steadied herself at once. "Am I bothering you?" she asked. "Why are you staring like that? It's as if I were a thorn stuck in your eye!"

"Of course I'm staring! I don't know if that thorn will ever come out. Better save it for a souvenir."

"What a joker! The sun's too strong here, let's go walk in the shade a bit."

They walked along together. George sighed. "I could hit myself. How come I never knew there was someone like you in Hong Kong?"

"You haven't come around much, not since I moved in with my aunt, and I seldom go out. Otherwise, we probably would have met by now. You get around a lot, I hear."

"And yet I almost missed this chance! What an amazing stroke of luck! We could have been born into separate worlds, or into the same world but with you twenty years older than me. Even ten years would be terrible. Of course, if I'd been born twenty years before you, that wouldn't matter so much. You don't think I'll be too disgusting when I'm old, do you?"

"What a way to talk!"

She looked at him again, trying to imagine what he would look like when he was old. He had even less color in his cheeks than Jijie; even his lips were whitish, almost like plaster. Under his thick black brows and lashes, his eyes were like fields of young rice when the wind blows across them and reveals, in flashes, the green gleam of water between the rice shoots— flashing, then darkening again. George Qiao was tall and well built, but his clothes fit him so perfectly, with such casual grace, that you didn't even notice his physique. He made Lu Zhaolin look rough and doltish. Weilong was feeling quite bitter toward Madame Liang because of Lu Zhaolin, and George was the only man she'd seen who could resist Madame Liang's charms. That made her heart warm toward him.

When he learned that she was from Shanghai, George asked her, "Which do you like better, Shanghai or Hong Kong?"

"Well, the scenery in Hong Kong is better of course. It's famous for its beaches. Perhaps if I could swim I'd like Hong Kong even more."

"I'd be happy to give you some lessons later on—if you're interested, that is."

Next, he praised her English.

"Oh, it's not that good," Weilong demurred. "Up until this year, I never spoke English outside of school. Lately I've been speaking a little English with my aunt's friends, but my grammar is all wrong."

"Probably you're just not used to it," he said. "It's a bit tiring, isn't it? Let's not speak English."

"Then what shall we speak? You don't understand Shanghainese, and my Cantonese is terrible."

"Then let's not talk at all. You've been entertaining these dreadful people all afternoon, you must need a break."

"Now that you mention it, I do feel a bit tired."

She sat down on a bench, and George sat next to her. After a moment, Weilong laughed. "Three minutes' silence, just as if we're in mourning!"

"Can't two people sit together without talking?" As he spoke, his arm went out along the backrest, behind Weilong.

"It would be better to talk a bit," Weilong hurriedly said.

"If you insist on conversation, then I'll speak in Portuguese." He started rattling away at once.

Weilong listened, her head to one side and her hands clasped around her knees. "I don't know what you're saying. Something unkind, no doubt!"

"Is that what my tone implies?" he asked gently.

Weilong blushed and hid her face.

"I'd translate it into English for you, but I'm afraid I'm not brave enough."

Weilong covered her ears. "Who wants to hear, anyway?" Then she stood up and walked back toward the crowd.

By that time the sky was already dark. The moon had just risen; it was dark and yellow, like the scorch mark left on jade-green satin when a burning ash of incense falls into someone's needlework. Weilong turned and saw that George was following her. "I can't go on dallying with you," she said. "And I'll thank you to refrain from annoying my aunt."

"Oh, I just wanted to fluster her a bit. She doesn't fluster easily. If a woman's too calm, too steady and self-controlled, then she's not so attractive."

Weilong gave a little hiss, then ordered him not to cause her aunt any further displeasure.

"Your aunt doesn't lose very often, but against me, she lost," George said, smiling lightly. "Today, just when she was most contented, she saw me, and had to remember the defeat she suffered. Naturally, she's angry."

"If you keep on talking nonsense, I'll get angry."

"If you want me to leave, I will. Just promise you'll go out with me tomorrow."

"I can't. You know I can't!"

"Does that mean I have to come here to see you? Your aunt won't let me in the door! The only reason she didn't have me chased off today is that she didn't want to be embarrassed in front of all these people."

Weilong bowed her head, not saying a word. Just then, Madame Liang and Lu Zhaolin, holding their cocktail glasses high, came walking—or rather, floating—over to Weilong. They were both tipsy. "Go find Jijie," Madame Liang said to Weilong, "and play something for us on the piano. Let's sing some songs while everyone's still here, liven things up a bit." Weilong nodded, then turned to George Qiao. He had vanished.

Weilong couldn't find Jijie anywhere, but when she asked the maids they said she was upstairs washing her face. Weilong went upstairs and saw that her aunt's bathroom light was on. Jijie was standing in front of the mirror, wiping her face with a tissue and some cleansing lotion.

"They want you to play the piano," said Weilong.

"And just who is the silver-throated diva this time? I really haven't got the patience it takes to back them up!"

"No one's doing a solo. They're going to sing popular tunes together, try to have some fun."

Jijie wadded up the tissue and threw it at the mirror. "So it's for fun, eh? Those people all have windpipes like cracked bamboo. One person singing, but it sounds like half a dozen voices at once."

Weilong laughed, then sat down sideways on the raised doorsill. "You're drunk!" she exclaimed.

"What if I am? They plied me with alcohol." When she'd had a few, her face grew even whiter. Only the rims of her eyes were red.

"You seem to know all the guests pretty well."

"I've met a lot of those South China University students before. Whenever they throw a tea dance, a dinner dance, or a picnic, they love to drag my sister and me along. Last year my sister entered the university, so now we're in even greater demand."

"Are you planning to go to the university after you graduate next year?"

"What I'd really like is to get as far away from here as possible, go to university in Australia maybe, or Hawaii. I'm sick of Hong Kong."

"Is George studying at South China?"

"Him! He's the Qiao family's most illustrious good-for-nothing. He got into the university five years ago, but quit after only half a year. He went back last year because of my sister Jimiao, and what he did then stirred up a lot of talk. It's a good thing he's his father's least favorite son; otherwise the old man would have been furious. Weilong, you probably don't know about mixed-blood boys; even the best are a bit sullen, like slave girls."

Weilong swallowed the words that had risen to her lips, and smiled at Jijie.

"It's true! I'm mixed-blood myself and I've been through it all. These mixed-blood boys are the ones we're most likely to marry. We can't marry a Chinese—we've got foreign-style educations, so we don't fit in with the pure Chinese types. We can't marry a foreigner, either—have you seen any whites here who aren't deeply influenced by race concepts? Even if one of them wanted to marry one of us, there'd be too much social pressure against it. Anyone who marries an Oriental loses his career. In this day and age, who would be that romantic?"

Weilong hadn't expected Jijie to pour out her heart. She nodded and bit her fingernails. "Really? I hadn't realized. Such a tiny group from which to choose!"

"That's why Jimiao is desperate to leave Hong Kong. It's too colonial here. If we go somewhere else, the race restrictions can't possibly be as severe, can they? There must be some place in the world where we can live." The rims of her eyes grew even redder as she spoke.

"You're really drunk!" said Weilong. "Here you are getting all emotional!" She waited a moment, then asked, "So what happened then?"

"When?" Jijie was confused.

"George Qiao and your sister."

"Oh, you mean them. Well, after that, a lot of ridiculous things happened! He made my sister really angry. You don't know what a loose tongue that George has. He spread all kinds of rumors..."

Before she had finished, there was a knock on the door and Glint entered. The two girls were wanted downstairs, she said. Jijie had to break off then and there. She and Weilong went downstairs together, chatting lightly.

As soon as the pair appeared in the living room, the others burst into applause. They demanded that Weilong sing. She tried to decline, but finally gave in and sang "Burmese Nights." When she had finished she surreptitiously searched Madame Liang's face; her aunt's hold over Lu Zhaolin was, she could see, still uncertain. If Weilong stepped too far into the limelight, if the company paid too much attention to her, she might well incur the wrath of her aunt. She decided not to sing again.

The garden party was an afternoon tea, and by seven or eight in the evening the crowd had dispersed. Madame Liang and Weilong had been too busy taking care of guests to eat anything, so they were ready for a meal. Madame Liang felt a bit guilty about Lu Zhaolin, so she was being very kind to Weilong. Neither had much to say.

"The chocolate cake wasn't very good today," remarked Madame Liang. "Remember, next time, to ask the Qiao family to lend us their cook for a day."

Weilong agreed. Madame Liang cut a slice of cold cow's tongue, then stared at it with a smile. A moment later she picked up her water glass; she stared at it with a smile. Picking up the pepper shaker seemed to trigger a further memory; the smile lines around her mouth grew deeper yet.

Weilong sighed. "A woman is such a pitiful thing!" she thought. "A man is only a little bit nice, and see how happy she is!"

Madame Liang glanced at Weilong sharply. "What are you smiling at?" she demanded, barely suppressing her own smile.

Weilong was startled. "Did I smile?"

Behind Madame Liang stood a pine cupboard in which a silver plaque was displayed, an award that she'd received for her donations to the Royal Medical Society's Hong Kong branch. It shone bright as a mirror. Weilong caught a glimpse of her smiling reflection in the silver. She quickly wiped off the smile.

"Liar! And such a child—invite a few people over, and see how happy she gets!" Then, smiling secretly, Madame Liang went back to eating her slice of cow's tongue.

Weilong had a new thought, and again the corners of her mouth lifted; what made her smile was what, in her heart, made her pretend to frown: "What's the matter with you?

You've got good reason to be angry—why are you so calm? People in the old days would 'dare to fume but dare not speak.' You don't even dare to get angry, is that it?" But her heart had slipped away from Liang and Lu as lightly as a dragonfly grazes the water, before carelessly flying off somewhere else. Aunt and niece had each invited an invisible guest: since there really were four at table, it was a most companionable meal.

After dinner, Weilong went back to her bedroom. Glint was turning down the bed. She folded up a moon-white nightgown and put it on the pillow. When she saw Weilong she said, "That George Qiao sure had eyes for you!"

"How bizarre," Weilong said with a sarcastic smile. "Qiao must be an amazing fellow. Everyone gets so worried if he talks to me for just a few minutes."

"That fellow, well, he's not so amazing, but still it's not a good idea to lead him on."

Weilong shrugged. "So who's leading him on?"

"You lead him on, or he leads you—what's the difference?"

Heading into the bathroom, Weilong said, "Yes, yes, you don't need to tell me. Zhou Jijie gave me an earful just now—told me all about his evil ways. You must have heard everything through the door."

She started to shut the bathroom door, but Glint wedged her foot in it. "Miss," she said, "you don't understand. The fact that he plays around doesn't matter that much. The bad thing's that his father doesn't like him. His mother fell out of favor soon after they got married, and she doesn't have any money to give him. His father has never taken him in hand, so he makes no effort to study. Even now, with his father still around, George is hard up, always strapped for cash. When Sir Cheng Qiao dies, he'll leave behind two dozen concubines and half a dozen sons. Even the favorites won't get much, so what do you think will be left for George? And he's good for nothing except playing around. He's got tough times ahead."

Weilong was silent. She looked Glint in the eye for quite a while and then she said, "Don't worry. I may be foolish, but I'm not that foolish."

Having said as much, she really did try to be careful. George didn't come charging into the Liang household again, but whenever Weilong attended a social function, he was sure to be there. Weilong was much cooler toward him than she had been when they first met. She was now going out surprisingly often; Madame Liang wanted her out of the house. Madame Liang and Lu Zhaolin were hitting it off beautifully, and because Weilong and Lu Zhaolin had once been attracted to each other, Madame Liang worried that her niece might resent her success. She also didn't want Zhaolin to be distracted. So she made sure that Weilong stayed out of sight, at least for the time being.

But good things never come without problems, and just at this point Madame Liang's old flame Situ Xie returned to Hong Kong. Although Situ Xie was no longer youthful, he was even touchier than a young man, and his suspicions were easily aroused. Madame Liang was not about to offend an old friend, just for the sake of a fling. She set Lu Zhaolin aside, and focused instead on keeping Situ Xie happy.

One night, Weilong and Madame Liang went to a banquet together. It was crowded and the guests included both George Qiao and Situ Xie. When the dinner was over, Madame Liang invited Situ Xie to her house to see the new cherry-red glass tile she'd had installed in the bathroom. Since Situ Xie was the head of a Shantou ceramics company, she wanted his expert opinion. She and Weilong rode home with Situ Xie in his car. Halfway there, a heavy rain began to fall. It was then early summer, right at the start of the plum-rain season. The mountain slopes were velvet-black, and the dark, plush wind came in urgent bursts, squeezing the hot, white raindrops into a round, whirling mass as big as a cartwheel; lit up by the car's headlights, it rolled on ahead of them like a white satin-covered ball. The thick trees on the mountainside leaned over and shrank together into another whirling mass, a green satin ball rolling behind the white one.

The three of them sat in the car, with Madame Liang in the middle. The heat was too much for Weilong, so she leaned against the seat in front of her, feeling the humid breeze. It blew on her, and she began to get tired, so she nestled her head in her elbow. This reminded her of one of George's little habits. When he had to make a bit of mental effort, he'd bury his face in the crook of his arm and sit silent for a moment; then he'd lift his head and say, with a smile: "Right! Now I've got it!" It was childlike, and it filled Weilong with an almost maternal love. She wanted to kiss the short hair on the back of his head, kiss the face that was making such an effort to think, kiss the wrinkled sleeves at his elbows. Now all of George's delightful little gestures came to mind, and her heart grew soft and warm. Her heart grew hot, but her hands and feet were very cold. First hard, then soft, a current of cold happiness raced through her body, while outside the car window the rain blew hard, then soft, then hard again.

Sunk in reverie, Weilong was paying no attention to the conversation between Madame Liang and Situ Xie. Madame Liang gave her a nudge. "Look, look at this!" she said. Then she thrust her wrist into Weilong's face, so that Weilong could admire a diamond bracelet that was a full three inches wide. The car's interior light hadn't been switched on, but the bracelet gleamed so brightly that it made Madame Liang's red fingernails shine. Weilong gasped in admiration. "He gave it to me," said Madame Liang. She turned her face back toward Situ Xie, pouting. "I've never seen anyone so impatient, giving out jewelry when we haven't even reached the house!"

Weilong held Madame Liang's wrist and admired the bracelet. While she was exclaiming over it, and in far less time than it takes to tell—faster even than a detective whips out the handcuffs and claps them onto a criminal—Situ Xie put another diamond bracelet, identical to the first, around Weilong's own wrist. Weilong was too startled to say a word. She fumbled in the dark, unable to find the clasp, struggling to remove the bracelet. In her impatience she started pulling at it, trying to force it over her hand. Situ Xie quickly took her hand in his. "Miss Weilong, you can't refuse me this honor. Wait a moment, and I'll explain the whole thing to you. These bracelets come as a pair, and I couldn't bear to see them separated. One goes to your aunt, so this one has to go to you, doesn't it? Someday your aunt's will be yours, so it all comes to the same thing. No, no! Don't take it off—give it to your aunt for safekeeping, if you like."

"I would never dare to accept anything so valuable."

"When one of your elders gives you something," said Madame Liang, "it is never wrong to accept it. A simple thank you will suffice!" Then, with a light kick, she pressed her lips to Weilong's ear. "Have you no sense?" she hissed. "Do you have to carry on like some low-bred idiot?"

Weilong controlled her feelings. "Thank you very much," she said to Situ Xie, "but really…"

"Oh, please don't mention it," Situ Xie said over and over. "After all, we're all good friends." And he squeezed her hand a few times, before withdrawing his and resuming his conversation with Madame Liang. Weilong couldn't find a way to break in; she didn't know what to do.

The car pulled up at the Liang mansion, the storm now blowing so hard that it seemed the mountains would be driven into the sea. None of them had brought an umbrella, so the driver honked the horn, alerting the servants to come down with umbrellas to escort each of them into the house. The white leather pumps that Madame Liang and Weilong wore were soaked and splattered; at each step they squeaked and oozed. No sooner had Weilong reached the door than she ran upstairs.

"Wash your feet and change your shoes," Madame Liang ordered, "then come down for brandy. Otherwise, you might catch cold."

Weilong consented, but to herself she thought, "Stay up late drinking with you two? I'd have to be brave enough to eat a leopard!"

When she reached her room she locked herself in. She started the water for her bath, then called out for someone to tell them that she'd caught a cold and gone to bed. Glint knocked a few minutes later, with some aspirin. Under the cover of the running water, Weilong pretended not to hear.

Her room, with its private bath and little balcony, was practically a separate apartment. Before going to bed, Weilong opened the glass door to the balcony to make the room less stuffy. Luckily, the wind wasn't blowing in her direction, and not much rain came in. There was an outcrop opposite the balcony—as if the mountain had reached out its tongue to give the balcony a lick. During plum-rain season, the trees on the mountain were steeped in mist; the scent of green leaves was everywhere. Plantains, Cape jasmine, magnolia, banana trees, camphor trees, sweet flag, ferns, ivorywoods, palms, reeds, and tobacco, all growing too fast and spreading too rapidly: it was ominous, with a whiff of something like blood in the air. The humidity was oppressive, and the walls and furniture were slick with moisture.

Weilong lay on her bed. The bedding was gummy; the pillowcase ready to grow moss. She had just had a bath, but already the humidity made her wish for another. She tossed and turned; she was painfully troubled. She kept thinking about Situ Xie and the change in his behavior toward her. He'd always been interested in her, but he'd never been so forward— certainly not in the presence of her aunt. Judging from his performance today, he must have reached an agreement with Madame Liang. Would he offer her such a valuable present for no reason? He wasn't that kind of a person! Having thought things through this far, Weilong glanced at the bracelet on her dressing table. She had taken it off and tossed it there; it glittered beneath the small table lamp. She sat up sharply. "Better put it away safely," she thought. "No matter what, I must find a way to return it to him. Losing it would be no fun." She opened the closet and got out a little leather case, then put the bracelet into it for safekeeping. The closet was set into the wall and fitted out with rows of bright lightbulbs to prevent mildew in the rainy season.

When Weilong opened the closet door again, she found herself thinking back to the spring, and how nervous she'd been that evening when she'd first arrived. She remembered how, after making sure no one could see her, she had tried on all her new clothes. Since then three months had passed in a flash; in that brief time she'd done a great deal of dressing up, eating out, and playing around—she'd even made something of a name for herself. Everything the average girl dreams of, she'd done. It was unlikely that all this would come free of charge. From that perspective, the little drama that had just unfolded was inevitable. No doubt this wasn't the first time that Madame Liang had sacrificed a girl in order to please Situ Xie. And Madame Liang would be sure to require other sacrifices from her as well. The only way to refuse would be to leave the house altogether.

Weilong leaned against the closet door and watched the rain on the balcony. When the drops of rain hit the cement and caught a bit of light, they twirled around and shot out beams of silver light—long, long beams of light, like the silver skirts of ballet dancers. Weilong sighed. After three months of this life, she was addicted. If she wanted to leave Madame Liang's house, she would have to find a rich man to marry. A husband who was both rich and charming? It was unlikely. Plumping for a man with money—that had been Madame Liang's approach.

Madame Liang had a clear head, and she was unabashedly materialistic: as a young woman, she'd ignored the opinions of others and married a sixty-year-old tycoon, waiting for him to die. He died all right but, sad to say, a bit late—Madame Liang was old now, with a hungry heart that she could not fill. She needed love, she needed it from lots and lots of people, but to a young person, her way of looking for love seemed ridiculous! Weilong didn't want to end up like that.

Her thoughts turned to George Qiao. After her emotions had been so deeply unsettled by the day's unexpected turn of events, she felt she had no strength left: she had to give up the battle against George that had been going on in her heart. She had to surrender to love. Maybe George wanted nothing more than a moment's pleasure; maybe he treated all women this way. But if he made a sincere declaration of love, she knew that she would accept him. True, George hadn't behaved very well in the past. He was too smart, too detached; the people he knew didn't understand him. Surrounded by Hong Kong people, he lived like a foreigner. It was a good thing that he was still young. If his wife loved him and believed in him, he was sure to succeed. He didn't have money, but the Qiao family had contacts throughout Hong Kong. He'd find a way to make a living.

Weilong had changed her mind about George, and her tone changed too. The next time they met, he felt it at once. That day, a group of young people set out for a picnic on one of the local mountain peaks. Weilong grew fatigued along the way, and George, after arranging to meet the others at the summit, stayed with her while she rested. It had been raining for the past several days and the rain had just ceased. The skies were overcast, and the green peaks pierced the fog. Sitting with their feet hanging over the edge of the road, Weilong and George looked down through the clouds to a misty mountain slope below. Two or three blue-clad peasant women in coolie hats were collecting tree limbs. Weilong felt a sort of swimming unreality, and because George was being especially gentle and kind that day, and was leaning against her quietly as they sat, she felt even more dazed, almost as if she were dreaming. She was wearing white slacks and a copper-red blouse with rusty green polka dots. A scarf of the same fabric had slipped from her head, revealing her long, wavy bangs. She picked at the grass blades. "George," she softly asked, "don't you have any plans for the future?"

"Of course I do. For instance, I plan to come and see you tonight, if the moon is shining."

Weilong's expression changed. Before she could speak, George continued. "I plan to come and see you because I have something important to tell you. I'd like to know what you think about marriage."

Weilong's heart did a somersault. Then George said, "I have no intention of getting married. Even if I could get married, I wouldn't be any good at it. I wouldn't be a satisfactory husband—not till I'm fifty, at least. Weilong, I'm telling you this straight out because you've never played games with me. You're too good—really, Weilong, you are. You let your aunt exploit you like this—and for whose benefit? When you're exhausted, all worn out, do you think she'll still want to keep you around? Weilong, you're worn out. You need a little happiness."

With that, he leaned down to kiss her, but her face stiffened. "Weilong, I can't promise you marriage, and I can't promise you love. All I can promise you is happiness."

This was a far cry from what Weilong had expected. She was confused, as if she'd suddenly tripped and fallen backward a long way. She pressed her hands against her temples, and turned away with a tiny smile. "What a tight-fisted guy!"

"I'm offering you happiness. Is there anything in the world that's harder to find than happiness?"

"You're offering me happiness? You're tormenting me, more than anyone ever has!"

"I'm tormenting you? Is that so?"

He wrapped his arm around her tightly and kissed her hard on the mouth. Just then, the sun came out and blazed right into their faces. George removed his lips, pulled a pair of dark sunglasses from his pocket. He put them on. "Look," he grinned, "the weather's clearing up! Tonight the moon is going to shine."

Weilong grabbed his coat collar, lifted her eyes, and stared into his face imploringly. She tried as hard as she could to find his eyes behind the dark lenses, but all she could see there was her own pale, shrunken reflection. She searched for a long time, then suddenly dropped her gaze. George clasped her tightly around her shoulders, and she buried her face in his chest. He discovered that she was trembling so hard that her teeth were chattering. "Weilong," he asked softly, "what are you so afraid of?"

"I—" she stuttered, "I—I'm afraid of myself! Maybe I'm going crazy!" She gasped loudly and started to cry.

George gave her a gentle shake, but she continued to tremble so violently that he could not hold her still.

Then she said, "No, I'm not crazy! What you say to me makes no sense—why on earth do I listen?"

There's an English saying in Hong Kong: "Hong Kong skies, Hong Kong girls." It's an apt comparison. Hong Kong girls are just as capricious, just as unpredictable, as the island's steamy climate. And the weather seemed to be listening to George, just like a girl: that night, the moon shone.

George came by moonlight, and he left by moonlight. The moon was still high in the sky when he climbed from Weilong's balcony to the cliff face nearby, clinging to the crooked tree branches as he went. The woods were still thick with humidity. It was hot and damp, the insects chirped, the frogs gurgled.

The entire hollow was like a huge cauldron that was slowly being heated by the dark blue blaze of the moon, heated till you could hear the water boiling. Even the firewood gatherers rarely came along this crest of the hill. George stepped cautiously. He was afraid of snakes and carried a stick. He took a step, pushed the tall grass back with his stick, swept it with the beam of his flashlight, then quickly turned off the light. Grass burrs stuck to his pants in itchy, prickly clumps. As he walked along, he heard a long, mournful wail that rose up from deep in the hills. It started suddenly and stopped as quickly—like a strangled cry for help. George knew it was only an owl, but fear chilled him to the bone. He stopped, listening intently. After a moment's rest, the wailing started again. George slipped; he almost fell down the slope. Grabbing a lemon tree, he steadied himself. Maybe it would be better to go across the garden, he thought. The gardener won't be there till daybreak, and that's awhile yet. Clinging to vines and creepers, he clambered down the cliff. George wasn't particularly athletic, but he'd been getting in and out of scrapes all his life, and this short scramble was well within his abilities. He climbed down till he was about ten feet above level ground, then hunched over to jump. He landed on the grass in the rear garden.

He walked around the corner of the veranda to the front lawn. Someone was standing by the little iron gate; he flinched in surprise. The person's back was clearly visible in the moonlight: a white linen blouse and wide black trousers of lightly lacquered silk; hair braided and coiled up on the head, serpentlike, because of the heat, the white neck surging naked above the collar. That small figure with the slender waist and bold curves—one he always watched, and remembered—it had to be Glint.

"The road down the hill," George thought. "It's famous as a lover's lane. In the summertime, people come and go all night long. The girl must have a date." He hesitated briefly, then stole up behind her. But Glint was on high alert; the moment she sensed someone at her back, she whipped around, confronting him head-on.

George fell back a step. "You scared me!" he laughed.

Glint's hand fluttered at her chest while she caught her breath. "I'm the one who should be saying that! My goodness, what a lot of trouble you are! You could scare a ghost to death!" Squinting, she looked him up and down and snickered. "I know what you're up to."

George brazened it out with a smile. "Your Young Mistress asked me to come. Didn't she tell you?"

"If she asked you, it would be open and aboveboard, and of course she'd want you to spend the night. What are you up to, sneaking away like this?"

George reached over and touched a stray hair at the back of her head. "Your braid wasn't pulled tight. It's about to come apart." His hand moved down her neck, then down her spine.

Glint twisted away, shaking her head. She heaved a long sigh. "I'd scream," she said, "but the mistress, with that terrible temper of hers—she'd throw a fit, without minding the consequences; the young lady's reputation would be harmed..."

"Oh, I suppose you could bear it if the young lady's reputation got hurt—but your reputation, now that's another matter. That's what's stopping you. Noble, virtuous sister, whatever are you doing in the garden so very late at night?"

Instead of rising to the bait, Glint gave him a wolfish glare. And she reproached him sternly: "This time you've really gone too far. What's your grudge against the Liang people? Even after what you did to Glance, you won't stop—you've got to come after *her* as well? And she's not at all the same as Glance!"

"Ah, so you're going to avenge them? Waylay me in the dark, kill me, take all my money?"

"And how much money do you have anyway? As if I would touch it!" Glint turned and walked off.

George scurried after her. He grabbed her around the waist. "Dear sister, don't be angry. Here's a little something, please accept it."

With his free hand, he reached into his trousers pocket and pulled out a roll of banknotes, planning to stuff it into her pocket. He fumbled around in her white linen fitted top, searching for the inside pocket, but in his haste he could not find it.

Glint slapped his hand sharply. She scolded: "Forget it! Do you really think I want your bribe?"

George now tried in earnest to pull away from her, but in the confusion he couldn't—Glint's fitted top was too tight. After several moments' struggle, he finally managed to wrest his hand free.

"I'm so very sorry," Glint remarked snippily as she did up the fastening of her top. "We servants aren't like you ladies and gentlemen; we haven't got so much leisure for lolling about in the open air, savoring the moonlight." She headed toward the house.

George followed close behind her, and while she was opening the side door with her key he came up behind, resting his face on the nape of her neck. Unwilling to call out, for fear of waking the household, Glint gnashed her teeth; she struck backward with her right foot, kicking George's knee as hard as she could. He cried out once, then stifled his voice. Again Glint struck, her left foot kicking him squarely in the left knee. George let go of her, and she walked through the door. He went in too, watching her sway gracefully up the stairs. There in the light of the hall lamp, he took out a handkerchief and, with a frown, dusted the black spots off his knees. Then he closed the door and followed Glint up the stairs.

In another corner of the house, Weilong lay curled on her bed in the heavy darkness, no lamp lit. She lay sleeping, motionless, but her body seemed to be in a car on the highway,

with a soft summer breeze tapping rhythmically on her cheeks.
But it wasn't a summer breeze, it was George's kisses. Weilong
lay like this longer than she could tell, then sat up abruptly. She
put on slippers and a dressing gown and went out onto the
little balcony. The moon had already set, but she had been
dipped in moonlight, steeped in moonlight, till her whole body
was transparent. She leaned back against the louvered door:
had the balcony been a black lacquer tea tray, she would have
been the inlaid flower.

She was surprised to find her mind so clear—never before
had she been so completely awake. Now, as she probed her feelings, she saw why she felt such stubborn love for George. This
abject infatuation of hers had been inspired by his very real
charm, of course; but in the end she loved him simply because
he did not love her. George had learned from experience, perhaps, this secret way to conquer women's unreasoning hearts.
He'd said many tender things, but never that he loved her. And
yet now she knew that George *did* love her. There were, of
course, some differences between his love and hers—and of
course his love had lasted only a moment. But her self-respect
had sunk so low that she was easily satisfied. Tonight, George
had loved her. The memory of this little happiness was all hers;
no one could take it away. Madame Liang, Situ Xie, and the
rest of that tiger-eyed crowd—they could do what they liked.
She had a new kind of security, a new sense of power and freedom. She was grateful that George hadn't married her. She'd
heard about the man who went on an excursion to Mount
Lu, and came back with half a dozen clay jugs: the jugs were
filled with the mountain's world-famous white clouds, which
he was going to release one after another to ornament his
garden. People who marry for love are as foolish as the man
with the cloud-filled jars! George was right, George was always
right. She leaned against the railing, and like George, she
buried her face in the crook of her elbow. Again it came—that

feeling of tingling ice-cold happiness, like golden bells ringing all over her body, the feeling she had when he clasped her shoulders tightly. Wanting to hug something herself, she gave a little whistle, and a white poodle came bounding out of the room wagging its tail. Murmuring softly, Weilong hugged the dog.

It was about four o'clock. The sky had begun to grow pale, but it was still full of stars, like a sheet of blue-green writing paper dusted with gold. Along the mountain face, the insects had fallen silent. There was a noiseless hush in the air. Suddenly, she heard footsteps—someone below walking toward the balcony. What a devoted gardener, Weilong thought. It's not even daybreak, and here he is already. Her heart was light and merry, playful like a little child's, and she pointed to the person in the distance, and whispered teasingly in the dog's ear: "Who do you think that is? Now just who do you think that is?" The dog began to bark.

Weilong looked more closely, and her heart started to pound—why did the gardener have such a monstrously swollen shape? Daybreak comes quickly in the tropics, and when the sky grew bright, the hazy oversize shadow resolved into two people walking together, wrapped in an embrace so close that they seemed to be one. When they heard the dog barking, they looked up and saw Weilong. There was no way for them to hide—right away she saw that it was George and Glint. Weilong had been holding the dog's lower jaw; now her grip tightened to a choke. The dog writhed furiously in her arms, then wriggled free and jumped down, yelping as it ran back into the room.

Weilong ran, stumbling, after the dog. Once she was in the room she stood stock-still; her arms hung stiffly at her sides. She stood there for a while, then fell onto the bed, arms still locked to her sides; she'd fallen flat on her face, but she didn't feel anything. She lay like that, face pressed downward, motionless, for the rest of the night. Gradually the sheet under her face grew damp. Icy tears soaked in under her shoulders.

The next day, when she got up, she was so cold that her whole body ached and her head felt swollen. The clock in her room had stopped, but the sunshine outside was bright and yellow—she couldn't tell if it was morning or afternoon. She sat on the edge of her bed for a long time. Then she stood up and went to look for Glint.

Glint was in the downstairs washroom rinsing out some things. She had plastered an entire wall with handkerchiefs—apple green, amber yellow, smoky blue, peach red, bamboo green—square upon square, some lined up neatly, others askew. The effect was almost painterly. Then she saw Weilong in the mirror, and her face froze. She tried to muster a smile, but Weilong pulled a sopping towel out of the sink and slapped her with it: one slashing sweep, right in the face, drenching her from head to foot. Glint cried out and turned away, raising her hands in defense, and the towel struck her hands as well. The towel was thick and sodden, so heavy it made Weilong's arm ache. She wrung it out with both hands, then slapped away furiously; Glint dodged the blows without making any effort to argue, apologize, or retaliate. Even so, there was a considerable noise in the washroom, and when the junior maids came running in, they were stopped dead in their tracks, unable to figure out what was going on.

Two of them grew restive; they huddled together and muttered, "A legitimate master doesn't trample on us like this—where did this Miss come from, that she has such a temper! And Glint, you hardly ever give in to others—what's wrong with you today?"

Glint sighed. "Leave her alone! She's the one to be sorry for!"

Her words pierced Weilong to the heart. She walloped Glint as hard as she could. Then, dropping the towel, she collapsed;

sitting on the edge of the bathtub, she buried her face in her hands and burst into tears.

By then, the commotion had reached Madame Liang's ears. When Madame Liang arrived at the scene, Glint was kneeling on the tiled floor mopping up the puddles. As she mopped, water dripped from her own clothes. "What's going on?" Madame Liang demanded. Glint made no reply. Weilong was questioned, but wouldn't say a word. All the junior maids who'd been watching said they didn't know why Miss was so angry. Holding her questions for the moment, Madame Liang ordered a maid to take Weilong upstairs to rest. Then she called Glint into her private room for a detailed examination.

There was no disguising the situation: Glint had to explain, in broken sentences, how Miss had made a date with George, and then she herself, upon hearing voices in Miss's bedroom, had grown suspicious. She hadn't dared to report it, for fear of causing a scene. Instead, she'd kept watch in the garden, planning to catch George as he was leaving and get to the bottom of things. But then Miss had found out, and not taking kindly to the thought of having tabs kept on her, she'd burst out in a rage against Glint.

Madame Liang listened and nodded, without saying a word; she had by now figured out the essentials of the true situation. After sending Glint away, she sat thinking, her anger growing till her face turned purple. She had been picking her teeth with a toothpick, and now she bit down so that it snapped. Grunting, she spat the end of the toothpick out. This George Qiao was an evil star in her astral house, forever playing tricks on her. She'd tried using Glance to hook him, but he'd merely swallowed the bait and gone on swimming about, free as he pleased. After that, she'd decided to take a loss, and to ignore him. But she couldn't keep Glance, not after all the ruckus he'd kicked up, and when Glance left it was like losing both of her hands. So she'd fired up the cooking pot again, and devoted all her energies to training Weilong. Putting her whole heart into the effort, she'd brought the girl along till she showed some promise. Weilong was just now making her debut, she was ten times more valuable than before, and now George turned up, once again, to feast on the fruits of others' toil. Even this was not enough; he'd casually taken Glint too. Madame Liang had lost a queen and a pawn. All her best personnel has been netted by this fellow—how could she not be angry?

Still, Madame Liang knew enough not to lose sight of what really mattered. She pondered for a while and then, her rage in check, proceeded with a slow, measured grace to Weilong's room. Weilong was lying with her face to the wall, and Madame Liang sat down on the edge of the bed. After a moment's silence, she said in a faltering tone, "Weilong, how can you do this to me?" She dabbed her eyes with a handkerchief. Weilong was silent. "How do you expect me to explain things to your father?" said Madame Liang. "While you're living here with me, I'm responsible for your behavior. It seems I've been too trusting. I've been negligent, and now this has happened!" She sighed. "You certainly have flouted my authority!"

Weilong knew that she was caught, and she let her aunt have her say. Her regrets were past repair. She steadied herself and gave a simple, straightforward reply: "My mistakes aren't your fault. I'll go back to Shanghai. If there's gossip, I'll take the blame myself. Of course I'm not going to involve you in this."

Madame Liang stroked her chin. "You say you'll go back, but this isn't the time to go back. Of course, I don't mean to detain you. I would be very happy, for my own sake, to send you back to your father; then I'd be free of this burden, and all these worries. But you know how people talk, and it's all too likely that before you even reached home, rumors would have come to your father's ears. You know what a terrible temper he has. If you go back now, that will only prove what people are saying. Your health has always been weak—how can you bear your father's constant displeasure, day after day?"

Weilong was silent. Madame Liang sighed. "Blame this, blame that—but in the end the blame's on you because of the scene you made in front of the servants. You're in a fix, and you've done it to yourself! Here you are all grown up, but you behave like a child, pay no attention to your own reputation— how are you going to face others now?"

Weilong blushed, before smiling bitterly. "Aunt will have to forgive me," she said. "I'm still young and reckless. When I've reached Aunt's age, then maybe, just maybe, I'll know how to fall in love with grace and style!"

Madame Liang responded with a sarcastic laugh. "If, at my age, you still have the opportunity to fall in love, that will be surprising indeed. You must have noticed that the average woman from the middle class and below, once she's past thirty or forty is nothing but an old crone. I have a nice place. I look after myself. Otherwise, I'd have turned old a long time ago. But you—you don't protect your own reputation. You've ruined your own prospects—an upper-class match will be out of reach, and there's no telling where you'll end up!"

These were words to hurt the ears and pain the heart. Weilong covered her face with her hands, just as if her powdery white, inky black good looks had already been leached away by the years that stream by like water.

Madame Liang twisted around, propping her elbow on Weilong's pillow. "For a woman, there's nothing more important than her reputation," she said in a low voice. "When I use the word 'reputation,' I mean something a bit different from a fusty old scholar's idea. These days, people who are even a little bit modern don't care that much about chastity. When a young lady goes out and mixes at banquets and parties, there's bound to be a certain amount of gossip. That kind of talk, the more it spreads, the more it stirs up interest, the more it increases your prestige. It certainly won't harm your future. The one thing that must be avoided at all costs is this: to love someone who doesn't love you, or who loves you and drops you. A woman's bones can't withstand a fall like that!

"In a situation like the one today, people who know the inside story will say that you run off and do whatever pops into your head, just like a child. But if outsiders come to hear of it, their poisonous tongues will say you scrapped with a maid over George Qiao. Now that would be unpleasant, wouldn't it?"

Weilong sighed heavily. "Well, I can't do anything about it. Anyway, I'm going back. I don't want to see Hong Kong ever again!"

Madame Liang furrowed her brow. "The same old tune! You keep saying you'll go back to Shanghai, as if going home would solve everything. It's not that simple. Of course you can do as like—you have your freedom! Still I'm worried about you; your father won't make life easy for you at home. This is no time for sulking. If you want to get your strength back, you have to make George Qiao submit. Once he's surrendered completely, then you can drop him—or keep him around for amusement's sake, that would show true skill! If you run away now, you'll be making it too easy for him!"

Weilong smiled wanly. "Aunt, George and I are finished."

"You think there's no hope left? That's because, from the very beginning, your attitude toward him has been all wrong. You're too straightforward. He's sure there's no one in your heart but him, so he's not serious and doesn't bother to take you seriously either. You should arrange to spend more time with other people; that way he'll be on edge all the time. He doesn't think much of you, but there are plenty of others who do—"

Weilong could see that she was working her way, in roundabout fashion, to the same old appeal on Situ Xie's behalf. She struggled to suppress a little burst of laughter. "Fool that I am," she thought, "I'm not yet such a fool as that." If, after falling into George's trap, she now turned around and fell into Situ Xie's, was that likely to make George respect her? She sat up straight, feet bare on the floor, with her head bowed. Smoothing her tangled hair with both hands, she slowly pushed it back from her brows. "Thank you, Aunt, for thinking things through so carefully for me. But I still think I should go back."

Madame Liang sat up straight also. "You're quite sure then?"

Weilong concurred, her voice low.

Madame Liang stood up and firmly laid her two hands on Weilong's shoulders. She looked deeply into her eyes. "When you came you were one kind of person. Now you are another kind of person. You have changed and your home must change along with you. You can try to go back to your previous life, but you might not be able to."

"I know I've changed. I didn't much like myself before, and now I like myself even less. I'm going back because I want to be a new person."

Upon hearing this, Madame Liang fell silent for a while. Then, bending from the waist, she solemnly kissed Weilong on the forehead and left the room. The gesture, with all its Catholic-style theatrics, appeared to have no effect on Weilong. She thrust both hands up into her hair again, and stared into space. Her face bore the trace of a smile, but her eyes were dead.

As soon as she'd left the room, Madame Liang telephoned George and told him they had something important to discuss. George knew that he'd been found out and, as per usual, gave lots of reasons why he couldn't come. So Madame Liang scared him: "Weilong is in tears and wants to go back to Shanghai, but her parents are sure to take this up. Her family in Shanghai will be hiring a lawyer to speak to you, and then it will be a big case! Your father, once he loses his temper, will clamp down hard on you. And since Weilong met you at my place, if this gets out, it's not going to help my reputation either, which is why I've been trying to reach you—to see if there's some solution. Who would have guessed you'd take it so calmly? The emperor does not worry—and that's what worries his advisers!"

George came, but he was smiling. "I'm no expert on the Chinese, but on this aspect of Chinese custom and lore, I've done my homework. If Weilong's family wants to talk with me, it'll only be to pressure me to marry her! Making this a public matter is the last thing they'd want."

Madame Liang stared him in the eye. "Marry her! Are you willing to marry her?"

"Weilong has her points."

"Answer me honestly. You can't marry her."

"Since you know, why are you asking? I don't have the right to marry as I please. I don't have any money and I'm used to the good life. Nature apparently intended me to be an imperial son-in-law."

Madame Liang stabbed him with her finger. "I always knew you for a money-loving materialist!" she scolded.

The two of them talked over the problem of getting Weilong to change her mind. By now, George realized that the threat of legal action had been made up by Madame Liang. His first step, in order to defuse the situation, was to render a full account of his behavior, and bare his heart to her. They talked through the night, and Madame Liang finally got an answer that satisfied her.

The next day, George's calls to Weilong rang the phone off the hook, and a steady stream of bouquets arrived for her, each with a note tucked inside. Weilong hurried down the hillside to the city to ask about the boat schedule and bought a ticket that same day. Madame Liang's attitude was one of strict noninterference, hearing nothing, asking nothing. Weilong hadn't taken the car—instead she'd caught a bus at the bottom of the hill—

and when she was on her way back up again, rain started coming down in buckets. The water swept smoothly down the steep asphalt road, and Weilong wrung out her dress as she walked, but no sooner had she wrung it out, than it was drenched again. For the past two days she'd been on the edge of catching a cold; now she was chilled through and through. Once she got home she fell ill, first the flu and then pneumonia.

Her temperature ran high, and she was feverishly anxious to return home. When she was sick at home, the room wasn't crowded with flowers from friends, the way this one was, but there was something more beautiful than flowers: a glass globe on her father's desk that he used as a paperweight—it would be given to her to hold, to cool her burning hands. There were tiny red, blue, and purple flowers all through the ball, neatly arranged in a simple pattern. It was very heavy in her hand. Thinking of it reminded her of everything in her life that seemed solid, substantial, reliable—her home; the black iron bed that she shared with her sister; the quilt on the bed, made of coarse red-and-white cloth; the old-fashioned boxwood dressing table; the darling little peach-shaped ceramic jar that shone red in the sunlight and was filled with talcum powder; the fashion-girl calendar tacked up on the wall, the girl's arms covered with phone numbers her mother had scribbled in a thick pencil script, numbers for the tailor, the employment agency, the soy-milk vender, and two different aunts. Twisting her hands in the sheets, Weilong thought about nothing but going home, going home, going home, but the more she wanted to go, the more her illness lingered. By the time her condition had started to improve, Hong Kong's incessantly rainy summer was over; it was fall, bracing and bleak.

Weilong was smitten with doubt—could she have fallen ill on purpose? Was she unconsciously unwilling to go home, seeking to delay her return? It was easy enough to say that she'd go back, become a new person, start a new life, and so on; but she no longer was the simple girl she'd once been. Go to school, then go out and get a job: perhaps this wasn't the best path for someone like her—pretty, but without much ability. Of course she'd have to get married. A new life meant a new man. A new man? She'd lost all her self-confidence because of George; she couldn't cope with other people now. The minute George had stopped loving her, she was in his power. She knew very well that he was only an ordinary playboy, that there was nothing especially terrifying about him—the terrifying thing was the passion, raging and wild beyond words, that he inspired in her.

She lay on her bed looking at the sky through the window. The afternoon sun shone brilliantly, the sky a cold metallic white, cutting the eyes like a knife. The air grew chilly, and a bird flew toward the mountaintop. High in the white sky, the dark bird gave a mournful cry, as if cut by the blade of the knife; then it dropped down over the mountain.

Weilong closed her eyes. Ah, George! One day he would need her, but by then she'd have lived in the narrow confines of some other household for too long. She'd have adapted to that place, her new flesh enmeshed in the fence around her life—no way to pull it free. If, at that point, George wanted her back, it would be too late.

Suddenly, she decided not to leave—no matter what, she would not leave. Then she went on changing her mind every five minutes: leave, don't leave, leave, don't leave. Lying on her bed, she rolled back and forth between the two extremes, her heart frying in hot oil. Seeking relief from the pain, she rushed off, the moment she was well enough to leave the house, and booked her passage. Later, as she was returning home, with darkness falling and the wind shuffling through the dwarf bamboos, the air grew sharp with cold. The sea beyond the bamboos, and the sky beyond the sea, were already gray and ocher; all along the road, in the gathering gloom, the ten-foot-high ivorywood trees bore their red flowers, high and low, as big as bowls.

As Weilong walked, a car came from behind; it drove right up to her, then stopped. Weilong recognized George's car but did not turn her head; staring straight ahead, she increased her pace. George followed slowly in the car, down a long stretch of road. Weilong had only just recovered from her illness and was still a little weak; soon she was sweating with the effort and had to stop and rest. The car also stopped. Weilong guessed that George wanted a chance to clear everything up, but when he didn't say a word, she glanced over. One of his arms was resting across the top of the steering wheel, and he was slumped against it, motionless. Weilong saw him, and pain tugged at her heart. Tears flowed down her face as she began to walk faster. This time George did not follow. At the next bend in the road, she turned back to look: his car was still there. Night had fallen, and the whole world looked like a gray Christmas card, everything shadowy and vague except the ivorywoods' enormous red flowers—simple, primitive, as big as bowls, as big as buckets.

When she got back to the house, Weilong asked where she could find Madame Liang, and was directed to the small study. She went straight there. The study was lit by a single small aquamarine desk lamp. Weilong sat at a distance from her aunt, in a yellow chair, and neither spoke for a long while. The room was full of the strong, almond-extract scent of Cutex. Madame Liang had just finished painting her nails and was stiffly holding her fingers out to dry. Her snow-white hands looked as if they'd been tortured in a finger clamp, the smashed fingertips dripping blood.

"Aunt," Weilong slowly asked, not looking at Madame Liang, "is George's not marrying due to financial reasons?"

"It's not that he doesn't have enough money to get married. The Qiao family isn't so poor that they can't afford to support a daughter-in-law. George's problem is that he's proud and he's set his sights higher; he wants his own place after he's married, since that would be more comfortable. Besides, the Qiao family is extremely complicated, and any daughter-in-law has a rough time of it there. If his wife had money, the two of them could avoid all sorts of provocations, all those ugly words and ugly faces."

"Then he wants to marry a young lady with a big dowry."

Madame Liang said nothing.

Weilong hung her head and continued in a tiny voice. "I don't have any money, but . . . I can earn money."

Madame Liang looked at her quizzically, biting her lips and smiling slightly.

Weilong's face went red. She continued: "Why can't I earn money? I didn't say anything to Situ Xie and he gave me that bracelet."

Laughter rose in Madame Liang's throat, and as she laughed she pointed a bloodred finger at Weilong, unable, for a moment, to get a word out. Finally she said, "Look at this child, fancy her remembering Situ Xie at this point! He was once very kind to you, but you were so vehement in your refusal, as if a diamond bracelet could bite you. If I hadn't acted quickly he probably would have been quite offended. And now you want to ask him for something. With a young lady so apt to balk at anything big, he won't know what to give—candy, maybe, or roses!"

Weilong hung her head. She sat in the dark, saying nothing.

"You shouldn't think that just because a person is reasonably good-looking, knows how to make chitchat and sing a few English songs, that people are going to come running to give her stacks and stacks of money. Speaking as a member of the family, and without mincing my words, I'd say you are too bashful, too weak, and too bad-tempered; you're indecisive, and you get too emotionally involved—you're not at all suited to this sort of thing."

Weilong let out a long, slow sigh. "Give me a chance to learn!"

"You do have a lot to learn, that's for sure! Well, why not give it a try."

And Weilong did try. She gave it her best effort, and with Madame Liang at her side to offer expert advice, the results were nothing short of excellent. At Christmastime, there was an item in the *South China Morning Post* announcing the engagement of George Qiao and Ge Weilong. On the day of the formal engagement, Situ Xie sent a very impressive gift, and even George Qiao's father, Sir Cheng Qiao, gave Weilong a wristwatch of white gold inlaid with diamonds. When Weilong went to offer her thanks in person, the old man was so pleased that he bought her a mink stole. Then, because he was afraid of displeasing Madame Liang, he bought her an ermine stole.

George was still apprehensive about the marriage, but Madame Liang gave him a talking to. "You should make the best of things! You want to marry a rich girl, but you've set your sights too high—if she's not high enough on the social register, you turn up your nose. A girl from a really rich family is used to getting her way, not nearly so easy to bring around as Weilong. You'd have to put up with all sorts of restrictions. The reason you want money is to have a good time, and if you're not having a good time, what's the point of the money? Weilong's earnings will decline sharply, of course, seven or eight years from now. When she can't bring in enough to pay the bills, get a divorce. Obtaining a divorce, in the British legal system, is quite difficult; the only legal grounds are adultery. How hard will it be to find evidence of that?"

After this talk, George was perfectly ready to go along. The wedding was announced right away. It was held at the Hong Kong Hotel, and was a great success.

Hong Kong doesn't have many apartments, and renting a whole house for just two people seemed too expensive. Sharing a house didn't appeal either, since it would mean a loss of privacy. Madame Liang couldn't do without Weilong just then, so she got George to move in with his wife's family, and gave the couple three rooms on the lower floor. It was just like having an apartment of their own.

From then on, it was as if Weilong had been sold to Madame Liang and George Qiao. She was busy all day long, getting money for George Qiao and people for Madame Liang. And sometimes she was happy—for instance, when she and George went to Wanchai on Chinese New Year's Eve, just the two of them, mingling with the crowds.

Wanchai isn't in the center of Hong Kong; in fact, it's quite far away from the city, and filled with low-class amusements. However once a year there's a New Year's market, not unlike the temple festivals in northern China. When the market opens, people flood in, and lots of fashionable people like to join in the throng and buy a few trinkets. Weilong spotted a jadeite potted plum in a stall that sold curios and antiques, and George squeezed forward to haggle with the vendor. The vendor squatted on top of a many-tiered stack of display shelves. He wore a tight-fitting padded jacket made of coarse blue cotton sackcloth, trousers of the same cloth, and a woolen hat pushed back from his brow. A gas lamp was hanging in the center of the street, and its greenish glare fell directly on his sharp Cantonese features, bringing out the prominences, deepening the ravines, darkening the hollows. He rested one hand on his knee and gestured with the other, but after a lot of haggling, he still shook his head.

Weilong pulled George away. "Come on, let's go!"

Pushed back and forth by the crowd, she had a strange sensation. The sky overhead was a dark purple-blue, and the sea at the end of the winter sky was purple-blue too, but here in the bay was a place like this, a place teeming with people and lanterns and dazzling goods—blue ceramic double-handled flowerpots, rolls and rolls of scallion-green velvet brushed with gold, cellophane bags of Balinese Shrimp Crisps, amber-colored durian cakes from the tropics, Buddha-bead bracelets with their big red tassels, light yellow sachets, little crosses made of dark silver, coolie hats—and stretching out beyond these lights and people and market goods, the clear desolation of sea and sky; endless emptiness, endless terror. Her future was like that—it didn't bear thinking about; if she did think, it was only endless terror. She had no lasting arrangement for her life. Her fearful, cringing heart could find a makeshift sort of rest only in little odds and ends, like these spread out before her.

Dirty as the place was, there were still moments of wild pleasure. Firecrackers flew headlong and at random up and down the street, and she and George hunched over as they walked, dodging the little green-and-red comets.

"Oh!" George suddenly cried out. "You're on fire!"

"There you go, tricking me again!" said Weilong, twisting her head around to check the back of her dress.

"When have I ever tricked you! Quick, kneel down. Let me stamp it out."

Weilong kneeled on the ground; George stamped on her dress, dirty shoes and all, and put out the fire that was burning at the hem. Her cotton-lined dress, made of violet satin that was embroidered with small silver "longevity" characters, had a hole burned through. They laughed, and went on walking.

After a moment, George said, "It's true, Weilong, I love to tell a lie, but I've never lied to you. Even I don't quite understand it."

"Still thinking of that?"

George insisted: "I've never lied to you, have I?"

Weilong sighed. "Never. You know very well that a tiny little lie could make me very happy, but you refuse. You don't want to be bothered."

"You don't need me to lie to you. You lead yourself on, all by yourself. Someday you'll have to admit that I'm despicable. When that happens, you'll regret having sacrificed so much for me. Who knows—maybe you'll be so enraged you'll murder me! It scares me, I tell you!"

"I love you, so I'm not going to blame you for anything."

"That's all very well, but our current division of rights and duties really is unfair."

Eyebrows raised, Weilong smiled slightly. "Fair? There's no such thing as 'fair' in relationships between people. But I have to ask, what's suddenly pricking your conscience today?"

"Because I can see how much you're enjoying the New Year, just like a child."

"I look happy, and you have to say something awful so I won't be—is that it?"

The two of them walked along examining the items on display. Every possible sort of thing was there, but pride of place went to the human goods. A group of girls was standing in the severe light of a gas lamp; the intense chiaroscuro turned their noses light blue and the sides of their faces green, while the rouge that was slathered over their cheeks looked purple. One girl was very young, thirteen or fourteen at most. Her skinny little body was dressed up Western-style, with a short, dark-violet serge coat over a bright red skirt of pleated silk. The cold made her shiver so hard that her smile rippled unevenly across her face like a reflection in water; her lower lip was bitten through by her chattering teeth. When a drunken English sailor came up to her from behind and laid a hand on her shoulder, she twisted her head around and shot him a flirtatious glance—and her eyes were truly luscious, with drooping corners that swept out to the hairline. It was a pity though that she had a bright pink chilblain on her ear. She clasped the sailor's arm with her two hands and leaned her head against him; pressed tight, they walked a few steps, and then another sailor arrived—two big, tall men, squeezing in on her from both sides. Her head only reached their elbows.

Along came a gang of sailors, drunk and throwing firecrackers in every direction. When they saw Weilong, they started to aim at her, and the firecrackers raced like meteors toward the moon. Weilong was so scared she turned and ran. George found their car, and pushed her toward it; they got in, started the engine, and left Wanchai.

"Those drunken mudfish," George said with a smile. "What do they take you for?"

"But how am I any different from those girls?"

Steering with one hand, George reached out with the other to cover her mouth. "Talk such nonsense again and—"

"Yes, yes! I was wrong, I admit it," Weilong apologized. "How could there not be any difference between us? They don't have a choice—I do it willingly!"

The car passed through Wanchai. The sharp pop-pop of the firecrackers faded behind them, and the red traffic lights chased each other across the windshield, then slipped into darkness. The car drove through the heavy blackness of the city streets. George hadn't looked—it was too dark to see—but he knew she must be crying. With his free hand he pulled out a cigarette case and lighter. Cigarette dangling from his lips, he struck a light. On that bitter winter's night, the flame flashed before his mouth like an orange blossom. The blossom bloomed, then died. The cold and the dark returned.

Here is the end of this Hong Kong story. Weilong's brazier of incense will soon go out too.

JASMINE TEA

THIS POT of jasmine tea that I've brewed for you may be somewhat bitter; this Hong Kong tale that I'm about to tell you may be, I'm afraid, just as bitter. Hong Kong is a splendid city, but a sad one too.

First, pour yourself a cup of tea, but be careful—it's hot! Blow on it gently. In the tea's curling steam you can see...a Hong Kong public bus on a paved road, slowly driving down a hill. A passenger stands behind the driver, a big bunch of azaleas in his arms. The passenger leans against an open window, the azaleas stream out in a twiggy thicket, and the windowpane behind becomes a flat sheet of red.

Sitting by that window was Nie Chuanqing, a young man of something like twenty. Twenty, perhaps, though he looked much older around the eyes and mouth. Then again, his skinny neck and thin shoulders could have been those of an adolescent. Wearing a blue gown of lined silk, he leaned sideways in the seat, with his head propped against the window and a stack of books in his lap. There, in the rosy sateen gleam of the flowers, his oval-shaped Mongolian face, with its faint eyebrows and with the downturned corners of the eyes, had a feminine kind of beauty. But the nose was too sharp; it clashed with the delicate softness of his face. A peach-colored bus ticket was stuck between his teeth, and he seemed to have dozed off.

The bus came to a sudden stop. Forcing his eyes open, Chuanqing saw one of his classmates boarding: it was Professor Yan's daughter, Yan Danzhu. He frowned. He hated bumping into people he knew on the bus, he couldn't hear what they said over the engine roar. He was a bit deaf, his hearing damaged by the blows to the ear he'd taken from his father.

Yan Danzhu's hair looked freshly shampooed, with the center part drawn straight while the hair was still wet and the ends touched up with a curling iron. Her hair fell vertically to her shoulders, like an Indian girl's in an American cartoon. She had a smooth, round face, tanned to a coppery color, with jet-black brows and shining eyes; she wasn't very tall, but she had a nicely curvy figure. Once on the bus, she smiled and nodded at Chuanqing, then came over to sit beside him.

"Going home?" she asked.

Chuanqing leaned over so he could hear. "Yeah."

The conductor came to collect the fare. Chuanqing reached for his wallet, but Danzhu said, "Oh—I've got a monthly pass."

"What classes will you be taking this semester?" she continued.

"Same as before, no big change."

"Are you still going to be in my father's History of Chinese Literature?"

Chuanqing nodded.

"Did you know I'm taking it too?" she laughed.

"You're going to be your father's student?" Chuanqing was surprised.

"That's right!" Danzhu giggled. "At first he wouldn't let me! He's never had a daughter sitting with the other students while he lectures, and he was afraid he'd be embarrassed. And then, since we're used to joking around at home, he thought maybe I'd be too casual in class, pester him with questions the way I usually do, maybe even argue back—and then how could he keep a stern face? So I gave my solemn promise never to open my mouth in his class, no matter how little I understood, and finally he agreed."

"Professor Yan . . . he's a nice man!" Chuanqing lightly sighed.

"What? So he's not a good teacher?" Danzhu laughed. "You don't like his class?"

"Take a look at my grades and you'll see that he doesn't like me."

"What do you mean? He's harder on you because you're from Shanghai, and your Chinese is better than the Hong Kong students' Chinese. He often praises you. He says you're a bit lazy, that's all."

Chuanqing made no reply, turning away instead, and pressing his face against the glass. He couldn't keep leaning toward her, listening so intently when she spoke. Anyone who saw them would draw the wrong conclusion. Already lots of people were spreading rumors, all because Danzhu kept coming up to him. At school, people gave him the cold shoulder, and since he knew he wasn't liked, he stayed away from the others. But he couldn't escape Danzhu.

Danzhu—he didn't know what she had in mind, since she certainly had plenty of friends. Even though she'd been at South China University for only half a year, she was one of the most popular girls on campus. Why on earth did she want to befriend him? He stole a sideways glance at her. Her full breasts and tiny waist were sculpted by a white wool-knit vest, as if she were a plaster statue. He turned away again, rubbing his forehead on the glass. He didn't like looking at girls, especially pretty girls with good figures: they made him feel especially dissatisfied with himself.

Danzhu was talking again. He frowned, forcing a smile. "Sorry, I didn't hear that."

Raising her voice, she repeated her words, but again, halfway through, he could not follow her. Fortunately, since he was so often silent, she wasn't at all disturbed by his failure to answer. But then he happened to catch one part of what she'd said, the very last part. She had lowered her head and was tugging at her wool-knit vest; she pulled it down, but it crept back up again.

"What I told you the other day—about the letter Dequan sent me—please forget about it," she said. "Just pretend I never said anything."

"Why?" asked Chuanqing.

"Why?...It's quite obvious. I shouldn't have told anyone. I'm such a child—I can't keep anything back!"

Chuanqing leaned forward, rested his elbows on his knees, and smiled. Danzhu leaned forward at his side. "Chuanqing," she said quite seriously, "you aren't taking this the wrong way, are you? When I told you about that, I wasn't showing off. I can't just...not talk to people. The words build up inside and I have to let them out. And then, when I refused him, I lost Dequan as a friend. I want to be friends with him, I want to be friends with lots of people. As for anything more than that, we're too young, we can't even talk about such things yet. But they...they all get so serious."

A few moments passed. "Chuanqing, are you upset?" He shook his head. "I don't know why, but there are some things I can't tell anyone except you."

"I don't know why either."

"I think it's because...well, to me, you're like a girl."

A bitter smile swept across his face. "Really? You have a lot of girlfriends, so why choose me?"

"Because you're the only one who can keep a secret."

But Chuanqing replied coldly, "Of course—I don't have any friends, so there's no one I could tell."

Quickly she replied, "You're taking it all wrong again!" They both fell silent. Then Danzhu sighed. "I didn't say it the right way, but...Chuanqing, why don't you try to make some friends? Then you'd have someone to study with or have fun with. Why don't you invite us to your house to play tennis? I know you have a tennis court."

Chuanqing laughed. "There isn't much chance of playing

tennis on our court. It's usually full of laundry hung out to dry, and when the weather's warm, they cook opium there."

Danzhu stopped, unable to say anything more.

Chuanqing turned back and looked out the window. The bus took a fast, hard turn, and the azaleas in the standing passenger's arms were sent flying about. When Chuanqing looked at Danzhu again, he gasped a little in surprise. "You're crying!"

"How could I be crying? I never cry!" But then, with a sad, hard sob, she confronted him: "You . . . you always make me feel as though I've done something wrong . . . as if I have no right to be happy! But my happiness doesn't do you any harm!"

Taking her books from her, Chuanqing wiped the cover of the top one dry. "Is this the new edition of Professor Yan's lecture notes? I haven't bought it yet. You might think it funny, but I've been in his class for half a year now, and I still don't know his given name."

"I like his name. I'm always telling him his name looks sharp—sharper than he does, by a long shot!"

Chuanqing had found the name on the book cover. He read it out loud: "Yan Ziye." Putting the book aside, he tilted his head in thought. Then he picked the book back up and read the name again: "Yan Ziye." He felt somehow doubtful the second time, as if he couldn't quite make out the characters.

"Not a good name?" Danzhu asked.

"Yes, of course it's good!" Chuanqing laughed. "We all know that you've got a good father! Good in every way, except that now you're way too spoiled!"

Danzhu hissed back at him through pursed lips. She stood up. "This is my stop. See you later!"

When she had gone, Chuanqing leaned his head against the windowpane. Once again he seemed to doze off. The passenger with the azaleas got off too—and with the azaleas gone from the window, there was only the gray street behind. When the backdrop changed, his face grew dark and yellow.

The bus turned another corner. Palm-tree leaves swished against the window. Chuanqing jumped up, pulled the bell cord, and descended at the next stop.

He lived in a big mansion. Within a few years of their moving here from Shanghai, all the flowers and trees that had once filled the yard had wilted, died, or been cut down, and now the sun beat down on a desolate scene. The housemaid had turned over a rattan chair on the grass. She was sluicing it out with a kettle of boiling water, killing bedbugs.

Inside, the hallway was heavy with darkness. The only gleam of light came from the dark red banister that twisted up, around, and away. Chuanqing crept up the stairs cautiously; then, seeing no one there, he slipped toward his room like a thin cloud of smoke. But the tired old floorboards squeaked loudly. Amah Liu heard, came out, and stopped him in his tracks.

"Young Master is home! Have you gone to see Master and Mistress?"

"I'll see them later, when we eat. What's the rush?"

Amah Liu grabbed him by the sleeve. "Here we go again! What have you done this time? Sneaking around, trying to avoid seeing anyone! Better go in right away, see them now and get it over with. If you don't, there'll be another angry scene!"

Chuanqing suddenly started acting like a boy of twelve or thirteen: he grit his teeth, he absolutely refused to go. The harder Amah Liu tugged at him, the harder he pulled away. Amah Liu was his mother's personal maid, the one who'd been sent along with her when she got married. The hatred he felt toward Amah Liu at home was the same hatred he felt toward Yan Danzhu at school. On a bitter-cold day, a person can be frozen numb and it won't bother him, but a little warmth will make him feel so cold that his heart hurts and his bones ache.

In the end, his loathing for Amah Liu made him give in; just to get rid of her, he agreed to see his father and stepmother. Nie Jiechen, his father, was wearing a grease-spotted vest of light green satin over his undershirt. Chuanqing's stepmother—all in black, her hair disheveled—was reclining on the two-person opium couch, facing her husband. Chuanqing stepped forward and greeted them. "Father, Mother!" They both gave barely attentive grunts. Then, at long last, the stone in his heart fell away: it looked as though they hadn't got wind of any offense of his today.

"Did you hand in the tuition fee?" his father asked.

Chuanqing sat down on an upholstered chair next to the smoking couch. "Yes."

"What courses are you taking?"

"History of the English Language, Nineteenth-Century English Prose—"

"All that English you're doing—why bother? A donkey can jounce along after the horses, jounce till his legs break, and still it won't amount to anything!"

His stepmother smiled. "He wants to put on the airs of a Young Master. No big deal—just get him a tutor, and the tutor can do his homework for him."

"I don't keep extra money lying around just so he can have a tutor," said his father. "What else are you taking?"

"History of Chinese Literature."

"That's too easy for you! Tang Dynasty poems, Song Dynasty lyrics—you've done all that before."

"Can't do anything new, but he sure can laze around!" said his stepmother.

Chuanqing's head dropped forward almost to the ground. He hunched his back, picked up the little metal end of his shoe-lace and scraped it lightly on his shoe. His father shifted around on the smoking couch, grabbed a rolled-up newspaper, and hit Chuanqing hard on the neck. "Idle hands, with nothing to do, will only find something to break!" he barked. "Go on! Go on! Get over there! Cook some opium pellets!"

Chuanqing sat on a little stool in the corner and cooked the opium on a low table. His stepmother was in excellent spirits today. She picked up a small gold-decorated teapot, drank a mouthful of tea, then pinched her lips together and smiled. "Chuanqing," she said, "do you have a girlfriend at school?"

"Him?" said his father. "He doesn't have any male friends, how could he get a girlfriend?"

"Chuanqing," his stepmother smiled, "I want to know. People are saying there's a girl from the Yan family—they're from Shanghai too—and that she's been chasing after you. Is there anything to it?"

Chuanqing's face reddened. "Yan Danzhu—she has a lot of friends, doesn't she? Why would she be interested in me?"

"Who says she's interested in you?" said his father. "It's your money she's interested in! You? What's there to see in you? Three parts human, seven parts ghost—"

But Chuanqing was thinking, "My money? My money?"

One day, the money would be his, and then he could sign his name on checks whenever he liked. He'd been waiting for this for years, since his early teens. Once, filled with urgency, he'd even practiced on a discarded check, signing his name at a slant: "Nie Chuanqing, Nie Chuanqing." Bravely, handsomely, on the left and on the right: "Nie Chuanqing, Nie Chuanqing." But his father had slapped him across the jaw, ripped the check away, and shoved the crumpled wad into his face. Why? Because Chuanqing had touched a raw nerve, one of his father's buried fears. When the money came into Chuanqing's hands, wouldn't he just go crazy and waste it, throw it all away? Such a timid, gloomy, idiotic boy. His father had certainly never intended him to turn out like this. Now, whenever he looked at his son, he felt helpless and full of rage. Underneath, there was an edge of fear. Nie Jiechen had once said, "Hit him, and he doesn't cry, he just stares at you with those big wide eyes. I can't stand to see him staring like that. It makes me furious!"

Chuanqing was cooking the opium. He couldn't keep his eyes—those big wide fearful staring eyes—off his father. Sooner or later... yes, his day would come. But by then, he'd have been trampled on for so long that nothing human would be left. What a bizarre victory it would be!

The opium paste dripped down the cooking wand and dropped into the lamp. Chuanqing started, afraid his parents would notice. Fortunately, a maid came in to announce the arrival of Second Aunt Xu. This distraction gave him the cover he needed.

"Go on, get out of here!" his father said to him. "A creepy sneak like you, not an ounce of manliness in you, a laughing-stock to everyone! Maybe you're not embarrassed, but I am!"

"The boy isn't suffering from a disease," his stepmother said, "and yet he's thin as a rail. If people see they'll think we mistreat him! And yet I've never known him to hold back when it comes to food and drink!"

His head hanging, Chuanqing left the room, only to glimpse the approaching female visitor. He ducked into a dark corner till the coast was clear, then went on to his bedroom and started flipping the pages of his schoolbooks. Thinking back to all the times Yan Danzhu had urged him to work harder, he felt a burst of energy; bracing himself, he decided to do some home-work.

His bedroom was clouded with smoke; opium fumes had drifted in from the other room. He lived in this air, had grown up in this air, but today for some reason the smell made him dizzy, nauseous. He'd go to the living room, where it was a bit cleaner. He ran down the stairs with his books under his arm, his mind surging with irritation. In the living room he found only dust motes and pale sunbeams. A translucent red flower vase held a feather duster. He took a seat at the square rosewood table that stood in the middle of the room, then leaned forward and lay half prone on the marble tabletop. The tabletop was cool, like the window on the bus.

Azaleas outside the window; inside, Yan Danzhu... and Danzhu's father was Yan Ziye. He'd seen that name when he was little, before he'd really learned to read. On the blank inside cover of a ragged old *Early Tide* magazine he'd deciphered, one by one, these words:

> To Miss Biluo,
> A trifle for your amusement.
> Best regards, Yan Ziye

His mother's name was Feng Biluo.

He reached for a textbook, pulled it over, and read a few pages, his head pillowed on his sleeve. It was as if he'd gone back to the age when he couldn't read very well; each word was a struggle, and he didn't know what any of it meant.

Suddenly he saw Amah Liu entering the room. "Move aside, Young Master." She tugged at the tablecloth draped across her shoulder, spread it out, and tied it to the legs of the table.

"What? Are they going to play mah-jongg?" Chuanqing asked.

"They need a fourth, so they telephoned Old Uncle and asked him to come."

Just then, the housemaid came in with a hundred-watt lightbulb. Chuanqing picked up his books to head back upstairs.

In the corner of his bedroom there was a big wicker trunk full of old, battered books—and, he remembered, a stack of *Early Tide* magazines. A leather strap was tied lengthwise across the top of the trunk, but undoing it would have required more energy than he had. He pried the lid up with his head, thrust his hands inside, and blindly fumbled around. Suddenly it came back to him: all the *Early Tide* magazines, every single one, had gotten lost when they moved.

He left his hands where they were, pinched by the lid of the trunk. His head drooped, as if he'd broken his neck. His gown of lined blue silk had a stiff standing collar, and the strong, hot sun shone down inside it, warming the back of his neck. He had a strange feeling, though, that the sky would soon be dark... that already it was dark. As he waited all alone by the window, his heart darkened along with the sky. An unspeakable, dusky anguish... Just as in a dream, that person waiting by the window was at first himself, and then in an instant he could see, very clearly, that it was his mother. Her long bangs swept down in front of her bowed head, and the pointed lower half of her face was a vague white shadow. Her eyes and eyebrows, so clouded and dim, were like black shadows in moonlight. But he knew for a certainty that it was his dead mother, Feng Biluo.

He hadn't had a mother since he was four years old, but he recognized her from her photograph. There was only one photo that showed her before her marriage, and in it she wore an old-style satin jacket embroidered with the faint shapes of tiny bats. The figure in the window was growing clearer now, and he could see the bats on the autumn-colored silk of her jacket. She was waiting for someone, waiting for news. She knew that the news wouldn't come. In her heart the sky was slowly darkening—Chuanqing flinched in pain. He couldn't tell whether it really was his mother, or himself.

But the nameless anguish pressing down on him? He knew now that that was love, a hopeless love some twenty years in the past. A knife will rust after twenty years, but it's still a knife. The knife in his mother's heart now twisted in his.

With an enormous effort, Chuanqing lifted his head. The entire illusion rapidly melted away. He had felt, for a moment, like an old-time portrait photographer, his head thrust into a tunnel of black cloth: there in the lens he'd caught a glimpse of his mother. He pulled his hands out from under the lid of the trunk; pressing them to his lips, he sucked fearfully at the red marks.

Chuanqing knew very little about his mother, but he did know that she had never loved his father. And so his father hated her. After she died, he turned his fury against her child; otherwise, even with the stepmother egging him on, Chuanqing's father wouldn't have become so vicious toward him.

His mother had never loved his father—had she loved someone else? A faint rumor to that effect had circulated among their relatives. His stepmother had been kin even before her marriage to his father, so she knew the rumors already. Of course she was unwilling to let the matter drop, and insisted on talking about Chuanqing's mother even in Chuanqing's presence. Anything that passed through her lips was sure to be grating and painful. Amah Liu, as Biluo's maid, couldn't stand hearing her deceased mistress slandered, and made sullen remarks in her mistress's defense to the other servants. That was how Chuanqing had picked up a few facts he thought he could depend on.

Viewed from a modern perspective, those few facts were pitifully simple. Feng Biluo was married at eighteen years of age. There had been a time, before her engagement, when she'd had ardent hopes of going to school and getting an education. In a conservative family like hers, this was most unlikely. But she and some female cousins kept talking about it, secretly, furtively. The cousins were quite a bit younger than Biluo, and their parents weren't so strict; at last they got their wish. They decided to take the entrance exam for a girls' elementary school that offered both Chinese and Western subjects; Yan Ziye, a distant relative, was invited to be their tutor. Ziye was their junior, in terms of family generations, but he was actually older in years, and he had two years of university study behind him.

Biluo hankered after her cousins' good fortune, she couldn't give up her dream of getting an education, so she followed every detail of their exam preparations. That was how, on several occasions, she happened to meet Yan Ziye at her cousins' house. The two of them were always in the company of others.

The Yan family engaged the services of a matchmaker. Before Biluo's mother could respond to the proposal, Biluo's grandfather's concubine, who was sitting in the corner smoking a water pipe, broke out in a loud cackle. "Well," the old woman chipped in, "it's a bit early to be talking about this!"

The matchmaker smiled back. "The young lady isn't little anymore..."

The old concubine laughed. "Her age is not the problem! The Yan family from Changshu is at best a family of traders. If their Young Master makes his way as a scholar, and they keep it up for a couple of generations, and *then* come to us with a marriage proposal—well, *then* we'll have something to discuss. But now? It's much too early!"

The matchmaker conveyed the rebuff to the Yan family. One way or another, Yan Ziye soon found out the exact nature of the Feng family's reply, and he was deeply angered. He wanted to let the whole matter drop.

But it seems that he and Biluo met yet one more time after this. It couldn't have been an accident, since the two of them would have gone out of their way not to encounter each other after the proposal. This last, brief meeting must have been Biluo's idea. Biluo hinted to Ziye that he should bring in another matchmaker to try to persuade her parents, since their refusal had not been absolute. But Ziye, who was young and hot tempered, didn't want to be accused of "social climbing," or to hear such terrible slurs on his own family's reputation. He told her that soon he'd be going abroad to study. If she wanted, she could take a drastic step: she could go with him. Biluo wouldn't do it.

When he thought back to this part, Chuanqing's heart rose up in resentment against his mother; still, he had to admit that she didn't have much choice. It was, after all, twenty years ago! She had to think of her family's reputation, and she had to think of Ziye's future.

Ziye went abroad by himself. By the time he returned, the Feng family had already married Biluo to Nie Jiechen, and Ziye had been through several romances. Chuanqing hadn't heard anything about how Ziye had come to marry Danzhu's mother, a southern girl, before moving his family, sometime in the past few years, to Hong Kong.

As for Biluo's life after her marriage—Chuanqing couldn't bear to imagine it. She wasn't a bird in a cage. A bird in a cage, when the cage is opened, can still fly away. She was a bird embroidered onto a screen—a white bird in clouds of gold stitched onto a screen of melancholy purple satin. The years passed; the bird's feathers darkened, mildewed, and were eaten by moths, but the bird stayed on the screen even in death.

She was dead, for her it was over, but what about Chuanqing? Why did Chuanqing have to endure such punishment? When Biluo was married into the Nie family, her sacrifice had at least been a conscious one. But Chuanqing, born into that family, had never had a choice. Another bird added to the screen—no matter how much he's beaten, he can't fly away. Twenty years with his father had crippled his spirit. Even if he did receive his freedom, escape was impossible for him.

He couldn't escape, couldn't escape! And since he'd never had the slightest hope of the whole situation being any different, he'd simply given in. But now, after taking all those bits that he garnered or guessed, and constructing from them, for the first time, a coherent story, he finally saw how it was: twentysome years ago, before his own birth, there had been a hope of deliverance for him. His mother had had a possibility of marrying Yan Ziye, so he himself almost could have been the

son of Yan Ziye. Then he'd be Yan Danzhu's elder brother—
maybe Yan Danzhu herself! If it had been him, then there'd be
no her.

The next day at school, in his History of Chinese Literature
class, Chuanqing's mind was a mess. He saw, as from a great
distance, Yan Danzhu slip quietly into the classroom, a bulky
patent-leather notebook clutched to her chest. She sat in the
front row, over to the left and out of the professor's line of
sight: no doubt trying not to disturb her father. Then she
looked around and smiled a bit at Chuanqing. There was an
empty seat beside her; the boy next to Chuanqing nudged him
and urged him to take it. Chuanqing shook his head. The boy
laughed. "What a fool you are! What have you got to lose? If
you don't go, I will!"

But as he was getting up, several other students pushed
ahead of him. The race was to the swift, and the one who got
there first promptly occupied the seat.

It was late-spring weather, and already the heat was ferocious. On top of her cheongsam, Danzhu wore a long-sleeved
jacket of thin white silk. Leaning over to laugh and chat with
someone next to her, she rested her cheek in one hand. Her
lively, copper-colored face and arms, complemented by that
gauzy silk, looked like amber liquor shimmering in a glass.
Simple appreciation of beauty was, however, just a small part of
Chuanqing's response to her. He thought: she doesn't look like
Yan Ziye at all, she must take after her mother, that southern
girl that Yan Ziye married. Yan Ziye was pale and fairly slim.
Most men don't get their looks till they're at least thirty—Yan
Ziye proved the point. He had to be—what—at least forty-
five? But he looked much younger.

Yan Ziye came in and walked to the podium. Chuanqing
suddenly felt that he'd never really seen him before. He saw, for
the first time, the debonair elegance of the long Chinese gown.
Chuanqing himself wore a gown and jacket, for reasons of

economy, though like most young men he would have preferred a Western suit. But Yan Ziye's loose gray silk gown, with its accumulation of soft, heavy folds, showed off the fine long lines of his body. Chuanqing was surprised by a sudden fantasy: If he were Yan Ziye's child, would he look like Yan Ziye? The resemblance would certainly have been close: unlike Danzhu, he was a man.

Yan Ziye opened the roll book. "Li Mingguang, Dong Dequan, Wang Lifen, Wang Zongwei, Wang Xiaoyi, Nie Chuanqing..." When Chuanqing answered, he thought his voice sounded strange, and he quickly blushed. But Yan Ziye kept going: "Qin Defen, Zhang Shixian..." One hand resting on the desktop, the other calmly bearing the roll book—a man who'd gone through hardship, but still had known some small measure of happiness.

A man whose blood could have flowed in my veins, Chuanqing thought to himself. "Suppose...suppose..." But how sweet a fruit the "suppose" must be, that people will sup and sup on it! A juicy fruit, like a lychee but without the pit, sparkling and light green; a fruit that hides the tart within the sweet. Suppose...suppose his mother, at the moment of saying her final farewell to Yan Ziye, had shown a bit of will, a bit of selfishness? If only, swept away by emotion, she had changed everything by saying: "In the past, my parents made all the decisions for me. Now you—you make the decision! Whatever you say, that's what I'll do." If she hadn't been so worried about the past, so concerned about the future...the future! Had she really shown any concern for the future? Had she given any thought to her future offspring? She'd done great harm, enormous harm, to her own child! Chuanqing himself knew that his accusations against his mother were unfair. For a girl of just seventeen or eighteen, as she was then, she'd held herself to an admirably high moral standard. But the most that anyone can do, when faced with a tough problem, is try to ease the heart's burden, try to take the pressure off. Could he really blame his mother?

Professor Yan turned around to write on the blackboard. The room filled with rustling sounds as the students copied after him, but Chuanqing couldn't keep his mind on his work.

He'd eaten one "suppose," and now he peeled another. If, for instance, his mother and Yan Ziye had gotten married, their life together would probably not have been perfectly blissful. Chuanqing knew from Amah Liu that Biluo was high-strung and emotional; Danzhu had once told him that Yan Ziye was suspicious and often quite rigid. Lovers love to fight; it's the absence of ties that makes mutual forbearance possible. And, at that time, society would have frowned on Biluo's breaking with her family, and the marriage would certainly have hurt Ziye's career. People's views had changed, of course, over the past ten years—but by then Ziye would have missed his chance, and he'd have lost his enthusiasm. When a man isn't happy in his career, all sorts of squabbles and petty misunderstandings will find their way into his home life. Wouldn't that have been bad for their children?

No, it would have been good for them! Little worries and small obstacles build character. If he were Ziye and Biluo's child, his mind would be so much deeper, so much more reflective, than Danzhu's. And a child with a loving family is always full of confidence and fellow-feeling—active, vigorous, and brave, whatever the vagaries of his life. So he would have all of Danzhu's strengths, and all the ones she lacked, too.

Danzhu sat in the front row: again his gaze fell on her. She was listening intently to Professor Yan's lecture, head tilted to one side, lips parted slightly as she tapped with a pencil on her small, white teeth. The line of her face, in profile, was smooth and lovely, especially that little snub nose, just like a child's. A trace of perspiration glistened on her nose; she looked like nothing so much as a shiny bronze fountain statue.

Danzhu was in the science division at the university, but still found time to study other things: literary history, for instance. Her interests were so wide-ranging that they touched on everything and everyone. Chuanqing suddenly thought of just the phrase to describe that undiscriminating approach that she took toward all their classmates: she was promiscuously friendly. Danzhu was happy to chat with anyone, but when anyone wanted more than that, she'd beg off, say they were all just students, not ready yet for love. But what did that mean? After Danzhu graduated, what was there for her to do? At the end of the day, she'd just go and get married! The more Chuanqing thought about Danzhu, the more boring and superficial she seemed. If he came from a family as wonderful as hers, he'd make the most of it, he'd be perfect. No, he did not like Danzhu.

Chuanqing's resentment against Danzhu—and his strange infatuation with Yan Ziye—grew stronger with each passing day. Under these psychological conditions, he was of course unable to study. At the end of the semester, his grades on his final exams were awful. Worst of all was History of Chinese Literature, which he hadn't even come close to passing. His father bawled him out, then sent someone to persuade the school administration to give him another chance, so he could stay with his class in the fall semester.

When Chuanqing went back to school, his misery had not lifted; instead it had grown worse. He had spent the whole summer vacation brooding endlessly on his pain and the reasons for it. Meanwhile the daily routine at home had brought him into closer contact with his father. He'd discovered how much he resembled Nie Jiechen, both in looks and in manners. Chuanqing loathed this Nie Jiechen who lived in his body. He had ways of avoiding his father, but he couldn't get away—not even by an inch—from this other self that was there, stuck inside of him.

Chuanqing daydreamed all day long, leaning on the wicker

trunk in the corner of his bedroom. An astonished Amah Liu kept coming by and saying, "Can't you feel the blazing sun beating down? The older you are, the more muddled you get— you can't even tell hot from cold! Sit up, get out of the sun!" Too lazy to get up, he'd sit there on the floor, then let his spinning head fall back on the wicker trunk; he'd stay that way a long while, until the wicker pattern was imprinted across his forehead.

When school started, his father called him in and delivered a stern warning. "Do badly again, and your studies are over! It's pointless anyway—you're just bringing shame on the Nie family!"

Chuanqing didn't want to drop out, so he worked hard. Scribbling through the homework, he managed to get by in lots of different subjects. But in the subject that his father thought should be easiest for him, History of Chinese Literature, he was lost, he couldn't make a showing at all. He had to keep taking the course, though, since replacing it with something else would cost him too many credits.

Final exams always came after the Christmas and New Year break. On the morning of Christmas Eve, classes were held as usual. Professor Yan wanted to see whether the students were adequately prepared for the exam, so he gave them an informal oral quiz. When he got to Chuanqing, he had to call out two or three times before Chuanqing heard him.

"Tell us about the rise of seven-character verse," Professor Yan said, already a bit annoyed.

Chuanqing stood bent over like a beggar, not daring to look at the teacher.

"The rise of seven-character verse..." He broke off. The whole room was silent. Chuanqing felt that Danzhu was certainly watching him—watching him disgrace the whole Nie family. No, it was his mother he was disgracing! The child of Yan Ziye's wife was watching the child of Feng Biluo making a fool of himself. The classroom was so quiet that he had to say something.

He licked his lips, and the words came out slowly. "The rise of seven-character verse . . . the rise of seven-character verse, the . . . uh . . . seven-character rise of verse!"

Behind him someone laughed. Even Danzhu couldn't help giggling. Most of the male students hadn't laughed at first, but when they heard Danzhu they let themselves go. When Professor Yan saw that the whole room was breaking out in laughter, he thought Chuanqing must be deliberately clowning around. He frowned and banged his book down on the lectern.

"I see," he said coldly. "That was supposed to be funny. Sorry, but I don't share your sense of humor."

Now the students stopped laughing, one by one.

"Nie Chuanqing," Professor Yan continued, "I've been watching you. For two whole semesters, you've been in a daze. Have you taken in anything I've said? Have you even taken a single note? If you don't choose to study, no one's forcing you. It would be better if you simply stopped coming, stopped wasting your classmates' time, and my time too!"

Professor Yan's tone matched his father's exactly, and Chuanqing's eyes filled with tears. He covered his face with his hands, but even so Yan Ziye could see that he was crying. Ziye had always hated crying—in his view, even a woman's tears were a kind of blackmail perpetrated by the weak, while a weeping man, tears rolling down his face, was an utterly shameless thing. He was outraged.

"Aren't you ashamed of yourself?" he shouted. "If all the youth of China were like you, China would be done for!"

The words fell like hammer blows, breaking Chuanqing's heart. Down he sat, slumping across the desktop, sobbing openly.

"If you're going to cry," Ziye said, "go outside to do it! I can't allow you to disturb the others. We're still holding class here!"

Once he'd started weeping, Chuanqing couldn't hold back his tears; the sound of his sobs grew louder and louder. Since he was hard of hearing, he hadn't caught the professor's last few words.

Ziye stepped forward, pointed at the door, and shouted, "Get out of here!"

Chuanqing stood and stumbled out.

That night, there was a Christmas Eve dance at the boys' dormitory, up on the mountainside. Chuanqing hadn't finished his first full year, but, like the other first-year students at South China University, he'd been pressured into buying a ticket. His father felt that with the ticket already purchased Chuanqing must go, otherwise the school would be taking advantage of them. And so, for the first time ever, he allowed Chuanqing to attend an event on his own. Chuanqing took a bus to the foot of the mountain and simply headed uphill. He had no intention of going to the dance. His plan was to wander around all evening, frittering away the whole joyous holiday. At home, he knew, he wouldn't have slept anyway; his heart was racked with turmoil.

Hong Kong lacks a true winter season, but even so Christmas Eve can be very cold. The mountain was covered with stubby pines and little firs; the sky was filled with clouds of azurite. A sighing wind stirred both trees and clouds, gathering them here, dispersing them there, pushing and piling them up; now they coalesced in a black mass, now they became green vapor. In the woods, the wind howled like a mad dog, but when it came across the distance from the sea, the sound was desperate and forlorn, like the cry of a lonesome hound.

Hunched over, with his hands thrust into his sleeves, Chuanqing raced up the stone steps. Ahead, beyond the last lamp, the way was pitch-black, but he knew the path well and could just make out the pale white edges of the cement. And he liked the dark. In the dark he could lose himself for a little while. That scraping sound on the sandstone under his feet—what was that? Was it Nie Chuanqing? "If all the youth of China were like him, China would be done for"—that one? Was it really him? Even he wasn't sure. It was too dark, he couldn't see.

When his father cursed him, called him "pig" or "dog" or worse, he couldn't care less, because he didn't respect his father in the least. But the words uttered so lightly by Yan Ziye had ravaged his heart and sickened his mind; he'd never forget them, not even in death.

Chuanqing pressed forward, for how long he didn't know, groping through the darkness, maybe even going in circles. Then he turned a corner, and a lamp appeared along the path. Some young people were approaching, talking and laughing together. Was the dance already over? Chuanqing ducked his head and headed back the other way. "Chuanqing! Chuanqing!" It was Danzhu's voice behind him, calling. He walked even faster.

Danzhu followed him a short distance, then stopped and turned around. "See you later!" she said to her companions from the dance. "I want to catch up with that awkward little miss of ours and have a chat."

"But we have to see you home!" the others said.

"Don't worry," said Danzhu. "I'll ask Chuanqing to see me home, that'll work just as well."

The others hesitated, but Danzhu said, "It's fine! It's fine! There's nothing to worry about!" Then she picked up the hem of her skirt and ran toward Chuanqing.

When Chuanqing saw that she really was coming after him, he had to slow down.

"Chuanqing," Danzhu asked, a bit breathless from running, "why didn't you come to the dance?"

"I can't dance."

"What are you doing here?"

"Nothing."

"Would you take me home?"

Chuanqing didn't say anything, but they began to make their way up the mountain. Danzhu's house was near the top. It was still completely dark, except for the flashing toes of her silver-white shoes.

Danzhu spoke again, and Chuanqing felt that never before had she spoken so haltingly. "You know," she said, "I looked for you for a long time after class today, but you'd already gone home. I know where you live, but then you never want us to go to your house..."

Chuanqing still didn't answer.

"About what happened today," Danzhu continued, "you should forgive my father. He...he is always too serious about things, and the situation at South China University, for anyone who's serious about teaching, is very discouraging. Most Hong Kong students have terrible Chinese, but they think Chinese is unimportant, and they're not willing to really study the language. How could he fail to be upset? You're the only one with a decent foundation in Chinese, and then you disappoint him. You...if you think about it...you can see how it is for him..."

Chuanqing said nothing.

"Do you see now," Danzhu said, "why he got angry with you?...Chuanqing, if you do forgive him, then go and explain things to him, tell him why you've been so preoccupied recently. You know my father is a kindhearted man, and I'm sure he'll do anything he can to help you. Tell me about it, and I'll pass the message on to my father, how's that?"

Tell Danzhu about it? Ask Yan Ziye, do you still remember Feng Biluo? Maybe he would remember, but he was a man who'd seen a lot over the years, and certainly he'd had other love affairs. But Biluo had loved only him...and in the old days women kept the tiniest little things locked in their hearts, turning them around, over and over again, musing at a window at dusk, on a rainy night, in the gloomy dawn. Yes, back in the old days, people were like that...

Chuanqing's chest was tight with pain and resentment; he couldn't relieve the pressure. Danzhu drew closer and asked, "Chuanqing, is it something to do with your family?"

"You're such a busybody!" he said with a weak laugh.

Danzhu didn't take offense; instead, she laughed with him. Everyone liked her—she had no idea that Chuanqing was standing there full of hate. The wind stirred a pine-tree branch and it brushed against her head; she cried out in surprise and dodged behind Chuanqing. This gave her a chance to take his arm. "Please tell me why," she asked softly.

Chuanqing swept her hand away. "Why? Why? Let me ask you something—why are you always hanging around me? Aren't girls supposed to be worried about their reputations? Shouldn't you be wondering what your father might think?"

When Danzhu heard this, she fell back a step. He walked ahead and she followed, but at a distance.

She sighed deeply and said, "I'm sorry. I forgot again. Boys and girls are different from each other! Here I am, always thinking that we're all still just children! Everyone in my family treats me like a little child."

"Can't stop talking about your family, can you?" Chuanqing retorted again. "As if everyone didn't know that you come from a model family! What a pity you're not a model daughter!"

"The way you talk, it seems that you can't stand me! As if my happiness made you unhappy. But, Chuanqing, I know you're not like that. So why—"

"Why? It must be that I'm jealous of you—because you're so pretty, so smart, so popular!"

"You're still not being open with me! Chuanqing, you know I'm your friend! I want you to be happy—"

"You want to give me a bit of your happiness, is that it? You've got enough, so you toss a scrap to the dog, is that it? I don't want it! I don't! I'd rather die!"

The mountain path turned a corner and the land dropped

away, opening out onto the ocean and sky. A cliff hung over the empty space, guarded by a semicircular metal railing. Chuan-qing was walking in front, but when he looked back he couldn't find Danzhu. He looked again, and saw her leaning against the railing. At the foot of the cliff the pines surged and bil-lowed, along with another kind of tree that stayed leafy even in winter; the leaves of that tree flashed green on one side, white on the other. The wind swallowed everything. All over the mountain leaves were fluttering, sprinkling a silver light every-where. When the clouds parted, the pale yellow winter moon came out; the dark white sea and sky stretched away, behind Danzhu, like a standing screen plated with mica. Danzhu was wearing a hooded cape of emerald green velvet with a white velvet lining. Even in very cold weather she liked to wear white, because the contrast with her dark complexion was so striking. Chuanqing had never seen her so dressed up before. Her hood was pushed halfway back, revealing the curls that were piled high on her head; the light was behind her, and her face was hidden, though he could feel her burning gaze fixed upon him.

Chuanqing's own gaze dropped. He clasped his hands be-hind his back and stood stiffly for a long moment. Finally, he raised his head. He spoke tersely: "Shall we go?"

She had already turned, and her back was to him. The wind blew wildly; it filled her cape until it billowed out, taut and bulging, then whipped it up over her head. Her white velvet cheongsam gleamed green in this light, and wafting up in the air her cape looked, at first glance, like an immense parachute from which her lustrous white body floated down—was she in fact a paratrooper who had been dispatched from the Moon Palace?

Chuanqing slowly approached her. Could Danzhu be in love with him? Surely that couldn't be, could it? And yet she had repeatedly found an opportunity to be with him. Right now, for instance—here she was running around with him on a deserted hillside in the middle of the night. Usually, no matter how much she laughed and played around with her classmates, she kept a certain distance—she really wasn't a flirt. Why did she treat him so differently? He thought back over her words and behavior just now. For a girl, wasn't that already clear enough?

He hated her, and yet what use was his hate? It was as utterly ineffectual as he was. If she loved him, he would have power over her, he could subject her to all sorts of subtle psychological tortures. That was his only hope for revenge.

"Danzhu," he asked, in a trembling voice, "do you like me a little? . . . Just a little?"

She really didn't mind the cold. She reached out from under the cape and rested her bare arm on the railing. He grasped the railing with both hands and leaned forward, meaning to press his cheek to her arm. But for some reason, he stopped in midair, his tears streaming down. He bent over the railing and pillowed his face on an arm—his own arm.

Did she love him, at least a little? He didn't want revenge, he just wanted love—especially from someone in the Yan family. Since he and the Yan family weren't, in fact, blood relations, a relation by marriage would be good enough. He simply had to have a link to the Yan family.

Danzhu pulled the flying cape back down and wound it tightly around her. "Not just a little," she smiled. "If I didn't like you, why would I want to be your friend?"

Straightening himself up, Chuanqing gulped and said, "Friends! But I don't want to be your friend."

"But you need friends."

"Just being friends isn't enough. I want a father and a mother."

Danzhu stared at him, dumbfounded. He seized the metal railing as if it were her arm. "Danzhu," he burst out, "if you fell in love with someone else, to him you'd only be someone to love. But to me, you'd be much more than that. You'd be creator, father, mother, a new world, a new everything. You'd be past and future. You'd be God."

There was a moment's silence, and then Danzhu spoke softly. "I'm afraid I don't have such wild ambitions. If I loved someone, I could be his beloved. I could be his wife. As for anything else, I—I think I know my limits."

The wind surged. Inside Chuanqing everything was blocked. He turned his head away, his hands gripped the rail even more tightly. In a low voice he said, "Then you don't love me. Not even a little."

"I've never thought about it before."

"Because you take me for a girl."

"No! No! Really...but..." At first she was embarrassed, then suddenly she was irritated. Frowning, she coughed wearily and said, "You won't want to hear this, so why are you pushing me to say it?"

Chuanqing turned his back to her and said through clenched teeth, "You take me for a girl. You...you...don't even take me for a person!" He'd lost control of his voice, and by the time he got to the end he was almost screaming.

Astonished, and without thinking about it, Danzhu stepped away from the railing above the cliff, finding a safer place. But then that struck her as an overreaction, a ridiculous one. She steadied herself and spoke gently. "If you want me to treat you like a man, that's fine. I'll do what you ask, and I'll certainly try to see you in a different light. But you have to show a bit of manliness too. It doesn't help when you keep crying all the time. So sickly, so easily upset—"

Chuanqing laughed rudely. "You really know how to sweet talk a child! 'Be good, don't cry! Such a big boy now, it's not good to cry!' Ha-ha! Ha-ha!" Laughing, he spun away and headed down the mountain on his own.

Danzhu stood there in confusion. It had never occurred to her that Chuanqing was in love with her. But of course, it wasn't at all unnatural. There wasn't anyone he was close to, and she was the only one who, time and time again, had shown him a little kindness. She had led him on (even though she hadn't meant to), but she couldn't satisfy his need. It was clear that lately something had been bothering him a lot. Was it because of her? When all was said and done, was all this fuss because of her? Here she'd wanted so much to help him, and she'd only hurt him! She couldn't let him go off in such a deranged state—if something happened to him she'd never forgive herself!

His selfishness, his rudeness, his unreasonable behavior—she could forgive him for everything, because he loved her. Such a weird person, and even he was in love with her—that was very satisfying. Danzhu was a good woman, but she was still a woman.

Already he was quite far away, but in the end she caught up. "Chuanqing! Wait!" she shouted as she ran.

Chuanqing pretended not to hear. When she was at his side everything seemed complicated again; she didn't know what to say. "Tell me... tell me..." she began, still gasping for breath.

Chuanqing's teeth were clenched. He spat the words out: "I'll tell you—I wish you were dead! If there's you, there's no me. And if there's me, there's no you. Get it?"

With one arm he squeezed her around the shoulders hard, then, with his free hand, he jammed her head down as sharply as he could, as if to jam it into her chest. She shouldn't have been born into this world, he wanted her to go back. He didn't know where his terrible strength came from; he seemed to have lost control of his hands and feet. She didn't cry out, but she struggled, and the two of them tumbled down the stone steps together. Clambering to his feet, Chuanqing kicked furiously at the body on the ground.

He kicked, and the curses came flooding from his mouth. He was speaking too fast, even he couldn't hear himself clearly, but it was something like: "So you think that I'm a goody-goody, do you? Out on the mountain in the middle of the night, just you and me...if it had been someone else you wouldn't have felt so safe? You think that I'm not going to kiss you, or beat you, or murder you, is that it? Is that it? It's Nie Chuanqing—don't worry! 'Don't worry, Chuanqing will see me home!'...You really think you know me!"

After the first kicks, she moaned softly. Then she was silent. He kept kicking fiercely. He had to. He was afraid that she might still be alive. And yet he was also scared to go on. His legs were shaky and numb from kicking. Torn between these two fears, he finally left her there. He began to run down the hill. His body seemed to be moving in a nightmare, sailing on the clouds, riding on the mist like an immortal, his feet skimming above the ground, the moon shining on row upon row of stone steps that pranced boldly before his eyes, like agile lines of calligraphy.

When he had run quite some distance, he stopped. No one else on the whole black mountain—just him and Danzhu. Seventy or eighty yards lay between them, but in his trance, he could hear her whispery, labored breathing. In that moment, his heart and hers were one. He knew that she hadn't died. And so? Did he have the courage to go back, to finish her off?

He stood there motionless for two or three minutes; to him it seemed two or three hours. Then he started running downhill again. He didn't stop this time, he ran all the way down the hill to the road and the traffic.

The house was so cold, even the white plaster walls were frozen green. There was no charcoal brazier in Chuanqing's room, and the air was so cold that his nose ached between breaths. The window had not been opened in a very long time. The room smelled like greasy hair.

Chuanqing lay facedown on the bed. He heard his father, speaking to his stepmother in the next room. "That child is getting crazy. See how late he's back from the dance!"

"It looks like we should find him a wife."

Chuanqing's tears ran, and his mouth twitched, as if he wanted to laugh. But he couldn't stir a muscle; it felt as if a shell of ice had frozen across his face. His body was encased in ice too.

Danzhu was not dead. In a few days, when classes started again, he would still have to see her at school. He couldn't escape.

LOVE IN A FALLEN CITY

SHANGHAI'S clocks were set an hour ahead so the city could "save daylight," but the Bai family said: "We go by the old clock." Ten o'clock to them was eleven to everyone else. Their singing was behind the beat; they couldn't keep up with the *huqin* of life.

When the *huqin* wails on a night of ten thousand lamps, the bow slides back and forth, drawing forth a tale too desolate for words—oh! why go into it? The tale of the *huqin* should be performed by a radiant entertainer, two long streaks of rouge pointing to her exquisite nose as she sings, as she smiles, covering her mouth with her sleeve... but here it was just Fourth Master Bai sunk in darkness, sitting alone on a ramshackle balcony and playing the *huqin.*

As he was playing, the doorbell rang downstairs. For the Bai household, this was most unusual; people didn't pay social calls after dark, not in the old etiquette. If a visitor came at night or a telegram arrived without warning, either it meant that some event of huge import had transpired or, most probably, someone had died.

Fourth Master sat still and listened, but since Third Master, Third Mistress, and Fourth Mistress were shouting all at once as they came up the stairs, he couldn't understand what they were saying. Sitting in the room behind the balcony were Sixth Young Lady, Seventh Young Lady, and Eighth Young Lady, along with the Third and Fourth Masters' children, all growing increasingly anxious. From where Fourth Master sat on the darkened balcony, he could see everything in the well-lit room. So when the door opened, there was Third Master in his undershirt and shorts, standing on the raised doorsill with his legs stuck out wide, reaching behind his thighs to slap at the mosquitoes, and calling out to Fourth Master: "Hey, Old Four, guess what? That fellow that Sixth Sister left, well, it seems he's caught pneumonia and died!"

Fourth Master put down the *huqin* and walked into the room. "Who brought the news?" he asked.

"Mrs. Xu," said Third Master. Then he turned to shoo away his wife with his fan. "Don't tag along like this just to gawk at things! Isn't Mrs. Xu still downstairs? She's a big lady, doesn't like climbing stairs—why aren't you looking after her?"

Third Mistress left and Fourth Master mulled things over. "Isn't Mrs. Xu a relative of the deceased?"

"Indeed," said Third Master. "It looks like their family has specially asked her to bring us the news, and that means something, of course."

"They don't want Sixth Sister to return and go into mourning, do they?"

Third Master scratched his scalp with the handle of the fan. "Well, according to the rules, it would only be right..."

They both looked over at their Sixth Sister. Bai Liusu sat in the corner of the room calmly embroidering a slipper; her brothers, it seems, had been so intent on their conversation that they hadn't given her a chance to speak. Now she simply said, "Go and be his widow, after we've divorced? People will laugh till their teeth fall out!" She went on sewing her slipper, apparently unperturbed, but her palms were clammy and her needle stuck—she couldn't draw it through anymore.

"Sixth Sister, that's no way to talk," said Third Master. "He didn't do right by you back then, we all know that. But now he's dead—you're not going to hold a grudge, are you? Those two concubines that he left behind, they won't go into widowhood. If you go back now, all serious and proper, to lead the mourning for him, who's going to dare to laugh? It's true you didn't have any children, but he has lots of nephews, and you can pick one of them to continue the line. There isn't a lot of property left, but they're a big clan; even if they only make you the keeper of his shrine, they're not going to let a mother and child starve."

Bai Liusu laughed sarcastically. "Third Brother has certainly planned out everything," she said, "but unfortunately it's a bit late. The divorce went through some seven or eight years ago. Are you saying that those legal proceedings were empty nonsense? You can't fool around with the law!"

"Don't you try to scare us with the law," Third Master warned. "The law is one thing today and another tomorrow. What I'm talking about is the law of family relations, and that never changes! As long as you live you belong to his family, and after you die your ghost will belong to them too! The tree may be a thousand feet tall, but the leaves fall back to the roots."

Liusu stood up. "Why didn't you say all this back then?"

"I was afraid you'd be upset and think that we weren't willing to take you in."

"Oh? But now you're not afraid of upsetting me? Now that you've spent all my money, you're not afraid of upsetting me?"

"I spent your money?" Third Master demanded, pressing his face close to hers. "I spent your few paltry coins? You live in our house, and everything you eat and drink comes out of our pockets. Sure, in the past, it was no problem. One more person, two more chopsticks, that's all. But these days? Well, just go and find out for yourself—what does rice cost now? I didn't mention money, but you had to bring it up!"

Fourth Mistress, who was standing behind Third Master, laughed. "They say you shouldn't talk about money with your own flesh and blood. Once you start the money talk, there's all too much to say! I've been telling Fourth Master, telling him for a long time now: 'Old Four, you'd better warn Third Master. When you two buy gold, or buy stocks, don't use Sixth Sister's money. It will bring you bad luck! As soon as she got married, her husband spent all his family's money. Then she came back here, and now her family, as everyone can see, is going bankrupt. A real bad-luck comet, that one!'"

Third Master said, "Fourth Mistress is right. If we hadn't let her into those stock deals, we never would have lost all our property!"

Liusu shook with fury; her lower jaw quivered so hard that it seemed ready to drop off. She clamped the half-embroidered slipper to it.

Third Master continued: "I remember how you came home crying, making all that fuss about getting a divorce. Well, I'm a man with a heart, and when I saw that he'd beaten you up like that, I couldn't bear it, so I struck my chest and said, 'All right! I, the third son of the Bai family, may be poor, but my home shall not lack my sister's bowl of rice.' Still, my thinking was: 'Oh, you young married folk—what hot tempers you've got! It's never so serious that, after a few years back with your parents, you won't up and change your mind one day, and be perfectly ready to go back.' If I'd known that you two really wanted to break it off, do you think I would have helped you get a divorce? Breaking up other peoples' marriages means there won't be any sons or grandsons. I, the third son of the Bai family, am a man with sons, and I fully expect their support in my old age."

Liusu had now reached the height of fury, but she simply laughed. "Yes, yes, everything is my fault. You're poor? It's because I've eaten you out of house and home. You've lost your capital? It must be that I've led you on. Your sons die? I've done it to you, I've ruined your fate."

At this, Fourth Mistress grabbed her son's collar and rammed his head into Liusu, shouting, "Cursing the children now! After what you've said, if my son dies, I'll come looking for you!"

Liusu quickly dodged out of the way, then clasped Fourth Master and said, "Fourth Brother, look, just look, and be fair about it!"

Fourth Master said, "Now don't get so excited. If you have something to say, then say it, and we'll take our time and consider the whole situation carefully. Third Brother is only trying to help you ..." Liusu angrily let go of him and headed straight for the inner bedroom.

No lamps were lit in there. Peering through the red gauze bed curtains in the darkness, Liusu could dimly see her mother lying on the big redwood bed, slowly waving a round white fan. Liusu walked over to the bed, then slipped down to her knees and fell forward against it. "Mother!" she sobbed.

Old Mrs. Bai's hearing was still good, so she hadn't missed anything that had been said in the outer room. She coughed, felt around next to her pillow for a small spittoon, spat into it, and only then began to speak. "Your Fourth Sister-in-law has a sharp tongue, but that doesn't mean you should follow suit. We all have our own problems, you know. Your Fourth Sister-in-law is naturally strong willed—she's always managed the household. But your Fourth Brother is not ambitious, and he threw himself into gambling and visits to prostitutes. It's bad enough that he made himself ill, but then he took money from the household accounts: your Fourth Sister-in-law lost face because of that, and now she has to let Third Sister-in-law manage things. She's boiling over with frustration, and that's a hard way to live. Your Third Sister-in-law doesn't have a lot of energy, and running this household is no easy matter! You should bear all this in mind. Try to make allowances."

When Liusu heard her mother's tone and the way she played things down, she felt that her point had been completely overlooked; she couldn't find any reply to make.

Old Mrs. Bai rolled over and faced the wall. "Lately we've had to hunt everywhere to scrape up any money at all. Time was, we could sell some land and live off the proceeds a few years. But that's no longer possible. I'm old, and when it's time for me to go, I'll go, and I won't be able to look after any of you. Every party ends sometime. Staying on with me is not a feasible long-term plan. Going back is the decent thing to do. Take a child to live with you, get through the next fifteen years or so, and you'll prevail in the end."

As she was speaking, the doorway curtain moved. "Who's there?" Old Mrs. Bai said.

Poking her head through the curtain, Fourth Mistress came in. "Mother," she said, "Mrs. Xu is still downstairs waiting to talk with you about Seventh Sister's marriage."

"I'm just getting up," Old Mrs. Bai said. "Let's have some light."

When the lamp had been lit, Fourth Mistress helped the old lady to sit up, then waited on her as she got dressed and out of bed.

"Has Mrs. Xu found a suitable match?" the old lady asked.

"An excellent one, from what she says, though he is a bit older."

Old Mrs. Bai coughed. "This child Baolu is twenty-four now, and she's a knot in my heart. All this worry for her sake, and yet people say I'm neglecting her because she's not my own daughter!"

Fourth Mistress helped the old lady toward the outer room. "Take out my new tea leaves from over there and brew a bowl for Mrs. Xu," said the old lady. "The Dragon Well tea that Great Aunt brought back last year is in the green tin canister, the Green Spring is in the tall canister. Be sure to get it right."

Fourth Mistress nodded, then called out: "We're coming! Turn up the lamps!" Footsteps pounded as a small throng of sturdy young servants hurried over to help an older maid carry the old lady down the stairs.

Fourth Mistress was alone in the outer room, rifling through cabinets and trunks in search of the old lady's private stock of tea leaves. Suddenly she cried out, "Seventh Sister! What hole did you climb out of? Scared me half to death! Where did you disappear to just now?"

"I was sitting in the cool air out on the balcony," Baolu murmured.

"Bashful, eh?" Fourth Mistress snickered. "I say, Seventh Sister, when you go to live with your in-laws, try to be a little careful. Don't feel you can make trouble whenever you like. Is divorce an easy thing? Can you just leave when you like, let everything fall apart? If it really was that easy, why haven't I divorced your Fourth Brother, since he's never amounted to much! I too have my own family, it's not as if I don't have a place to run to. But in times like these I have to think of their needs too. I've got a conscience, and I have to think of them—can't weigh them down and drive them into poverty. I still have some sense of shame!"

Bai Liusu was kneeling forlornly by her mother's bed. When she heard these words, she crushed the embroidered slipper against her chest. The needle that was stuck in the slipper pierced her hand, but she didn't feel any pain. "I can't live in this house any longer," she whispered. "I just can't!" Her voice was faint and floating, like a trailing tendril of dust. She felt as if she were dreaming, tendrils streaming from her face and head. Falling forward in a daze, she thought she was clasping her mother's knees, and she started sobbing aloud. "Mother, Mother, please help me!" Her mother's face remained blank as she smiled on without saying a word. Wrapping her arms around her mother's legs, Liusu shook her violently and cried, "Mother! Mother!"

In her daze, it was many years before: she was about ten

years old, coming out of a theater, and in the middle of a torrential downpour she was separated from her family. She stood alone on the sidewalk staring at people, the people staring back at her, and beyond the dripping bus windows, on the other side of those blank glass shields, were strangers, an endless number of them, all locked inside their own little worlds, against which she could slam her head till it split—and still she'd never manage to break through. It seemed that she was trapped in a nightmare.

Suddenly she heard the sound of footsteps behind her, and guessed that her mother had returned. With a fierce effort she steadied herself, not saying anything. The mother she was praying to and the mother she really had were two different people.

Someone walked over to the bed and sat down, but when she spoke, it was in Mrs. Xu's voice. Mrs. Xu chided her, "Sixth Young Lady, don't be upset. Get up, get up, the weather is so hot..."

Bracing herself against the bed, Liusu struggled to her feet. "Auntie," she said, "I can't stay here in this house any longer. I've known for ages how much they resent me, even if they bite their tongues. But now that they've beat the drums, banged the gongs, and said it straight out, I've lost too much face to go on living here!"

Mrs. Xu made Liusu sit down with her on the edge of the bed. "You're too good, no wonder people bully you," she said tenderly. "Your older brothers played the market with your money until they'd spent it all! Even if they supported you for the rest of your life, it would only be right."

Liusu rarely heard such a decent remark. Without pausing to weigh its sincerity, she let her heart well up and her tears rain down. "Why was I such a fool? All because of that fuss over money, little bits of money, now I have no way out of here!"

Mrs. Xu said, "Someone so young can always find a way to make a life."

"If there were a way, I'd be long gone! I haven't studied much, and I can't do manual labor, so what kind of job can I do?"

"Looking for a job won't get you anywhere. But looking for a somebody, that's the way to go."

"No, I don't think so. My life is over already."

"That kind of talk is for the rich, for people who don't have to worry about food and clothing. People who don't have money can't just give up, even if they want to. Shave your head, become a nun, and when you beg for alms you'll still have to deal with people—you can't just leave the human race!"

Liusu bowed her head.

Mrs. Xu said, "If you'd come to me about this a few years ago it would have been better."

"Yes, that's right," said Liusu. "I'm already twenty-eight."

"For a person with your qualities, twenty-eight doesn't matter. I'll keep you in mind. But I really should scold you—you've been divorced for seven or eight years now. If only you'd made up your mind earlier, you could have set yourself free and saved yourself a lot of grief!"

"Auntie, of course you know the situation. Would a family like mine ever let us go out and meet people? And I can't depend on them to find me a match. First of all, they don't approve, and even if they did, I have two younger sisters who are still unmarried, and then there are Third and Fourth Brothers' daughters, all growing up fast. They can't even manage for the younger ones. Why would they do anything for me?"

"Speaking of your sister," Mrs. Xu said, "I'm still waiting for their reply."

"Do things look good for Seventh Sister?" asked Liusu.

"I think we're getting close," said Mrs. Xu. "I wanted to let the ladies talk it over among themselves, so I said I'd come up here to look in on you. I'd better be getting back now. Would you go down with me?"

Liusu had to help Mrs. Xu down the stairs. The stairs were old and Mrs. Xu was large: they creaked and squeaked down the stairs together. They entered the drawing room, and Liusu wanted to light the lamps, but Mrs. Xu said, "Don't bother, we can see well enough. The others are in the east wing. You come with me, and we'll all have a nice chat, and that way everything will be smoothed over. Otherwise, tomorrow when it's time to eat, and you can't avoid seeing them, it will be awkward and unpleasant."

Liusu couldn't bear hearing that phrase "time to eat." Her heart ached and her throat went dry. Forcing a smile, she demurred. "Thank you very much, Auntie, but I'm not feeling very well right now—I really can't see anyone. I'm afraid I'd be so nervous that I'd say something disastrous, and that would be a terrible way to repay all your kindness."

Seeing that Liusu refused to budge, Mrs. Xu decided to leave things where they stood. She went in by herself.

As soon as the door closed behind her, the drawing room fell into shadow. Two squares of yellow light streamed in through the glass panes in the upper part of the door, landing on the green tile floor. In spite of the gloom, one could see, on the bookshelves that lined the walls, long rows of slipcases made of purplish sandalwood into which formal-script characters had been carved, then painted green. On a plain wooden table in the middle of the room, there was a cloisonné chiming clock with a glass dome over it. The clock was broken; it hadn't worked in years. There were two hanging scrolls with paired verses; the crimson paper of the scrolls was embossed with gold "longevity" characters, over which the verses had been inscribed in big, black strokes. In the dim light, each word seemed to float in emptiness, far from the paper's surface. Liusu felt like one of those words, drifting and unconnected. The Bai household was a fairyland where a single day, creeping slowly by, was a thousand years in the outside world. But if you spent a thousand years here, all the days would be the same, each one as flat and dull as the last one.

She crossed her arms and clasped her neck with her hands. Seven, eight years—they'd gone by in the blink of an eye. Are you still young? Don't worry, in another few years you'll be old, and anyway youth isn't worth much here. They've got youth everywhere—children born one after another, with their bright new eyes, their tender new mouths, their quick new wits. Time grinds on, year after year, and the eyes grow dull, the minds grow dull, and then another round of children is born. The older ones are sucked into that obscure haze of crimson and gold, and the tiny flecks of glinting gold are the frightened eyes of their predecessors.

Liusu cried out, covered her eyes, and fled; her feet beat a rapid retreat up the stairs to her own room. She turned on the lamp, moved it to her dressing table, and studied her reflection in the mirror. Good enough: she wasn't too old yet. She had the kind of slender figure that doesn't show age—her waist eternally thin, her breasts girlishly budding. Her face had always been as white as porcelain, but now it had changed from porcelain to jade—semitranslucent jade with a tinge of pale green. Once, her cheeks had been plump; now they were drawn, so that her small face seemed smaller yet, and even more attractive. Her face was fairly narrow, but her eyes were set well apart. They were clear, lively, and slightly coquettish.

Out on the balcony, Fourth Master had once again taken up his *huqin*. The tune rose and fell, and Liusu's head tilted to one side as her eyes and hands started moving through dance poses. As she performed in the mirror, the *huqin* no longer sounded like a *huqin*, but like strings and flutes playing a solemn court dance. She took a few paces to the right, then a few to the left. Her steps seemed to trace the lost rhythms of an ancient melody.

Suddenly, she smiled—a private, malevolent smile; the music

came to a discordant halt. The *huqin* went on playing outside, but it was telling tales of fealty and filial piety, chastity and righteousness: distant tales that had nothing to do with her.

Fourth Master had retreated to the balcony because he knew he lacked standing in the family council downstairs. Once Mrs. Xu had left, the Bai family had to thoroughly assess every aspect of her proposal. Mrs. Xu planned to help Baolu make a match with a Mr. Fan, who had recently been working quite closely with Mr. Xu in the mining business. Mrs. Xu had always kept track of his family and their situation, and she believed him to be entirely reliable. Mr. Fan's father was a well-known overseas Chinese with properties scattered throughout Ceylon, Malaya, and other such places. Fan Liuyuan was now thirty-two years old, and both of his parents had passed away.

Everyone in the Bai family kept asking Mrs. Xu how such a perfect son-in-law could still be single, and she told them that when Fan Liuyuan returned from England, a whole passel of mothers had forcefully, insistently, pushed their daughters at him. They had schemed and squabbled, pulling every trick in the book and making a huge fuss over him. This had completely spoiled Mr. Fan; from then on he took women to be so much mud under his feet. He'd always been a bit odd anyway, due to his unusual childhood—his parents weren't officially married. His father met his mother in London, when he was touring Europe. She was an overseas Chinese, a girl often seen at parties, and the marriage had been kept secret. Then Fan's first wife got wind of it. Fearing that the first wife would take revenge, the couple never dared to go back to China, and Fan Liuyuan grew up in England. After his father's death, Liuyuan sought legal recognition of his rights; even though the first wife had only daughters, two of them, there was still quite a bit of nastiness. He was all alone in England, and went through some hard times, but at last he got the right to inherit his father's estate. The Fan family was still very hostile toward him, so he lived in Shanghai most of the time, returning to the family home in Guangzhou only when absolutely necessary. The unstable emotional environment of his early years had left its mark on him, and gradually he became a playboy—he gambled, he gourmandized, he visited prostitutes. The only pleasure he denied himself was married bliss.

"A man like this is probably very picky," said Fourth Mistress. "I'm afraid he might look down on Seventh Sister because she's the daughter of a concubine. It would be a shame to lose so good a connection!"

"But he too is the child of a secondary wife," said Third Master.

"He's a very clever man, though," said Fourth Mistress. "Can our Number Seven, who is such a dolt, ever hope to catch him? My eldest daughter, on the other hand, is very quick. Don't be fooled by looks—she is still young but she is smart! She knows how to behave."

"But there's such a difference in their ages," said Third Mistress.

Fourth Mistress snorted. "You don't know! This kind of man likes them young. If my eldest won't do, there's always her younger sister."

Third Mistress laughed. "Your second daughter is twenty years younger than Mr. Fan!"

Fourth Mistress quietly tugged at her sister-in-law's arm, a serious look on her face. "Third Sister, don't be so foolish! You're protecting Number Seven, but what is she to the Bai family? Having another mother really makes a big difference. No one here should hope for any benefit after she gets married! What I'm saying is for the good of the family."

But Old Mrs. Bai's chief concern was her fear that relatives would say she'd wronged a motherless girl. She decided to pursue the plan that had been first proposed. Mrs. Xu would set up a meeting, and Baolu would be introduced to Fan Liuyuan.

Mrs. Xu, in a two-pronged attack, also scouted for Liusu. She found a Mr. Jiang, who worked in the customs office. His wife had recently died, leaving five children behind, and now he was very anxious to remarry. Mrs. Xu thought it best to take care of Baolu first, and then make a match for Liusu, because Fan Liuyuan would soon be leaving for Singapore. The Bai household looked at Liusu's remarriage as some kind of joke, but since they wanted to get her out of the house they ignored the whole business, letting Mrs. Xu manage it. For Baolu, however, they fell all over themselves, bustling about with great fanfare, turning the house upside down. Two daughters in the same house, but one got lots of attention and the other got cold silence. The contrast was painfully obvious.

Old Mrs. Bai was not satisfied until she had dressed Baolu in every last stitch of the family's best finery. Third Mistress's daughter had received a length of silk as a birthday present from her godmother. Old Mrs. Bai forced Third Mistress to hand it over, and then she had it made into a cheongsam for Baolu. The old lady's private cache of fine goods consisted mostly of furs, and since furs couldn't be worn in the summertime, she had to pawn a sable jacket, then use the money to have several old pieces of jewelry reset. Of course Baolu was also given pearl earrings, jade bracelets, and emerald rings to wear. Everyone wanted to make sure she was fully adorned, a glittering beauty.

On the appointed day, Old Mrs. Bai, Third Master, Third Mistress, Fourth Master, and Fourth Mistress all wanted to go along. Baolu had learned, in a roundabout way, of Fourth Mistress's plot against her. She fumed in secret, determined not to let Fourth Mistress's daughters anywhere near her when she made her entrance. But since she couldn't very well say that she didn't want the girls there, she insisted instead that Liusu go with her. After seven people had been crammed into the taxi-cab, there really wasn't room for any more, so the two girls, Jinzhi and Jinzhan, forlornly stayed behind.

They left at five o'clock in the afternoon, and didn't return until eleven that evening. How could Jinzhi and Jinzhan relax and go to sleep? They were wide-eyed with anticipation when everyone came home, but no one had anything to say. Baolu walked into Old Mrs. Bai's room with a long face, stripped off all her jewels and ornaments, gave them back to the old lady and, without a word, went to her room. Jinzhi and Jinzhan dragged their mother out to the balcony and begged her to tell them what had happened.

"I've never seen anything like you girls," Fourth Mistress snapped. "You're not the ones whose match is being made—and here you are all hot and bothered!"

Third Mistress followed them onto the balcony. "Don't say things she might take the wrong way," she said softly.

Fourth Mistress turned to face Liusu's room and shouted, "I may be pointing at the mulberry but I'm cursing the locust tree. And why shouldn't I curse her? It's not as if she hadn't seen a man for a thousand years! So why does she act crazy, all worked up and woozy the minute she catches a whiff of one?"

Jinzhi and Jinzhan were bewildered by their mother's outburst. Third Sister managed to calm her down, then told the girls, "First we went to see a movie."

"See a movie?" Jinzhi was quite surprised.

"Yes—quite quite strange, isn't it?" Third Mistress said. "The whole point of the meeting was for them to see each other, but there in the dark you can't see anything. Later, Mrs. Xu said this was all Mr. Fan's idea—that it was a ploy of his. He wanted her to sit around for a couple hours, till the sweat made her makeup run and he could get a better look. That's what Mrs. Xu thinks. I think Mr. Fan never was sincere about this. He wanted to see a movie because he didn't want to talk with us. Didn't he try to slip away as soon as the movie ended?"

Fourth Mistress couldn't hold back. "What do you mean?

Everything was going very well. If it hadn't been for that troublemaker we took with us, we'd be halfway there by now!"

"Then what? Then what?" Jinzhi and Jinzhan frantically implored their aunt.

"Well, then Mrs. Xu stopped Mr. Fan and said we should all go and get something to eat. Mr. Fan said it would be his treat."

Fourth Mistress clapped her hands together. "If we were going to get a bite to eat, then that's what we should have done. It's obvious that Seventh Sister doesn't know how to dance, so why'd we go to a dance hall and then just sit around? You won't hear me saying it, but, really, this was Third Master's fault. He goes out. He knows the town. He should have said something when Mr. Fan told the cabdriver to go to a dance hall."

"So many restaurants in Shanghai," Third Mistress rose in defense. "How could he know which ones have dancing, and which ones don't? He hasn't got the leisure to go around finding out things like that—the way Fourth Master does!"

Jinzhi and Jinzhan still wanted to hear the rest of the story, but Third Mistress had been challenged by Fourth Mistress so many times that now she lost interest. "So we went to get a bite to eat, and then we came home."

"What kind of person is this Mr. Fan?" Jinzhan asked.

"How should I know?" said Third Mistress. "I don't think we got three whole sentences out of him." She thought for a moment. "He dances pretty well, though."

Jinzhi let out a small gasp. "Who did he dance with?"

Fourth Mistress cut in. "Who else? Your Sixth Aunt of course! People who are properly brought up, people like us, aren't taught to dance. But your Sixth Aunt learned it all from that no-good husband of hers. Utterly shameless! Someone asks you to dance, can't you say you don't know how, and let it go at that? There's no shame in not knowing how to dance. Look at your Third Aunt—look at me—we're all from good families, we've been around long enough to see something of the world. We don't dance!"

Third Mistress sighed. "One dance, well, you could say it was just to be polite. But two, three dances!"

Jinzhi and Jinzhan were flabbergasted.

Fourth Mistress turned again toward a certain doorway and vented her ire. "You've got a heart smeared with pig fat! If you think that by ruining your sister's chances you are going to get lucky, you'd better forget it! He's turned down so many ladies, do you think he'd want a soiled flower like you?"

Liusu and Baolu shared a room, and Baolu had already gone to bed. Liusu crouched down in the dark and lit a stick of mosquito-repellant incense. She'd heard everything that had been said out on the balcony, but this time she was perfectly calm. She struck the match and watched it burn, the little three-cornered pennant of flaming red flickering in its own draft, coming closer and closer toward her fingers. With a puff of her lips, she blew it out, leaving only the glowing red flagpole. The pole twisted and shrank into a curly gray fiendish shape. She tossed the dead match into the incense pan.

She hadn't planned the evening's events, but in any case she'd shown them a thing or two. So they thought she was finished, that her life was already over? The game was just beginning! She smiled. Baolu must be cursing her silently, far more fiercely even than Fourth Mistress. But she knew that as much as Baolu hated her, the younger woman's heart was also full of respect and admiration. No matter how amazing a woman is, she won't be respected by her own sex unless she's loved by a member of the opposite one. Women are petty this way.

Was it really true that Fan Liuyuan liked her? Not certain in the least. All those things he'd said—she didn't believe a word of it. She could tell that he was used to lying to women, she'd have to be very careful. Family, family everywhere, and no one to turn to—she was on her own. Her moon-white silk gauze cheongsam hung from the bed frame. Twisting around, she sat on the floor and hid her face in the long skirt. Puff after steady puff, the green smoke of the mosquito-repellent incense floated up, seeping into her brain. Her eyes gleamed with tears.

A few days later, Mrs. Xu returned to the Bai residence. Fourth Mistress had already predicted: "After the scene Sixth Sister made, Seventh Sister's chances are ruined. How could Mrs. Xu fail to be angry? And if Mrs. Xu was angry with Sixth Sister, would she still be willing to help her by making useful introductions? This was a case of 'trying to steal a chicken with a handful of grain, and losing both bird and bait.'"

And it was true: Mrs. Xu was not as enthusiastic as she had been. She started out by beating around the bush, explaining why she hadn't come by in a while. Her husband had some business to take care of in Hong Kong, and, if all went well, they would be going there, renting a house, and staying for about a year. That was why she'd been so busy the last few days, packing up and getting ready to go. As for the Baolu project, Mr. Fan had already left Shanghai, so they'd have to let it rest for the time being. And Mrs. Xu had just found out that Mr. Jiang, Liusu's potential match, had another woman in his life. Trying to drive a wedge between them would be no easy matter. Anyway, this kind of person really wasn't reliable; it might be better to give it up. When Third and Fourth Mistress heard this, they exchanged glances and smirked.

Mrs. Xu furrowed her brow and continued: "My husband has a lot of friends in Hong Kong, but the problem is that 'distant water can't put out a nearby fire' . . . If Sixth Young Lady could go to Hong Kong for a bit, probably she'd find a lot of opportunities. Over the past few years, so many Shanghainese men have gone to Hong Kong that the place is teeming with talented types. Naturally, Shanghai men prefer to be with other Shanghainese, and people are saying that young ladies from back home are very popular. If Sixth Young Lady went, there's no doubt she'd find a good match. She could grab a handful and take her pick."

Everyone felt that Mrs. Xu really had a way with words. A few days ago her grand plans had come to naught, leaving her high and dry, and yet here she was putting up a good front, etc. Old Mrs. Bai sighed. "Going to Hong Kong," she said. "Easier said than done! After all—"

To everyone's surprise, Mrs. Xu cheerfully interrupted. "If Sixth Young Lady wants to go, she can go as my guest. I agreed to help her, so I should see it through."

At this, they all turned to one another, blinking with amazement. Even Liusu was taken aback. Mrs. Xu's volunteering to make a match for her—that had been impulsive and good-hearted, born of a real sympathy for her situation. Running around fixing things up, arranging a dinner party, inviting that Mr. Jiang—such generosity was not unheard of. But paying Liusu's fare and expenses and taking her to Hong Kong— Mrs. Xu would be shelling out a lot of money, and for what? There may be lots of virtuous people in this world, but they aren't so stupid as to throw good money away for virtue's sake. Mrs. Xu must have a backer. Could it be a plot hatched by that Fan Liuyuan? Mrs. Xu had said that her husband had close business ties with Fan Liuyuan, and she and her husband were probably eager to help him out. Sacrificing some poor and lonely little relative to score points with him—that was a distinct possibility.

While Liusu's mind was racing, Old Mrs. Bai said, "Oh, this won't do. We can't let you—"

Mrs. Xu laughed this off. "It's no problem. A little thing like this—of course I can manage it! Anyway, I want Sixth Young Lady to help me. I've got two children, and high blood pressure, and I shouldn't let myself get too tired. If she travels with us, there will be someone to take care of things. I won't pamper her, I'll want her to help out quite a lot!"

Old Mrs. Bai came up with a stream of polite replies on Liusu's behalf. Mrs. Xu turned, and opened a direct attack. "Well, Sixth Young Lady, you really should agree to go with us. Just think of it as sightseeing, and it will be worth it!"

Liusu bowed her head, and said with a smile, "You're really too good to me."

She made a rapid calculation. There was no hope of getting that Mr. Jiang, and even if someone made another match for her, it wouldn't be much different from Jiang, maybe not even that good. Liusu's father had been a famous gambler. He'd gambled away the family's fortune and started its descent into the ranks of poor, declining households. Liusu had never touched cards or dice, but she too liked to gamble. She decided to wager her future. If she lost, her reputation would be ruined, and even the role of stepmother to five children would be far above her. If she won, she'd get the prize the whole crowd was eyeing like so many greedy tigers—Fan Liuyuan—and all her stifled rancor would be swept clean away.

She agreed to Mrs. Xu's plan, which called for leaving within the week. Liusu rushed to get ready. Even though she didn't have much, and there really wasn't anything to pack, she was intensely busy for several days. She raised some cash by selling a few trinkets, then had some outfits made. Mrs. Xu, though she too was very busy, found time to give Liusu the benefit of her advice. When the Bai family saw Mrs. Xu being so kind to Liusu, they became freshly interested in her. They were still very distrustful, but now they were more cautious, holding long whispered consultations behind Liusu's back instead of spitefully scolding her to her face. Once in a while they even addressed her quite respectfully, thinking that if she really married a rich man in Hong Kong and returned home in glory, they'd better be on speaking terms with her. It wouldn't do to offend her.

The Xu family took Liusu with them, in a car, to the dock.

They had a first-class cabin on a Dutch ship. But the ship was small and pitched violently, and as soon as they had boarded, Mr. and Mrs. Xu collapsed into their berths. What with the adults retching and the children crying, Liusu really did wait on them for several days.

Not until the ship had finally reached the shore did she have a chance to go up on deck and gaze out at the sea. It was a fiery afternoon, and the most striking part of the view was the parade of giant billboards along the dock, their reds, oranges, and pinks mirrored in the lush green water. Below the surface of the water, bars and blots of clashing color plunged in murderous confusion. Liusu found herself thinking that in a city of such hyperboles, even a sprained ankle would hurt more than it did in other places. Her heart began to pound.

Suddenly someone rushed up from behind, grabbing her legs and almost knocking her down. Liusu gasped, then realized that it was one of the Xu children. She quickly steadied herself, and went back to help Mrs. Xu. The dozen suitcases and two children refused to match up; no sooner were the bags in order than a child went missing again. Worn out by her labors, Liusu stopped gazing at the scenery.

After disembarking, they took two taxis to the Repulse Bay Hotel. They left the teeming city behind, the taxis rising and dipping across the hilly terrain. Soon cliffs of yellow-and-red soil flanked the road, while ravines opened up on either side to reveal dense green forest or aquamarine sea. As they approached Repulse Bay, the cliffs and trees grew gentler and more inviting. Returning picnickers swept past them in cars filled with flowers, the sound of scattered laughter fading in the wind.

When they arrived at the hotel entrance, they couldn't actually see the hotel. They got out of the car and climbed up a broad flight of stone steps. Not until they had reached the top, where an ornamental garden was laid out, could they see two yellow buildings farther up. Mr. Xu had already reserved their rooms, so the hotel staff led them along a small gravel path, through the amber dimness of the lobby and hallway, then up to the second floor. They turned a corner, and there, through a doorway, was a small balcony, with vines flowering on a trellis and sunlight slanting across one section of the wall.

Two people were standing on the balcony and talking. One was a woman. She stood with her back toward them, her long black hair hanging down to her ankles. She wore anklets of twisted gold over her bare feet; it wasn't clear whether she was wearing slippers or not, but above the anklets one could just make out the slim, Indian-style trousers. The man called out, "Ah, Mrs. Xu!" and then walked toward them; he greeted the couple and nodded, with a suppressed smile, at Liusu.

Liusu saw that it was Fan Liuyuan and her heart raced again, even though she'd already guessed that he'd be here. The woman who'd been standing on the balcony went off somewhere. Liuyuan accompanied them up the stairs. As they walked, everyone kept saying how surprised and happy they were, just as if they'd run into an old friend, quite unexpectedly, while traveling far from home.

Fan Liuyuan couldn't really be called handsome, but he was attractive in a rugged sort of way. Mr. and Mrs. Xu supervised the porters with their luggage, and Liuyuan and Liusu walked ahead. "Mr. Fan," inquired Liusu with a glint of a smile, "it seems you haven't gone to Singapore."

"No, I've been waiting here for you," Liuyuan said lightly.

It had never occurred to Liusu that he would be so direct. She didn't inquire further, afraid that if he went on to say that it was he, not Mrs. Xu, who had invited her to Hong Kong, she wouldn't know how to respond. She treated it as a joke, and replied with a smile.

Having learned that she was in room 130, Liuyuan stopped in front of a door and said, "Here it is." The porter unlocked the door. Liusu walked in and was immediately drawn to the window. The whole room seemed to be a dark picture frame around the big ocean painting there. Roaring breakers spilled onto the curtains, staining their edges blue.

"Put the trunk in front of the wardrobe," Liuyuan said to the porter.

His voice sounded next to Liusu's ear, startling her. She turned and saw that the porter had gone, though the door had not been closed. Liuyuan leaned against the window with one hand stretched along the frame, blocking her line of vision and smiling as he gazed at her. Liusu bowed her head.

Liuyuan laughed. "Did you realize? Your specialty is bowing the head."

Liusu raised her head. "What? I don't understand."

"Some people are good at talking, or at laughing, or at keeping house, but you're good at bowing your head."

"I'm no good at anything," said Liusu. "I'm utterly useless."

"It's the useless women who are the most formidable."

Liusu walked away laughing. "I'm not going to discuss this with you anymore. I'm going next door to have a look around."

"Next door? My room or Mrs. Xu's room?"

Liusu was startled again. "You're staying in the next room?"

Liuyuan had already swung the door open for her. "Sorry... my room's a mess, no visitors allowed."

He knocked at room 131, and Mrs. Xu opened the door to let them in. "Come and some have tea with us. We have a sitting room." Then she rang the bell to call for refreshments.

Mr. Xu came out of the bedroom and said, "I telephoned my friend Mr. Zhu, and he insists on throwing a party tonight to welcome us. He's invited us to the Hong Kong Hotel." He turned to Liuyuan. "Of course you're included."

"My, you've got a lot of energy," said Mrs. Xu. "After all those days seasick on the boat, shouldn't we go to bed early? Let's not go out tonight."

"The Hong Kong Hotel has the most old-fashioned ballroom

I've ever seen," said Liuyuan. "Everything about the place—building, lights, decor, orchestra—is very English and, forty or fifty years ago, was very up-to-date. But nowadays it's not much of a draw. There's nothing to see there, except maybe the funny little waiters. Even on a very hot day, they wear those northern-style trousers, gathered tight at the ankles."

"Why?" asked Liusu.

"Chinese flavor!"

Mr. Xu laughed. "Well, since we're here we might as well go and have a look. Sorry, but you'll just have to keep us company!"

"I'm not sure I'm going, so don't wait for me."

Liuyuan seemed quite uninterested in going, while Mr. Xu, who was not in the habit of frequenting ballrooms, was unusually excited, as if he truly wanted to introduce her to his friends. Liusu felt quite unsure about what was going on.

But when they got to the Hong Kong Hotel that night, the group that had gathered to welcome them was largely composed of old married couples. The few single men were all youths in their early twenties. While Liusu was dancing, Fan Liuyuan suddenly appeared and cut in on her partner. In the lychee-red light of the ballroom, she couldn't see his darkened face clearly, but she could tell that he was unusually withdrawn.

"Why so quiet?" she teased.

"Everything that can be said to a person's face, I've already said."

Liusu chuckled. "And just what is it that you sneak around and say behind a person's back?"

"There are some kinds of foolishness that you don't want other people to hear, don't even want yourself to hear. Even hearing yourself say it makes you feel embarrassed. For instance, I love you, I will love you for the rest of my life."

Liusu turned away and chided him softly. "Such nonsense!"

"If I don't say anything, you complain because I'm too quiet, but if I talk, you complain that I talk too much."

"Tell me," said Liusu, "why is it that you don't want me out on the dance floor?"

"Most men like to lead a woman astray, then make appeals to the bad woman's bad conscience, and reform her till she's good. I don't go around making so much work for myself. I think the important thing, for a good woman, is steady honesty."

Liusu gave him a sideways glance. "You think you're different from them? It seems to me you're just as selfish."

"Selfish? How?"

To herself, she thought: "Your idea of the perfect woman is someone who is pure and high-minded but still ready to flirt. The pure high-mindedness is for others, but the flirting is for you. If I were an entirely good woman, you would never have noticed me in the first place!"

She leaned her head to one side and said, "You want me to be good in front of others, but bad when I'm with you."

Liuyuan thought for a moment. "I don't understand."

Liusu explained again. "You want me to be bad to others, but good only to you."

"Now you've turned it around again! You're just making me more confused."

He was silent for a while, then said, "What you're saying isn't so."

Liusu laughed. "Ah, so now you understand."

"I don't care if you're good or bad. I don't want you to change. It's not easy to find a real Chinese girl like you."

Liusu sighed softly. "I'm old-fashioned, that's all."

"Real Chinese women are the world's most beautiful women. They're never out of fashion."

"But for a modern man like you—"

"You say 'modern,' but what you probably mean is Western.

It's true I am not a real Chinese. It's just that in the past few years I've become a little more like a Chinese. But you know, a foreigner who's become Chinese also becomes reactionary, more reactionary even than an old-fashioned scholar from the dynastic era."

Liusu laughed. "You're old-fashioned, and I'm old-fashioned. And you've already said that the Hong Kong Hotel is the most old-fashioned ballroom ever..."

They both laughed, and just then the music ended. Liuyuan led her back to her seat. He told the others that Miss Bai had a headache, and that he would see her home.

This was entirely unexpected. Liusu had no time to think, though she knew that she didn't want to cross him. They didn't know each other well enough to argue openly. So she let him help her with her coat, made her apologies all around, and went out with him.

Directly in their path a group of Western gentlemen stood clustered around a woman, like stars around the moon. Liusu first noticed the woman's long black hair; it had been done up in two long braids and then coiled on top of her head. She was Indian, and even in Western apparel, her aura was intensely Oriental. She was wearing a dark, sheer cape over a long, close-fitting gown, goldfish-red, that covered even her hands, leaving only her pearly fingernails exposed. The plunging neckline of her dress formed a narrow "V" all the way to her waist; it was the latest fashion from Paris, called *ligne du ciel*. Her complexion was rich and tawny, like a gold-plated Buddha, but a devil lurked in her dark eyes. Her nose was classically straight, though a bit too sharp and thin. Her mouth was small, with lips so pink and full they looked swollen.

Liuyuan stopped and made a slight bow in her direction. Liusu looked at the woman, and the hauteur with which the woman returned her gaze put a thousand miles between them.

Liuyuan introduced them. "This is Miss Bai. This is Princess Saheiyini."

Liusu couldn't help but be impressed. Saheiyini reached out and touched Liusu's hand with her fingertips. "Is Miss Bai from Shanghai?" she asked Liuyuan, who nodded. "She doesn't seem like someone from Shanghai," she said, with a smile.

"Then what does she seem like?" Liuyuan asked.

Saheiyini placed a finger on one cheek and thought for a moment. Then she brought her hands together, fingers pointing upward, as if she had something to say but words simply failed her. She laughed, shrugging her shoulders, and walked into the ballroom. Liuyuan headed toward the door again, taking Liusu with him. Liusu couldn't understand much English, but she had followed their expressions. Now she said, with a smile, "I *am* a country bumpkin."

"As I said, you are a real Chinese. That of course is different from her notion of a Shanghainese."

They got in a taxi, and Liuyuan said, "Don't be bothered by the airs she puts on. She struts around saying that she's the daughter of Prince Krishna Karumpa, but that her mother lost the prince's favor and was told to commit suicide, and she too had to flee. Now she wanders in exile, unable to return. And in fact, it is true that she can't go back to her native land—but nothing else in her story has been proven."

"Has she been to Shanghai?"

"She's very well-known in Shanghai. She came to Hong Kong with an Englishman. Did you see that old man standing behind her? He's the one who's keeping her these days."

"You men are always like this. When you're talking to her, you can't think of enough polite things to say, but behind her back you say she's worthless. I can just imagine what you say to others about me, the daughter of a poor old Qing official, even lower ranking than she is!"

Liuyuan laughed. "Who would dare speak of you two in the same breath?"

Pursing her lips, Liusu said, "Maybe that's because her name is too long. Can't get it all out in one breath."

"You needn't worry. I promise to treat you the way you should be treated."

Liusu smoothed her face and murmured a half-persuaded "Really?" to herself, as she leaned against the car window. His tone did not seem sarcastic, and she had noticed that when the two of them were alone together, he was a perfect gentleman. For reasons that she failed to fathom, he was a model of self-restraint when no one else was around to see, but when people were watching, he liked to take liberties. Was this just a peculiarity of his? Or was he up to something? She couldn't quite figure it out.

When they reached Repulse Bay, he helped her out of the taxi, then pointed to the dense copse alongside the road. "Do you see that tree? It's a southern variety. The English call it 'flame of the forest.'"

"Is it red?" asked Liusu.

"Red, red, red!"

In the darkness, Liusu couldn't see the red, but she knew instinctively that it was the reddest red, red beyond belief. Great masses of little red flowers, nestled in a huge tree that reached up to the sky, a riotous welter burning all the way up, staining the indigo sky with red. Leaning her head back, she gazed upward.

"The Cantonese call it the 'shadow tree,'" said Liuyuan. "Look at this leaf."

The leaf was as light as a fern; when a slight breeze made the delicate silhouette flutter, they seemed to hear a faint, almost melodic sound, like the tinkling of wind chimes in the eaves.

"Let's walk over there a bit," said Liuyuan.

Liusu didn't say anything. But as he walked, she slowly followed. After all, it was still early, and lots of people go out for walks on a road—it would be all right. A short distance past the Repulse Bay Hotel, an overhead bridge arched through the air. On the far side of the bridge there was a mountain slope; on the near side, a gray brick retaining wall. Liuyuan leaned against the wall, and Liusu leaned too, looking upward at its great height, the wall so high that the upper edge faded out of sight. The wall was cool and rough, the color of death. Pressed against that wall, her face bloomed with the opposite hues: red lips, shining eyes—a face of flesh and blood, alive with thought and feeling.

"I don't know why," said Liuyuan, looking at her, "but this wall makes me think of the old sayings about the end of the world. Someday, when human civilization has been completely destroyed, when everything is burned, burst, utterly collapsed and ruined, maybe this wall will still be here. If, at that time, we can meet at this wall, then maybe, Liusu, you will honestly care about me, and I will honestly care about you."

"So you admit you like to play games," Liusu sniffed coyly. "That doesn't mean you can drag me along too! When have you caught me lying?"

"Fair enough," Liuyuan said with a snicker. "There's no one more openhearted than you."

"That's enough . . . stop patronizing me."

Liuyuan was silent for a long time. Then he sighed.

"Something you're unhappy about?" Liusu asked.

"Lots."

"If someone as free as you are thinks life is unfair, then someone like me ought to just go and hang herself."

"I know you're not happy," said Liuyuan. "You've certainly seen more than enough of all these awful people, and awful things that are everywhere around us. But if you were seeing them for the first time, it would be even harder to bear, even harder to get used to. That's what it's been like for me. When I arrived in China I was already twenty-four. I had such dreams of my homeland. You can imagine how disappointed I was. I couldn't bear the shock, and I started slipping downward. If...if you had known me before, then maybe you could forgive me for the way I am now."

Liusu tried to imagine what it would be like to see her Fourth Sister-in-law for the first time. Then she burst out: "That would still be better. When you see them for the first time, then no matter how awful, no matter how dirty they are, they—or it—is still outside of you. But if you live in it for a long time, how can you tell how much of it is them, and how much of it is you?"

Liuyuan fell silent. After a long pause he said, "Maybe you are right. Maybe what I'm saying is just an excuse, and I'm only fooling myself." Then he laughed suddenly. "Actually, I don't need any excuses! I like to have a good time—and I have plenty of money, plenty of time—do I need any other reason?"

He thought it over, and again grew frustrated. He said to her, "I don't understand myself—but I want you to understand me! I want you to understand me!" He spoke like this, and yet in his heart he'd already given up hope. Still, stubbornly, plaintively he went on: "I want you to understand me!"

Liusu was willing to try. She was willing to try anything, within limits. She leaned her head in his direction, and answered softly, "I do understand. I do." But while comforting him, she suddenly thought of her moonlit face. That delicate profile, the eyes, the brow—beautiful beyond reason; misty, ethereal. Slowly she bowed her head.

Liuyuan began chuckling. "That's right, don't forget," he said, in a new tone of voice. "Your specialty is bowing the head. But there are those who say that only teenage girls can bow the head well. If you're good at it, then it becomes a habit. And when you've bowed the head for many years, you might end up with a wrinkled neck."

Liusu turned away, but not without raising her hand to her neck. "Don't worry," laughed Liuyuan, "of course you don't have any wrinkles. When you get back to your room, when no one else is around, you can unbutton your collar and check."

Liusu didn't reply. She just turned and started walking. Liuyuan caught up to her. "I'll tell you why you'll keep your good looks. Saheiyini once said she didn't dare get married because Indian women, once they start relaxing at home, sitting around all day, just get fat. I told her that Chinese women, when they sit around, aren't even good at fattening up—since even that takes some kind of effort. So it turns out that laziness has its advantages!"

Liusu utterly ignored him, and from then on he held himself in check, making conversation and small jokes all the way back. She did not soften until they'd arrived at the hotel. Quietly they returned to their respective rooms.

Liusu assessed the situation. It turned out that what Liuyuan cared about was spiritual love. She approved entirely, because spiritual love always leads to marriage, while physical love tends to reach a certain level and then stop, leaving little hope of marriage. There was just one small problem with spiritual love: while courting, the man always says things that the woman doesn't understand. Not that it matters all that much. In the end the marriage goes through anyway, and then you buy a house, arrange the furniture, hire some servants—and in such matters the woman is much more expert than the man. Given all that, Liusu felt that the little misunderstanding of that evening was not anything to worry about.

The next morning there was not a peep from Mrs. Xu's room, which meant she must be sleeping in. Liusu remembered that Mrs. Xu had told her that in this hotel there was an extra charge for room delivery, not to mention the tip, so she decided to go to the dining room and save a bit of expense. She washed and dressed, and walked out the door. There was a porter waiting outside. Seeing her, he immediately knocked at Liuyuan's door. Liuyuan appeared at once. "Let's have breakfast together," he smiled.

"Mr. and Mrs. Xu haven't raised the bed curtain yet?" he asked, as they walked together.

"They must be tuckered out from their good time last night!" returned Liusu. "I didn't hear them come in. It must have been close to dawn."

They took a table on the veranda outside the dining room. Beyond the stone railing stood an enormous palm tree, its feathery fronds trembling slightly in the sun, like a fountain of light. Under the tree was a pool with its own fountain, much less magnificent.

"What are Mr. and Mrs. Xu going to do today?" asked Liuyuan.

"I think they're going to look at houses."

"Let them look at houses—we'll go have our own fun. Would you rather go to the beach or go have a look at the city?"

Liusu had, on the previous afternoon, surveyed the beach scene through binoculars. Strapping youths and lovely girls. Very exciting but a little too rowdy. Preferring to err on the side of caution, she suggested that they go into town. So they caught one of the buses provided by the hotel and went into the city center.

Liuyuan took her to the Great China to eat. Liusu heard the waiters speaking Shanghainese, filling the air with her native tongue. "Is this a Shanghai restaurant?" she asked with some surprise.

"Don't you feel homesick?" Liuyuan laughed.

"But . . . coming to Hong Kong so that we can eat Shanghai cuisine seems a bit silly."

"I do a lot of silly things when I'm with you. For instance, take a tram around in circles, go to a movie I've seen two times already—"

"Because you've caught silliness from me, right?"

"Take it to mean whatever you please."

When they had finished eating, Liuyuan raised his glass and drained the remaining tea, then lifted the glass high and stared at it.

"If there's something worth seeing, let me look too," Liusu said.

"Hold it up to the light," said Liuyuan. "The scene inside reminds me of the forests of Malaya."

When the glass was tilted, a hatching of green tea leaves stuck to one side; held up to the light, they became a waving plantain tree, while the tangled swirl of tea leaves clumped at the bottom looked like knee-high grass and undergrowth. Liusu peered up at the glass, and Liuyuan leaned over, pointing all this out. Through the dusky green glass, Liusu suddenly saw him watching her with eyes that seemed to laugh, yet didn't. She put the glass down and smiled.

"I'll take you to Malaya," Liuyuan said.

"What for?"

"To go back to nature." He thought for a moment. "But there's just one problem—I can't imagine you running through the forest in a cheongsam. But neither can I imagine you not wearing a cheongsam."

Liusu's face stiffened. "Stop talking nonsense."

"But I'm serious. The first time I saw you, you were wearing one of those trendy tunics, and I thought you shouldn't bare your arms like that. But Western-style clothes aren't right for you either. A Manchu-style cheongsam might suit you better, if its lines weren't so severe."

"In the end, if a person is ugly, then no matter how she dresses it still won't look right!"

Liuyuan laughed. "You keep twisting my words! What I mean is that you're like someone from another world. You have all these little gestures, and a romantic aura, very much like a Peking opera singer."

Liusu raised her eyebrows. "An opera singer—indeed!" she said sarcastically. "But of course it takes more than one to put on a show, and I've been forced into it. A person acts clever with me, and if I don't do the same, he takes me for a fool and insults me!"

When Liuyuan heard this, he was rather crestfallen. He raised the empty glass, tried to drink from it, then put it down again and sighed. "Right," he said. "My fault. I'm used to throwing out lines because everyone throws lines at me. But to you I have said a few sincere things, and you can't tell the difference."

"I'm not the worm in your innards—I can't read your mind."

"Right. My fault. But I really have thought up a great many schemes because of you. When I first met you in Shanghai, I thought that if you could get away from your family, maybe you could be more natural. So I waited and waited till you came to Hong Kong... and now, I want to take you to Malaya, to the forest with its primitive peoples..." He laughed at himself, his voice hoarse and dry, and called for the check. By the time they had paid, he had already recovered his good spirits; he resumed his excessively courteous, unflappably chivalrous manner.

Every day he took her out, and they did everything there was to do... movies, Cantonese opera, casinos, the Gloucester Hotel, the Cecil Hotel, the Bluebird Coffee Bar, Indian fabric shops, Szechuan food in Kowloon... and they often went for walks, even very late at night. She could hardly believe it, but he rarely so much as touched her hand. She was continually on edge, fearing that he would suddenly drop the pretense and launch a surprise attack. But day after day he remained a gentleman; it was like facing a great enemy who stood perfectly still. At first this threw her entirely off balance, like missing a step when going down a flight of stairs; her heart pulsated, throbbing irregularly. After a while, though, she got used to it.

Then something happened out on the beach. By this time Liusu knew Liuyuan a little better; she didn't think a beach outing would be a problem. So they whiled away a whole morning there. They even sat together on the sand, though facing opposite directions. Suddenly Liusu squealed: mosquito bite, she said.

"It's not a mosquito," said Liuyuan. "It's a little insect called a sand fly. Its bite leaves a red mark, just like a mole on your skin."

"There's too much sun," Liusu complained again.

"Let's sit out a bit longer, and then we can go into one of those cabanas. I've already got one rented."

The thirsty sun sucked in the seawater, gargling and spitting in steady rhythm. It lapped up all the moisture in their bodies, so that they grew light and empty, like dry, golden leaves. Liusu started to feel that strange, light-headed happiness, but then she had to cry, "Ouch! Mosquito!" She twisted around and slapped her own bare back.

"That's the hard way," said Liuyuan. "Here, I'll slap for you, and you slap for me."

And Liusu did watch over his back, slapping at the sand flies whenever she saw one. "Aiiya, he got away!" And Liuyuan watched her back for her. They hit and slapped at each other, then broke into laughter. Suddenly Liusu took offense, stood up, and walked back toward the hotel. This time Liuyuan didn't follow her. When she had reached the trees and the stone path that ran between two rush-mat cabanas, Liusu stopped, shook the sand out of her little skirt, and looked back. Liuyuan was still there, stretched out with his arms folded under his head, a man daydreaming in the sun, turning into a golden leaf again. Liusu went into the hotel, got some binoculars, and looked from her window. Now a woman reclined next to him, a big braid coiled on top of her head. Saheiyini could be burned to ashes, and Liusu would still know her.

From that day on, Liuyuan spent all his time with Saheiyini; apparently he had decided to let Liusu cool her heels for a while. Liusu had been going out every day; now, with nothing to do and no good explanation to make to Mrs. Xu, she thought it best to come down with a cold and keep to her room for a few days. Fortunately, the gods were very considerate; they sent a nice, kind rain. That was one more excuse, leaving her free not to go out.

One afternoon, Liusu came back to the hotel with her umbrella, having gone for a walk in the hotel garden. It was getting dark, and she guessed that Mr. and Mrs. Xu would soon return from house hunting, so she sat on the veranda waiting for them. She opened her shiny oil-paper umbrella and set it out on the railing, blocking her face from view. The umbrella was pink and painted with malachite-green lotus leaves, and the raindrops slipped along its ribs. It was raining hard. Car tires scuffed by in the rain, and then a laughing group of men and women scrambled up to the hotel, led by Fan Liuyuan. Saheiyini was leaning on his arm, but she was a mess, her bare legs flecked with mud. She took off her big straw hat, splashing water on the ground. Catching sight of Liusu's umbrella, Liuyuan said a few words to Saheiyini at the foot of the stairs, and Saheiyini went on up by herself. Liuyuan came over, and pulled out a handkerchief to wipe the rain from his face and clothes. Liusu was forced to offer a brief greeting. Liuyuan sat down. "I heard you haven't been feeling well."

"Just a summer cold."

"This weather is so muggy. We've just gone out on that Englishman's yacht to have a picnic, sailed out to Tsing Yi Island."

So Liusu asked him about the scenery on Tsing Yi Island. Just then, Saheiyini returned in an Indian outfit, with a gosling-yellow wrap that hung down to the ground and was embossed all over with two-inch-wide silver flowers. She too sat down by the railing, at a table far away, one arm draped casually over the back of her chair, silver polish glinting on her fingernails.

"Why don't you go over?" Liusu said to Liuyuan with a smile.

"There's someone with a controlling interest."

"How can that Englishman tell her what to do?"

"He can't control her, but you can control me."

Liusu puckered her lips. "Oooh! I could be the governor of Hong Kong or the local city god, with everyone here under me, and still you wouldn't be under my control!"

Liuyuan shook his head. "A woman who doesn't get jealous is not quite right in the head."

Liusu let out a laugh. There was a short silence. "Why are you watching me?" she asked.

"I'm trying to see if you'll be nice to me from now on."

"Whether I'm nice to you or not, what difference could it make to you?"

Liuyuan clapped his hands together. "Ah! That's more like it! Now there's just a bit of venom in her voice!"

Liusu had to laugh. "I've never seen anyone like you, so intent on making people jealous!"

After that, they became friendly again and went to dinner together. On the surface Liusu seemed to have warmed to him again, but deep down she was depressed. Stirring up her jealousy was his way of taunting her so that she'd run into his arms of her own accord. But she'd kept him at a distance for so long now; if she softened toward him at this point, she'd be sacrificing herself for nothing. He wouldn't really feel obligated; he'd just think that she'd fallen for a trick. She was dreaming if she thought he'd marry her after that ... Clearly, he wanted her, but he didn't want to marry her. Since her family, poor as they were, was a respectable family, and since he and they all moved in the same circle, he was worried about getting a reputation as a seducer. That was why he put on that open and aboveboard manner. Now she knew that his innocence was fake. He didn't want to be held responsible. If he abandoned her, no one would listen to her side of things.

When Liusu had thought all this through, she couldn't help grinding her teeth in anger. Outwardly, she went along with Liuyuan as usual. Mrs. Xu had already rented a house in Happy Valley and planned to move in soon. Liusu would have liked to go with them, but since she had troubled them for more than a month, the idea of being their long-term guest was quite embarrassing. Staying at the hotel was also out of the question. She suffered the agony of indecision, not knowing whether to advance or retreat.

Then one night, after tossing and turning in bed for hours before finally drifting off, the telephone suddenly rang. It was Liuyuan's voice. "I love you," he said. And hung up. Liusu held the receiver in her hand and stared into space, her heart pounding. Softly she put it back in the cradle. No sooner had she hung up than it rang again. Again she raised the receiver. Liuyuan said, "I forgot to ask—do you love me?"

Liusu coughed. When at last she spoke her throat was still dry and raspy. "You must have known long ago," she said in a low voice. "Why else did I come to Hong Kong?"

Liuyuan sighed. "I knew, but even with the truth staring me in the face, I still don't want to believe it. Liusu, you don't love me."

"Why do you say that?"

Liuyuan didn't say anything. Then, after a long while, he said "In *The Book of Songs* there's a verse—"

"I don't understand that sort of thing," Liusu cut in.

"I know you don't understand," Liuyuan said impatiently. "If you understood, I wouldn't need to explain! So listen:

"Facing life, death, distance
Here is my promise to thee—
I take thy hand in mine:
We will grow old together.

"My Chinese isn't very good, and I don't know if I've got it right, but I think this is a very mournful poem which says that life and death and parting are enormous things, well beyond human control. Compared to the great forces in the world, we people are so very, very small. But still we say 'I will stay with you forever, we will never, in this lifetime, leave each other'—as if we really could decide these things!"

Liusu was silent for a while, but finally she burst out: "Why not go ahead and just say, flat out, that you don't want to marry me, and leave it at that! Why beat around the bush, with all this talk of not being able to decide things? Even a conservative person like me can say 'First marriage for the family, second marriage for oneself.' If someone as free and unburdened as you are can't decide for himself, then who can decide for you?"

"You don't love me—is that something you can simply decide for yourself?" Liuyuan said coldly.

"If you really love me, why worry if I do?"

"I'm not such a fool that I'll pay to marry someone who has no feelings for me, just so that she can tell me what to do! That's simply too unfair. And it's unfair to you, too. Well, maybe you don't care. Basically, you think that marriage is long-term prostitution—"

Liusu didn't wait for him to finish. She slammed the receiver down, her whole face crimson with rage. How dare he talk to her like this? How dare he! She sat on the bed, the feverish darkness wrapped around her like a purple wool rug. Her body was covered with sweat and she itched all over; her hair, stuck to her neck and back, irritated her terribly. She pressed her hands against her cheeks: her palms were ice-cold.

The phone rang again. She didn't answer, just let it ring. "Brring... Brring..." The sound was especially ear-piercing in that quiet room, in the quiet hotel, on quiet Repulse Bay. Liusu suddenly realized that she couldn't wake up the entire Repulse Bay Hotel. Starting, of course, with Mrs. Xu next door... Trembling with fear, she picked up the receiver and laid it on the bedsheet. But the night was so still that even from a distance she could hear Liuyuan's perfectly calm voice saying "Liusu, from your window, can you see the moon?"

She didn't know why, but suddenly she was sobbing. The moon shone bright and blurry through her tears, silver, with a slightly greenish tint. "In my window," said Liuyuan, "there is a flowering vine that blocks half the view. Maybe it's a rose. Or maybe not." He didn't say anything more, but the phone stayed off the hook. After a very long while, Liusu began to wonder if he had dozed off, but finally there was a gentle little click. Her hand still shaking, Liusu took the receiver from where it lay on the bed and put it back in the cradle. She feared he would call a fourth time, but he didn't. It was all a dream—the more she thought about it, the more it seemed like a dream.

The next day, she didn't dare ask him about it because he would be sure to tease her—"Dreams are just your heart's desire." Was she really so infatuated with him, that even in her sleep she dreamed of him calling her to say, "I love you"? There was no change in his attitude. They went out for the day, just as usual. Liusu suddenly noticed that there were lots of people who took them for husband and wife—the porters, the wives and old ladies that she chatted with in the hotel—and they could hardly be blamed for this. She and Liuyuan had rooms right next to each other, they came in and went out side by side, they took late-night walks on the beach, totally unconcerned about what other people might think. A nanny wheeled a baby carriage by, nodded to Liusu, and greeted her as "Mrs. Fan." Liusu froze, unable to either smile or not smile.

She could only look at Liuyuan from under her brows and say, in a low voice, "I wonder what they think!"

"Don't worry about those who call you 'Mrs. Fan.' But those who call you 'Miss Bai'—what must they think?"

The color drained from Liusu's face. Liuyuan stroked his chin and laughed. "Why content yourself with appearances only?"

Liusu stared at him in shock, suddenly seeing how wicked this man was. Whenever they were in public, he made sure to give the impression of affectionate intimacy, so that now she had no way to prove that they had not slept together. She was riding the tiger now, no way to go home, no way to rejoin her family; she had no option except to become his mistress. But if she relented at this point, all her efforts would have been wasted, with no hope of recovery. She wouldn't do it! Even if she was trapped by appearances, he'd taken advantage of her in name only. The real truth was that he had not gotten her. And since he hadn't, he might come back someday, ready to make peace on better terms.

She made up her mind, and told Liuyuan that she wanted to go back to Shanghai. Liuyuan didn't try to keep her; instead he volunteered to see her home. "Oh, that's not necessary," said Liusu. "Aren't you going to Singapore?"

"I've already put it off this long, delaying a little longer won't matter. I've got things to do in Shanghai too."

Liusu knew that he was still playing the same hand, afraid that others wouldn't talk about them enough. The more that people had to talk about, the less she'd be able to defend herself, and Shanghai would become a very uncomfortable place for her. But Liusu reasoned that even if he didn't go back with her, she wouldn't be able to keep things from her family. Having braved damnation thus far, she might as well let him see her home.

When Mrs. Xu saw that the pair that had seemed to be

getting along so well suddenly wanted to break things off, she was surprised, to say the least. She asked each of them, and they both made excuses for the other, but of course Mrs. Xu didn't believe a word they said.

On the ship, they had many chances to be together, but if Liuyuan could resist the moon in Repulse Bay, he could resist the moon on shipboard. He didn't say a single concrete thing to her. He seemed nonchalant, but Liusu could tell that it was the nonchalance of a man who is pleased with himself—he was sure she couldn't escape him now, sure that he had her in the palm of his hand.

When they got to Shanghai, he took her to her house in a taxi, without getting out himself. The Bai household had heard the news long before, and were entirely aware that Young Sixth Lady and Fan Liuyuan had cohabited in Hong Kong. Going off with a man for a whole month, then waltzing back as if nothing were the matter—clearly she meant to disgrace the entire family.

Liusu had taken up with Fan Liuyuan—for his money, of course. If she'd landed the money, she wouldn't have crept back so very quietly; it was clear that she hadn't gotten anything from him. Basically, a woman who was tricked by a man deserved to die, while a woman who tricked a man was a whore. If a woman tried to trick a man but failed and then was tricked by him, that was whoredom twice over. Kill her and you'd only dirty the knife.

Ordinarily, when anyone in the Bai family made a mistake the size of a sesame seed it got blown all out of proportion. Now that they had uncovered an enormous, truly sensational crime, they stammered with overexcitement, unable for a moment to get a word out. Their first move, since they agreed that "dirty laundry shouldn't be aired in public," was to go around to all their friends and relatives and make them swear to keep their mouths shut. Then they went back around to the same friends and relatives, and sounded them out, one by one. Did they know? If so, how much? In the end they decided it couldn't be kept quiet, so they announced it cheerfully and openly, slapping their thighs, moaning and sighing about the whole thing. Orchestrating all this took up the entire autumn, and left them no time to do anything definite about Liusu herself.

Liusu knew very well that returning like this would make things even worse than they'd been before. The ties of affection and loyalty between her and this family had been severed long ago. Of course she considered looking for a job, anything to earn a bowl of rice. No matter how rough it was, it would still be better than living with a hostile family. But if she took some menial job, she would lose her social status. Even though status wasn't something you could eat, losing it would be a pity. And she had not yet given up all hope concerning Fan Liuyuan. She couldn't sell herself cheaply now, or else he'd have a perfect excuse for refusing to marry her. So she just had to hang on a little while longer.

Finally, at the end of November, Fan Liuyuan sent a telegram from Hong Kong. Everyone in the family had eyeballed the telegram before Old Mrs. Bai called Liusu, and put it in her hand. The message was terse: "PLS COME HK. PASSAGE BOOKED VIA THOMAS COOK." Old Mrs. Bai gave a long sigh. "Since he's sent for you, you should go!"

Was she worth so little? Tears dropped from her eyes. Crying made her lose all her self-control; she found she could not bear it anymore. Already she'd aged two years in one autumn—she couldn't afford to grow old! So for the second time she left home and went to Hong Kong. This time, she felt none of her earlier eagerness for adventure. She had lost. Of course, everyone likes to be vanquished, but only within bounds. To have been vanquished solely by Fan Liuyuan's charms, that was one thing. But mixed with that was the pressure from her family—the most painful factor in her defeat.

Fan Liuyuan was waiting for her at the dock in a light, drizzling rain. He said that her green rain slicker looked like a bottle. "A medicine bottle," he explained. She thought he was teasing her because she'd grown so frail, but then he whispered into her ear, "You're just the medicine I need." She blushed, averting her eyes.

He had reserved her old room for her. By the time they got to the hotel, it was already two in the morning. In the bathroom, getting ready for bed, she turned off the light. Then she remembered that the bedroom light switch was by the bed. Blundering around in the dark, she stepped on a shoe and almost fell. She cursed herself for being so careless, leaving her shoes lying around. There was a laugh from the bed: "Don't be frightened! It's my shoe!"

Liusu stopped. "What are you doing here?"

"I always wanted to see the moon from your window. You can see it much better from this room than from the room next door."

So he had phoned her that night—it wasn't a dream! He did love her. What a cruel and spiteful man! He loved her, and still he treated her like this! Her heart went cold. Turning away, she walked over to the dressing table. The late-November crescent moon was a mere hook of white; its pale light made the window look like a pane of ice. But moonbeams reached the sea and were reflected from the water through the window and then into the mirror, so that even though the beams were faint, they made the mirror glow. Liusu slowly stripped off her hairnet, mussing her hair; the hairpins came loose and fell clattering to the floor. She pulled the hairnet on again, holding the ties in her mouth between tightly pinched lips. She frowned, crouched down, and, one by one, picked up the hairpins.

By then, Liuyuan had walked over behind her in his bare feet. He put one hand on her head, turned her face toward his, and kissed her mouth. The hairnet slipped off her head. This was the first time he had kissed her, but it didn't feel like the first time to either of them—they had both imagined it so many times. They'd had many opportunities—the right place, the right moment—he'd thought of it; she had worried it might happen. But they were both such clever people, always planning carefully, that they'd never dared to risk it. Suddenly it was reality, and they were both dazed. Liusu's head was spinning. She fell back against the mirror, her back tightly pressed to its icy surface. His mouth did not leave hers. He pushed her into the mirror and they seemed to fall into it, into another shadowy world—freezing cold, searing hot, flame of the forest flowers burning them all over.

The next day, he told her he was going to England in a week. She asked him to take her with him, but he said it wasn't possible. He offered to rent a house for her in Hong Kong so she could wait for his return, which would be in about a year. If she'd rather live with her family in Shanghai, that would be fine too.

Of course she wasn't willing to go back to Shanghai. The more distance she could put between those people and herself, the better. Living on her own in Hong Kong would be lonely, but she could bear that. The problem was whether anything would change after he'd returned—and that depended entirely on him. How could a week's love hold his heart? But, on the other hand, maybe it was to her advantage: Liuyuan was not a man of stable affections, and meeting and parting so quickly as this meant he had no time to grow tired of her. One short week...always more memorable than a year. Then again, even if he did come back with a heart full of warm memories, wanting her again, she might have changed by then! A woman near thirty can be unusually attractive, but she can also grow haggard in a moment. In the end, trying to hold on to a man without the surety of marriage is a difficult, painful, tiring business, well nigh impossible. But what did it matter, anyway? She had to admit that Liuyuan was delightful, and he really made the sparks fly, but what she wanted from him was, after all, financial security. And on that point, she knew she could rest assured.

They took a house on Babington Road, up on a mountain slope. When the rooms had been painted, they hired a Cantonese maid called Ah Li. They only managed to set up the basic furnishings before Liuyuan had to leave. Liusu could take her time with the rest. There wasn't any food in the house, so on the winter evening when she saw him off at the pier, they grabbed some sandwiches in the ship's dining hall. Feeling dejected, Liusu had a few drinks and stood in the roar of the sea wind; by the time she got home, she was rather drunk.

When she came in, Ah Li was in the kitchen heating water so she could wash her child's feet. Liusu went through the whole house, turning on all the lights. The green paint on the sitting room door and window was still wet. She touched it with her index finger, then pressed her sticky finger against the wall, leaving a green mark each time. Why not? Was it against the law? This was her house! Laughing, she put a fresh green handprint on the dandelion white of the plaster wall.

She sashayed into the next room. Empty rooms, one after another—pure empty space. She felt that she could fly up to the ceiling. Walking around on those big empty floors was like being on the smooth, dust-free ceiling. The room was too empty, she had to fill it with light. But the light was too dim. She'd have to remember to put in brighter bulbs tomorrow.

She went up the stairs. Emptiness was good—she needed absolute peace and quiet. She was worn out. Trying to please Liuyuan was hard work. He was an odd person to begin with, and because he really was attached to her, he was especially odd with her—always unhappy about something. It was just as well that he was gone; finally she could relax. She didn't want anyone now—hateful people, lovable people—she didn't want any of them. From her earliest youth, she'd lived in an overcrowded world. Pushing, squeezing, trampling, hugging, hauling, old people, young people, people everywhere. Twentysome people in a family, all in one house; you sat in a room clipping a fingernail—someone was watching you from the window. Now at last she had flown far away, to this unpeopled place. If she were Mrs. Fan officially, she would have all sorts of responsibilities, there'd be no getting rid of people. But now she was just Fan Liuyuan's mistress, kept in the background. She should avoid people and people should avoid her.

Peace and quiet is well and good. But, apart from people, she had no interests in life. All of her learning, such as it was, came from her aptitude for performing in the human sphere: she knew how to be a grave, good daughter-in-law, a fussy, caring mother. But now she was a warrior without a battlefield. How was she supposed to "mind the house" when there was nothing to mind? Raise children? Liuyuan didn't want children. Economize and save for the future? There wasn't the slightest need for her to worry about money. So how would she while away all this time? Play mah-jongg with Mrs. Xu, watch operas? Start flirting with actors, smoke opium, go the route of the concubine? She pulled herself up short and straightened her shoulders, clenching her clasped hands behind her back. It was not going to come to that! She was not that kind of person, she could control herself. But... could she keep from going mad? Six rooms, three up and three down, all ablaze with light. The newly waxed floors as bright as snow. And no sign of anyone. One room after another, echoing emptiness. Liusu lay on the bed. She wanted to turn off all the lights, but she couldn't move an inch. Finally she heard Ah Li coming up the stairs in her wooden clogs, clomping back and forth as she turned the lights off—and then at last her mind slowly relaxed.

———

That was on December 7, 1941. On December 8, the bombing started. In between the explosions, the silvery winter mist slowly cleared, and on the peaks and in the valleys, all the people on the island looked toward the sea and said, "The war has started, the war has started." No one could believe it, but the war had started. Liusu was alone on Babington Road, unaware of what was happening. By the time Ah Li had gone around to all the neighbors to get the news, then roused her from sleep, in a complete panic, the fighting had begun in earnest. There was a scientific research station near Babington Road, with an anti-aircraft gun, and stray bullets kept whizzing down with a sharp whistling sound, before dropping to the earth with a "crump." The whistling noise split the air, shredded the nerves. The light blue sky was ripped into strips that drifted on the winter wind. Countless shreds of nerves also floated by.

Liusu's rooms were empty, her heart was empty, and there wasn't any food in the house, so her belly was empty too. Emptiness sharpened everything, and the pangs of fear hit her especially hard. She tried to phone the Xus in Happy Valley but couldn't get through—everyone who had a phone was calling around to ask where the safest refuges might be. Finally, in the afternoon, Liusu got through, but the phone just rang and rang, no answer; Mr. and Mrs. Xu must have fled to a safer place already. Liusu didn't know what to do, and the shell fire intensified. Then the bombers targeted the antiaircraft gun near her house. They circled overhead, droning like flies, like a dentist's drill boring painfully into the soul. Ah Li sat on the sitting-room threshold hugging her crying child. She seemed dazed, rocking from side to side, singing as though in a dream, patting and soothing her child. Again the whistling sound—a "crump" broke off a corner of the roof, spilling rubble down. Ah Li screamed, jumped up, and rushed toward the door, still carrying her child. Liusu ran after and caught her at the front door. "Where are you going?" she asked, grabbing the woman tightly.

"We can't stay here! I'm taking her to the sewers to hide!"

"You're crazy!" said Liusu. "You'll be killed out there!"

"Let me go! This child...she's my only one...can't let her die...we'll go hide in the sewers..."

Liusu held her back with all her might, but Ah Li pushed, and Liusu fell. Then Ah Li rushed to the door. Just as she reached it, there was an earth-shattering boom, and the whole world went black, as if a giant lid had slammed down on some stupendously huge trunk. Untold, immeasurable fear and fury—all shut inside.

Liusu thought her life was over, but, strangely enough, she was still alive. She blinked: the floor was covered with glass shards and sunlight. She struggled to her feet, and went to look for Ah Li. Ah Li was still clutching her child, her head drooping, her forehead propped against the porch wall. She'd been knocked silly. Liusu pulled her back inside, and they heard the cries of people outside. They were saying that a bomb had fallen next door, blowing a huge crater in the garden. But even after that great boom and the closing of the lid, still they had no peace. The crumping sounds continued, as if someone were hammering nails into the lid of the trunk, hammering on and on; hammering from day to dark, then dark to day again.

Liusu thought of Liuyuan, wondering if his ship had left the harbor, if it had been sunk. But he seemed vague to her, like someone in another world. Her present and her past were disconnected, like a song on the radio that had played halfway through and then was cut short by static. Maybe the song would continue, after the crackling stopped. But if the end of the song had been blasted off, then it would be over, nothing left to hear.

The next day, Liusu, Ah Li, and Ah Li's child shared the last biscuits from a tin. Liusu was weak and exhausted, each crack of a screaming bomb slapping her hard in the face. The lumbering sound of an army truck came from the street. It stopped at their door. The doorbell rang, and Liusu answered it. It was Liuyuan. She grabbed his hand and clutched his arm, like Ah Li clutching her child; then she fell forward, hitting her head on the porch wall.

Liuyuan lifted her face with his other hand. "Frightened? Don't worry," he urged her. "Go get your things together. We're going to Repulse Bay. Hurry!"

Liusu ran back in and started rushing around. "Is it safe in Repulse Bay?"

"They say a navy can't land there. Anyway, the hotel has huge stocks of food. There'll be something to eat."

"Your ship..."

"The ship never left. They took the first-class passengers to the Repulse Bay Hotel. I tried to come yesterday, but I couldn't get a car, and the buses were jammed. Today, I finally managed to get this truck."

Liusu couldn't think clearly enough to pack her things, so she just grabbed a little bag and stuffed it full. Liuyuan gave Ah Li two months' salary and told her to watch the house. Then the two of them got into the truck, lying facedown and side by side in the truck bed, with a canopy of khaki oilcloth overhead. The ride was so bumpy that their knees and elbows were scraped raw.

Liuyuan sighed. "This bombing blasted off the ends of an awful lot of stories!"

Liusu was filled with sorrow. Then, after a moment, she said, "If you were killed, my story would be over. But if I were killed, you'd still have a lot of story left!"

"Were you planning on being my faithful widow?"

They were both a little unnerved, and for no reason at all they began to laugh. Once they started they could not stop. But when they were finished laughing, they shuddered from head to toe.

The truck drove through a rain of bullets back to Repulse

Bay. Army troops were stationed on the ground floor, so they stayed in their old room on the second floor. After they had settled in, they found out that the stores of food were all reserved for the troops. Besides canned milk, beef, mutton, and fruit, there were sacks and sacks of bread, both whole wheat and white. But the guests were only allotted two soda crackers, or two lumps of sugar, per meal. Everyone was famished.

For a couple of days all was quiet at Repulse Bay, then suddenly the action heated up. There was nowhere on the second floor to take cover, so they had to leave. Everyone went downstairs to the dining hall. The glass doors were opened wide, with sandbags piled up in front: the British troops were firing artillery from behind the sandbags. When the gunboats in the bay figured out where the shooting was coming from, they returned fire. Shells flew over the palm tree and the fountain in both directions. Liuyuan and Liusu, along with everyone else, squeezed back against the wall.

It was a dark scene, like an ancient Persian carpet covered with woven figures of many people—old lords, princesses, scholars, beauties. Draped over a bamboo pole, the carpet was being beaten, dust flying in the wind. Blow after blow, it was beaten till the people had nowhere to hide, nowhere to go. The shells flew this way, and the people ran over there; the shells flew that way, and the people all ran back. In the end, the whole hall was riddled with holes. One wall had collapsed, and they had nowhere to hide. They sat on the ground, awaiting their fate.

By this time, Liusu wished that Liuyuan wasn't there: when one person seems to have two bodies, danger is only doubled. If she wasn't hit, he still might be, and if he died, or was badly wounded, it would be worse than anything she could imagine. If she got wounded, she'd have to die, so as not to be a burden to him. Even if she did die, it wouldn't be as clean and simple as dying alone. She knew Liuyuan felt the same way. Now all she had was him; all he had was her.

The fighting ended. The men and women who'd been trapped in the Repulse Bay Hotel slowly walked toward the city. They walked past yellow cliffs, then red cliffs, more red cliffs, then yellow cliffs again, almost wondering if they'd gotten lost, and were going in circles. But no, here was a pit they hadn't seen before, blasted out of the road and full of rubble.

Liuyuan and Liusu spoke very little. It used to be that whenever they took a short trip in a car there was a dinner-party's worth of conversation, but now, walking together for miles, they had nothing to say. Once in a while, one of them would start a sentence, but since the other knew exactly what would come next, there was no need to finish it.

"Look, on the beach," said Liuyuan.

"Yes."

The beach was covered with tangled coils of barbed wire. Past the barbed wire, the white seawater gurgled, drinking in and spitting out the yellow sand. The clear winter sky was a faint blue. The flame of the forest was past its flowering season.

"That wall..." asked Liusu.

"Haven't gone to check."

Liusu sighed. "Doesn't matter."

Liuyuan was hot from walking, he took off his coat and slung it over his shoulder, but his back was still covered with perspiration.

"You're too warm," Liusu said. "Let me take it."

Before, Liuyuan would never have agreed, but now he wasn't so chivalrous; he handed his coat to her.

As they walked farther, the mountains got taller. Either it was the wind blowing in the trees, or it was the moving shadow of a cloud, but somehow the greenish yellow lower slopes slowly darkened. Looking more closely, you saw that it wasn't the wind and it wasn't the clouds but the sun moving slowly over the mountain crest, blanketing the lower slope in a giant blue shadow. Up on the mountain, smoke rose from burning houses—white on the shaded slopes, black on the sunlit slopes—while the sun kept on moving slowly over the mountain crest.

They were home. They pushed open the half-shut door, and a little flock of pigeons took wing and fled. The hallway was full of dirt and pigeon droppings. Liusu went to the staircase and cried out in surprise. The brand-new trunks she had put in the rooms upstairs were strewn about wide open, and two of them had slid partway down to the ground floor, so that the stairs were buried in a flowing mass of satins and silks. Liusu bent down and picked up a brown wool-lined cheongsam. It wasn't hers. Sweat marks, dirt, cigarette burns, the scent of cheap perfume. She found more women's things, old magazines, and an open can of lychees, the juice dripping out onto her clothes. Had some troops been staying here? British troops who had women with them? They seemed to have left in a hurry. The local poor who'd turned to looting hadn't been here; otherwise, these things would be gone. Liuyuan helped her call for Ah Li. A last gray-backed pigeon scurried past, whirred through the sunlit doorway, and flew off.

Ah Li was gone, who knew where. But even with the servant gone from the house, the masters must go on living. They couldn't worry about the house yet; first they had to think about food. Scrambling around, they finally turned up a bag of rice, which they bought at a very high price. Fortunately the gas lines had not been cut, but there wasn't any running water. Liuyuan took a lead-lined bucket up the mountain to fetch some springwater for cooking. In the days that followed, they spent all their time preparing meals and cleaning house. Liuyuan did all kinds of chores—sweeping, mopping, and helping Liusu wring out the heavy laundered sheets. Even though she'd never cooked before, Liusu managed to give the food some real Shanghainese flavor. Liuyuan was fond of Malayan food, so she also learned how to make satay and curried fish. Food became a major source of interest, but they had to be very careful about expenses. Liuyuan didn't have a lot of Hong Kong dollars with him; they'd have to go back to Shanghai as soon as they could get a boat.

Anyway, staying on in Hong Kong after the disaster was not a feasible long-term plan. They had to scramble around all through the day just to get by. Then, at night, in that dead city, no lights, no human sounds, only the strong winter wind, wailing on and on in three long tones—oooh, aaah, eeei. When it stopped here, it started up there, like three gray dragons flying side by side in a straight line, long bodies trailing on and on, tails never coming into sight. Oooh, aaah, eeei—wailing until even the sky dragons had gone, and there was only a stream of empty air, a bridge of emptiness that crossed into the dark, into the void of voids. Here, everything had ended. There were only some broken bits of leveled wall and, stumbling and fumbling about, a civilized man who had lost his memory; he seemed to be searching for something, but there was nothing left.

Liusu sat up hugging her quilt and listening to the mournful wind. She was sure that the gray brick wall near Repulse Bay was still as strong and tall as ever. The wind stopped there, like three gray dragons coiling up on top of the wall, the moonlight glinting off their silver scales. She seemed to be going back in a dream, back to the base of that wall, and there she met Liuyuan, finally and truly met him.

Here in this uncertain world, money, property, the permanent things—they're all unreliable. The only thing she could rely on was the breath in her lungs, and this person who lay sleeping beside her. Suddenly, she crawled over to him, hugging him through his quilt. He reached out from the bedding and grasped her hand. They looked and saw each other, saw each other entirely. It was a mere moment of deep understanding, but it was enough to keep them happy together for a decade or so.

He was just a selfish man; she was a selfish woman. In this age of chaos and disorder, there is no place for those who stand on their own, but for an ordinary married couple, room can always be found.

One day, when they were out shopping for food, they ran into Princess Saheiyini. Her complexion was sallow; her loosened braids had been piled up in a fluffy topknot. She was dressed in a long black cotton gown she had picked up god knows where, though on her feet she still wore a pair of fancy Indian slippers, colorfully embroidered and bejeweled. She shook their hands warmly, asked where they were living, and wanted very much to come and see their new house. Noticing the shelled oysters in Liusu's basket, she wanted to learn how to make steamed oyster soup. So Liuyuan invited her for a simple meal, and she was very happy to go home with them. Her Englishman had been interned, and she was living now with an Indian policeman's family, people she knew well, people who had often done little things for her. She hadn't eaten a full meal in a long time. She called Liusu "Miss Bai."

"This is my wife," said Liuyuan. "You should congratulate us!"

"Really? When did you get married?"

Liuyuan shrugged and said, "We just put a notice in the Chinese newspaper. You know, wartime weddings are always a bit slapdash."

Liusu didn't understand their English. Saheiyini kissed him, then kissed her. The meal was skimpy, and Liuyuan made sure Saheiyini understood that oyster soup was a treat. Saheiyini did not come back to their house.

After they had seen their guest off, Liusu stood on the threshold and Liuyuan stood behind her. He closed her hands in his and said, "Well, when should we get married?"

Liusu didn't say a thing. She bowed her head and let the tears fall.

"Now, now..." Liuyuan said, gripping her hands tightly. "We can go and put a notice in the paper today—unless of course you'd rather wait, and throw a big bash when we get back to Shanghai, invite all the relatives—"

"Those people! Who'd want them?" Saying that she laughed, leaned back, and let herself go, falling against him. Liuyuan ran his finger down her face. "First you cry, and then you laugh!" he said.

They walked into town together. Where the road took a sharp turn, the land suddenly fell away—in front of them was only empty space, a damp, pale gray sky. From a little iron gate frame hung an enameled sign with the words DR. ZHAO XIANGQING, DENTIST. The sign creaked on its chains in the wind. Behind it there was only that empty sky.

Liuyuan stopped in his tracks to stare. Feeling the terror in this ordinary scene, he shivered. "Now you must believe 'Facing life, death, distance...' How can we decide these things? When the bombing was going on, just one little slip..."

Liusu chided him: "Are you still saying you're unable to make this decision?"

"No, no, I'm not giving up halfway! What I mean is..." He saw her face, then laughed. "Okay, I won't try to say it!"

They went on walking, and Liuyuan said, "The gods must be behind this; we really did find out what love is!"

"You said a long time ago that you loved me."

"That doesn't count. We were way too busy falling in love— how could we have found time to really love each other?"

When the marriage announcement was posted in the paper, Mr. and Mrs. Xu rushed over to offer their congratulations. Liusu wasn't altogether pleased with them, since they had moved off to a safe place when the city was besieged, not worrying a bit whether she lived or died. Still she had to greet them with a smile. Liuyuan brought out some wine and a few dishes for a belated celebration. Not much later, travel between Hong

Kong and Shanghai became possible again, and they returned to Shanghai.

Liusu went back to the Bai household just once, afraid that with so many blabbermouths, something was sure to go wrong. And trouble could not be avoided: Fourth Mistress had decided to divorce Fourth Master, and everyone blamed Liusu for this. Liusu had divorced and married again with such astonishing success—no wonder other people wanted to follow her example. Liusu crouched down in the lamplight, lighting mosquito-repellant incense. When she thought of Fourth Mistress, she smiled.

Liuyuan even stopped teasing her, saving all his daring talk for other women. That was a good sign, worth celebrating, since it meant that she was his own—his wife in name and in truth. Still, it made her a little sad.

Hong Kong's defeat had brought Liusu victory. But in this unreasonable world, who can distinguish cause from effect? Who knows which is which? Did a great city fall so that she could be vindicated? Countless thousands of people dead, countless thousands of people suffering, after that an earth-shaking revolution . . . Liusu didn't feel there was anything subtle about her place in history. She stood up, smiling, and kicked the pan of mosquito-repellant incense under the table.

Those legendary beauties who felled cities and kingdoms were probably all like that.

Legends exist everywhere, but they don't necessarily have such happy endings.

When the *huqin* wails on a night of ten thousand lamps, the bow slides back and forth, drawing forth a tale too desolate for words—oh! why go into it?

THE GOLDEN CANGUE

Translated by Eileen Chang

SHANGHAI thirty years ago on a moonlit night...maybe we did not get to see the moon of thirty years ago. To young people the moon of thirty years ago should be a reddish-yellow wet stain the size of a copper coin, like a teardrop on letter paper by To-yün Hsüan,[1] worn and blurred. In old people's memory the moon of thirty years ago was gay, larger, rounder, and whiter than the moon now. But looked back on after thirty years on a rough road, the best of moons is apt to be tinged with sadness.

The moonlight reached the side of Feng-hsiao's pillow. She was a slave girl brought by the bride, the new Third Mistress of the Chiangs. She opened her eyes to take a look and saw her own blue-white hand on the half-worn blanket faced with quilted Korean silk. "Is it moonlight?" she said to herself. She slept on a pallet on the floor under the window. The last couple of years had been busy with the changing of dynasties. The Chiangs coming to Shanghai as refugees did not have room, so the servants' quarters were criss-crossed with people sleeping.

Feng-hsiao seemed to hear a rustle behind the big bed and guessed that somebody had got up to use the chamber pot. She turned over and, just as she thought, the cloth curtain was thrust aside and a black shadow emerged, shuffling in slippers

1. To-yün Hsüan (Solitary Cloud Studio) was famous for its fine red-striped letter paper, popular down to the thirties.

trodden down in the back. It was probably Little Shuang, the personal maid of Second Mistress, and so she called out softly, "Little Sister Shuang."

Little Shuang came, smiling, and gave a kick to the pallet. "I woke you." She put both hands under her old lined jacket of dark violet silk, worn over bright oil-green trousers. Feng-hsiao put out a hand to feel the trouser leg and said, smiling:[2]

"Colorful clothes are not worn so much now. With the people down river,[3] the fashions are all for no color."

Little Shuang said, smiling, "You don't know, in this house we can't keep up with other people. Our Old Mistress is strict, even the young mistresses can't have their own way, not to say us slave girls. We wear what's given us—all dressed like peasants." She squatted down to sit on the pallet and picked up a little jacket at Feng-hsiao's feet. "Was this newly made for your lady's wedding?"

Feng-hsiao shook her head. "Of my wardrobe for the season, only the few pieces on view are new. The rest is just made up of discards."

"This wedding happened to run into the revolution, really hard on your lady."

Feng-hsiao sighed. "Don't go into that now. In times like this, one should economize, but there was still a limit! That wedding really lacked style. That one of ours didn't say anything, but how could she not be angry?"

"I shouldn't wonder Third Mistress is still unhappy about it. On your side the trousseau was passable, the wedding preparations we made were really too dismal. Even that year we took our Second Mistress it was better than this."

2. Editor's note: The repetition of the phrase "said, smiling" (*hsiao tao*) may seem tiresome to the reader. However, this and similar phrases are routinely prefixed to reported speeches in traditional Chinese fiction, and Eileen Chang, a dedicated student of that fiction, has deliberately revived their use in her early stories. It is to be regretted that their English equivalents cannot be equally unobtrusive.

3. On the lower Yangtze.

Feng-hsiao was taken aback. "How? Your Second Mistress..."

Little Shuang took off her shoes and stepped barefoot across Feng-hsiao to the window. "Get up and look at the moon," she said.

Feng-hsiao scrambled quickly to her feet. "I was going to ask all along, your Second Mistress..."

Little Shuang bent down to pick up the little jacket and put it over her shoulders. "Be careful you don't catch cold."

Feng-hsiao said, smiling, as she buttoned it up, "No, you've got to tell me."

"My fault, I shouldn't have let it out," Little Shuang said, smiling.

"We are like sisters now. Why treat me like an outsider?"

"If I tell you, don't you tell your lady though. Our Second Mistress's family owns a sesame oil shop."

"Oh!" Feng-hsiao was surprised. "A sesame oil shop! How on earth could they stoop so low! Now your Eldest Mistress is from a titled family; ours can't compare with Eldest Mistress, but she also came from a respectable family."

"Of course there was a reason. You've seen our Second Master, he's crippled. What mandarin family would give him a daughter for wife? Old Mistress didn't know what to do, First was going to get him a concubine, and the matchmaker found this one of the Ts'ao family, called Ch'i-ch'iao[4] because she was born in the seventh month."

"Oh, a concubine," said Feng-hsiao.

"Was to be a concubine. Then Old Mistress thought, since Second Master was not going to take a wife, it wouldn't do either for the second branch to be without its proper mistress. Just as well to have her for a wife so she would faithfully look after Second Master."

4. The old phrase *ch'i-ch'iao*, clever seven, refers to the skill of the Weaving Maid, a star that is reunited with the Cowherd, another star, across the Milky Way every year on the seventh of the seventh moon.

Feng-hsiao leaned her hands on the window sill, musing. "No wonder. Although I'm new here, I've guessed some of it too."

"Dragons breed dragons, phoenixes breed phoenixes—as the saying goes. You haven't heard her conversation! Even in front of the unmarried young ladies she says anything she likes. Lucky that in our house not a word goes out from inside, nor comes in from outside, so the young ladies don't understand a thing. Even then they get so embarrassed they don't know where to hide."

Feng-hsiao tittered. "Really? Where could she have picked up this vulgar language? Even us slave girls—"

Little Shuang said, holding her own elbows, "Why, she was the big attraction at the sesame oil shop, standing at the counter, and dealing with all kinds of customers. What have we got to compare with her?"

"Did you come with her when she was married?"

Little Shuang sneered. "How could she afford me! I used to wait on Old Mistress, but Second Master took medicine all day and had to be helped around all the time, and since they were short of hands, I was sent over there. Why, are you cold?" Feng-hsiao shook her head. "Look at you, the way you pulled in your neck, so cuddlesome!" She had hardly finished speaking when Feng-hsiao sneezed. Right away Little Shuang gave her a push. "Go to bed, go to bed. Warm yourself."

Feng-hsiao knelt down to take her jacket off. "It's not winter, you don't catch cold just like that."

"The window may be closed but the wind squeaks in through the crevices."

They both lay down. Feng-hsiao asked in a whisper, "Been married for four, five years now?"

"Who?"

"Who else?"

"Oh, she. That's right, it's been five years."

"Had children too, and gave people nothing to talk about?"

"As to that—! Plenty to talk about. The year before last

Old Mistress took everybody in the house on a pilgrimage to Mount P'u-t'o. She didn't go because it was just after her lying-in, so she was left at home to look after the house. Master-in-law[5] called a bit too often and a batch of things was lost."

Feng-hsiao was startled. "And they never got to the bottom of it?"

"What would have come of that? It would have been embarrassing for everybody. Anyway, the jewelry would have gone to Eldest Master, Second Master, and Third Master one day. Eldest Master and Eldest Mistress couldn't very well say anything on account of Second Master. Third Master was in no position to, he himself was spending money like water and had borrowed a lot from the family accounts."

The two of them talked across ten feet. Despite their effort to lower their voices, a louder sentence or two woke up old Mrs. Chao on the big bed. She called out, "Little Shuang." Little Shuang did not dare answer. Old Mrs. Chao said, "Little Shuang, if you talk more nonsense and let people hear you, be careful you don't get skinned tomorrow!" Little Shuang kept still. "Don't think you're still in the deep halls and big courtyards we lived in before, where you had room to talk crazy and act silly. Here it's cheek by jowl, nothing can be kept from other people. Better stop talking if you want to avoid a beating."

Immediately the room became silent. Old Mrs. Chao, who had inflamed eyes, had stuffed her pillow with chrysanthemum leaves, said to make eyes clear and cool. She now raised her head to press down the silver hairpin tucked across her bun and the chrysanthemum leaves rustled with the slight stir. She turned over, her whole frame pulled into motion, all her bones squeaking. She sighed, "You people—! What do you know?" Little Shuang and Feng-hsiao still dared not reply. For a long time nobody spoke, and one by one they drifted off to sleep.

5. *Chiu-yeh*, lit., Master Brother-in-law, in this case Ch'i-ch'iao's elder brother.

It was almost dawn. The flat waning moon got lower, lower and larger, and by the time it sank, it was like a red gold basin. The sky was a cold bleak crab-shell blue. The houses were only a couple of stories high, pitch-dark under the sky, so it was possible to see far. At the horizon the morning colors were a layer of green, a layer of yellow, and a layer of red like a watermelon cut open—the sun was coming up. Gradually wheelbarrows and big pushcarts began rattling along the road, and horse carriages passed, hoofs tapping. The beancurd soup vender with the flat pole on his shoulder hawked his wares slowly, swingingly. Only the long-drawn last syllable carried, "Haw...O! Haw...O!" Farther off, it became "Aw...O! Aw...O!"

In the house the slave girls and amahs had also got up, in a flurry to open the room doors, fetch hot water, fold up bedding, hook up the bed-curtains, and do the hair. Feng-hsiao helped Third Mistress Lan-hsien get dressed. Lan-hsien leaned close to the mirror for a careful look, pulled out from under her armpit a pale green blossom-flecked handkerchief, rubbed some powder off the wings of her nose, and said with her back to Third Master on the bed. "I'd better go first to pay my respects to Old Mistress. I'd be late if I waited for you."

As she was speaking, Eldest Mistress Tai-chen came and stood on the doorstep, saying with a smile, "Third Sister, let's go together."

Lan-hsien hurried up to her. "I was just getting worried I'd be late—so Eldest Sister-in-law hasn't gone up yet. What about Second Sister-in-law?"

"She'll still be a while."

"Getting Second Brother his medicine?"

Tai-chen looked around to make sure there was no one about before she said, smiling, "It's not so much taking medicine as—" She put her thumb to her lips, made a fist with the three middle fingers, sticking out the little finger, and shushed softly a couple of times.

Lan-hsien said, surprised, "They both smoke this?"

Tai-chen nodded. "With your Second Brother it's out in the open, with her it's kept from Old Mistress, which makes things difficult for us, caught in between—have to cover up for her. Actually Old Mistress knows very well. Purposely pretends she doesn't, orders her around and tortures her in little ways, just so that she can't smoke her fill. Actually, to think of it, a woman and so young, what great worries could she have, to need to smoke this to take her mind off things?"

Tai-chen and Lan-hsien went upstairs hand in hand, each followed by the slave girl closest to her, to the small anteroom next door to Old Mistress's bedroom. The slave girl Liu-hsi came out to them whispering, "Not awake yet."

Tai-chen glanced up at the grandfather clock and said, smiling, "Old Mistress is also late today."

"Said she didn't sleep well the last couple of days, too much noise on the street," Liu-hsi said. "Probably used to it now, making up for it today."

Beside the little round pedestal table of purple elm covered with a strip of scarlet felt sat Yün-tse, the second daughter of the house, cracking walnuts with a little nutcracker. She put it down and got up to greet them. Tai-chen laid a hand on her shoulder. "Sister Yün, you are really filial. Old Mistress happened to be in the mood yesterday to want some sugared walnuts made, and you remembered."

Lan-hsien and Tai-chen sat down around the table and helped to peel the walnut skin. Yün-tse's hands got tired and Lan-hsien took the nutcracker that she put down.

"Be careful of those nails of yours, as slender as scallions. It would be a pity to break them when you've grown them so long," said Tai-chen.

"Have somebody go and get your gold nail sheath," Yün-tse said.

"So much bother, we might as well have them shelled in the kitchen," said Lan-hsien.

As they were talking and laughing in undertones, Liu-hsi raised the curtain with a stick, announcing, "Second Mistress is here."

Lan-hsien and Yün-tse rose to ask her to sit down but Ts'ao Ch'i-ch'iao would not be seated as yet. With one hand on the doorway and the other on her waist, she first looked around. On her thin face were a vermilion mouth, triangular eyes, and eyebrows curved like little hills. She wore a pale pink blouse over narrow mauve trousers with a flickering blue scroll design and greenish-white incense-stick binding.[6] A lavender silk crepe handkerchief was half tucked around the wrist in one narrow blouse sleeve. She smiled, showing her small fine teeth, and said, "Everybody's here. I suppose I'm late again today. How can I help it, doing my hair in the dark? Who gave me a window facing the back yard? I'm the only one to get a room like that. That one of ours is evidently not going to live long anyway, we're just waiting to be widow and orphans—whom to bully, if not us?"

Tai-chen blandly said nothing. Lan-hsien said, smiling, "Second Sister-in-law is used to the houses in Peking, no wonder she finds it too cramped here."

Yün-tse said, "Eldest Brother should have got a larger one when he was house-hunting, but I'm afraid this counts as a bright and airy house for Shanghai."

Lan-hsien said, "That is so. It's true it's a bit crowded, really, so many people in the house—"

Ch'i-ch'iao rolled up her sleeve and tucked the handkerchief in her green jade bracelet, glanced sideways at Lan-hsien, and said, smiling, "So Third Sister feels there're too many people. If

6. So called because the binding is rounded and narrow.

it's too crowded for us, who have been married for years, naturally it's too crowded for newlyweds like you."

Before Lan-hsien could say anything, Tai-chen blushed, saying, "Jesting is jesting, but there's a limit. Third Sister has just come here, what will she think of us?"

Ch'i-ch'iao pulled up a corner of her handkerchief to cover her mouth. "I know you're all young ladies from respectable homes. Just try and change places with me, I'm afraid you couldn't put up with it for even one night."

Tai-chen made a spitting noise. "This is too much. The more you talk, the more impertinent you get."

At this Ch'i-ch'iao went up and took Tai-chen by her sleeve. "I can swear—I can swear for the last three years. Do you dare swear? You dare swear?"

Even Tai-chen could not help a titter, and then she muttered, "How is it that you even got two children?"

Ch'i-ch'iao said, "Really, even I don't know how the children got born. The more I think about it the more I can't understand."

Tai-chen held up her right hand and waved it from side to side. "Enough talk in this vein. Granted that you take Third Sister as one of our own, and feel free to say anything you like, still Sister Yün's here. If she tells Old Mistress later, you'll get more than you want."

Yün-tse had walked off long ago, and was standing on the veranda with her hands behind her back, whistling at the canary to make it sing. The Chiangs lived in a modern foreign-style house of an early period, tall arches supported by thick pillars of red brick with a floral capital, but the upstairs veranda had a wooden floor. Behind the railings of willow wood was a row of large baskets of bamboo splits, in which dried bamboo shoots were being aired. The worn sunlight pervaded the air like gold dust, slightly choking and dizzying when rubbed in the eyes. Far away in the street a peddler shook a rattle-drum whose sleepy beat, *bu lung dung...bu lung dung*, held the memory of many children now grown old. The private rickshas tinkled as they ran past and an occasional car horn went *ba ba*.

Because Ch'i-ch'iao knew that everybody in this house looked down on her, she was especially warm to the newcomer. Leaning on the back of Lan-hsien's chair, she asked her this and that and spoke admiringly of her fingernails after giving her hand a thorough inspection. Then she added, "I grew one on my little finger last year fully half an inch longer than this, and broke it picking flowers."

Lan-hsien had already seen through Ch'i-ch'iao and understood her position at the Chiangs'. She kept smiling but hardly answered. Ch'i-ch'iao felt the slight. Ambling over to the veranda, she picked up Yün-tse's pigtail and shook it, making conversation, "*Yo!* How come your hair is so thin? Only last year you had such a head of glossy black hair—must have lost a lot?"

Yün-tse turned aside to protect her pigtail, saying with a smile, "I can't even lose a few hairs without your permission?"

Ch'i-ch'iao went on scrutinizing her and called out, "Eldest Sister-in-law, come and take a look. Sister Yün has really grown much thinner. Could it be that the young lady has something on her mind?"

With marked annoyance Yün-tse slapped Ch'i-ch'iao's hand to get it off her person. "You've really gone crazy today. As if you're not enough of a nuisance ordinarily."

Ch'i-ch'iao tucked her hands in her sleeves. "What a temper the young lady has," she said, smiling.

Tai-chen put her head out, saying, "Sister Yün, Old Mistress is up."

Each of them straightened her blouse hastily, smoothed her hair in front of her ears, lifted the curtain to go into the next room, curtsied, and waited on Old Mistress at breakfast. The old women holding trays went in through the living room; the slave girls inside took the dishes from them and they returned to wait in the outer room. It was quiet inside, scarcely anybody saying anything; the only sound was the rustle of the thin silver chain aquiver at the top of a pair of silver chopsticks.

Old Mistress believed in Buddha and made it a rule to worship for two hours after breakfast. Coming out with the others, Yün-tse managed to ask Tai-chen without being overheard, "Isn't Second Sister-in-law in a hurry to go for her smoke? Why is she still hanging around inside?"

Tai-chen said, "I suppose she has a few words to say in private."

Yün-tse could not help laughing. "As if Old Mistress would listen to anything she had to say!"

Tai-chen laughed cynically. "That you can't tell. Old people are always changing their minds. When it's dinned into your ears all day long, it's just possible you'll believe one sentence out of ten."

As Lan-hsien sat cracking walnuts, Tai-chen and Yün-tse went to the veranda, though not purposely to eavesdrop on the conversation in the main chamber. Old Mistress, being of advanced age, was a little deaf, so her voice was especially loud. Intentionally or not, the people on the veranda heard much of the talk. Yün-tse turned white with anger; she first held her fists tight, then flicked her hands forcibly and ran toward the other end of the veranda. After a couple of running steps she stood still and bent forward with her face in her hands, sobbing.

Tai-chen hurried up to hold her. "Sister, don't be like this! Stop it quick. It's not worth your while to heed the likes of her. Who takes her words seriously?"

Yün-tse struggled free and ran straight to her own room. Tai-chen came back to the living room and clapped her hands once. "The damage is done."

Lan-hsien hastened to ask, "What happened?"

"Your Second Sister-in-law was just telling Old Mistress, 'A grown girl won't keep,' and Old Mistress is to write to the P'engs to come for the bride quick. Look, what kind of talk is this?"

Lan-hsien, also stunned, said, "Wouldn't it be slapping one's own face, for the girl's family to say a thing like this?"

"The Chiangs will only lose face temporarily, but not Sister Yün. How are they to respect her over there when she gets married? She still has her life to live."

"Old Mistress is understanding, she's not likely to share that person's views."

"Of course Old Mistress didn't like it at first, saying a daughter of our house would never have such ideas. So *she* said, '*Yo!* you don't know the girls nowadays. How can they compare with the girls when you were a girl? Times have changed, and people also change, otherwise why is there trouble all over the world?' You know, old people like to hear this sort of thing. Old Mistress is not so sure any more."

Lan-hsien sighed, saying, "How on earth did she have the gall to make up such stories?"

Tai-chen rested both elbows on the table and stroked an eyebrow with a little finger. After a moment of reflection she snickered, "She thinks she's being specially thoughtful toward Sister Yün! Spare me her thoughtfulness."

Lan-hsien grabbed hold of her. "Listen—that can't be Sister Yün?" There seemed to be loud weeping in a back room and the rattle of brass bedposts being kicked and a hubbub of voices trying to soothe and reason to no avail.

Tai-chen stood up. "I'll go and see. This young lady may be good-tempered, but she can fight back if cornered."

Tai-chen was gone when Third Master Chiang came in yawning. A robust youth, tending toward plumpness, Chiang Chi-tse sported down his neck a big shiny three-strand pigtail loosely plaited. He had the classic domed forehead and squarish lower face, chubby bright red cheeks, glistening dark eyebrows, and moist black eyes where some impatience always showed through. Over a narrow-sleeved gown of bamboo-root green he wore a little sleeveless jacket the color of sesame-dotted, purplish-brown soy paste, buttoned across with pearls from shoulder to shoulder. He asked Lan-hsien, "Who's talking away to Old Mistress inside there?"

"Second Sister-in-law."

Chi-tse pressed his lips tight and shook his head.

"You've had enough of her, too?" Lan-hsien said, smiling.

Chi-tse said nothing, just pulled a chair over, pushed its back against the table, threw the hem of his gown up high and sat down astride the chair, his chin on the chair back, and picked up and ate one piece of walnut after another.

Lan-hsien gave him a look from the corners of her eyes. "People peeling them the whole morning, was it all for your sake?"

Just then Ch'i-ch'iao lifted the curtain and came out. The minute she saw Chi-tse she involuntarily circled over to the back of Lan-hsien's chair, put both hands around Lan-hsien's neck and bent her head down, saying with a smirk, "What a ravishing bride! Third Brother, you haven't thanked me yet. If I hadn't hurried them to get this done for you early, you might have had to wait eight or ten years for the war to be over. You'd have died of impatience."

Lan-hsien's greatest regret was that her wedding had happened in a period of national emergency and lacked pomp and style. As soon as she heard these jarring words, her narrow little face fell to its full length like a scroll. Chi-tse glanced at her and said, smiling, "Second Sister-in-law, a good heart does not get rewards, as of old. Nobody feels obliged to you."

"That's all right with me, I'm used to it," said Ch'i-ch'iao, "Ever since I stepped inside the Chiang house, just nursing your Second Brother all these years, watching over the sickbed day and night, just for that alone you'd think I've done some good and nothing wrong, but who's ever grateful to me? Who ever did me half a good turn?"

Chi-tse said, smiling, "You're full of grievances the minute you open your mouth."

With a long-drawn-out groan she kept fingering the gold triad[7] and key chain buttoned on Lan-hsien's lapel. After a long pause she suddenly said, "At least you haven't fooled around outside for a month or so. Thanks to the bride, she made you stay home. Anybody else could beg you on bent knees and you wouldn't."

"Is that so? Sister-in-law never asked me, how do you know I won't?" he said, smiling, and signaled Lan-hsien with his eyes.

Ch'i-ch'iao doubled up laughing. "Why don't you do something about him, Third Sister? The little monkey, I saw him grow up, and now he's joking at my expense!"

While talking and laughing she felt bothered; her restless hands squeezed and kneaded Lan-hsien, beating and knocking lightly with a fist as if she wished to squash her out of shape. No matter how patient Lan-hsien was, she could not help getting annoyed. With her temper rising, she applied more strength than she should using the nutcracker, and broke the two-inch fingernail clean off at the quick.

"*Yo!*" Ch'i-ch'iao cried. "Quick, get scissors and trim it. I remember there was a pair of little scissors in this room. Little Shuang!" she called out. "Liu-hsi! Come, somebody!"

Lan-hsien rose. "Never mind, Second Sister-in-law, I'll go and cut it in my room." She went.

Ch'i-ch'iao sat down in Lan-hsien's chair. Leaning her cheek on her hand and lifting her eyebrows, she gazed sideways at Chi-tse. "Is she angry with me?"

"Why should she be?" he said, smiling.

"I was just going to ask that. Could I have said anything wrong? What's wrong with keeping you at home? She'd rather have you go out?"

7. A toothpick, tweezers, and ear-spoon.

He said, smiling, "The whole family from Eldest Brother and Eldest Sister-in-law down, all want to discipline me, just for fear that I'll spend the money in the general accounts."

"By Buddha, I can't vouch for the others but I don't think like that. Even if you get into debt and mortgage houses and sell land, if I so much as frown I'm not your Second Sister-in-law. Aren't we the closest kin? I just want you to take care of your health."

He could not suppress a titter. "Why are you so worried about my health?"

Her voice trembled. "Health is the most important thing for anybody. Look at your Second Brother, the way he gets, is he still a person? Can you still treat him as one?"

Chi-tse looked serious. "Second Brother is not like me, he was born like this. It's not that he ruined his health. He's a pitiful man, it's up to Second Sister-in-law to take care of him."

Ch'i-ch'iao stood up stiffly, holding on to the table with both hands, her eyelids down and the lower half of her face quivering as if she held scalding hot melted candlewax in her mouth. She forced out two sentences in a small high voice, "Go sit next to your Second Brother. Go sit next to your Second Brother." She tried to sit beside Chi-tse and only got onto a corner of his chair and put her hand on his leg. "Have you touched his flesh? It's soft and heavy, feels like your feet when they get numb..."

Chi-tse had changed color too. Still he gave a frivolous little laugh and bent down to pinch her foot. "Let's see if they are numb."

"Heavens, you've never touched him, you don't know how good it is not to be sick... how good..." She slid down from the chair and squatted on the floor, weeping inaudibly with her face pillowed on her sleeve; the diamond on her hairpin flashed as it jerked back and forth. Against the diamond's flame shone the solid knot of pink silk thread binding a little bunch of hair at the heart of the bun. Her back convulsed as it sank lower and lower. She seemed to be not so much weeping as vomiting, churning and pumping out her bowels.

A little stunned at first, Chi-tse got up. "I'm going, if that's all right with you. If you're not afraid of being seen, I am. Have to save some face for Second Brother."

Holding onto the chair to get up, she said, sobbing, "I'll leave." She pulled out a handkerchief from her sleeve to dab at her face and suddenly smiled slightly. "You're so protective of your Second Brother."

Chi-tse laughed. "If I don't protect him, who will?" Ch'i-ch'iao said, walking toward the door, "You're a good one to talk. Don't try to act the hypocrite in front of me. Why, just in these rooms alone . . . nothing escapes my eyes—not to mention how wild you are once outside the house. You probably wouldn't even mind having your wet nurse, let alone a sister-in-law."

"I've always been easygoing about things. How am I supposed to defend myself if you pick on me?" he said, smiling.

On her way out she again leaned her back against the door, whispering, "What I don't get is in what way I'm not as good as the others. What is it about me that's no good?"

"My good sister-in-law, you're all good."

She said with a laugh, "Could it be that staying with a cripple, I smell crippled too, and it will rub off on you?" She stared straight ahead, the small, solid gold pendants of her earrings like two brass nails nailing her to the door, a butterfly specimen in a glass box, bright-colored and desolate.

Looking at her, Chi-tse also wondered. But that would not do. He loved to play around but had made up his mind long ago not to flirt with members of the family. When the mood had passed one could neither avoid them nor kick them aside, they would be a burden all the time. Besides, Ch'i-ch'iao was so outspoken and hot-tempered, how could the thing be kept secret? And she was so unpopular, who would cover up for her, high or low? Perhaps she no longer cared and would not even mind if it got known. But why should a young man like him take the risk? He spoke up: "Second Sister-in-law, young as I am, I'm not one who'd do just anything."

There seemed to be footsteps. With a flip of his gown he ducked into Old Mistress's room, grabbing a handful of shelled walnuts by the way. She had not quite come to her senses, but when she heard someone pushing the door she roused herself, managing the best she could and hiding behind the door. When she saw Tai-chen walk in, she came out and slapped her on the back.

Tai-chen forced a smile. "You're in better spirits than ever." She looked at the table. "My, so many walnuts, practically all eaten up. It couldn't be anybody but Third Brother."

Ch'i-ch'iao leaned against the table, facing the veranda and saying nothing.

"People had to shell them all morning, and he came along to enjoy himself." Tai-chen grumbled as she took a seat.

Ch'i-ch'iao scraped the red table cover with a piece of sharp walnut shell, one hard stroke after another until the felt turned hairy and was about to tear. She said between clenched teeth, "Isn't it the same with money? We're always told to save, save it so others can take it out by the handfuls to spend. That's what I can't get over."

Tai-chen glanced at her and said coldly, "That can't be helped. When there're too many people, if it doesn't go in the open it will go in the dark. Control this one and you can't control that one."

Ch'i-ch'iao felt the sting and was just about to reply in kind when Little Shuang came in furtively and walked up to her, mumbling, "Mistress, Master-in-law is here."

"Master-in-law's coming here is nothing to hide. You've got a growth in your throat or what?" Ch'i-ch'iao cursed. "You sound like a mosquito humming."

Little Shuang backed off a step and dared not speak.

Tai-chen said, "So your brother has come to Shanghai too. It seems all our relatives are here."

Ch'i-ch'iao started out of the room. "He's not to come to Shanghai? With war inland, poor people want to stay alive too." She stopped at the doorstep and asked Little Shuang, "Have you told Old Mistress?"

"Not yet," said Little Shuang.

Ch'i-ch'iao thought for a moment and went downstairs quietly because she didn't have the courage after all to go in and tell Old Mistress of her brother's arrival.

Tai-chen asked Little Shuang, "Master-in-law came alone?"

"With Mistress-in-law, carrying food in a two-decked set of round wooden boxes."

Tai-chen chuckled, "They went to all that expense."

Little Shuang said, "Eldest Mistress needn't feel sorry for them. What comes in full will go out full too. To them even remnants are good, for making slippers and waistbands, not to mention round or flat pieces of gold and silver."

"Don't be so unkind. You'd better go down," Tai-chen said, smiling. "Her family seldom comes here. Not enough service and there'd be trouble again."

Little Shuang hurried out. Ch'i-ch'iao was just cross-questioning Liu-hsi at the top of the stairs to see if Old Mistress knew. Liu-hsi replied, "Old Mistress was at her prayers, Third Master was leaning against the window looking out, and he said there were guests coming in the front gate. Old Mistress asked who it was. Third Master looked hard and said he was not sure that it wasn't Master-in-law Ts'ao, and Old Mistress left it at that."

Fire leaped up inside Ch'i-ch'iao as she heard this. She stamped her feet and muttered on her way downstairs, "So— just going to pretend you don't know. If you are going to be so snobbish, why did you bother to carry me here in a sedan chair, complete with three matchmakers and six wedding gifts? Ties of kinship not even a sharp knife can sever. Even if you're not just feigning death today but are really dead, he will have to come to your funeral and kowtow three times and you will have to take it."

Her room was screened off by a stack of gold-lacquered trunks right inside the door, leaving just a few feet of space. As she lifted the curtain, all she saw was her brother's wife bent over the box set to remove the top section containing little pies so as to see if the dishes underneath had spilled. Her brother Ts'ao Ta-nien bowed down to look, hands behind his back. Ch'i-ch'iao felt a wave of acid pain rising in her heart and could not restrain a shower of tears as she leaned against the trunks, her face pressed against their padded covers of sandy blue cloth. Her sister-in-law straightened up hastily and rushed up to hold her hand in both of hers, calling her Miss over and over again. Ts'ao Ta-nien also had to rub his eyes with a raised sleeve. Ch'i-ch'iao unbuttoned the frogs on the trunk jackets with her free hand, only to button them up again, unable to say anything all the while.

Her sister-in-law turned to give her brother a look. "Say something! Talking about Sister all the time, now that you see her you're again like the gourd with its mouth sawed off."[8]

Ch'i-ch'iao said in a quavering voice, "No wonder he has nothing to say—how could he face me?" and turning to her brother, "I thought you would never want to come here! You have ruined me well and good. You walked away just like that, but I couldn't leave. You don't care if I live or die."

Ts'ao Ta-nien said, "What are you saying? It's one thing for other people to talk like this, but you too! If you don't cover up for me you won't look so good either."

"Even if I say nothing, I can't keep other people from talking.

8. An idiomatic expression in Chinese.

Just because of you I've got all kinds of illnesses from anger. After all this, you still try to gag me with these words!"

Her sister-in-law interposed quickly, "It was his fault, his fault! Miss has been put upon. However, Miss has not suffered just on that account alone—be patient anyway, there will be happiness in the end." The words "However, Miss has not suffered just on that account alone" struck Ch'i-ch'iao as so true that she began to weep. It made her sister-in-law so nervous she kept shaking a raised hand from side to side, saying, "Be careful you don't wake up *Ku-yeh*."[9] The net curtains hung still on the big dark bed of purple cedar over on the other side of the room. "Is *Ku-yeh* asleep? He'd be angry if we disturbed him."

Ch'i-ch'iao called out loudly, "If he can react like a human being, it won't be so bad."

Her sister-in-law was so frightened she covered Ch'i-ch'iao's mouth. "Don't, *Ku-nai-nai*![10] Sick people feel bad to hear such talk."

"He feels bad and how do I feel?"

Her sister-in-law said, "Is *Ku-yeh* still suffering from the soft bone illness?"

"Isn't that enough to bear, without further complications? Here the whole family avoids mentioning the word tuberculosis, actually it's just tuberculosis of the bones."

"Does he sit up for a while sometimes?"

Ch'i-ch'iao started to chuckle. "Huh huh! Sit up and the spine slides down, not even as tall as my three-year-old, to look at."

Her sister-in-law ran out of comforting words for the moment and all three were speechless. Ch'i-ch'iao suddenly stamped her feet, saying, "Go, go, you people. Every time you come I have to review once more in my mind how everything has led to this, I can't stand the agitation. Go away quick."

9. Honorific for the son-in-law of the family.
10. Honorific for the married daughter of the house.

Ts'ao Ta-nien said, "Listen to a word from me, Sister. Having your own family around makes it a little better anyhow, and not just now when you're unhappy. Even when your day of independence comes, the Chiangs are a big clan, the elders keep browbeating people with high-sounding words, and those of your generation and the next are like wolves and tigers, every one of them, not a single one easy to deal with. You need help too for your own sake. There will be times aplenty when you could use your brother and nephews."

Ch'i-ch'iao made a spitting noise. "I'd be out of luck indeed if I had to rely on your help. I saw through you long ago—if you could fight them, the more credit to you and you'd come to me for money; if you're no match for them you'd just topple over to their side. The sight of mandarins scares you out of your wits anyway: you'll just pull in your neck and leave me to my fate."

Ta-nien flushed and laughed sardonically. "Wait till the money is in your hands. It will not be too late then to keep your brother from getting a share."

"Then why bother me when you know it's not yet in my hands?"

"So we're wrong to come all this distance to see you!" he said. "Come on, let's go. To be perfectly frank though, even if I use a bit of your money it's only fair. If I'd been greedy for wedding gifts and asked for another several hundred taels of silver from the Chiangs and sold you for a concubine, you'd have been sold."

"Isn't a wife better than a concubine? Kites go farther on a longer string, you have big hopes yet."

Ta-nien was just going to retort when his wife cut in, "Now hold your tongue. You'll still meet in days to come. One day when *Ku-nai-nai* thinks of you she'll know she only has this one brother."

Ta-nien hustled her into tidying the box set, picked it up, and started out.

"What do I care?" Ch'i-ch'iao said. "When I have money I won't have to worry about your not coming, only how to get rid of you." Despite her harsh words she could not hold back the sobs that got louder and louder. This quarrel had made it possible for her to release the frustrations pent up all morning long.

Her sister-in-law, seeing that she was evidently clinging to them a little, succeeded by cajoling and lecturing in pacifying her brother, and at the same time, with her arm around her, led her to the carved pearwood couch, set her down, and patiently reasoned with her, until she gradually dried her tears. The three now talked about everyday affairs. It was more or less peaceful in the north, with business as usual at the Ts'aos' sesame oil shop. Their present trip to Shanghai had to do with their future son-in-law, a bookkeeper who happened to be in Hupeh when the revolution started. He had left the place with his employer and finally come to Shanghai. So Ta-nien had brought his daughter here to be married, visiting his sister on the side. Ta-nien asked after all the Chiangs of the house and wanted to pay his respects to Old Mistress.

"Just as well that you don't see her," said Ch'i-ch'iao. "I was just being mad at her."

Ta-nien and his wife were both startled.

"How can I help myself?" Ch'i-ch'iao said. "The whole family treading me down, if I'd been easy to bully I'd have been trampled to death long ago. As it is, I'm full of aches and pains from anger."

"Do you still smoke, Miss?" her sister-in-law said. "Opium is still better than any other medicine for soothing the liver and composing the nerves. Be sure that you take good care of yourself, Miss, we're not around, who else is there to look after you?"

Ch'i-ch'iao went through her trunks to take out lengths of silks of new designs to give to her sister-in-law and also a pair of gold bracelets weighing four taels, a pair of carnelian hairpins the shape of lotus pods, and a quilting of silk fluff. She had for each niece a gold ear-spoon and each nephew a miniature gold ingot or a sable hat, and handed her brother an enameled gold watch shaped like a cicada. Her brother and sister-in-law hastened to thank her.

"You didn't come at the right moment," Ch'i-ch'iao said. "When we were just about to leave Peking, what we couldn't take was all given to the amahs and slave girls, several trunkfuls they got for nothing."

They looked embarrassed at this. Taking their leave, her sister-in-law said, "When we've got our daughter off our hands, we'll come and see *Ku-nai-nai* again."

"Just as well if you don't," Ch'i-ch'iao said, smiling. "I can't afford it."

When they got out of the Chiangs' house her sister-in-law said, "How is it this *ku-nai-nai* of ours has changed so? Before she was married she may have been a bit proud and talked a little too much. Even later, when we went to see her, she had more of a temper but there was still a limit. She was not silly as she is now, sane enough one minute and the next minute off again, and altogether disagreeable."

Ch'i-ch'iao stood in the room holding her elbows and watched the two slave girls, Little Shuang and Ch'iang-yün, carrying the trunks between them and stacking them back one by one. The things of the past came back again: the sesame oil shop over the cobbled street, the blackened greasy counter, the wooden spoons standing in the buckets of sesame butter and iron spoons of all sizes strung up above the oil jars. Insert the funnel in the customer's bottle. One big spoon plus two small spoons just make a bottle—one and a half catties. Counts as one catty and four ounces if it's somebody she knows. Sometimes she went marketing too, in a blouse and pants of blue linen trimmed with mirror-bright black silk. Across the thick row of brass hooks from which pork dangled she saw Ch'ao-lu of the butcher shop. Ch'ao-lu was always after her, calling her Miss Ts'ao, and on rare occasions Little Miss Ch'iao,[11] and she would give the rack of hooks a slap that sent all the empty hooks swinging across to poke him in the eye. Ch'ao-lu plucked a piece of raw fat a foot wide off the hook and threw it down hard on the block, a warm odor rushing to her face, the smell of sticky dead flesh... she frowned. On the bed lay her husband, that lifeless body...

A gust of wind came in the window and blew against the long mirror in the scrollwork lacquered frame until it rattled against the wall. Ch'i-ch'iao pressed the mirror down with both hands. The green bamboo curtain and a green and gold landscape scroll reflected in the mirror went on swinging back and forth in the wind—one could get dizzy watching it for long. When she looked again the green bamboo curtain had faded, the green and gold landscape was replaced by a photograph of her deceased husband, and the woman in the mirror was also ten years older.

Last year she wore mourning for her husband and this year her mother-in-law had passed away. Now her husband's uncle, Ninth Old Master, was formally invited to come and divide the property among the survivors. Today was the focal point of all her imaginings since she had married into the house of Chiang. All these years she had worn the golden cangue but never even got to gnaw at the edge of the gold. It would be different from now on. In her white lacquered silk blouse and black skirt she looked rouged, from the eyes rubbed red to the feverish cheekbones. She lifted her hand to touch her face. It was flushed but the rest of her body was so cold she was actually trembling. She told Ch'iang-yün to pour her a cup of tea. (Little Shuang had been married long ago; Ch'iang-yün was also mated with a page.) The tea she drank flowed heavily into her chest cavity

11. A familiar form of address, as to a child of the family.

and her heart jumped, thumping in the hot tea. She sat down with her back to the mirror and asked Ch'iang-yün, "All this time Ninth Old Master has been here this afternoon, he's just been going over the accounts with Secretary Ma?"

Ch'iang-yün answered yes.

"Eldest Master and Eldest Mistress. Third Master and Third Mistress, none of them is around?"

Ch'iang-yün again answered yes.

"Who else did he go to see?"

"Just took a turn in the schoolroom," said Ch'iang-yün.

"At least our Master Pai's studies could bear checking into... The trouble with the child this year is what happened to his father and grandmother, one after the other. If he still feels like studying, he's born of beasts." She finished her tea and told Ch'iang-yün to go down and see if the people of the eldest and third branches were all in the parlor, so she would not be too early and be laughed at for seeming eager. It happened that the eldest branch had also sent a slave girl to find out, who came face to face with Ch'iang-yün.

Ch'i-ch'iao finally came downstairs slowly, gracefully. A foreign-style dining table of ebony polished like a mirror was set up in the parlor for the occasion. Ninth Old Master occupied one side by himself, the account books with blue cloth covers and plum-red labels heaped before him along with a melon-ribbed teacup. Around him besides Secretary Ma were the specially invited *kung ch'in*, relatives no closer to one than to the other, serving more or less in the capacity of assistant judges. Eldest Master and Third Master represented their respective branches, but Second Master having died, his branch was represented by Second Mistress. Chi-tse, who knew very well that this day of reckoning bode no good for him, arrived last. But once there he never showed any anxiety or depression: that same plump red smile was still on his cheeks and in his eyes still that bit of dashing impatience.

Ninth Old Master gave a cough and made a brief report on the Chiangs' finances. Leafing through the account books, he read out the main holdings of land and houses and the annual incomes from these. Ch'i-ch'iao leaned forward with hands locked tight over her stomach, trying hard to explain to herself every sentence he uttered and match it with the results of her past investigations. The houses in Tsingtao, the houses in Tientsin, the land in the hometown, the land outside Peking, the houses in Shanghai... Third Master had borrowed too much from the general accounts and for too long. Apart from his share, now canceled out, he still owed sixty thousand dollars, but the eldest and second branches had to let it go at that since he had nothing. The only house he owned, a foreign-style building with a garden bought for a concubine, was already mortgaged. Then there was just the jewelry that Old Mistress had brought with her as a bride to be divided evenly among the three brothers. Chi-tse's share could not very well be confiscated, being mementos left by his mother.

Ch'i-ch'iao suddenly cried out, "Ninth Old Master, this is too hard on us."

The parlor had been dead quiet before, now the silence became a sandy rustle that sawed straight into the ears like the damaged sound track of a movie grating rustily on. Ninth Old Master opened his eyes wide to look at her. "What? You wouldn't even let him have the bit of jewelry his mother left?"

" 'Even brothers settle their accounts openly,' " Ch'i-ch'iao quoted. "Eldest Brother and Sister-in-law say nothing, but I have to toughen my skin and speak out this once. I can't compare with Eldest Brother and Sister-in-law. If the one we lost were able to go out and be a mandarin for a couple of terms and save some money, I'd be glad to be generous, too—what if we cancel all the old accounts? Only that one of ours was pitiful, ailing and groaning all his life, never earned a copper coin. Left us widow and orphans who're counting on just this small fixed sum to live on. I'm a crab without legs and Ch'ang-pai is not yet fourteen, with plenty of hard days ahead." Her tears came down as she spoke.

"What do you want then if you may have your way?" said Ninth Old Master.

"It's not for me to decide," she said, sobbing. "I'm only begging Ninth Old Master to settle it for me."

Chi-tse, cold-faced, said nothing. The whole roomful of people felt it was not for them to speak. Ninth Old Master, unable to keep down a bellyful of fire, snorted, "I'd make a suggestion, only I'm afraid you won't like it. The second branch has land and nobody to look after it, the third branch has a man but no land. I'd have Third Master look after it for you for a consideration, whatever you see fit, only you may not want him."

Ch'i-ch'iao laughed sardonically. "I'd have it your way, only I'm afraid the dead one will not. Come, somebody! Ch'iang-yün, go and get Master Pai for me. Ch'ang-pai, what a hard life your father had! Born with ailments all over, went through life like a wretch, and for what? Never even had a single comfortable day. In the end he left you, all there is of his bone and blood, and people still won't let you be, there're a thousand designs on your property. Ch'ang-pai, it's your father's fault that he dragged himself around with all his illnesses, bullied when he was alive, to have his widow and orphan bullied when he's dead. I don't matter, how many more scores of years can I live? At worst I'd go and explain this before Old Mistress's spirit tablet and kill myself in protest. But Ch'ang-pai, you're so young, you still have your life to live even if there's nothing to eat or drink except the northwest wind!"

Ninth Old Master was so angry he slapped the table. "I wash my hands of this! It was you people who begged and kowtowed to make me come. Do you think I like to go looking for trouble?" He stood up, kicked the chair over and, without waiting to be helped out of the room, strode out of sight in a gust of wind.

The others looked one another in the face and slipped out one by one. Only Secretary Ma was left behind busy tidying up the account books. He thought that, with everybody gone and Second Mistress sitting there alone beating her breast and wailing, it would be embarrassing if he just walked off, and so he went up to her, bowing repeatedly, holding his own hands and moving them up and down in obeisance, and calling, "Second Mistress! Second Mistress!... Second Mistress!" Ch'i-ch'iao just covered her face with a sleeve. Secretary Ma could not very well pull her hand away. Perspiring in despair, he took off his black satin skullcap to fan himself.

The awkward situation lasted for a few days, then the property was divided quietly according to the original plans. The widow and orphans were still taken advantage of.

Ch'i-ch'iao took her son Ch'ang-pai and daughter Ch'ang-an and rented another house to live in, and seldom saw the Chiangs' other branches. Several months later Chiang Chi-tse suddenly came. When the amah announced the visit upstairs, Ch'i-ch'iao was secretly worried that she had offended him that day at the family conference over the division of property and wondered what he was going to do about it. But "an army comes and generals fend it off," so why should she be afraid of him? She tied on a black skirt of iron-thread gauze under the Buddha-blue solid gauze jacket she was wearing and came downstairs. When Chi-tse got up all smiles to give his best regards to Second Sister-in-law, and asked if Master Pai was in the schoolroom and if Little Miss An's ringworm was all cured, Ch'i-ch'iao suspected he was here to borrow money. Doubly on guard, she sat down and said, smiling, "You've gained weight again lately, Third Brother."

"I seem like a man without a thing on his mind," Chi-tse said, smiling.

"Well, 'A blessed man need never be busy.' You're never one to worry," she said, smiling.

"I'd have fewer worries than ever after I'd sold my landed property," he said, smiling.

"You mean the house you mortgaged? You want to sell it?"

"Quite a lot of thought went into it when it was built and I loved some of the fixtures; of course I wouldn't want to part with it. But later, as you know, land got expensive over there, so the year before last I tore it down and built in its place a row of houses. But it was really too much bother collecting rent from house to house, dealing with those tenants; so I thought I'd get rid of the property just for the sake of peace and quiet."

Ch'i-ch'iao said to herself, "How grand we sound! Still acting the rich young master in front of me when I know all about you!"

Although he was not complaining of poverty to her, any mention of money transactions seemed to lead them onto dangerous ground, and so she changed the subject. "How is Third Sister? Her kidneys haven't been bothering her lately?"

"I haven't seen her for some time, either," Chi-tse said, smiling.

"What is this? Have you quarreled?"

"We haven't quarreled either all this time," he said, smiling. "Exchange a few words when we have to but that's also rare. No time to quarrel and no mood for it."

"You're exaggerating. I for one don't believe it."

He rested his elbows on the arms of the rattan chair, locking his fingers to shade his eyes, and sighed deeply.

"Unless it's because you play around too much outside. You're in the wrong and still sighing away as if you were wronged. There's not one good man among you Chiangs!" she said, smiling, and lifted her round white fan as if to strike him. He moved his interlocked fingers downward with both thumbs pressed on his lips and the forefingers slowly stroking the bridge of his nose, and his eyes appeared all the brighter. The irises were the black pebbles at the bottom of a bowl of narcissus, covered with cold water and expressionless. It was impossible to tell what he was thinking. "I must beat you," she said.

A bubble of mirth came up in his eyes. "Go ahead, beat me."

She was about to hit him, snatched back her hand, and then again mustered her strength, saying, "I'd really beat you!" She swung her arm downward, but the descending fan remained in mid air as she started to giggle.

He raised a shoulder toward her, smiling. "You'd better hit me just once. As it is, my bones are itching for punishment."

She hid the fan behind her, chuckling.

Chi-tse moved his chair around and sat facing the wall, leaning back heavily with both hands over his eyes, and heaved another sigh.

Ch'i-ch'iao chewed on her fan handle and looked at him from the corners of her eyes. "What's the matter with you today? Can't stand the heat?"

"You wouldn't know." After a long pause he said in a low voice, enunciating each word distinctly. "You know why I can't get on with the one at home, why I played so hard outside and squandered all my money. Whom do you think it's all for?"

Ch'i-ch'iao was a bit frightened. She walked a long way off and leaned on the mantelpiece, the expression on her face slowly changing. Chi-tse followed her. Her head was bent and her right elbow rested on the mantelpiece. In her right hand was her fan whose apricot-yellow tassel trailed down over her forehead. He stood before her and whispered, "Second Sister-in-law!...Ch'i-ch'iao!"

Ch'i-ch'iao turned her face away and smiled blandly. "As if I'd believe you!"

So he also walked away. "That's right. How could you believe me? Ever since you came to our house I couldn't stay there a minute, only wanted to get out. I was never so wild before you came; later it was to avoid you that I stayed out. After I was married to Lan-hsien, I played harder than ever because aside from avoiding you I had to avoid her too. When I did see you, scarcely two sentences were exchanged before I lost my temper—how could you know the pain in my heart? When you were good to me, I felt still worse—I had to control myself—I couldn't ruin you just like that. So many people at home, all watching us. If people should know, it wouldn't matter too much for me, I was a man, but what was going to happen to you?"

Ch'i-ch'iao's hands trembled until the yellow tassel on the fan handle rustled against her forehead.

"Whether you believe it or not makes little difference," he said. "What if you believe it? Half our lives are over anyway, it's no use talking about it. I'm just asking you to understand the way I felt, then it wouldn't be unfair that I suffered so much on your account."

Ch'i-ch'iao bowed her head, basking in glory, in the soft music of his voice and the delicate pleasure of this occasion. So many years now, she had been playing hide-and-seek with him and never could get close, and there had still been a day like this in store for her. True, half a lifetime had gone by—the flower-years of her youth. Life is so devious and unreasonable. Why had she married into the Chiang family? For money? No, for meeting Chi-tse, because it was fated that she should be in love with him. She lifted her face slightly. He was standing in front of her with flat hands closed on her fan and his cheek pressed against it. He was also ten years older, but he was after all the same person. Could he be lying to her? He wanted her money—the money she had sold her life for? The very idea enraged her. Even if she had him wrong there, could he have suffered as much for her as she did for him? Now that she had finally given up all thoughts of love he was here again to provoke her. She hated him. He was still looking at her. His eyes—after ten years he was still the same person. Even if he was lying to her, wouldn't it be better to find out a little later? Even if she knew very well it was lies, he was such a good actor, wouldn't it be almost real?

No, she could not give this rascal any hold on her. The Chiangs were very shrewd; she might not be able to keep her money. She had to prove first whether he really meant it. She took a grip on herself, looked outside the door, gasped under her breath, "Somebody there!", and rushed out. She went to the amahs' quarters to tell P'an Ma to get the tea things for Third Master.

Coming back to the room, she frowned, saying, "So hateful —amah peering outside the door, turned and ran the minute she saw me. I went after her and stopped her. Who knows what stories they'd make up if we'd talked, however briefly, with the door shut. No peace even living by yourself."

P'an Ma brought the tea things and chilled sour plum juice. Ch'i-ch'iao used her chopsticks to pick the shredded roses and green plums off the top of the honey layer cake for Chi-tse. "I remember you don't like the red and green shreds," she said.

He just smiled, unable to say anything with people around.

Ch'i-ch'iao seemed to be making conversation. "How are you getting on with the houses you were going to sell?"

Chi-tse answered as he ate, "Some people offered eighty-five thousand; I haven't decided yet."

Ch'i-ch'iao paused to reflect. "The district is good."

"Everybody is against my getting rid of the property, says the price is still going up."

Ch'i-ch'iao asked for more particulars, then said, "A pity I haven't got that much cash at hand, otherwise I'd like to buy it."

"Actually there's no hurry about my property, it's your land in our part of the country that should be gotten rid of before long. Ever since we became a republic it's been one war after another, never missed a single year. The area is so messed up and with all the squeeze—the collectors and bookkeepers and the local powers—how much do we get when it comes to our turn, even in a year of good harvest? Not to say these last few years when it's either flood or drought."

Ch'i-ch'iao pondered. "I've done some calculating and kept putting it off. If only I'd sold it, then I wouldn't be caught short just when I want to buy your houses."

"If you want to sell that land it had better be now. I heard Hopeh and Shantung are going to be at war again."

"Who am I to sell it to in such a hurry?"

He said after a moment of hesitation, "All right, I'll see if I can find out for you."

Ch'i-ch'iao lifted her eyebrows and said, smiling, "Go on! You and that pack of foxes and dogs you run with, who is there that's halfway reliable?"

Chi-tse dipped a dumpling that he had bitten open into the little dish of vinegar, taking his time, and mentioned a couple of reliable names. Ch'i-ch'iao then seriously questioned him in detail and he set his answers out tidily, evidently well prepared.

Ch'i-ch'iao continued to smile but her mouth felt dry, her upper lip stuck on her gum and would not come down. She raised the lidded teacup to suck a mouthful of tea, licked her lips, and suddenly jumped up with a set face and threw her fan at his head. The round fan went wheeling through the air, knocked his shoulder as he ducked slightly to the left, and upset his glass. The sour plum juice spilled all over him.

"You want me to sell land to buy your houses? You want me to sell land? Once the money goes through your hands what can I count on? You'd cheat me—you'd cheat me with such talk—you take me for a fool—" She leaned across the table to hit him, but P'an Ma held her in a desperate embrace and started to yell. Ch'iang-yün and the others came running, pressed her down between them, pleaded noisily. Ch'i-ch'iao struggled and barked orders at the same time, but with a sinking heart she quite realized she was being foolish, too foolish, she was making a spectacle of herself.

Chi-tse took off his drenched white lacquered silk gown. P'an Ma brought a hot towel to wipe it for him. He paid her no attention but, before sauntering out the door with his gown on his arm, he said to Ch'iang-yün, "When Master Pai finishes his lesson for the day, tell him to get a doctor for his mother." Ch'iang-yün, who was too frightened by the proceedings not to say yes, received a resounding slap on the face from Ch'i-ch'iao. Chi-tse was gone. The slave girls and amahs also hurriedly left her after being scolded. Drop by drop, the sour plum juice trickled down the table, keeping time like a water clock at night—one drip, another drip—the first watch of the night, the second watch—one year, a hundred years. So long, this silent moment. Ch'i-ch'iao stood there, supporting her head with a hand. In another second she had turned around and was hurrying upstairs. Lifting her skirt, she half climbed and half stumbled her way up, continually bumping against the dingy wall of green plaster. Her Buddha-blue jacket was smudged with patches of pale chalk. She wanted another glimpse of him from the upstairs window. No matter what, she had loved him before. Her love had given her endless pain. Just this alone should make him worthy of her continuing regard. How many times had she strained to suppress herself until all her muscles and bones and gums ached with sharp pain. Today it all had been her fault. It wasn't as if she did not know he was no good. If she wanted him she had to pretend ignorance and put up with his badness. Why had she exposed him? Isn't life just like this and no more than this? In the end what is real and what is false?

She reached the window and pulled aside the dark green foreign-style curtains fringed with little velvet balls. Chi-tse was just going out the alley, his gown slung over his arm. Like a flock of white pigeons, the wind on that sunny day fluttered inside his white silk blouse and trousers. It penetrated everywhere, flapping its wings.

A curtain of ice-cold pearls seemed to hang in front of Ch'i-ch'iao's eyes. A hot wind would press the curtain tight on her face, and after being sucked back by the wind for a moment, it would muffle all her head and face before she could draw her breath. In such alternately hot and cold waves her tears flowed.

The tiny shrunken image of a policeman reflected faintly in the top corner of the window glass ambled by swinging his arms. A ricksha quietly ran over the policeman. A little boy with his long gown tucked up into his trouser waist ran kicking a ball out of the edge of the glass. The postman in green riding a bicycle superimposed his image on the policeman as he streaked by. All ghosts, ghosts of many years ago or the unborn of many years hence...What is real and what is false?

The autumn passed, then the winter. Ch'i-ch'iao was out of touch with reality, feeling a little lost despite the usual flares of temper which prompted her to beat slave girls and change cooks. Her brother and his wife came to Shanghai to see her twice and stayed each time not longer than ten days, because in the end they could not stand her nagging, even though she would give them parting presents. Her nephew Ts'ao Ch'un-hsi came to town to look for work and stayed at her house. Though none too bright, this youth knew his place. Ch'i-ch'iao's son Ch'ang-pai was now fourteen, and her daughter Ch'ang-an about a year younger, but they looked only about seven or eight, being small and thin. During the New Year holidays the boy wore a bright blue padded gown of heavy silk and the girl a bright green brocade padded gown, both so thickly wadded that their arms stuck out straight. Standing side by side, both looked like paper dolls, with their flat thin white faces. One day after lunch Ch'i-ch'iao was not up yet. Ts'ao Ch'un-hsi kept the brother and sister company throwing dice. Ch'ang-an had lost all her New Year money gifts and still would not stop playing. Ch'ang-pai swept all the copper coins on the table toward himself and said, smiling, "I won't play with you any more."

"We'll play with candied lotus seeds," Ch'ang-an said.

"The sugar will stain your clothes if you keep them in your pocket," Ch'un-hsi said.

"Watermelon seeds will do, there's a can of them on top of the wardrobe," said Ch'ang-an. So she moved a small tea table over and stepped on a chair to get on it and reach up.

Ch'un-hsi was so nervous he called out, "Don't you fall down, Little Miss An, I can't shoulder the blame." The words were scarcely out of his mouth when Ch'ang-an suddenly tipped backwards and would have toppled down if he had not caught her. Ch'ang-pai clapped his hands, laughing, while Ch'un-hsi, though he muttered curses, also could not help laughing. All three of them dissolved in mirth. Lifting her down, Ch'un-hsi suddenly saw in the mirror of the rosewood wardrobe Ch'i-ch'iao standing in the doorway with her arms akimbo, her hair not yet done. Somewhat taken aback, he quickly set Ch'ang-an down and turned around to greet her, "Aunt is up."

Ch'i-ch'iao rushed over and pushed Ch'ang-an behind her. Ch'ang-an lost her balance and fell down but Ch'i-ch'iao continued shielding her with her own body while she cried harshly to Ch'un-hsi, "You wolf-hearted, dog-lunged creature, I'll fix you! I treat you to three teas and six meals, you wolf-hearted, dog-lunged thing, in what way have I not done right by you, and yet you'd take advantage of my daughter? You think I can't make out what's in your wolf's heart and dog's lungs? Don't you go around thinking if you teach my daughter bad things I'll have to hold my nose and marry her to you, so you can take over our property. A fool like you doesn't look to me as if he'd think of such a trick, it must be your parents who taught you, guiding you by the hand. Those two wolf-hearted, dog-lunged, ungrateful, old addled eggs, they are determined to get my money. When one scheme fails another comes up."

Ch'un-hsi, staring white-eyed in his anger, was just about to defend himself when Ch'i-ch'iao said, "Aren't you ashamed? You'd still answer back? Get out of my sight right away, don't wait for my men to drive you out with rods." So saying, she pushed her son and daughter out and then left the room herself, supported by a slave girl. Being a quick-tempered youth, Ch'un-hsi rolled up his bedding and left the Chiang house forthwith.

Ch'i-ch'iao returned to the living room and lay down on the opium couch. With the velvet curtains drawn it was dark in the room. Only when the wind came in through the crevices and moved the curtains was a bit of sky hazily visible under their hems fringed with green velvet balls. There was just the opium lamp and the dim light of the stove burning red. Having had a fright, Ch'ang-an sat stunned on a little stool by the stove.

"Come over here," Ch'i-ch'iao said.

Ch'ang-an didn't go over right away, thinking her mother would hit her. She fiddled with the laundry hung on the tin screen around the stove and turned over a cotton undershirt with little pink checks, saying, "It's almost burned." The shirt gave out a hot smell of cloth fuzz.

But Ch'i-ch'iao, not quite in the mood to beat or scold her, merely went over everything and added, "You'll be thirteen this year after the New Year, you should have more sense. Although Cousin is no outsider, men are all rotten without exception. You should know how to take care of yourself. Who's not after your money?" A gust of wind passed, showing the cold white sky between the velvet balls on the curtains, puncturing with a row of little holes the warm darkness in the room. The flame of the opium lamp ducked and the shadows on Ch'i-ch'iao's face seemed a shade deeper. She suddenly sat up to whisper, "Men...leave them alone! Who's not after your money? Your mother's bit of money didn't come easy nor is it easy to keep. When it comes to you two, I can't look on and see you get cheated. I'm telling you to be more on guard from now on, you hear?"

"I heard," Ch'ang-an said with her head down.

One of Ch'i-ch'iao's feet was going to sleep, and she reached over to pinch it. Just for a moment a gentle memory stirred in her eyes. She remembered a man who was after her money.

Her bound feet had been padded with cotton wool to simulate the reformed feet, half let out. As she looked at them, something occurred to her and she said with a cynical laugh, "You may say yes, but how do I know if you're sensible or silly at heart? You're this big already, and with a pair of big feet, where can't you go? Even if I could control you, I wouldn't have the energy to watch you all day long. Actually at thirteen it's already too late for foot-binding, it is my fault not to have seen to it earlier. We'll start right now, there's still time."

Ch'ang-an was momentarily at a loss for an answer, but the amahs standing around said, smiling, "Small feet are not fashionable any more. To have her feet bound will perhaps mean trouble when the time comes for Little Miss to get engaged."

"What nonsense! I'm not worried about my daughter having no takers; you people needn't bother to worry for me. If nobody really wants her and she has to be kept all her life, I can afford it too."

She actually started to bind her daughter's feet, and Ch'ang-an howled with great pain. By then even women in conservative families like the Chiangs were letting out their bound feet, to say nothing of girls whose feet had never been bound. Everybody talked about Ch'ang-an's feet as a great joke. After binding them for a year or so, Ch'i-ch'iao's momentary enthusiasm had waned and relatives persuaded her to let them loose, but Ch'ang-an's feet would never be entirely the same again.

All the children of the Chiangs' eldest and third branches

went to foreign-style schools. Ch'i-ch'iao, always purposely competing with them, also wanted to enroll Ch'ang-pai in one. Aside from playing mahjong for small stakes, Ch'ang-pai liked only to go to amateur Peking opera clubs. He was working hard day and night training his singing voice, and was afraid that school would interfere with his lessons, so he refused to go. In desperation Ch'i-ch'iao sent Ch'ang-an instead to the Hu Fan Middle School for girls and through connections got her into one of the higher classes. Ch'ang-an changed into a uniform of rough blue "patriotic cloth" and in less than six months her complexion turned ruddy and her wrists and ankles grew thicker. The boarders were supposed to have their clothes washed by a laundry concession, Ch'ang-an could not remember her own numbers and often lost pillowcases, handkerchiefs, and other little items, and Ch'i-ch'iao insisted on going to speak to the principal about it. One day when she was home for holidays, in going over her things Ch'i-ch'iao found a sheet was missing. She fell into a thunderous rage and threatened to go to the school herself the next day to demand satisfaction. Ch'ang-an in dismay tried just once to stop her and Ch'i-ch'iao scolded, "You good-for-nothing wastrel. Your mother's money is not money to you. Did your mother's money come easy? What dowry will I have to give you when you get married? Whatever I give you will be given in vain."

Ch'ang-an dared not say anything in reply and cried all night. She could not bear to lose face like this in front of her schoolmates. To a fourteen-year-old that seems of the greatest importance. How was she to face people from now on if her mother went and made a scene? She would rather die than go to school again. Her friends, the music teacher she liked, they would soon forget there was such a girl who had come for half a year and left quietly for no reason. A clean break—she felt this sacrifice was a beautiful desolate gesture.

At midnight she crawled out of bed and put a hand outside

the window. Pitch-dark, was it raining? No raindrops. She took a harmonica from the side of her pillow and half squatted, half sat on the floor, blowing it stealthily. Hesitantly the little tune of "Long, Long Ago" twirled and spread out in the huge night. People must not hear. Held down strictly, the thin, wailing music of the harmonica kept trailing off and on like a baby sobbing. Short of breath, she stopped for a while. Through the window the moon had come out of the clouds. A dark gray sky dotted sparsely with stars and a blurred chip of a moon, like a lithographed picture. White clouds steaming up underneath and a faint halo over the street lamp showing among the top branches of a tree. Ch'ang-an started her harmonica again. "Tell me the tales that to me were so dear, long, long ago, long, long ago..."

The next day she summoned up enough courage to tell her mother, "I don't feel like going back to school, Mother."

Ch'i-ch'iao opened her eyes wide. "Why?"

"I can't keep up with the lessons, and the food is too bad, I can't get used to it."

Ch'i-ch'iao took off a slipper and slapped her with its sole just by the way, saying bitterly, "Your father was not as good as other people, you're also not as good? You weren't born a freak, you're just being perverse so as to disappoint me."

Looking down, Ch'ang-an stood with her hands behind her back and would not speak. So the amahs intervened, "Little Miss is grown up now, and it's a bit inconvenient for her to go to school where there're all sorts of people. Actually, it's just as well for her not to go."

Ch'i-ch'iao paused to reflect. "At least we have to get the tuition back. Why give it to them for nothing?" She wanted Ch'ang-an to go with her to collect it. Ch'ang-an would have fought to the death rather than go. Ch'i-ch'iao took two amahs with her. The way she told it when she returned, although she did not get the money back, she had thoroughly humiliated the principal. Afterwards, when Ch'ang-an met any of her school-mates on the street, she reddened and paled alternately. Earth had no room for her. She could only pretend not to see and walk past them hastily. When friends wrote her, she dared not even open the letters and just sent them back. Thus her school life came to an end.

Sometimes she felt the sacrifice was not worth it and was secretly sorry, but it was too late. She gradually gave up all thought of self-improvement and kept to her place. She learned to make trouble, play little tricks, and interfere with the run-ning of the house. She often fell out with her mother, but she looked and sounded more and more like her. Every time she wore a pair of unlined trousers and sat with her legs apart and the palms of both hands on the stool in front of her, her head tilted to one side, her chin on her chest, looking dismally but intently at the woman opposite and telling her, "Every family has its own troubles, Cousin-in-law—every family has its own troubles!" she appeared Ch'i-ch'iao's spit and image. She wore a pigtail and her eyes and eyebrows had a taut expressiveness about them reminiscent of Ch'i-ch'iao in her prime, but her small mouth was a bit too sunken, which made her look older. Even when she was younger, she did not seem fresh, but was like a tender bunch of vegetables that had been salted.

Some people tried to make matches for her. If the other side was not well off, Ch'i-ch'iao would always suspect it wanted their money. If the other side had wealth and influence, it would show little enthusiasm. Ch'ang-an had only average good looks, and since her mother was not only lowborn but also known for her shrewishness, she probably would not have much upbring-ing. So the high were out of reach and the low Ch'i-ch'iao would not stoop to—Ch'ang-an stayed home year after year. But Ch'ang-pai's marriage could not be delayed. When he gam-bled outside and showed enough personal interest in certain Peking opera actresses to attend their performances regularly,

Ch'i-ch'iao still had nothing to say; she got alarmed only when he started to go to brothels with his Third Uncle Chiang Chi-tse. In great haste she betrothed and married him to a Miss Yuan, called Chih-shou as a child.

The wedding ceremony was half modern, and the bride, without the customary red kerchief over her head and face, wore blue eyeglasses and a pink wedding veil instead, and a pink blouse and skirt with multi-colored embroidery. The glasses were removed after she entered the bridal chamber and sat with bowed head under the turquoise-colored bed curtains. The guests gathered for the "riot in the bridal chamber" surrounded her, making jokes. Ch'i-ch'iao came out after taking a look. Ch'ang-an overtook her at the door and whispered, "Fair-skinned, only the lips are a bit too thick."

Ch'i-ch'iao leaned a hand on the doorway, took a gold ear-spoon from her bun to scratch her head with, and laughed sardonically. "Don't start on that now. Your new sister-in-law's lips, chop them up and they'll make a heaping dish!"

"Well, it's said that people with thick lips have warm feelings," said a lady beside her.

Ch'i-ch'iao snorted; pointing her gold ear-spoon at the woman; she lifted an eyebrow and said with a crooked little smile, "It isn't so nice to have warm feelings. I can't say much in front of young ladies—just hope our Master Pai won't die in her hands." Ch'i-ch'iao was born with a high clear voice, which had grown less shrill as she grew older, but it was still cutting, or rather rasping, like a razor blade. Her last remark could not be called loud, nor was it exactly soft. Could the bride, surrounded by a crowd as she was, possibly have registered a quiver on her severely flat face and chest? Probably it was just a reflection of the flames leaping on the tall pair of dragon-and-phoenix candles.

After the Third Day Ch'i-ch'iao found the bride stupid and unsatisfactory in various things and often complained to relatives. Some said placatingly, "The bride is young. Second Sister-in-law will just have to take the trouble to teach her. It just happens that the child is naïve."

Ch'i-ch'iao made a spitting noise. "Our new young mistress may look innocent—but as soon as she sees Master Pai she has to go and sit on the nightstool. Really! It sounds unbelievable, doesn't it?"

When the talk reached Chih-shou's ears. she wanted to kill herself. This was before the end of the first month, when Ch'i-ch'iao still kept up appearances. Later she would even say such things in front of Chih-shou, who could neither cry nor laugh with impunity. And if she merely looked wooden, pretending not to listen, Ch'i-ch'iao would slap the table and sigh, "It's really not easy, to eat a mouthful of rice in the house of your son and daughter-in-law! People pull a long face at you at the drop of a hat."

One night Ch'i-ch'iao was lying on the opium couch smoking while Ch'ang-pai crouched on a nearby upholstered chair cracking watermelon seeds. The radio was broadcasting a little-known Peking opera. He followed it in a book, humming the lyrics word by word, and as he got into the mood, swung a leg up over the back of the chair rocking it back and forth to mark the rhythm.

Ch'i-ch'iao reached out a foot to give him a kick. "Come Master Pai, fill the pipe for me a couple of times."

"With an opium lamp right there why put me to work? I have honey on my fingers or something?" Ch'ang-pai stretched himself while replying and slowly moved over to the little stool in front of the opium lamp and rolled up his sleeves.

"Unfilial slave, what kind of answer is that! Putting you to work is an honor." She looked at him through slitted smiling eyes. All these years he had been the only man in her life. Only with him there was no danger of his being after her money—it was his anyway. But being her son, he amounted to less than half a man. And even the half she could not keep, now that he was married. He was a slight, pale young man, a bit hunched, with gold-rimmed glasses and fine features meticulously drawn, often smiling vacantly, his mouth hanging open and something shining inside, either too much saliva or a gold tooth. The collar of his gown was open, showing its pearly lamb lining and a white pajama shirt. Ch'i-ch'iao put a foot on his shoulder and kept giving him light kicks on the neck, whispering, "Unfilial slave, I'll fix you! When do you get so unfilial?"

Ch'ang-pai quoted with a smile, "'Take a wife and the mother is forgotten'"

"Don't talk nonsense, our Master Pai is not that kind of person, nor could I have had a son like that either," said Ch'i-ch'iao. Ch'ang-pai just smiled. She looked fixedly at him from the corners of her eyes. "If you're still my Master Pai as before, cook opium for me all night tonight."

"That's no problem," he said, smiling.

"If you doze off, see if I don't hammer you with my fists."

The living room curtains had been sent to be washed. Outside the windows the moon was barely visible behind dark clouds, a dab of black, a dab of white like a ferocious theatrical mask. Bit by bit it came out of the clouds and a ray of light shone disconcertingly from under a black strip of cloud, an eye under the mask. The sky was the dark blue of the bottomless pit. It was long past midnight, and Ch'ang-an had gone to bed long ago. As Ch'ang-pai started to nod while rolling the opium pills, Ch'i-ch'iao poured him a cup of strong tea. The two of them ate honeyed preserves and discussed neighbors' secrets. Ch'i-ch'iao suddenly said, smiling, "Tell me, Master Pai, is your wife nice?"

"What is there to say about it?" Ch'ang-pai said, smiling.

"Must be nice if there is nothing to criticize," said Ch'i-ch'iao.

"Who said she's nice?"

"Not nice? In what way? Tell Mother."

Ch'ang-pai was vague at first but under cross-examination he had to reveal a thing or two. The amahs handing them tea turned aside to chuckle and the slave girls covered their mouths trying not to laugh and slipped out of the room. Ch'i-ch'iao gritted her teeth and laughed and muttered curses, removed the pipe bowl to knock out the ashes with all her strength, banging loudly. Once started, Ch'ang-pai found it hard to stop and talked all night.

The next morning Ch'i-ch'iao told the amahs to bring a couple of blankets to let the young master sleep on the couch. Chih-shou was up already and came to pay her respects. Ch'i-ch'iao had not slept all night but was more energetic than ever and asked relatives over to play mahjong, women of different families including her daughter-in-law's mother. Over the mahjong table she told in detail all her daughter-in-law's secrets as confessed by her son, adding some touches of her own that made the story still more vivid. Everybody tried to change the subject, but the small talk no sooner started than Ch'i-ch'iao would smilingly switch it back to her daughter-in-law. Chih-shou's mother turned purple. Too ashamed to see her daughter, she just put down her mahjong tiles and went home in her private ricksha.

Ch'i-ch'iao made Ch'ang-pai cook opium for her for two nights running. Chih-shou lay stiffly in bed with both hands on her ribs curled upward like a dead chicken's claws. She knew her mother-in-law was questioning her husband again, although heaven knew how he could have anything fresh to say. Tomorrow he would again come to her with a drooling, mock-pleading look. Perhaps he had guessed that she would center all her hatred on him. Even if she could not fight savagely with tooth and nail, she would at least upbraid him and make a scene. Very likely he would steal her thunder by coming in half drunk, to pick on her and smash something. She knew his ways. In the end he would sit down on the bed, raise his shoulders, reach inside his white silk pajama shirt to scratch himself, and smile unexpectedly. A little light would tremble on his gold-rimmed spectacles and twinkle in his mouth, spit or gold tooth. He would take off his glasses... Chih-shou suddenly sat up and parted the bed curtains with the sound of a bucket of water crashing down. This was an insane world, a husband not like a husband, a mother-in-law not like a mother-in-law. Either they were mad or she was. The moon tonight was better than ever, high and full like a white sun in a pitch-black sky, not a cloud within ten thousand li. Blue shadows all over the floor and blue shadows on the canopy overhead. Her feet, too, were in the deathly still blue shadows.

Thinking to hook up the bed curtains, Chih-shou reached out groping for the hook. With one hand holding on to the brass hook and her face snuggled against her shoulder, she could not keep the sobs from starting. The curtain dropped by itself. There was nobody but her inside the dark bed. Still she hastened to hook the curtains up in a panic. Outside the windows there was still that abnormal moon that made one's body hairs stand on end all over—small white sun brilliant in the black sky. Inside the room she could clearly see the embroidered rosy-purple chair covers and table cloths, the gold-embroidered scarlet screen with five phoenixes flying in a row, the pink satin scrolls embroidered with seal-script characters embellished with flowers. On the dressing table the silver powder jar, silver mouth-rinsing mug, and silver vase were each caught in a red and green net and filled with wedding candies. Along the silk panel across the lintel of the bed hung balls of flowers, toy flower pots, *ju-yi*,[12] and rice dumplings, all made of multicolored gilded velvet, and dangling underneath them glass balls the size of finger tips and mauvish pink tassels a foot long. In

12. Literally, "as you wish." An odd-shaped ornamental piece, usually of jade.

such a big room crammed full of trunks, spare bedding, and furnishings, surely she could find a sash to hang herself with. She fell back on the bed. In the moonlight her feet had no color of life at all—bluish, greenish, purplish, the tints of a corpse gone cold. She wanted to die, she wanted to die. She was afraid of the moonlight but dared not turn on the light. Tomorrow her mother-in-law would say, "Master Pai fixed me a couple more pipes and our poor young mistress couldn't sleep the whole night, kept her light on to all hours waiting for him to come back—can't do without him." Chih-shou's tears flowed along the pillow. She did not wipe her eyes with a handkerchief; rubbing would get them swollen and her mother-in-law would again say, "Master Pai didn't sleep in his room for just one night and Young Mistress cried until her eyes were like peaches!"

Although Ch'i-ch'iao pictured her son and daughter-in-law as a passionate couple, Ch'ang-pai was not very pleased with Chih-shou and Chih-shou on her part hated him so much her teeth itched to bite. Since the two did not get along, Ch'ang-pai again went strolling in "the streets of flowers and the lanes of willows." Ch'i-ch'iao gave him a slave girl called Chüan-erh for a concubine and still could not hold him. She also tried in various ways to get him to smoke opium. Ch'ang-pai had always liked a couple of puffs for fun but he had never got into the habit. Now that he smoked more he quieted down and no longer went out much, just stayed with his mother and his new concubine.

His sister Ch'ang-an got dysentery when she was twenty-four. Instead of getting a doctor, Ch'i-ch'iao persuaded her to smoke a little opium and it did ease the pain. After she recovered she also got into the habit. An unmarried girl without any other distractions, Ch'ang-an went at it singlemindedly and smoked even more than her brother. Some tried to dissuade her. Ch'i-ch'iao said. "What is there to be afraid of? For one thing we Chiangs can still afford it, and even if I sold two hundred *mou* of land today so the brother and sister could smoke, who is there who'd dare let out half a fart? When the girl gets married she'll have her dowry, she'll be eating and drinking out of her own pocket, so even if *Ku-yeh* stints on it he can only look on."

All the same Ch'ang-an's prospects were affected. The matchmakers, who had never come running to begin with, now disappeared altogether. When Ch'ang-an was nearly thirty, Ch'i-ch'iao changed her tune, seeing that her daughter was fated to be an old maid. "Not married off because she's not good-looking, and yet blames her mother for putting it off, spoiling her chances. Pulls a long face all day as if I owed her two hundred copper coins. It's certainly not to make myself miserable that I've kept her at home, feeding her free tea and rice!"

On the twentieth birthday of Chiang Chi-tse's daughter Ch'ang-hsing, Ch'ang-an went to give her cousin her best wishes. Chiang Chi-tse was poor now but fortunately his wide social contacts kept him more or less solvent. Ch'ang-hsing said to her mother in secret, "Mother, try to introduce a friend to Sister An, she seems so pitiful. Her eyes reddened with tears at the very mention of conditions at home."

Lan-hsien hastily held up her palm, shaking it from side to side. "No, no! This match I dare not make. Stir up your Second Aunt with her temper?"

But Ch'ang-hsing, young and meddlesome, paid her no heed. After some time she by chance mentioned Ch'ang-an's case to her schoolmates, and it happened that one of them had an uncle newly returned from Germany, a northerner, too, even distantly related to the Chiangs, as it turned out when they really investigated his background. The man was called T'ung Shih-fang, and was several years older than Ch'ang-an. And Ch'ang-hsing took matters into her own hands and arranged everything. Her schoolmate's mother would play hostess. On Ch'ang-an's side her family was kept as much in the dark as if sealed in an iron barrel.

Ch'i-ch'iao had always had a strong constitution but ever since Chih-shou had got tuberculosis Ch'i-ch'iao thought her daughter-in-law disgustingly affected, making much of herself, eating this and that, unable to stand the least fatigue and seemingly having a better time than usual, so she, too, got sick out of spite. At first it was just weak breath and thin blood, but even then it sent the entire household into a spin, so that they had no time for Chih-shou. Later Ch'i-ch'iao got seriously ill and took to her bed and there was more fuss than ever. Ch'ang-an slipped out in the confusion and called a tailor to her Third Uncle's house, where Ch'ang-hsing designed a new costume for her. On the day of the dinner Ch'ang-hsing accompanied her in the late afternoon to see the hairdresser, who waved her hair with hot tongs and plastered close-set little kiss-curls from the temple to the ears. Upon returning home, Ch'ang-hsing made her cousin wear "glassy-green" jadeite[13] earrings with pagoda-shaped pendants two inches long and change into an apple-green georgette gown with a high collar, ruffled sleeves, and fine pleats below the waist, half Western style. As a young maid squatted on the floor buttoning her up, Ch'ang-an scrutinized herself in the wardrobe mirror and could not help stretching out both arms and kicking out the skirt in a posture from "The Grape Fairy."[14] Twisting her head around, she started to laugh, saying, "Really dolled up to look like the celestial maiden scattering flowers!"[15]

Ch'ang-hsing signaled the maid in the mirror with her eyes

13. The most valued kind of jadeite, translucent and dark green in color.
14. A short musical by Li Ching-hui, a most popular choice for school productions during the twenties and thirties.
15. *T'ien-nü san-hua* (The celestial maiden scatters flowers) is the title of a Peking opera made popular by Mei Lan-fang. It is based on an episode from the Vimalakirti Sutra.

and they both laughed. After Ch'ang-an had finished dressing, she sat down straight-backed on a high chair.

"I'll go and telephone for a taxi," Ch'ang-hsing said.

"It's early yet," said Ch'ang-an.

Ch'ang-hsing looked at her watch. "We're supposed to be there at eight. It's now five past."

"It probably wouldn't matter if we were half an hour late."

Ch'ang-hsing thought it both infuriating and laughable for her cousin to want to put on airs. She opened her woven silver handbag to examine its contents. On the pretext that she had forgotten her compact, she went to her mother's room and told her all about it, adding, "T'ung is not the host today, so for whom is she putting on airs? I won't bother to talk her out of it, let her dawdle till tomorrow morning, it's none of my business."

Lan-hsien said, "Look how silly you are! You made the appointment, you're making the match, how can you not be responsible? I've told you so many times you should have known better, Little Miss An is just as petty as her mother and not used to company. She'll make a spectacle of herself and she's your cousin after all. If you lose face you deserve it—who told you to get into this? Gone crazy from having nothing to do?"

Ch'ang-hsing sat pouting in her mother's room for a long while.

"It looks as if your cousin is waiting to be pressed," Lan-hsien said, smiling.

"I'm not going to press her."

"Silly girl, what's the use of your pressing? She's waiting for the other side to telephone."

Ch'ang-hsing broke out laughing. "She's not a bride, to be urged three, four times and forced into the sedan chair."

"Ring up the restaurant anyway and be done with it—tell them to call. It's almost nine. If you wait any longer it's really off."

Ch'ang-hsing had to do as she was told and finally set out with her cousin.

Ch'ang-an was still in good spirits in the car, talking and laughing away. But once in the restaurant, she suddenly became reserved, stealing into the room behind Ch'ang-hsing, timidly removed her apple-green ostrich cape and sat down with bowed head, took an almond and bit off a tenth of it every two minutes, chewing slowly. She had come to be looked at. She felt that her costume was impeccable and could stand scrutiny but her body was altogether superfluous and could as well be shrunk in size and put away if she knew how to do this. She kept silent throughout the meal. While waiting for the dessert, Ch'ang-hsing pulled her to the window to watch the street scene and walked off on some pretext, and T'ung Shih-fang ambled over to the window.

"Has Miss Chiang been here before?" he said.

"No," Ch'ang-an said in a small voice.

"The first time for me too. The food is not bad, but I'm not quite used to it yet."

"Not used to it?"

"Yes, foreign food is more bland, Chinese food is more greasy. When I had just come back friends and relatives made me eat out for several days running and I easily got an upset stomach."

Ch'ang-an looked at her fingers back and front as if intent on counting how many of the whorls were "snails" and how many "shovels."

Out of nowhere a little neon light sign in the shape of a flower bloomed on the windowpane, reflected from the shop opposite, red petals with a green heart. It was the lotus of the Nile set before the gods and also the lily emblem of French royalty...

Shih-fang, who had nor seen any girls of his homeland for many years, was struck by Ch'ang-an's pathetic charm and rather liked it. He had been engaged long before he went abroad, but having fallen in love with a schoolmate he violently opposed the match. After endless long-distance negotiations he almost broke with his parents who for a time stopped sending money, causing him much hardship. They finally gave in, however, and put an end to his engagement. Unfortunately his schoolmate fell in love with somebody else. In his disappointment he dug in and studied for seven, eight years. His conviction that old-fashioned wives were best was also a rebound.

After this meeting with Ch'ang-an, they were both interested. Ch'ang-hsing thought she should finish her good deed but, however enthusiastic, she was not qualified to speak to Ch'ang-an's mother. She had to beg Lan-hsien, who refused adamantly, saying, "You know very well your father and your Second Aunt are like enemies, never see each other. Although I've never quarreled with her there's no love lost. Why ask to be cold-shouldered?"

Ch'ang-an said nothing when she saw Lan-hsien, merely shed tears. Lan-hsien had to promise to go just once. The sisters-in-law met and after the amenities Lan-hsien explained the purpose of her visit. Ch'i-ch'iao was glad enough when she first heard of it.

"Then I'll leave it to Third Sister," she said. "I haven't been at all well, I can't cope with it, will just have to trouble Third Sister. This girl has been a dead weight on my hands. As a mother I can't be said to have not done right by her. When old-fashioned rules were in force I bound her feet, when newfangled rules were in force I sent her to school—what else is there? A girl I dug out my heart and liver to train, as it were, she shouldn't have no takers as long as she's not scarred or pock-marked or blind. But this girl was born an Ah-tou[16] that can't be propped up. I get so angry I keep yelling: 'Oh, for the

16. The inept heir of Liu Pei, founder of the Shu Han kingdom during the Three Kingdoms period.

day that I shut my eyes and am gone!'——her marriage will then be in the hands of heaven and left to fate."

So it was agreed that Lan-hsien would ask both sides to dinner so they could take a look at each other. Ch'ang-an and T'ung Shih-fang met again as if for the first time. Ch'i-ch'iao, sick in bed, did not appear, so Ch'ang-an got engaged in peace. At the dinner table Lan-hsien and Ch'ang-hsing forcibly took Ch'ang-an's hand and placed it in T'ung Shih-fang's. Shih-fang put the ring on her finger in public. And the girl's family gave gifts in return, not the traditional stationery but a pen set in a velvet-lined box plus a wrist watch.

After the engagement Ch'ang-an furtively went out alone with T'ung Shih-fang several times. The two of them walked side by side in the park in the autumn sun, talking very little, each content with a partial view of the other's clothes and moving feet. The fragrance of her face powder and his tobacco smell served as invisible railings that separated them from the crowd. On the open green lawn where so many people ran and laughed and talked, they alone walked an enchanted porch that wound on endlessly in silence. Ch'ang-an did not feel there was anything amiss in not talking. She thought this was all there was to social contact between modern men and women. As to T'ung Shih-fang, from painful experience in the past he was dubious anyway of the exchange of thought. He was satisfied that someone was beside him. Formerly he had been disgusted by the character in fiction who would say, when asking a woman to live with him, "Please give me solace." Solace is purely spiritual but it is used here as a euphemism for sex. But now he knew the line between the spiritual and the physical could not be drawn so clearly. Words are no use after all. Holding hands for a long time is a more apt consolation, because not many people talk well and still fewer really have anything to say.

Sometimes it rained in the park. Ch'ang-an would open her umbrella and Shih-fang would hold it for her. Upon the translucent blue silk umbrella myriad raindrops twinkled like a skyful of stars that would follow them about later on the taxi's glistening front window of crushed silver and, as the car ran through red and green lights, a nestful of red stars would fly humming outside the window and a nestful of green stars.

Ch'ang-an brought back some of the stray dreams under the starlight and became unusually silent, often smiling. Ch'i-ch'iao saw the change and could not help getting angry and sarcastic. "These many years we haven't been very attentive to Miss, no wonder Miss seldom smiled. Now you've got your wish and are going to spring out of the Chiangs' door. But no matter how happy you are, don't show it on your face so much— it's simply sickening."

In former days Ch'ang-an would have answered back, but now that she appeared a transformed person she let it go and concentrated on curing herself of the opium habit. Ch'i-ch'iao could do nothing with her.

Eldest Mistress Tai-chen, who had not been present when Ch'ang-an got engaged, came to the house to congratulate her sometime afterward. Ch'i-ch'iao whispered, "Eldest Sister-in-law, it seems to me we still have to ask around a bit. This is not a matter to blunder into. The other day I seemed to have heard something about a wife in the country and another across the seas."

"The one in the country was sent back before marriage," said Tai-chen. "The same with the one overseas. It's said that they were friends for several years, nobody knew why nothing came of it."

"What's so strange about that? Men's hearts change faster than you can say change. He didn't even acknowledge the one who came with the three matchmakers and six gifts, not to say the hussy that's neither fish nor flesh. Who knows whether he has anybody else across the seas? I have only this one daughter,

I can't muddle along and ruin her whole life. I myself have suffered in matchmakers' hands."

Ch'ang-an sat to one side pressing her fingernails into her palm until the palm reddened and the nails turned white from the strain. Ch'i-ch'iao looked up and saw her. "Shameless girl, pricking up your ears to listen! Is this anything that you should hear? When we were girls we couldn't get out of the way fast enough at the very mention of marriage. You Chiangs had generations of book learning in vain, you may have to go and learn some manners from your mother's family with their sesame oil shop."

Ch'ang-an ran out crying. Ch'i-ch'iao pounded her pillow and sighed. "Miss couldn't wait to marry, so what can I do? She'd drag home any old smelly stinking thing. It's supposed to be her Third Aunt that found him for her—actually she's just using her Third Aunt for a blind. Probably the rice was already cooked before they asked Third Aunt to be matchmaker. Everybody ganged up to fool me—and just as well. If the truth came out, where should the mother and brother look?"

Another day Ch'ang-an slipped out on some excuse. When she got back she was going to report every place she had been before Ch'i-ch'iao had even asked.

"All right, all right, save your words," Ch'i-ch'iao barked. "What's the use of lying to me? Let me catch you red-handed one day—humph! don't you think that because you're grown up and engaged I can't beat you any more!"

'I went to give Cousin Hsing those slipper patterns, what's wrong in that?" Ch'ang-an was upset. "If Mother doesn't believe me, she can ask Third Aunt."

"Your Third Aunt found you a man and she's the father and mother of your rebirth! Never seen anybody as cheap as you ... Disappears in the twinkling of an eye. Your family kept you and honored you all these years—short of buying a page to serve you, where have we been remiss, that you can't even stay home for a moment?"

Ch'ang-an blushed, tears falling straight down.

Ch'i-ch'iao paused for breath. "So many good ones were turned down before and now you go and marry a ne'er-do-well, the leftover of the lot, isn't that slapping one's own face? If he's a man, how did he live to be thirty-something, cross oceans and seas over a hundred thousand li, and never get himself a wife?"

But Ch'ang-an remained obdurate. Both parties being none too young, several months after the engagement Lan-hsien came to Ch'i-ch'iao as Shih-fang's deputy and asked her to set a date for the wedding.

Ch'i-ch'iao pointed at Ch'ang-an. "Won't marry early, won't marry late, has to choose this year when there's no money at hand. If we have a better harvest next year, the trousseau would be more complete."

"Modern-style weddings don't go in for these things. Might as well do it the new way and save a little," Lan-hsien said.

"New ways, old ways, what's the difference? The old ways are more for show, the new ways more practical—the girl's family is the loser anyway."

"Just do whatever you see fit, Second Sister-in-law, Little Miss An is not going to argue about getting too little, is she?" At this everybody in the room laughed; even Ch'ang-an could not help a little smile.

Ch'i-ch'iao burst out, "Shameless! You have something in your belly that won't keep or what? Can't wait to get over there, as if your eyebrows were on fire. Will even do without the trousseau—you're willing, others may not be. You're so sure he's after your person? What vanity! Have you got a presentable spot on you? Stop lying to yourself. This man T'ung has his eyes on the Chiangs' name and prestige, that's all. Your family sounds so grand with its tides and its eminent generals and ministers, actually it's not so at all. It's been strong outside and shriveled up inside long since, and for these last few years couldn't even keep up appearances. Moreover, each generation of your family is worse than the one before, no regard for heaven and earth and king and parent any more. The young masters know nothing whatsoever and all the young ladies know is to grab money and want men—worse than pigs and dogs. My own family was a thousand times and ten thousand times to blame in making this match—ruined my whole life. I'm going to tell this man T'ung not to make the same mistake before it's too late."

After this quarrel Lan-hsien washed her hands of the match. Ch'i-ch'iao, convalescing, could get out of bed a bit and would sit astride the doorway and call out toward Ch'ang-an's room day after day, "You want strange men, go look for them, just don't bring them home to greet me as mother-in-law and make me die of anger. Out of sight, out of mind, that's all I ask. I'd be grateful if Miss will let me live a couple of years longer." She had just these few sentences arranged in different orders, shouted out so that the whole street could hear. Of course the talk spread among relatives, boiling and steaming.

Ch'i-ch'iao then called Ch'ang-an to her, suddenly in tears. "My child, you know people outside are saying this and that about you, have smirched you till you're not worth a copper coin. Ever since your mother married into the Chiang family, from top to bottom there's not one that's not a snob. Man stands low in dogs' eyes. I took so much from them in the open and in the dark. Even your father, did he ever do me a good turn that I'd want to stay his widow? I stayed and suffered endless hardships these twenty years, just hoping that you two children would grow up and win back some face for me. I never knew it'd come to this." And she wept.

Ch'ang-an was thunderstruck. Never mind if her mother made her out to be less than human or if outsiders said the same; let them. Only T'ung Shih-fang—he—what would he think? Did he still want her? Was there any change in his manner last time she saw him? Hard to say... She was too happy, she wouldn't notice little differences... Between the discomfort of taking the cure and these repeated provocations Ch'ang-an was already having a hard time but, forcing herself to bear up, she had endured. Now she suddenly felt as though all her bones were out of joint. Explain to him? Unlike her brother, he was not her mother's offspring and could never thoroughly understand her mother. It would have been all right if he never had to meet her mother but sooner or later he would make her acquaintance. Marriage is a lifelong affair; you can be a thief all your life but you can't always be on guard against thieves. Who knew what her mother would resort to? Sooner or later there would be trouble, sooner or later there would be a break. This was the most beautiful episode of her life, better finish it herself before other people could add a disgusting ending to it. A beautiful, desolate gesture... She knew she would be sorry, she knew she would, but unconcernedly she lifted her eyebrows and said, "Since Mother is not willing to make this match I'll just go and tell them no."

Ch'i-ch'iao held still for a moment before she went on sobbing.

Ch'ang-an paused to collect herself and went to telephone T'ung Shih-fang. Shih-fang did not have time that day, and arranged to meet her the next afternoon. What she dreaded most was the night in between, and it finally passed, each minute and every chime of the quarter hour sinking its teeth into her heart. The next day, at the old place in the park he came up smiling without greeting her; to him this was an expression of intimacy. He seemed to take special notice of her today, kept looking into her face as they walked shoulder to shoulder. With the sun shining brightly she was all the more conscious of her swollen eyelids and could hardly lift her eyes. Better say it while he was not looking at her. Hoarse from weeping, she whispered, "Mr. T'ung." He did not hear her. Then she'd better say it while he was looking at her. Surprised that she was still smiling slightly, she said in a small voice, "Mr. T'ung, I think—about us—perhaps we'd better—better leave it for now. I'm very sorry." She took off her ring and pushed it into his hand—cold gritty ring, cold gritty fingers. She quickened her pace walking away. After a stunned moment he caught up with her.

"Why? Not satisfied with me in some way?"

Ch'ang-an shook her head, looking straight ahead.

"Then why?"

"My mother . . ."

"Your mother has never seen me."

"I told you, it's not because of you, nothing to do with you. My mother . . ."

Shih-fang stood still. In China must her kind of reasoning be taken as fully adequate? As he hesitated, she was already some distance away.

The park had basked in the late autumn sun for a morning and an afternoon, and its air was now heavy with fragrance, like rotten-ripe fruit on a tree. Ch'ang-an heard, coming faintly in slow swings, the sound of a harmonica clumsily picking out "Long, Long Ago"—"Tell me the tales that to me were so dear, long, long ago, long, long ago..." This was *now*, but in the twinkling of an eye it would have become long, long ago and everything would be over. As if under a spell Ch'ang-an went looking for the person blowing the harmonica—looking for herself. Walking with her face to the sunlight, she came under a *wu-t'ung* tree with a boy in khaki shorts astride one of its forked branches. He was rocking himself and blowing his harmonica, but the tune was different, one she had never heard before. The tree was not big, and its sparse leaves shook in the sun like golden bells. Looking up, Ch'ang-an saw black as a shower of tears fell over her face. It was then that Shih-fang found her, and he stood quietly beside her for a while before he said, "I respect your opinion." She lifted her handbag to ward off the sun from her face.

They continued to see each other for a time. Shih-fang wanted to show that modern men do not make friends with women just to find a mate, and so although the engagement was broken he still asked her out often. As to Ch'ang-an, in what contradictory hopes she went out with him she herself did not know and would not have admitted if she had known. When they had been engaged and openly going out together she still had had to guard her movements. Now her rendezvous were more secret than ever. Shih-fang's attitude remained straightforward. Of course she had hurt his self-respect a little, and he also thought it a pity more or less, but as the saying goes, "a worthy man needn't worry about not having a wife." A man's highest compliment to a woman is a proposal. Shih-fang had pledged himself to relinquish his freedom. Although Ch'ang-an had declined his valuable offer, he had done her a service at no cost to himself.

No matter how subtle and awkward their relations were, they actually became friends. They even talked. Ch'ang-an's naïveté often made Shih-fang laugh and say, "You're a funny one." Ch'ang-an also began to discover that she was an amusing person. Where matters could go from here might surprise Shih-fang himself.

But rumors reached Ch'i-ch'iao. Behind Ch'ang-an's back she ordered Ch'ang-pai to send T'ung Shih-fang a written invitation to an informal dinner at home. Shih-fang guessed that the Chiangs might want to warn him not to persist in a friendship with their daughter after the break. But while he was talking with Ch'ang-pai over two cups of wine about the weather, current politics, and local news in the somber and high-ceilinged dining room, he noticed that nothing was mentioned of Ch'ang-an. Then the cold dishes were removed. Ch'ang-pai suddenly leaned his hands against the table and stood up. Shih-fang looked over his shoulder and saw a small old lady standing at the doorway with her back to the light so that he could not see her face distinctly. She wore a blue-gray gown of palace brocade embroidered with a round dragon design, and clasped with both hands a scarlet hot-water bag; two big tall amahs stood close against her. Outside the door the setting sun was smoky yellow, and the staircase covered with turquoise plaid linoleum led up step after step to a place where there was no light. Shih-fang instinctively felt this was a mad person. For no reason there was a chill in all his hairs and bones.

"This is my mother," Ch'ang-pai introduced her.

Shih-fang moved his chair to stand up and bow. Ch'i-ch'iao walked in with measured grace, resting a hand on an amah's arm, and after a few civilities sat down to offer him wine and food.

Where's Sister?" Ch'ang-pai asked. "Doesn't even come and help when we have company."

"She's coming down after smoking a couple of pipes more," Ch'i-ch'iao said.

Shih-fang was greatly shocked and stared intently at her.

Ch'i-ch'iao hurriedly explained, "It's such a pity this child didn't have proper prenatal care. I had to puff smoke at her as soon as she was born. Later, after bouts of illness, she acquired this habit of smoking. How very inconvenient for a young lady! It isn't that she hasn't tried to break it, but her health is so very delicate and she has had her way in everything for so long it's easier said than done. Off and on, it's been ten years now."

Shih-fang could not help changing color. Ch'i-ch'iao had the caution and quick wits of the insane. She knew if she was not careful people would cut her short with a mocking incredulous glance, she was used to the pain by now. Afraid that he would see through her if she talked too much, she stopped in time and busied herself with filling wine cups and distributing food. When Ch'ang-an was mentioned again she just repeated these words lightly once more, her flat sharp voice cutting all around like a razor blade.

Ch'ang-an came downstairs quietly, her embroidered black slippers and white silk stockings pausing in the dim yellow sunlight on the stairs. After stopping a while she went up again, one step after another, to where there was no light.

Ch'i-ch'iao said, "Ch'ang-pai, you drink a few more cups with Mr. T'ung. I'm going up."

The servants brought the soup called *i-p'in-kuo*, the "highest ranking pot," and changed the wine to Bamboo Leaf Green, newly heated. A nervous slave girl stood in the doorway and signaled the page waiting at the table to come out. After some whispering the boy came back to say a few words into Ch'ang-pai's ear. Ch'ang-pai got up flustered and apologized repeatedly to Shih-fang, "Have to leave you alone for a while, be right back," and also went upstairs, taking several steps in one.

Shih-fang was left to drink alone. Even the page felt apologetic. "Our Miss Chüan is about to give birth," he whispered to him.

"Who's Miss Chüan?" Shih-fang asked.

"Young Master's concubine."

Shih-fang asked for rice and made himself eat some of it. He could not leave the minute he set his bowl down, so he waited, sitting on the carved pearwood couch. Flushed from the wine, his ears hot, he suddenly felt exhausted and lay down. The scrollwork couch, with its ice-cold yellow rattan mat, the wintry fragrance of pomelos... the concubine having a baby. This was the ancient China he had been homesick for... His quiet and demure well-born Chinese girl was an opium smoker! He sat up, his head in his hands, feeling unbearably lonely and estranged.

He took his hat and went out, telling the page, "Later please inform your master that I'll thank him in person another day."

He crossed the brick-paved courtyard where a tree grew in the center, its bare branches printed high in the sky like the lines in crackle china. Ch'ang-an quietly followed behind, watching him out. There were light yellow daisies on her navy blue long-sleeved gown. Her hands were clasped and she had a gentle look seldom seen on her face.

Shih-fang turned around to say, "Miss Chiang..."

She stood still a long way off and just bent her head. Shih-fang bowed slightly, turned, and left. Ch'ang-an felt as though she were viewing this sunlit courtyard from some distance away, looking down from a tall building. The scene was clear, she herself was involved but powerless to intervene. The court, the tree, two people trailing bleak shadows, wordless—not much of a memory, but still to be put in a crystal bottle and held in both hands to be looked at some day, her first and last love.

Chih-shou lay stiffly in bed, her two hands placed palms up on her ribs like the claws of a slaughtered chicken. The bed curtains were half up. Night or day she would not have them let down; she was afraid.

Word came that Miss Chüan had given birth to a son. The slave girl tending the steaming pot of herb medicine for Chih-shou ran out to share the excitement. A wind blew in through the open door and rattled the curtain hooks. The curtains slid shut of their own accord but Chih-shou did not protest any more. With a jerk to the right, her head rolled off the pillow. She did not die then, but dragged on for another fortnight.

Miss Chüan was made a wife and became Chih-shou's substitute. In less than a year she swallowed raw opium and killed herself. Ch'ang-pai dared not marry again, just went to brothels now and then. Ch'ang-an of course had long since given up all thoughts of marriage.

Ch'i-ch'iao lay half asleep on the opium couch. For thirty

years now she had worn a golden cangue. She had used its heavy edges to chop down several people; those that did not die were half killed. She knew that her son and daughter hated her to the death, that the relatives on her husband's side hated her, and that her own kinsfolk also hated her. She groped for the green jade bracelet on her wrist and slowly pushed it up her bony arm as thin as firewood until it reached the armpit. She herself could not believe she'd had round arms when she was young. Even after she had been married several years the bracelet only left room enough for her to tuck in a handkerchief of imported crepe. As a girl of eighteen or nineteen, she would roll up the lavishly laced sleeves of her blue linen blouse, revealing a pair of snow-white wrists, and go to the market. Among those that liked her were Ch'ao-lu of the butcher shop; her brother's sworn brothers, Ting Yü-ken and Chang Shao-ch'üan, and also the son of Tailor Shen. To say that they liked her perhaps only means that they liked to fool around with her; but if she had chosen one of these, it was very likely that her man would have shown some real love as years went by and children were born. She moved the ruffled little foreign-styled pillow under her head and rubbed her face against it. On her other cheek a teardrop stayed until it dried by itself: she was too languid to brush it away.

After Ch'i-ch'iao passed away, Ch'ang-an got her share of property from Ch'ang-pai and moved out of the house. Ch'i-ch'iao's daughter would have no difficulty settling her own problems. Rumor had it that she was seen with a man on the street stopping in front of a stall where he bought her a pair of garters. Perhaps with her own money but out of the man's pocket anyway. Of course it was only a rumor.

The moon of thirty years ago has gone down long since and the people of thirty years ago are dead but the story of thirty years ago is not yet ended—can have no ending.

SEALED OFF

THE TRAMCAR driver drove his tram. The tramcar tracks, in the blazing sun, shimmered like two shiny worms oozing out from water: stretch, then shrink, stretch, then shrink. Soft and slippery, long old worms, slinking on and on and on... the driver stared at the wriggling rails, and did not go mad.

The tramcar would have gone on forever, if the city hadn't been shut down. It was. The streets were sealed off. "Ding-ding-ding-ding" rang the bell. Each "ding" was a small, cold dot: dot after dot, they formed a line that cut through space and time.

The tramcar stopped, but the people on the street started rushing around: those on the left rushed over to the right, those on the right rushed over to the left. The metal shop gates came rattling down, all in a single sweep. Matrons tugged madly at the bars. "Let us in!" they cried. "At least for a little while! There are children here, and old people too!" But the gates stayed tightly shut. The two sides glared at one another through the bars, feeding off each other's fear.

On the tram, people were fairly calm. They had somewhere to sit, and though the tram interior was shabby, it was still quite a bit better, for most passengers, than their rooms at home.

Gradually the street grew quiet too—not a complete silence but voices turned blurry, like the soft rustling of a marsh-grass pillow, heard in a dream. The huge, shambling city sat dozing in the sun, its head resting heavily on people's shoulders, its drool slipping slowly down their shirts, an inconceivably enormous weight pressing down on everyone. Never before, it seemed, had Shanghai been this quiet—and in the middle of the day! A beggar, taking advantage of the breathless, birdless quiet, lifted up his throat and began to chant: "Good master, good lady, kind sir, kind ma'am, won't you give alms to this poor soul? Good master, good lady..." But soon he stopped, overawed by the eerie quiet.

Then a braver beggar, a man from Shandong Province, broke the silence firmly. His voice was round and resonant: "Sad, sad, sad! No money do I have!" An old, old song, sung from one century down to the next. The tram driver, also from Shandong, succumbed to the sonorous tune. Heaving a long sigh, he folded his arms across his chest, leaned against the tram door, and joined in: "Sad, sad, sad! No money do I have!"

A few passengers got off. There was some scattered conversation among those who stayed, and a group of office workers, over by the door, resumed the discussion they'd been having. One of them flicked his fan open—it made a quick ripping sound—and delivered his conclusion: "Well, in the end, his problem is simply that he doesn't have any manners." Someone else snorted, and smiled sarcastically. "No manners, you say? He sure knows how to kiss up to the bosses!"

A middle-aged couple who looked very much like brother and sister stood together in the middle of the tram, holding on to the leather straps. "Careful!" she yelped. "Don't get that on your trousers!" The man flinched, then lifted his hand, dangling a parcel of smoked fish. He held the greasy paper parcel with gingery care, several inches out from his trousers. His wife did not let up. "Do you know what dry cleaning costs these days? Or what it costs to have new trousers made?"

Lu Zongzhen, accountant for Huamao Bank, was sitting in the corner. When he saw that smoked fish, he remembered the steamed spinach buns that his wife had asked him to buy at a noodle stand near the bank. Women are always like that!

Buns that are bought in the hardest-to-find, most twisty-wisty of little alleys have to be the cheapest and the best. She didn't consider how it made him look—a man smartly dressed in dapper suit and tie, with tortoiseshell glasses and a leather briefcase, and then, tucked under his arm, these steaming hot buns wrapped in newspaper—how ridiculous! Still, if the city was sealed long enough to affect his dinner hour, the buns would do, in a pinch.

He glanced at his watch; it was only four-thirty. The power of suggestion? Already he felt hungry. He loosened one corner of the paper wrapping and peeked inside. Snowy white mounds, giving off soft little whiffs of sesame oil. A piece of newspaper had stuck to a bun, and gravely he peeled it away; the ink had transferred to the bun, and the writing was in reverse, as in a mirror. He pored over the words till he could make them out: "Obituaries...Positions Wanted...Stock Market Developments ...Now Playing..."—all normal, useful expressions, though funny, somehow, seen on a bun. Eating, it seems, is serious business; it turns everything else, by way of contrast, into a joke. Lu Zongzhen thought the words looked funny, but he didn't laugh: he was a very straightforward fellow. He went from bun-print to newsprint, but after perusing half a page of old news, he had to stop: if he turned the page, all the buns would fall out.

While Lu read his newspaper, the others did likewise. People who had newspapers read newspapers; those who didn't have newspapers read receipts, or rules and regulations, or business cards. People who were stuck without a single scrap of printed matter read shop signs along the street. They simply had to fill this terrifying emptiness—otherwise, their brains might start working. Thinking is painful business.

Not a problem, however, for the old man across from Lu Zongzhen, clacking two polished walnuts around and around in his hand: a rhythmic little gesture can fill in for thought.

The old man had a clean-shaven pate, a ruddy yellow complexion, and an oily sheen on his face. When his brows were furrowed, his whole head looked like a walnut. And his brains were like walnut meat—sweet, slightly moist, and in the end, very bland.

To the old man's right sat Wu Cuiyuan, who looked very much a young Christian wife, even if she was unmarried. She wore a white linen cheongsam with narrow blue piping all around—the navy blue, next to the white, looked like the dark border around an obituary—and she carried a little blue-and-white-checked parasol. Her hairstyle was utterly banal, afraid of attracting attention. Actually, she had little reason to be afraid. She wasn't bad-looking, but hers was an uncertain, unfocused, timid kind of beauty, always trying not to offend. Her whole face was bland, limp, undefined: even her own mother couldn't say for certain whether it was long or round.

At home she was a good daughter, at school she was a good student. After graduating from college, Cuiyuan had become an English instructor at her alma mater. Now, with the city sealed off, she decided to make use of the time by grading a few papers. The first one was a male student's. It railed against the evils of the big city, full of righteous anger, the prose stiff, choppy, ungrammatical. "Lipstick-wearing prostitutes . . . cruising the Cosmo . . . seedy bars and dance halls." Cuiyuan paused for a moment, then pulled out her red pencil and gave the paper an "A." Ordinarily, she would have gone right on to the next one, but now, because of all this time for thought, she couldn't help wondering why she had given this student such a high mark. If she hadn't asked herself this question, she could have ignored the whole thing, but once she did ask, her whole face flushed red. Suddenly she understood: it was because this student was the only man who, with perfect frankness, no qualms whatsoever, raised such topics with her.

He treated her like someone who had been places and done

things; he treated her like a man, like a trusted friend. He respected her. Cuiyuan usually felt that no one at school—from the president on down to the professors, the students, and even the janitors—respected her. The students' griping was especially hard to take: "S. U. is really falling apart—getting worse all the time! A Chinese person teaching us English is already bad enough, and this one's a Chinese who's never even been abroad..."

Cuiyuan took abuse at school, and she took abuse at home. The Wu household was a modern, model household, devout and serious. The family had pushed their daughter to study hard, to climb upward step by step, right to the very top...A girl in her twenties teaching at a university! It set a new record for women's professional achievement. But her parents were losing their enthusiasm; now they wished that she had slacked off a bit as a student and worked harder at getting them a wealthy son-in-law.

She was a good daughter, a good student. All the people in her family were good people. They took baths every day; they read the newspaper every day. When they turned on the radio, they never listened to local folk opera, comic opera, that sort of thing, just symphonies by Beethoven or Wagner; they didn't understand what they were listening to, but they listened anyway. In this world, there are more good people than real people ...Cuiyuan wasn't very happy.

Life was like the Bible, translated from Hebrew to Greek, from Greek to Latin, from Latin to English, from English to Mandarin Chinese. When Cuiyuan read it, she translated the Mandarin into Shanghainese. Some things did not come through.

Cuiyuan put the student's essay down and buried her chin in her hands. The hot sun beat down on her back.

Sitting next to Cuiyuan was a nanny with a small child stretched out on her lap. The sole of the child's foot pushed against Cuiyuan's thigh. Tiny red cloth shoes, decorated with tigers, on a soft but tough little foot... this at least was real.

A medical student who was also on the tram had taken out a sketch pad and was carefully putting the last touches on a diagram of the human body. The other passengers thought he was sketching the man who sat dozing across from him. Since they had nothing else to do, they crowded around, clumping together in threes and fours, leaning on one another with their hands behind their backs, watching the man sketching from life. The man with the smoked fish whispered to his wife: "I can't get used to this cubism, this impressionism, that's so popular these days!" "Your trousers!" she hissed.

The medical student meticulously wrote in the name of every bone, nerve, muscle, and tendon. One of the office workers half covered his face with a folding fan, and quietly informed his colleague: "That's the influence of Chinese painting. Nowadays, a bit of writing is often added to Western art too—clearly a case of 'Eastern ways spreading westward.'"

Lu Zongzhen didn't join the crowd; he stayed in his seat. He had decided that he was hungry. With everyone gone, he could comfortably munch his spinach-stuffed buns. But then he looked up and glimpsed one of his relatives, his wife's cousin's son, back in the third-class car. He deeply disliked this Dong Peizhi. Peizhi was a man of humble origins who harbored a great ambition: to marry a young lady of means, to serve as a starting point for his climb to the top. Lu Zongzhen's eldest daughter had just turned thirteen; even so, she had caught Peizhi's eye. The mental calculations he had made pleased him no end, and his manner grew ever more assiduous.

When Lu Zongzhen caught sight of the young man, back in the other car, he gasped softly in alarm, afraid that Peizhi, seeing the father of his intended, might seize this golden opportunity to go on the attack. Trapped in the same car with Dong Peizhi while the city was shut down—that would be unbearable! Zongzhen quickly closed his briefcase, wrapped up the buns, and fled to a seat on the opposite side of the tram. Now Wu Cuiyuan, sitting next to him, conveniently obstructed the view. There was no way his nephew could see him.

Cuiyuan turned her head and shot him a look. What a mess! This woman must think that he was making a pass, switching seats like that, for no apparent reason. He recognized that look women get—face rigid as can be, not a trace of a smile in the eyes or on the lips, not even in the little hollows by the nose, and yet, somewhere, a trembling hint of a tiny smile that is on the verge of breaking out. When a woman feels that she really is *very* attractive, she just can't help but smile.

But—damn it! Dong Peizhi had spotted him after all and was coming toward the first-class car, very self-deprecating, bowing even at a distance, with his long, red, blushing face, and his long, gray, monkish gown—a chaste, long-suffering young man, the perfect social-climber son-in-law. Thinking fast, Zongzhen decided to steal a page from Peizhi's book and move in on an opportunity. So he stretched one arm out across the windowsill behind Cuiyuan, soundlessly announcing his flirtatious intent. He knew this would not scare Dong Peizhi into immediate retreat, because in Peizhi's eyes he already was a dirty old man. According to Peizhi, everyone over thirty was old, and everyone who was old was nasty. After he'd witnessed Zongzhen's disgraceful behavior, Peizhi would feel compelled to go and tell his wife all about it. Well, if she got riled up, that was fine with him. Her fault for saddling him with a nephew like that. Let her get angry—it would serve her right.

He didn't care too much for this woman sitting next to him. Her arms were white, true enough—white like squeezed-out toothpaste. Her whole body was like squeezed-out toothpaste, no shape at all.

"Whenever will this blockade end?" he said in a low, smiling voice. "It's awful!"

Cuiyuan jumped and turned to look at him, at which point she saw his arm stretched out behind her. Her whole body froze. But come what may, Zongzhen could not let himself pull that arm back. His nephew stood just across the way, watching him with brilliant, glowing eyes and the hint of an understanding smile. If, at this moment, he looked his nephew in the eye, maybe the young fool would get scared and drop his gaze, flustered like some sweet young thing; then again, Peizhi might give him a knowing wink—who could tell?

Zongzhen gritted his teeth, and renewed the attack. "Aren't you bored? We could chat a bit, no harm in that! Let's...let's talk!" He couldn't keep the plaintiveness out of his voice.

Once again, she was startled and turned to look at him. Now he remembered, he had seen her get on the tram—a striking image, thrown up by chance, and nothing she could have planned. "You know, I saw you getting on the tram," he said softly. "In the window at the front of the tram, there's an advertisement with a piece torn out, and I saw part of your face, just a bit of your chin, through the tear." It was an ad for Lacova powdered milk, and it showed a fat little child. Under the child's ear, this woman's chin had suddenly appeared; it was a little spooky, when you thought about it. "Then you looked down to search for change in your purse, and I saw your eyes, then your eyebrows, then your hair." When you considered her features in isolation, one after another, you had to admit she did have a certain charm.

Cuiyuan smiled. You'd never guess that this man could talk so sweetly—he looked like such a respectable businessman! She looked at him again. At the edges of his nostrils, the cartilage glowed red in the sunlight. The hand at the end of his sleeve, the hand that rested on the newspaper, was a tanned, living hand—a real person! Not too honest, not too bright, but a real person! Suddenly she felt flushed, happy. "You shouldn't be talking like that," she murmured, and turned her face away.

"Huh?" Zongzhen had already forgotten what he'd said. His eyes were fixed on his nephew's back—that tactful young man had decided that three's a crowd, and he didn't want to offend his uncle. Anyway, they'd meet again, since they were such a close family, no knife sharp enough to sever their ties; so Peizhi retreated to the third-class car. Once he was gone, Zongzhen withdrew his arm, and acted like a respectable man. Casting about for something to say, he glanced at the notebook lying on Cuiyuan's lap. "Shenguang University," he read out. "Are you a student there?"

Did he think she was so young? That she was still a student? She laughed without answering.

"I graduated from Huaqi." He repeated the name. "Huaqi." On her neck there was a small, dark mole, as if someone had given her a sharp pinch. Zongzhen rubbed the fingers of his right hand across the nails of his left, absentmindedly. He coughed slightly, then continued. "What field are you in?"

Cuiyuan saw that he had moved his arm. She thought that his change of attitude had come in response to the subtle influence of her own fine character, and that she therefore owed him an answer. "Literature. And you?"

"Business." Suddenly he felt their conversation was getting stuffy. "When I was in school, I ran around joining student movements. Now that I'm out, I run around trying to earn a living. I can't say I've ever studied much."

"Does your job keep you very busy?"

"Terribly busy. In the morning I take the tram to work, and in the evening I take it home, but I don't know why I'm going to work, or why I'm going home! I'm not the least bit interested in my job. Sure, it's a way to earn money, but I don't know who I'm earning it for!"

"Everyone has family to think of."

"Oh, you don't know—my family—" A short cough. "We'd better not talk about it!"

"Here it comes!" thought Cuiyuan. "His wife doesn't understand him. Every married man in the world seems to be in desperate need of another woman's understanding."

Zongzhen hesitated, swallowed hard, and forced the words out: "My wife—she doesn't understand me at all."

Cuiyuan looked at him, and frowned to show her sympathy.

"I don't know why, every evening when the time rolls around, I go home. What home? I don't really have a home." He removed his glasses, held them up to the light, wiped off the moisture with his handkerchief. Another little cough. "So—I just have to keep going on, and try not to think about it. I can't start thinking about it!" Cuiyuan always felt a certain revulsion when a nearsighted person removed his glasses in front of others. It was indecent, like taking off your clothes in public.

"You—you have no idea what this woman is like!" Zongzhen continued.

"Then why, back then, did you ...?"

"Even back then, I was against it. It was my mother who chose her. Of course I wanted to choose for myself, but, well, she was very beautiful, and I was quite young ... a young man, you know ..." Cuiyuan nodded.

"And then she changed into *this* kind of person. She even got into a huge fight with my mother, who turned around and blamed me for marrying her! She has such a temper ... she didn't even make it through elementary school."

Cuiyuan couldn't help saying, with a tiny smile, "You seem to think that diplomas matter a lot! Education doesn't make that much difference—for a woman." She didn't know why she said that, hurting her own pride.

"Well of course, you can laugh about it because you've been to college. You don't know what kind of—" He stopped, breathing hard, and took off the glasses he had just put back on.

"It can't be that bad, now can it?" Cuiyuan said.

Zongzhen made a jerky, awkward gesture with the glasses in his hand. "You don't know what kind of—"

Cuiyuan responded quickly: "I know, I know." She knew that if he and his wife didn't get along, it couldn't be only his wife's fault. He too was a person of limited intellect. What he wanted was a woman who'd forgive him and accept him for what he was.

The street erupted in noise as two trucks full of soldiers rumbled by. Cuiyuan and Zongzhen stuck their heads out to see what was going on; to their surprise, their faces were drawn into sudden proximity. Seen near up, anyone's face is somehow different—tension-charged like a close-up on the movie screen. Zongzhen and Cuiyuan suddenly felt they were seeing each other for the first time. To his eyes, her face was the spare, simple peony of a watercolor sketch, and the strands of hair fluttering at her temples were pistils ruffled by a breeze.

He looked at her, and she blushed. When she let him see her blush, he grew visibly happy. Then she blushed even more deeply.

Zongzhen had never thought he could make a woman blush, make her smile, make her turn her face away, then turn it back again. In this he was a man. Usually Zongzhen was an accountant, a father, a head of household, a passenger on the tram, a customer in the store, a local citizen. But to this woman who knew nothing about him, he was only and entirely a man.

They were in love. He told her all kinds of things: who at the bank was his real friend, and who was just pretending; how his family squabbled; his secret sorrows; his schoolboy dreams ... unending talk, but she was not put off. A man in love likes to talk; a woman in love changes her ways and doesn't want to talk. She knows, without even knowing that she knows, that after a man really understands a woman, he won't love her anymore.

Zongzhen was sure that Cuiyuan was a lovely woman—

pale, wispy, warm, like breath in winter. You don't want her, and quietly she drifts away. Being part of you, she understands everything, forgives everything. You tell the truth, and her heart aches for you; you tell a lie, and she smiles as if to say, "Go on—you're just pulling my leg!"

Zongzhen was quiet for a moment. Then, suddenly: "I'm thinking of marrying again."

Cuiyuan quickly assumed an air of shocked surprise. "You want to divorce your wife? You can't do that, can you?"

"I can't get a divorce. I have to consider my children's happiness. My oldest daughter is thirteen this year and she's just passed the secondary school entrance exam, with a good score too."

"What's that got to do with it?" Cuiyuan thought.

"Oh," she said aloud, and coldly, "you plan to take a concubine."

"I plan to treat her like a wife," said Zongzhen. "I'll—I'll take good care of her. I won't let her suffer in any way."

"But," said Cuiyuan, "a girl from a good family won't want to be a concubine, will she? And so many legal problems..."

Zongzhen sighed. "Yes, you are right. I can't do it. Shouldn't have even mentioned it... I'm too old. Thirty-five already."

Cuiyuan spoke very deliberately. "Well, these days that's not considered old at all."

Zongzhen was still. Finally he asked, "How... how old are you?"

Cuiyuan ducked her head. "Twenty-five."

Zongzhen was silent for a while. "Are you available?" he finally asked. Cuiyuan didn't answer. "You aren't," Zongzhen said. "And even if you were willing, your family would oppose it... that's the problem, isn't it?"

Cuiyuan pursed her lips. Her family—her prim and proper family—how she hated them! She'd had enough of their lies. They wanted her to find them a wealthy son-in-law; Zongzhen didn't have money but he did have a wife. Well, if they got mad, that would be just fine with her! It would serve them right!

The tram was filling up again. Apparently the people outside were saying that the "all clear" would come any minute now. One after another, the passengers got on and sat down; they squeezed against Zongzhen and Cuiyuan, forcing them to sit closer, then closer again.

Zongzhen and Cuiyuan wondered how they could have been so dense, not sitting closer on their own. Zongzhen felt he was too happy—he had to fight against it. "No, no, it just won't work!" His voice was agonized. "I can't let you sacrifice your future! You're a fine person, with such a good education . . . and I, I don't have much money. I can't ask you to bury yourself like that!"

Well, of course, it always comes down to money. He was only being reasonable. "It's over," Cuiyuan thought. In the end she'd probably marry, but her husband could never be as dear as this stranger met by chance . . . this man on a tram in the middle of a sealed-off city . . . it could never be this natural again. Never again . . . oh, this man, he was so stupid! So very stupid! All she wanted was one small part of him, a little part that no one else wanted. He was throwing away his own happiness. Such an idiotic waste! She wept, but it wasn't a gentle, maidenly weeping. She pretty much spit the tears all over his face. He was a good man—the world had gained one more good man!

What use would it be to explain things to him? A woman who has to use words to touch a man's heart is a sorry figure.

Once Zongzhen became anxious, he couldn't get any words out, just kept shaking the umbrella Cuiyuan was holding. She ignored him. Then he tugged at her hand. "Hey—hey—there are people here, you know! Don't! Don't get so upset! Wait a bit, and we'll talk it over on the telephone. Give me your number."

Cuiyuan didn't answer. He pressed her. "You have to give me your telephone number."

"Seven-five-three-six-nine." Cuiyuan spoke as fast as she could.

"Seven-five-three-six-nine?"

She would not answer.

"Seven-five-three-six-nine, seven-five..." Mumbling the number over and over, Zongzhen searched his pockets for a pen, but the more frantic he became, the harder it was to find one. Cuiyuan had a red pencil in her bag, but she purposely did not take it out. He ought to remember her telephone number; if he didn't, then he didn't love her, and there was no point in continuing the conversation.

The city started up again. "Ding-ding-ding-ding" rang the bell. Each "ding" was a small, cold dot: dot after dot, they formed a line that cut through space and time.

Cheers rippled through the vast city. The tram started clanking its way forward. Zongzhen suddenly stood up, pushed into the crowd, disappeared. Cuiyuan turned her head away, as if she didn't care. He had gone. To her, it was as if he were dead.

The tram picked up speed. On the evening street, a seller of curdled tofu had set his shoulder pole down and lifted his rattle; eyes shut, he shook it back and forth. A big-boned blonde with a straw hat slung across her back bantered with an Italian sailor. All her teeth showed when she grinned. Cuiyuan's eyes saw them and they lived, lived for that one moment. The tram clanked onward, and one by one they died away.

Cuiyuan shut her eyes fretfully. If he telephoned her, she wouldn't be able to control her voice; it would be filled with emotion for him, a man who had died and come back to life again.

The lights inside the tram went on; she opened her eyes and saw him sitting in his old seat, looking remote. She trembled with shock—he hadn't gotten off the tram after all! Then she understood his meaning: everything that had happened while the city was sealed off was a nonoccurrence. The whole city of Shanghai had dozed off and dreamed an unreasonable dream.

The tramcar driver raised his voice in song: "Sad, sad, sad! No money do I have! Sad, sad, sad—" An old beggar woman, thoroughly dazed, limped across the street in front of the tram. The driver bellowed at her. "Swine!"

RED ROSE, WHITE ROSE

THERE were two women in Zhenbao's life: one he called his white rose, the other his red rose. One was a spotless wife, the other a passionate mistress. Isn't that just how the average man describes a chaste widow's devotion to her husband's memory —as spotless, and passionate too?

Maybe every man has had two such women—at least two. Marry a red rose and eventually she'll be a mosquito-blood streak smeared on the wall, while the white one is "moonlight in front of my bed." Marry a white rose, and before long she'll be a grain of sticky rice that's gotten stuck to your clothes; the red one, by then, is a scarlet beauty mark just over your heart.

But Zhenbao wasn't like that; he was logical and thorough. He was, in this respect, the ideal modern Chinese man. If he did bump into something that was less than ideal, he bounced it around in his mind for a while and—poof!—it was idealized: then everything fell into place.

Zhenbao had launched his career the proper way, by going to the West to get his degree and factory training. He was smart and well educated, and having worked his way through school, he had the energy and determination of a self-made man. Now he held an upper-level position in a well-known foreign textile company. His wife was a university graduate, and she came from a good family. She was gentle and pretty, and she'd never been a party girl. One daughter, age nine: already they'd made plans for her college tuition.

Never had a son been more filial, more considerate, than

Zhenbao was to his mother; never was a brother more thoughtful or helpful to his siblings. At work he was the most hardworking and devoted of colleagues; to his friends, the kindest, truest, and most generous of men. Zhenbao's life was a complete success. If he had believed in reincarnation—he didn't—he'd have hoped simply to pick up a new name, then come back and live the same life all over again.

Rich idlers laughed at Zhenbao and called him vulgar—literary youths and progressive types did too. But since he was vulgar in a Western way, they didn't really hold it against him. Zhenbao wasn't tall, but he was vigorous and quick. He had a soy-brown face and wore black-rimmed glasses, with something peculiarly unresolved in his facial expression. His posture was excellent and he didn't joke around—unless, that is, it was appropriate to joke. He seemed frank and open, a man you could take in at a glance—and if you couldn't quite pinpoint the sincerity in his eyes, those eyeglasses were proof enough.

Zhenbao came from a poor family. If he hadn't struggled to rise in the world, he probably would have had to stand behind a counter in a shop, and then his whole existence would have been one tiny round of ignorance and stupidity. Instead, starting in on his new job after his studies abroad, his window opened up on the whole world: he had plenty of opportunities to look forward to and the benefits of an unfettered mind. An amazing degree of freedom, all in all. And yet the average man's life, no matter how good, is only a "peach blossom fan." Like the loyal, beleaguered beauty in the story, you bang your head and blood drips on the fan. Add a few strokes of ink, and the bloodstain becomes a peach blossom. Zhenbao's fan was still blank, but he had a dry brush, a wet inkstone, a sunny window, and a clean table—all just waiting for him to lower his brush and begin.

That blank fan did have some hazy figures in the background, like the images of people in old-fashioned clothes that one sees printed in light purple ink on elegant, mock-antique stationery. Before the wife and mistress, there had been two insignificant women.

The first was a Paris whore.

Zhenbao had studied textile manufacturing at a school in Edinburgh. Poor students don't have a chance to see much when abroad, and all that Zhenbao remembered of Britain was the Underground, cabbage, fog, hunger, and stuffing himself sick. As for things like opera, not until he returned home to Shanghai did he have an opportunity to see a Russian company perform. But one summer he'd laid out some money, taken off some time, and gone on a tour of the Continent. When he got to Paris, naturally he wanted to see how very naughty the Parisians were, except that he didn't have any friends who knew the town well enough to show him around. He couldn't afford—and didn't want—that kind of friend. So he plunged in all on his own, afraid of what it might cost, afraid of being cheated too.

One evening in Paris, he found himself with nothing to do. He'd eaten supper early and was walking to his lodgings in a quiet back street. "And all my friends will think that I've really seen Paris," he said to himself, almost plaintively. The streetlamps had already been lit but overhead the sun still shone, dropping bit by bit down to the roofs of the square cement buildings, dropping farther and farther. The shimmering white of the roofs seemed to be crumbling away. Zhenbao walked down the street, feeling forlorn. In one of the houses someone was playing a piano with one hand, picking out the notes: Christmas songs played very slowly, one after another. Christmas carols are joyful on Christmas Eve, but this was a summer afternoon on a long quiet street flooded with sunlight. The timing felt all wrong, like a dream so mixed-up and meaningless that it was almost funny. Zhenbao didn't know why, but he couldn't bear the sound of that one-finger melody.

He picked up his pace; his hand started to sweat in his pocket. He walked quickly, but then the woman in front of him, wearing a black dress, slowed down; she turned her head just a bit and gave him a glance. She was wearing a red slip under her black lace dress. Zhenbao liked red lingerie. He hadn't realized that a woman of this sort would be in this neighborhood, with a little hotel nearby.

Years later, when Zhenbao was telling the story to friends, he would adopt a mocking manner, happy but a tad rueful. "Before I went to Paris," he'd say, "I was just a boy! I really ought to go back someday, for old times' sake." The memory should have been a romantic one, but oddly enough he couldn't recall any of the romantic parts, only the upsetting ones. Foreigners always have more body odor than Chinese people do; this woman couldn't stop worrying about it. He noticed how she'd half consciously raise one arm and turn her head to sniff. The armpits of her clothing were sprayed with perfume; cheap perfume mixed with armpit odor and sour sweat made for a strange smell that he couldn't get out of his head. But what he hated most was her constant worrying. When she came out of the bathroom in her slip, she rested her hand high on the wall, tilted her head to the side, and smiled at him—but he knew that at some level she was sniffing herself.

With a woman like this—even with a woman like this!— though he could spend money on her, he couldn't be her master. The half hour he spent with her filled him with shame.

There was another detail he could never forget. She was putting her clothes back on, pulling her dress over her head, and when she was half there, with the fabric still piled up around her shoulders, she stopped for a moment as if she'd thought of something. Right then, he saw her in the mirror. She had a mass of tousled blond hair, pulled tight by the dress so that only her long, thin face showed. Her eyes were blue, a blue that ran down into the shadows under her eyes, while the eyes themselves were like two transparent glass balls. It was a cold, severe, masculine face, the face of an ancient warrior. Zhenbao was badly shaken.

When he came out, the sun was still shining, with the shadows of the trees lying crooked in the sunlit street. This too was not right. It was terrifying.

Whoring can be sleazy, low-class, filthy-miserable, and it won't matter—that just makes it all the earthier. But it wasn't like that, not this time. Later, when Zhenbao had figured out how to get what he wanted out of a whore, he'd think back to that time in Paris, his first time, when he'd been such a fool. Now he was the master of his own world.

From that day on, Zhenbao was determined to create a world that was "right," and to carry it with him wherever he went. In that little pocket-size world of his, he was the absolute master.

Zhenbao lived in England for a considerable time. His factory internship paid a stipend, and he rustled up odd jobs on the side. Once he'd made himself a bit more comfortable, financially speaking, he acquired a few girlfriends. He was a nice fellow, and he wanted to meet a nice girl, not some prostitute. But he was also a busy man who couldn't spend lots of time on courting; naturally he liked girls who were a little more forthright. There were only a few Chinese girls in Edinburgh, two of them classmates who hailed from the inland provinces—he found them too affected, too churchy, altogether too pious. Nowadays the churches have become something of a social scene, with quite a few beauties on display, but ten years ago, the fervent churchgoers who had love in their hearts weren't, in fact, lovely. The lively ones were the overseas Chinese; mixed-blood girls went even farther.

Zhenbao met a girl named Rose. She was his first love, which is why he also likened his two later women to roses. Rose's father was a good-looking English businessman who'd lived in southern China for many years and then, thanks to a passing fancy, married a Cantonese girl and brought her home to Edinburgh. The wife had to be living in the house still, but she was practically invisible and never took part in social events. Rose attended an English school, and because she wasn't completely English she acted more English than the English themselves. The English students liked to affect a certain dashing indifference, and when something really important was at stake, the affectation grew even stronger. Zhenbao couldn't figure out whether or not Rose really loved him; he, for his part, was rather dazzled. They both liked to do things fast, and on Saturday nights they made the rounds of different dance halls. When they weren't out on the dance floor, but just sitting around and talking, Rose never seemed to pay much attention. She'd take out some matches and try to balance a glass on top of them. Zhenbao was supposed to help. That was Rose: solemn as could be when she was horsing around. There was a canary at her place, and whenever it sang she thought it was calling to her. "Yes, bird?" she'd answer right off, standing on tiptoe with her hands behind her back, and her face tilted up toward the birdcage. Her tan face was long, not round like a child's, but at such moments she seemed remarkably childlike. She'd gaze wide-eyed at the bird in the cage, the whites of her eyes tinged blue, as if she were staring into deep blue skies.

Rose may have been the most ordinary of girls, but her very youth made her remarkably hard to read. Like that canary—calling out but not really saying anything to anyone.

Her short skirt ended above her knees, and her legs were light and nimble, as delicately made as wooden legs in a shop window; her skin was as smooth and glistening as freshly planed and oiled wood. Her hair was cut very short, shaved down to a little point at the nape of her neck. No hair to protect her neck, no sleeves to protect her arms—Rose did not watch her words, and her body was open for the taking. She was carefree with Zhenbao, and he put that down to her being innocent, but her being so carefree with everyone struck him as slightly nutty. This kind of woman was common enough in foreign countries, but in China it would never do. Marrying her, then transplanting her to his hometown—that would be a big waste of time and money, not a good deal at all.

One evening he drove her home, as he often did. But this time it seemed different because he was going to leave England soon and if he had anything to say he should have said it by now. He hadn't. Her house was quite far from town. The faint black-and-white of the late-night road patted their faces like a powder puff. The conversation in the car was desultory in the English fashion, starting and stopping again. Rose knew that she had already lost him. Then, out of a kind of hopeless obstinacy, her heart caught fire. "Stop here," she said, when they had almost reached her house. "I don't want to let my family see us saying good-bye." "I'd kiss you even in front of them," Zhenbao said, smiling. He reached out to wrap his arm around her shoulder, and she buried her face into his chest. The car kept going—they were well past her house before it stopped. Zhenbao slid his hand under her velvet coat and pulled her toward him. Behind her aching-cold diamonds, crinkly silver lace, hundreds of exquisite nuisances, her young body seemed to leap out of her clothes. Zhenbao kissed her, and tears streamed over her face till neither of them could tell who was crying. Outside the car, a damp, limitless fog floated in the wind. Its emptiness sapped their strength, and all they could do was hang on to each other. Rose clung to his neck, this way then that, trying to pull ever closer, wishing she could fuse her body with his, press herself into it. Zhenbao was so confused that he couldn't think. He had never dreamed that Rose loved him so much; he could have done whatever he wanted. But ... this would not do. Rose, after all, was a decent girl. This sort of thing was not for him.

Rose's body leapt out of her clothes, leapt onto his body, but he was his own master.

Afterward, even he was surprised by his self-control. He'd hardened his heart and taken Rose home. Just before he left, he held her moist face, with its sniffles and tears and quivering eyelashes that fluttered in his palms like some tiny winged creature. In later days, he'd recall this experience whenever he needed to rally his strength: "If you could control yourself then, in that situation, surely you can do so now."

His behavior that evening filled him with astonishment and admiration, and yet in his heart he felt regret. Without admitting it, he felt quite a lot of regret.

He seldom mentioned the incident, but there was not one of his friends who was unaware of Zhenbao's reputation as a regular Liu Xiahui, a man who could keep perfectly calm with a beautiful woman in his lap. Word had gotten around.

Zhenbao's grades were excellent, and before he'd even graduated he was offered a position at Great Beneficence, an English dyeing and weaving company; he started there immediately upon his return to Shanghai. Zhenbao's family home was in Jiangwan, quite far from his job, and at first he stayed with some old family friends. But when his younger brother, Tong Dubao, finished his secondary schooling, Zhenbao made arrangements for Dubao to come and live with him, so he could help him with his studies; he wanted Dubao to take the entrance exam for the technical school that was affiliated with the Great Beneficence Dyeing and Weaving Company. They couldn't both stay in the friends' home; that would be too great an imposition. As it happened, an old classmate of Zhenbao's, Wang Shihong, had an empty room in his place. Wang Shihong had been abroad and had come back to Shanghai two years before Zhenbao; now he was living in an apartment on Ferguson Road. He and Zhenbao struck a deal—the room was even furnished.

On the day he was to move in, Zhenbao left work just after dusk. He and his brother were busy supervising the coolies as they carried the trunks in, and Wang Shihong was standing arms akimbo in the doorway, when a woman walked in from the room behind. She was washing her hair, which was all lathered up with shampoo, the white curls standing high on her head like a marble sculpture. "While the workmen are here," she said to Shihong, holding her hair with her hands, "have them arrange all the furniture and things. It's no use asking our majordomo to help: he'll just make excuses—if he's not in the mood he won't do anything."

"Let me introduce everyone," said Wang Shihong. "Zhenbao, Dubao, my wife. I believe you haven't met yet?"

The woman withdrew her hand from her hair to shake hands with the guests, but seeing the shampoo on her fingers, she hesitated. She nodded and smiled instead, then wiped her fingers on her dressing gown. A little shampoo splashed the back of Zhenbao's hand. Instead of rubbing it off, he let it dry there. The skin puckered up slightly, as if a mouth were lightly sucking at the spot.

Mrs. Wang turned and went back into the other room. Zhenbao directed the workers as they moved the bed and wardrobe, but he felt troubled, and the sucking sensation was still there. His mind wandered as he headed to the bathroom to wash his hands, thinking about this Mrs. Wang. He'd heard that she was an overseas Chinese from Singapore who, when she was studying in London, was quite a party girl. She and Wang Shihong got married in London, but Zhenbao had been too busy to attend the wedding. Seeing her was much better than hearing about her: under her white, shampoo-sculpted hair was a tawny gold face, the skin glistening and the flesh so firm that her eyes rose at a long upward slant, like the eyes of an actress. Her striped dressing gown, worn without a belt, hugged her body loosely, and the black-and-white stripes

263

hinted at her figure, each line, each inch, fully alive. People like to say that the wide, long-sleeved gowns of former times didn't flatter curvaceous beauties, but Zhenbao had just discovered that this was not the case. He turned on the faucet. The water wasn't very hot, though the water heater downstairs was certainly on, and yet the lukewarm stream seemed to have a lighted wick running through it. Twisting and winding, the water ran from the faucet, every inch of it alive, while Zhenbao's mind went running off to who knows where.

Wang Shihong heard the sound of running water and came into the bathroom. "Do you want to take a bath? The water never comes up hot in this bathroom. The hot water pipe wasn't connected properly. That's one bad thing about this apartment. If you want to wash, come into our bathroom."

"Oh no, please don't bother," Zhenbao said. "Isn't your wife washing her hair?"

"She must be finished by now. I'll go and have a look."

"Oh, really, it's not that important."

Wang Shihong went to speak with his wife, and his wife said, "I'm just finishing. Tell the amah to draw him a bath."

A little later, Wang Shihong told Zhenbao to bring his soap, towel, and clothes into their bathroom. Mrs. Wang was still in front of the mirror, struggling to get a comb through her tightly permed hair. The bathroom was full of steam, and the night wind blew in through the open window. On the floor, clusters of fallen hair swirled about like ghostly figures.

Zhenbao stood outside the door holding his towel and watching the tangled hair, in the glare of the bathroom light, drifting across the floor. He felt quite agitated. He liked women who were fiery and impetuous, the kind you couldn't marry. Here was one who was already a wife, and a friend's wife at that, so there couldn't be any danger, but... look at that hair! It was everywhere. She was everywhere, tugging and pulling at him.

The couple stood in the bathroom talking, but the water filling the tub was loud and Zhenbao couldn't hear what they said. When the tub was full, they came out so he could take his bath. After his bath, Zhenbao crouched down and started picking up stray hairs from the floor tiles and twisting them together. The permed hair had turned yellow at the ends; it was stiff, like fine electrical wire. He stuffed it into his pocket. His hand stayed there, and his whole body tingled. But this was too ridiculous. He extracted the hair from his pocket and tossed it into the spittoon.

Carrying his soap and towel, he returned to his own room—Dubao was opening the trunks and arranging things. "What kind of person could the previous tenant have been?" Dubao asked. "Look, here under the chair slipcovers, and under the carpet here—those have got to be cigarette burns! And these marks under the table—they won't come off. Mr. Wang isn't going to blame us is he?"

"Of course not. They must know about it already. Besides, we're classmates from way back, so they won't be as petty as you are!" Zhenbao smiled.

Dubao fell silent. Then he asked, "Do you know who the previous tenant was?"

"His family name is Sun I think; he's back from England, teaching at a university now. Why do you ask?"

Dubao smiled before he spoke. "Just now when you were gone, the majordomo and the amah came to put up the curtains. They said something about not knowing how long we'll stay, and they said that Mr. Wang had wanted to kick out the man who lived here before. Mr. Wang was planning to go to Singapore on business, and he should have left a long time ago, but something happened and he got nervous—he wouldn't leave till the other fellow was out. Neither of them budged—not for two whole months."

Zhenbao told him to shush. "How can you believe such

nonsense! When you live in someone's house, the first rule is never to discuss the family with the servants. That only leads to trouble!" Dubao didn't say anything more.

A bit later, the amah came to call them to dinner, and the brothers went into the dining room together. The cooking in the Wang household had a slightly Southeast Asian flavor, Chinese food prepared Western style, and the main dish was lamb curry. Mrs. Wang had nothing but a thin slice of toast and a piece of ham in front of her. She even cut the fatty part off the meat and gave it to her husband.

"Such a small appetite?" Zhenbao smiled.

"She's afraid of getting fat," said Shihong.

Zhenbao's face expressed disbelief. "Mrs. Wang looks just right. She's not fat at all."

"I've just lost five pounds, so I'm a lot thinner than I was," she said.

Shihong grinned and reached over to pinch her cheek. "A lot thinner? Then what's this?"

His wife gave him a sharp glance. "That's the London lamb I ate last year." Everyone laughed hard at this.

Even though the Tong brothers and Mrs. Wang had just met for the first time, their hostess hadn't bothered to change before coming to the dinner table. She was still in her dressing gown and her hair was still wet. A white towel was wrapped carelessly around it, and every so often the towel dripped, spangling her eyebrows. Dubao was a country boy, and Mrs. Wang's free-and-easy ways struck him as strange indeed. But even Zhenbao found her pretty remarkable. Mrs. Wang was extremely attentive, asking all sorts of questions. She wasn't very good at keeping house, that was clear, but she did know how to entertain.

"I haven't had time to tell you," Shihong said to Zhenbao, "but I'm leaving tomorrow. I have some business in Singapore. It's good that you've moved in and can take care of things here."

"Mrs. Wang is very capable," Zhenbao said with a smile.

"She'll be taking care of us, I'm sure. I very much doubt that it will be us taking care of her."

"Don't be fooled by her chatter," said Shihong. "She doesn't understand a thing. She's been in China for three years now, but she still isn't used to it here, and she can't really speak Chinese well."

Mrs. Wang smiled slightly and didn't disagree. She merely summoned the amah to fetch a bottle of medicine from the cabinet, and poured out a spoonful. Zhenbao saw the thick liquid, like white paint, in the spoon, and winced. "Is that cream of calcium? I've taken that before—it tastes terrible."

Mrs. Wang emptied the spoon down her throat. For a moment she was speechless, but then she swallowed the medicine. "It's like drinking a wall!" she said. Zhenbao smiled again. "When Mrs. Wang talks, she hits the nail right on the head!"

"Mr. Tong," said Mrs. Wang, "don't keep calling me Mrs. Wang." She got up and went over to a desk near the window. It's true, Zhenbao was thinking to himself, the name "Mrs. Wang" is just too commonplace. She sat at the desk, apparently writing something. Shihong went over to her, put his hand on her shoulder, and bent down to ask, "You're perfectly healthy, so why are you taking doses of that?"

Mrs. Wang kept on writing, without turning her head. "The heat is rising in my system—I've got a pimple on my face."

"Where?" said Shihong, leaning his face close. She moved aside lightly, frowning and smiling at once. "Hey there, hey there!" she warned him.

Dubao, raised in an old-fashioned family, had never seen a husband and wife like this. He was unable to sit still and left to admire the scenery. He opened the glass door and walked onto the balcony. Zhenbao went on peeling an apple with a fair degree of composure. But Mrs. Wang came back across the room, and thrust a piece of paper at him. "There, I too have a given name," she said.

"The way you write Chinese characters, you shouldn't show them around," Shihong said with a smile. "People will just laugh."

When Zhenbao saw the three crooked words on the paper, each one bigger than the last, and the last one breaking apart into three distinct fragments—wang jiAO RUI—he really had to laugh.

"I told you people would laugh, didn't I?" Shihong said with a clap of his hands.

"No, no," said Zhenbao, controlling himself. "Really it's a pretty name!"

"Those overseas Chinese—the names they pick never have any style," said Shihong.

Pouting, Jiaorui grabbed the piece of paper and crumpled it up. She turned on her heels and walked off, seemingly in a huff. Not thirty seconds later she came back with an open jar of candied walnuts, which she'd already started to eat, and she offered them to Zhenbao and Dubao.

"I thought you were afraid of getting fat!" laughed Shihong.

"It's true," said Zhenbao. "Sweets are very fattening."

"You don't know about those overseas Chinese, they—" Shihong started to say, but Jiaorui hit him. "It's always 'they, them, those overseas Chinese'!" she said. "Don't call me 'them'!"

Shihong went right on. "They have the bad habits of the Chinese and the bad habits of foreigners as well. From the foreigners they learn to be afraid of getting fat, won't eat this, won't eat that, always taking purgatives but can't stop eating sweets. But then—go ahead, just ask her! If you ask her why she's eating this, she'll say she's had a little cough recently, and candied walnuts are good for a cough."

"That really is the old Chinese way," Zhenbao said with a smile. "Anything you like to eat is, of course, good for something."

Jiaorui picked up a walnut and slid it between her teeth. She pointed her little finger at Zhenbao. "Stop that now—there really is some truth to it!"

To Zhenbao, she seemed drunk. Fearing the kind of faux pas that so often follows drink, he mumbled something inconsequential and strolled onto the balcony. The breeze was cool on his skin: most likely his face had been pretty red a moment before. Now he was even more troubled. He'd just put an end to his relationship with Rose, and here she was again, in a new body, with a new soul—and another man's wife. But this woman went even further than Rose. When she was in the room, the walls seemed to be covered with figures in red chalk, pictures of her half naked, on the left, on the right, everywhere. Why did he keep running into this kind of woman? Was it his fault that he always reacted the way he did? Surely that couldn't be. After all, there really weren't many women of this sort, not among the pure Chinese. He'd just returned to China, so he was running with the half-Chinese, half-Western crowd. Any Chinese he met while abroad was "an old friend found in a faraway land." When he returned home and saw those "old friends" again, the first time they met they were bosom friends, the second time mere acquaintances, and by the third time they were strangers to each other.

And yet, when it came to this Wang Jiaorui, hadn't Shihong done pretty well for himself by marrying her? Of course, Wang Shihong's father had money; if a man had to forge ahead on his own, as Zhenbao did, such a woman would be a major impediment. And he wasn't easygoing like Wang Shihong, who let a woman flout every rule. What was the point if you had to argue all day long? That was sure to sap a man's energy and drain him of ambition. Of course...she was like this precisely because her husband couldn't control her; if Wang Shihong had managed to get a handle on her, she wouldn't be quite so unruly.

Zhenbao leaned on the railing, his arms folded. Down below, an electric tram with a brightly burning lamp stopped at the entrance of the building. Several people got on and off, and the lamp moved away. Wide and quiet, the street stretched beyond him; the only light was from a little restaurant on the first floor. Two leaves skittered by in the wind like ragged shoes not worn by anyone, just walking along by themselves. So many people in the world—but they won't be coming home with you. When night fell and silence took over—or when, as could happen at any time, you stood at the brink of death —there in the dark, you needed a wife you really loved, otherwise there would be nothing but loneliness. Zhenbao didn't think this through clearly, but he was overwhelmed by a sense of foreboding.

Shihong and his wife were chatting as they walked onto the balcony. "Is your hair dry?" Shihong asked. "If you stand in the breeze your cough is going to get worse."

"It doesn't matter," said Jiaorui, unwrapping the towel and shaking out her hair.

Zhenbao figured that since Shihong was leaving the next day, the couple would want to speak in privacy. Raising a hand to disguise a forced yawn, he said, "We'll go to bed now. Dubao has to get up very early tomorrow so he can go to school and get a student handbook."

"I'm leaving in the afternoon," Shihong said, "so I probably won't see you." The two men shook hands and said good-bye. Zhenbao and Dubao went to their room.

The next day, when Zhenbao came back from work and pressed the doorbell, Jiaorui opened the door, phone receiver in hand. It was dim in the hallway, which made it hard to see, but Shihong's hat and coat were gone from the coatrack, along with the leather suitcase that had been under the rack. He must have left already. Taking off his coat and hanging it on the rack, Zhenbao heard Jiaorui dial a phone number in the other room. "Please ask Mr. Sun to come to the phone," she said. Zhenbao listened. He heard her ask, "Is this Timmy? No, I'm not going out today, I'm at home waiting for a boyfriend." She started to giggle. "Who is he? I'm not telling you. Why should I tell you? ...Ah, so you're not interested? Not even interested in yourself, are you...Anyway, I'm waiting for him to come for tea at five o'clock. I'm waiting specially for him, so don't come over."

Zhenbao went to his room without waiting for her to finish. His brother wasn't there, or in the bathroom either. He went out to see if he was on the balcony, and Jiaorui emerged from the living room to greet him. "Dubao asked me to tell you that he's making the rounds of the used bookstores to see if he can find some books."

"Oh, thank you," said Zhenbao. He took a good long look. She was wearing a long dress that trailed on the floor, a dress of such intense, fresh, and wet green that anything it touched turned the same color. When she moved a little, the air was streaked with green. The dress had been cut a bit too small, it seemed: the seams along the side were split open an inch and a half, then laced together, in a crisscross pattern, over a green satin strip that didn't fully cover a startling pink slip. Looked at too long, those eye-popping colors would prove blinding. Only Jiaorui could wear a dress like that with such utter insouciance.

"Would you like some tea?" she asked, turning back into the living room. She sat down at the table, and lifted the pot to pour the tea. The table was set for two, with a plate of butter biscuits and toast. Zhenbao stood by the glass door.

"Isn't there a guest coming?"

"We won't wait for him. Let's go ahead and have something to eat."

Zhenbao hesitated, unable to figure out what she had in mind. Then, just for the time being, he sat down.

"Do you take milk?" Jiaorui asked.

"Either way."

"Oh, that's right, you like green tea. You were abroad so

many years and couldn't get it there—that's what you said yesterday."

"You have a good memory."

Getting up to ring the bell, Jiaorui threw him a glance. "No, you don't know. Usually my memory is terrible."

Zhenbao's heart jumped, and he was knocked off balance. The amah came in. "Make two cups of green tea," Jiaorui ordered.

"Ask her to bring another teacup and plate while she's at it," said Zhenbao, "for the guest who's coming later."

Jiaorui gave him a sharp look. "Who is this guest that you're so anxious about? Amah, bring me a pen and a piece of paper." She dashed off a note, then pushed it across to Zhenbao. Two lines, simple and succinct: *Dear Timmy, So very sorry, but I have something to do today. I've gone out.—Jiaorui*. She folded the paper over and gave it to the amah. "Mr. Sun will come in a little while. When he does, give this to him and tell him I'm not home."

The amah went out. Zhenbao took a biscuit. "I don't understand you," he said. "Why go to so much trouble, asking a man to come to your house, then turn him away empty-handed?"

Jiaorui leaned forward, carefully considering the selection of biscuits on the plate, but she couldn't find any that she liked. "When I asked him to come I didn't plan to turn him away."

"Oh? A last-minute decision?"

"Don't you know the saying? It's a woman's prerogative to change her mind."

The amah brought the green tea, leaves floating all over the surface of the water. Zhenbao held the glass in both hands without drinking. His eyes were fixed on the tea but his mind was elsewhere, working things out. Jiaorui was still carrying on with that Mr. Sun behind her husband's back, and evidently she was worried that Zhenbao would see what was going on. That's why she'd put on this sweet act today. She wanted to win him over so he'd keep his mouth shut. But in fact Zhenbao had no intention of interfering in their private lives. It wasn't that his bond with Wang Shihong was too weak—even if they'd been blood brothers, stirring up disputes between a husband and wife was not his style. Even so, this woman could cause a lot of trouble. Zhenbao redoubled his caution.

Jiaorui set down her tea glass and rose to get a jar of peanut butter from the cabinet. "I'm a trashy person, and I like to eat trashy things."

"Oh, my! This stuff is very rich, very fattening!"

Jiaorui took off the lid. "I love breaking the rules. Don't you approve of rule-breaking?"

Zhenbao put his hand on top of the glass jar. "No."

Jiaorui hesitated for a long moment. Then she said, "How about this? You put some on the bread for me. I'm sure you won't give me too much."

Her expression was so pitiful that he couldn't help laughing. Zhenbao spread peanut butter on the bread. Jiaorui watched him closely over the edge of her cup, pursed her lips, and laughed. "Do you know why I had you do it for me? If I did it myself, all of a sudden I might turn conscientious and spread it as thin as possible. But I know that you'd feel bad if you only gave me a little!" At this they both laughed. Unable to resist Jiaorui's childlike charm, Zhenbao gradually softened.

As they were drinking their tea, the doorbell sounded. Zhenbao got restless. For the third time now he asked, "Is that the guest you invited? Don't you feel embarrassed?" Jiaorui shrugged.

Taking his glass with him, Zhenbao went out to the balcony. "When he comes back through the door, I want to see the kind of person he is."

"Him?" said Jiaorui, following behind. "Very pretty. Too, too pretty."

"You don't like pretty men?" said Zhenbao, leaning against the railing.

"Men should not be pretty. Men get spoiled even more easily than women do."

Zhenbao lowered his eyelids, then looked at her. "You shouldn't talk about others," he said with a smile. "You've been terribly spoiled."

"Maybe. But you're just the opposite. You deny yourself when in fact you like to eat and play around as much as I do."

"Really?" Zhenbao laughed. "And you know all about it!"

Jiaorui looked down and started picking tea leaves out of her glass. She kept picking away, until at last she took a sip. Zhenbao too drank his tea in silence.

A little while later, a man in a Western suit came out of the building. Zhenbao couldn't see much from the third floor, but it looked like the man rushed around the corner, his body tense with anger.

"Poor guy," Zhenbao couldn't help saying. "He came all this way for nothing!"

"So what? He has nothing to do all day long! I too have nothing to do, but I have no respect for people like me. What I like most is to wrest a bit of time from a man who's already very busy—the way a tiger seizes its prey. Pretty despicable, don't you think?"

Zhenbao was leaning against the railing. He tapped his foot against the railing and then, bit by bit, not entirely intentionally, he started kicking at her rattan chair. When the chair shook, the flesh on her arm trembled slightly. She wasn't fat at all, but because of her small frame she seemed plump. "So you like busy men?" Zhenbao smiled.

Jiaorui hid her eyes with her hand. "Actually, it doesn't matter. My heart's an apartment."

"So—is there an empty room for rent?" Jiaorui didn't answer. "I'm not used to living in an apartment. I want to live in a single-family house."

She gave a little grunt of disbelief. "Well," she said, "let's see if you can tear one down and build the other!"

Zhenbao gave her chair a good hard kick. "Just watch me!"

Jiaorui took her hand from her eyes and gave him a long look. "You're wicked!"

"Can't help myself, with you."

"Come on, be serious," Jiaorui said. "Why don't you tell me something about your past."

"What past?"

Jiaorui's leg swept out, almost spilling the tea in his hand. "Faker! I already know all about it."

"If you know, why ask? Wouldn't it be better if you told me something about your past?"

"My past?" She leaned her head to one side and rubbed her cheek on her shoulder. After a long moment's silence, she softly said, "There isn't much to tell." There was another long silence.

"Well then, please tell," Zhenbao urged. But Jiaorui fell into thought and said nothing, her eyes fixed straight ahead. "How did you and Shihong meet?" he asked.

"In a very ordinary way," she said. "The student associations held a meeting in London. I was a representative and so was he."

"Were you at the University of London?"

"My family sent me to London to study, but the real reason was to find a suitable husband. I was quite young and had no wish at all to get married, but I used this as an excuse to escape from home and have a good time. After a few years of having a good time, my reputation wasn't all that good, so I looked around and grabbed this Shihong fellow."

Zhenbao kicked her chair lightly. "And you still haven't had enough of the good times?"

"It's not a question of having enough or not. Once you've learned to do something, you can't just put it aside and give it up."

"Don't forget that you're in China now," Zhenbao said with a smile.

Jiaorui finished her tea in one swallow, stood, and spat the tea leaves over the railing. "In China, you have Chinese freedoms: you can spit on the street if you want."

The doorbell rang again, and Zhenbao guessed that it was his brother. It was in fact Dubao, and now that he was back, things took a different turn.

Later on, Zhenbao reviewed the whole scene in his mind. Out on the dusky balcony he hadn't been able to see her clearly; he'd only heard her soft voice secretly rustling, tickling his ear like a breath. There in the dark, her heartrending body slipped out of his mind for a moment, and he had a chance to see what else there was to her. She seemed smart and straightforward, but with the emotions of a still-maturing girl—even though she was a wife already. That, for him, was her most appealing feature. There was a danger here, a danger much greater than simple lust. He could not, must not, get serious about her! It would only be looking for trouble. Maybe . . . maybe it was just her body after all. When a man yearns for a woman's body, then starts to care about her mind, he fools himself into believing that he's in love. Only after possessing her body can he forget her soul. This may be the only way to free himself. And why not? Jiaorui had a lot of lovers—one more or one less wouldn't make much difference. He couldn't pretend that Wang Shihong wouldn't care, but then again it wouldn't make things any worse than they already were, for him.

Suddenly, Zhenbao realized that he was digging for reasons to justify sleeping with this woman. He was mortified, and resolved to avoid her from this point on. He would look for another place to live. As soon as he found something, he would move. Zhenbao asked someone to help him get a bed for his brother in the dormitory at the technical school. With only himself to look after, things were easy to arrange. He'd been taking his lunches at a restaurant near the office; now he went out for dinner too. He stayed away until late at night and went straight to bed.

But one night the phone rang for a long time, and no one picked up. Zhenbao had just run out of his room to get it when he thought he heard Jiaorui's door opening. Afraid of running into her in the dark hallway, he beat a retreat. Jiaorui was groping around in the dark, seemingly unable to find the phone, and since Zhenbao was right by the light switch, he turned it on. He was stunned when he saw Wang Jiaorui in the light. She was wearing pajamas made out of a sarong fabric often worn by overseas Chinese in Southeast Asia, and it looked like she had just come from her bath. The design on the fabric was so heavy and dark that he couldn't tell whether it was snakes and dragons, or grasses and trees, the lines and vines all tangled up together, black and gold flecked with orange and green. Night deepened in the house. The dim lamp-lit hallway felt like a train car traveling from one strange place to another. On the train you meet a woman quite by accident—a woman who could be a friend.

Jiaorui lifted the receiver with one hand, the other hand searching along her side to find a little golden peach-stone button and slip it through its loop. She couldn't get it to button properly. Zhenbao didn't see anything, but he was shaken. His heart hung in midair. Jiaorui had turned sideways, and swept her loose, uncombed hair back across her shoulders. Her face was shadowy and golden, like an idol's; her lowered eyelashes cast long shadows that touched her cheek like the fingers of a small hand. She'd been in such a hurry that she'd lost one of her leather slippers. The bare foot rested on the slippered one.

Zhenbao noticed a trace of heat-rash powder on her ankle. Jiaorui hung up the phone. It was a wrong number. She stood there unsteadily, then sank into a chair, the phone still in her hand. Zhenbao put his hand on the doorknob to show that he didn't intend to chat. He nodded. "How is it that I haven't seen you lately?" he said. "I thought you'd melted away like candy." He knew, of course, that it was he who'd been avoiding her, not the other way around, but jumping in before she'd had a chance to speak was a form of self-defense. It was tiresome, no doubt, but when he saw her, he had to flirt. Some women are like that.

"Am I so sweet?" she replied nonchalantly, feeling around for her slipper with her bare foot.

"I don't know," Zhenbao replied boldly. "Haven't tasted."

Jiaorui gave a little laugh. She still couldn't find the slipper, and Zhenbao couldn't stand it anymore. He walked over and leaned down to pick it up for her, but just then her foot slipped in.

Now he was embarrassed. "Where have your servants gone?" he demanded, for no reason.

"An old hometown neighbor came to visit the majordomo and amah, and the three of them went off to the Cosmo to have some fun."

"Oh." Then, with a smile, he said, "Aren't you afraid of being alone in the house?"

Jiaorui stood up. Her slippers scuffed along as she went toward her room. "Afraid of what?"

"You're not afraid of me?"

"What?" she said without turning her head. "I'm not afraid of being alone with a gentleman!"

Now Zhenbao leaned back against the doorknob, his hand behind him, as if he had no intention of leaving. "I've never pretended to be a gentleman."

"A real gentleman doesn't need to pretend." She had opened her door, but then reached back to flick off the hall light. Zhenbao stood in the darkness, thoroughly shaken. In spite of his excitement, she was gone.

Zhenbao tossed and turned all night, telling himself that it wouldn't matter, that Jiaorui and Rose were not the same, that a married woman who did what she liked was the loosest of women, that he didn't owe her anything. But he felt a sense of duty toward himself. When he thought about Rose, he thought of that night in the car in the open fields when his conduct had been so sterling: How could he shrug off the man he'd shown himself to be?

Two weeks passed, and all at once the weather turned warm. Zhenbao went to work in his shirtsleeves, but before long it started to sprinkle and a chill blew in. He went back during his lunch break to get his coat. It had been hanging on the rack in the hall, but now it was gone. He searched and searched for it and eventually he started to worry. He saw that the living-room door had been left ajar. He pushed it open and there was his coat, hooked on the frame of an oil painting: Jiaorui was sitting on the sofa beneath, quietly lighting a cigarette. Surprised, Zhenbao quickly retreated, squeezing himself out of sight. But he couldn't resist taking another peek. Jiaorui, it turned out, wasn't smoking at all. There was an ashtray on the arm of the sofa, and she struck a match, lit the stub of an old cigarette, and watched it burn all the way down. When at last it singed her fingers, she threw the butt aside, lifted her fingers to her mouth and blew on them lightly, a look of utter content-ment on her face. The cloisonné ashtray, he realized, was from his room.

Zhenbao was bewildered, and he slipped away like a thief. It seemed incomprehensible at first, and even after thinking it through, he was mystified: Jiaorui, smitten, sitting near his coat and letting the cigarette scent from his clothes waft down over her. As if that weren't enough, she'd lit his used cigarette butts ... she really was a child, spoiled rotten, someone who'd always gotten whatever she wanted, and now that she'd run into some-one with an ounce of resistance, she dreamed only of him. The mind of a child and the beauty of a grown woman: the most tempting of combinations. Zhenbao could no longer resist.

He still ate dinner in a restaurant and arranged to meet several friends there, but the longer he sat in the crowd the more insipid he found the talk, the more detestable the company. He was impatient throughout the meal, and afterward he jumped on a bus to go back to the apartment. Jiaorui was playing the piano: "Shadow Waltz," a tune popular at the time. Hands thrust into his pockets, Zhenbao paced the balcony. The lamp on the piano lit up Jiaorui's face; he had never seen her looking so peaceful. Zhenbao hummed along with the piano, but she seemed not to hear; she just kept playing, beginning a new tune. Zhenbao didn't have the courage to sing. Standing in the doorway, he watched Jiaorui for a long time, tears welling up in his eyes, because he and she were really in the same place now, two people together, body and soul. He wished that she'd look up and see his tears, but instead she kept on playing. Zhenbao started to worry. He came over to turn the pages, intending to distract her. She paid no attention. She wasn't even looking at the music, she knew it all by heart and was focusing only on the unhurried flow of it from the tips of her fingers. Suddenly Zhenbao was angry and afraid. It was as if there were no connection between them. He sat down next to her on the piano bench, put his arm around her, and pulled her close. The music stopped abruptly; she tilted her face—all too skillfully. They kissed. Zhenbao's passion mounted. With a deafening crash he pushed her down onto the keyboard. There was a chaotic tempest of sound. Surely this was different from all the other times she'd been kissed.

Jiaorui's bed was too fancy for Zhenbao; he didn't sleep well on the thick bedding. Even though he rose early, he still felt as if he'd overslept. Combing his hair he found a sliver of clipped fingernail, a tiny red crescent moon. She'd scratched him with her long nails; as he was drifting off to sleep, he'd seen her sitting on the bed clipping them. Had there been a moon that night? He hadn't checked, but it must have been a red crescent moon.

After that, he came straight home after work, sitting on the top of a double-decker bus and facing the setting sun, the windowpane a sheet of light as the bus roared toward the sun, toward his happiness, his shameful happiness. How could it not be shameful? His woman ate another man's rice, lived in another man's house, went by another man's name. But feeling that he shouldn't be doing this only made his happiness more perfect.

It was if he'd fallen from a great height. An object that falls from high above is many times heavier than its original weight. Jiaorui, struck by that startlingly great weight, was knocked dizzy.

"I really love you," she said. But she was mocking him still, just a little. "Want to know something? Every day, when I sit here waiting for you to come back, I hear the elevator slowly clanking its way up. When it goes past our floor without stopping, it feels like my own heart's gone up, that it's just hanging in midair. But when the elevator stops before it reaches our floor, it seems like my breath's been cut off."

"So—there's an elevator in your heart. It looks as though your heart is still an apartment."

Jiaorui smiled gently, then walked over to the window and looked out, hands clasped behind her back. After a moment, she said, "The house that you wanted has been built."

At first Zhenbao didn't understand; when he did, he was staggered. He'd never been one to fool around with words, but now he tried something new. Taking a pen from the desk, he wrote "Happy heartwarming! Many congratulations on your new home!" And yet he couldn't really say that he was pleased. The thrill of pleasure had made his whole body sing, but all at once it was quiet. Now there was only a desolate calm; he felt sated and empty at the same time.

When they embraced again, Jiaorui wrapped herself around him, she held him so tightly that she blushed. "It's the same, isn't it, even if there's no love? If I could be like this with you, without any real feeling of love, you'd certainly lose all respect for me." She gripped him still more tightly. "Don't you feel the difference? Don't you?"

"Of course I do." But actually he couldn't tell. The old Jiaorui had been too good at feigning love.

Never before had she been in love like this. Even she didn't know why she loved Zhenbao so much. She'd watch him closely, her gaze both tender and mocking, mocking him and mocking herself.

He was a man with a future, of course, a top-notch textile engineer. His working style was special: nose to the grindstone, too busy to lift his head. The foreign boss was constantly calling for him: "Tong! Tong! Where's Tong?" Zhenbao pushed a lock of hair from his forehead, eyes gleaming behind his glasses, the frames flashing. He liked summer, but even when it wasn't summer he'd be so busy that he'd work up a sweat. The elbows and knees of his Western-style suit were full of creases like laugh lines. Chinese colleagues would complain about the shabby way he looked.

He told Jiaorui how competent he was and how efficient. She praised him, rubbing his hair. "Oh yes. My little one is really talented. But you know that. If you didn't, where would we be? It's in other ways that you're not so clever. I love you—did you know that? I love you."

He showed off in front of her, and she showed off in front of him. The only thing she was really good at was leading men on. Like the tumbler who excelled at turning somersaults and turned somersaults for the Virgin Mary, Jiaorui was sincerely pious: she offered up her art to her beloved. She'd provoke a man, and when he responded accordingly, she'd glance over at Zhenbao with a humble smile, as if to say, "This is what *I* know—and if I didn't, where would we be?" That Timmy Sun of hers was still in a sulk, and yet she found ways to tease him. Zhenbao understood what she was doing; it was tiresome, he thought, but he put up with it because it was just her childishness. Being with Jiaorui was like living with a swarm of teenagers—enough to make you old in no time.

Sometimes they discussed her husband's return. Zhenbao would wear a dark, defeated smile. His eyes and his eyebrows drooped; his whole face hung down in a mess like a mop. The entire relationship was illicit, but he kept using this sinfulness as a spur, pushing himself to love her even more fiercely. Jiaorui didn't understand the full nature of his feeling, but it made her happy to see him suffer. Back when she was a student in England—jumping out of bed, putting on lipstick without even bothering to wash her face, and running out to see her boyfriends—men had of course threatened to kill themselves for her sake. "I spent the whole night pacing under your window," they'd say. "I couldn't sleep." That meant nothing. But making a man suffer for real—that was something else again.

One day she said, "I've been thinking about how to tell him when he comes back," just as if it had already been decided that she would inform Shihong about everything, divorce him, and marry Zhenbao. Zhenbao wasn't brave enough to say anything then. But his dark, defeated smile was not having the desired effect, so later on he said, "Let's not rush into this blindly. Let me talk to a lawyer friend of mine first—get things clear. You know, if this isn't handled properly, there could be quite a price to pay." As a businessman, he felt that merely by uttering the word "lawyer" he'd gotten seriously involved in something—much too seriously. But Jiaorui didn't notice his qualms. She was full of confidence, sure that once the problem on her side was solved, it would all be clear sailing.

Jiaorui often called him at his office. She had no restraint, and it upset him. One day she phoned to say, "Why don't we go out later and have some fun?"

Zhenbao wanted to know why she was so happy.

"You like me to wear those prim and proper Chinese fashions, don't you? I had a new outfit made, and it came today. I want to wear it someplace."

"How about a movie?"

He and some colleagues had chipped in together to buy a small car, and Jiaorui liked to go out for a ride. She had a plan that Zhenbao was going to teach her to drive. "After I've learned I'll buy a car too," she announced. So Shihong would buy it for her? Her words stuck in Zhenbao's craw; he couldn't quite digest it.

Jiaorui didn't seem all that excited about seeing a movie. "Okay," she said, "if we can take the car."

"So what are your feet for?" he laughed.

"Chasing you!" And she laughed too. After that, things got busy at the office. Zhenbao had to get off the phone.

But that day another colleague happened to need the car, and Zhenbao was always self-sacrificing, especially when it came to pleasures. He was dropped off at the street corner— from the apartment window Jiaorui saw him stop to buy the evening paper, though she couldn't tell if he was looking at ads for the movies. She rushed out to meet him at the street door. "If we don't have the car, we can't make it to the 5:15 movie. Let's forget about it."

Zhenbao looked at her and smiled. "So do you want to go someplace else? You look great."

Jiaorui hooked her arm in his. "Won't it be fun just to walk along the avenue?"

But Zhenbao kept fretting, wanting to know how she felt about this place, then that one. They passed a Western-style restaurant with music. She turned it down. "The truth is, I'm pretty broke these days!" he said.

"Oh, dear," she laughed. "If I'd known that, I'd never have gotten mixed up with you!"

Just then, Zhenbao recognized an old foreign lady that he knew—somebody through whom his family had sent money and packages when he was studying abroad. Mrs. Ashe was British but she'd married a Eurasian, which made her self-conscious and as British as British can be. She was tall and stooped and wore an elaborate dress, a foreign-style print that sagged around her frame and made her look like an old beggar. Her hat was a robin's egg blue, mottled with black, and she'd stuck a pearl-headed hatpin and a swallow feather in it. Under the hat was a circle of gray hair, pressed flat like a wig, and her eyes looked as if they were made of pale blue porcelain. Her English came out very softly, her voice breathy and conspiratorial. Zhenbao shook hands with her. "Are you still living in the same place?" he asked.

"At first we were going to go home this summer, but my husband just can't get away!" Going to England was "going home" even though her husband's family had lived in China for three generations, and she herself had no living relatives in England.

Zhenbao introduced Jiaorui. "This is Mrs. Shihong Wang. Wang was in Edinburgh also, and Mrs. Wang spent many years in London. I'm living at their place now."

Mrs. Ashe was accompanied by her daughter. Zhenbao, of course, had considerable experience with mixed-blood girls. Miss Ashe pursed her red lips but didn't say much. She had dark brown eyes peering out of a pointed, white-peach face. A woman who doesn't yet have her own household, her own portion of worry and duty and joy, will often have that watchful, waiting look. And yet Miss Ashe, young as she was, didn't yearn for domesticity; she wasn't a girl with a heart "launched like an arrow toward home." Career girls in the city often have a harried look, and Miss Ashe's eyes were puffy, her face drawn and pale. In China, as elsewhere, the constraints imposed by the traditional moral code were originally constructed for the benefit of women: they made beautiful women even harder to obtain, so their value rose, and ugly women were spared the prospect of never-ending humiliation. Women nowadays don't have this kind of protective buffer, especially not mixed-blood girls, whose status is so entirely undefined. There was a razor edge to Miss Ashe's exhausted peering gaze.

Jiaorui could see at a glance that in going home mother and daughter would be headed straight into the English lower middle class. But they were Zhenbao's friends, and she was eager to make a good impression; also, for some reason, the presence of other females made her feel like a "proper woman" again. She was a full-status wife. She ought to exude an air of dignified affluence. Zhenbao rarely saw her smiling so serenely, almost like a movie star; suddenly she became a sapphire from whose depths a flickering lamp draws waves of light and shadow. Jiaorui was wearing a cheongsam of dark purple-blue georgette, and a little heart-shaped gold pendant gleamed faintly at her breast, cold and splendid—as if she had no other heart. Zhenbao looked at her, and he was both pleased and suspicious; if there'd been a man around how different things would have been!

Mrs. Ashe asked about Mrs. Tong, and Zhenbao said, "My mother's health is fine. She still looks after the whole family." He turned to Jiaorui. "My mother often does the cooking, and she's a very good cook. I always say we're very lucky to have a mother like that!" Whenever he praised his widowed mother, he was reminded of the many years of grievous hardship his family had endured, and he couldn't help gnashing his teeth. He smiled, but as the full weight of his ambitions bore down on him, his heart was like a rock.

Mrs. Ashe asked about his younger brother and sisters. "Dubao is a good kid, he's in technical school now, and later on our factory might send him to England to study." Even the two sisters were praised—the whole family was ideal—until Mrs. Ashe had to exclaim, "You really are something! I've always said that your mother must be very proud of you!" Zhenbao was suitably modest. He asked how things were going for everyone in the Ashe family.

Seeing the newspaper rolled up in his hand, Mrs. Ashe inquired if there was any news this evening. Zhenbao handed her the paper, but her eyesight was so poor that even when she held it at arm's length she still couldn't make anything out. She asked her daughter to read it for her.

"I was planning to take Mrs. Wang to see a movie, but there aren't any good ones," Zhenbao said. In front of other people his attitude toward Jiaorui was a little stiff—he wanted to show that he was only a family friend—but Miss Ashe's quiet, watchful eyes made him feel he was giving everything away. Zhenbao leaned close to Jiaorui. Very familiarly, he said, "I'll make it up to you another time, okay?" He looked at her with shining eyes and laughed. Immediately after, he was sorry—as if he'd gotten too excited while talking and sprayed spit in someone's face. He had always taken this Miss Ashe for a keen observer. She was young and she had nothing, not even a personality; she was just waiting for the approach of everything in the world. Already its huge shadow had fallen across her otherwise expressionless features.

Jiaorui was young, and she had all sorts of things, but somehow they didn't count. She seemed scatterbrained, like a child who goes out and picks dozens of violets, one by one, gathers them into a bunch and tosses them all away. Zhenbao had only his future to bank on, a future he'd prepared for all on his own. How could he bear to see it thrown to the wind? Rich young men and women are free to be careless—security is an inheritance for them—but for him it was not so easy! The four of them walked slowly down the same street, Mrs. Ashe in the

safety and comfort of a room full of flowered wallpaper, while
the three young people faced menace on every side—it boomed
beneath them like a drum.

It was not yet dark, but the neon lights were shining; in the
daylight they looked even more artificial, like costume jewelry.
They passed a shop with lamps for sale, innumerable lamps under the neon glow, the whole place blazing with light. Behind
the tin grill of a snack shop, a waitress leaned forward to pick
up a piece of pastry; her rouge-red cheeks looked good enough
to eat. Did old people also see it like that? Walking next to the
old woman, Zhenbao couldn't help feeling the brevity of youth.
A row of shiny round-head spikes, their heads indented on four
sides, marked off a pedestrian crosswalk; beside them the asphalt road looked as dark and soft as rubber. Zhenbao swayed
along, letting his body go. He couldn't tell whether it was his
own gait that was rubbery or the road underfoot.

Mrs. Ashe praised the fabric of Jiaorui's dress. Then she said,
"I saw a piece like that, last time I was at the Huilou fine goods
shop. Dolly turned it down because she thought it was too
dark. I still wanted to buy it, but then I thought, well, I don't
often have an occasion for wearing such clothes..." She didn't
seem to feel that what she said was sad, but the others all fell
silent, unable to respond. "So Mr. Ashe must be very busy?"
Zhenbao finally asked.

"Oh, yes. Otherwise, we'd go home for a visit this summer.
But he really can't get away!"

"Some Sunday when I have the car, I'll come and fetch you
all and take you to Jiangwan to have some Chinese snacks
made by my mother."

"That would be wonderful! My husband simply dotes on
Chinese things!"

She sounded just like a rich foreign visitor; no one would
have guessed that her husband was half Chinese.

After saying good-bye to Mrs. Ashe and her daughter,

Zhenbao remarked to Jiaorui, as if in explanation, "That Mrs. Ashe is a really good person."

Jiaorui looked at him and smiled. "I think you are a really good person."

"Just how am I so very good?" Suddenly his face was right in hers.

"I'll tell you—don't get angry. When a woman sees a man who's good like you, she wants to fix him up with someone else. She doesn't even think of keeping him for herself."

"So you don't like good men?"

"When a woman likes a good man it's because she thinks she can trap him."

"Oh-ho! So you're planning to trap me, is that it?"

Jiaorui paused. She gave him a sideways glance and started to smile but she stopped. "This time, it's the bad girl who's been trapped!"

That sideways glance, those soft words—they were intolerable to him at the moment. Later that evening, stretched out in Jiaorui's bed, he thought about the meeting with Mrs. Ashe on the street, about his studies in Edinburgh, when his family had sent him money and packages, and about how it was now time to repay his mother. He wanted to get ahead, move up in the world, and the first step was to rise in his profession. After he'd made it to a suitably high position, he'd contribute something to society—for instance, he could set up an industrial-science school for poor boys, or a model textile factory in his hometown, Jiangwan. Vague as it all was, even now he had a fuzzy intimation of the warm welcome awaiting him—not just from his own mother but from a whole world of mothers, tearful, and with eyes only for him.

Jiaorui was fast asleep, curled up close to him, the sound of her breathing loud in his ear. Suddenly she seemed a thing apart, and somehow alien. He sat up on the edge of the bed and groped around in the dark until he found a cigarette and lit it. He didn't think Jiaorui had noticed, but in fact she was awake. After a long while she reached out, feeling for his hand. "Don't worry," she said softly, "I'll be good." She laid his hand on her shoulder.

Her words made him weep, but the tears too were a thing apart, and somehow alien.

Zhenbao didn't answer, letting his hands roam over familiar places. Soon the sun would rise. The city was full of the muffled noise of crowing cocks.

The next day, they spoke again of her husband's return. "Anyway, he'll be back sometime in the next few days," Jiaorui said with great certainty.

Zhenbao asked her how she knew, and only then did she tell him that she'd sent Shihong a letter by airmail telling him everything and asking for her freedom. Zhenbao gasped, the sound coming from deep within. He stood up and ran out onto the street. When he looked back at the towering apartment building, with its tall, flowing red-and-gray lines, it looked like a roaring train—incredibly huge and barreling straight down upon him, blocking out sun and moon. The situation was beyond repair. He'd thought that he had it all under control and that he could stop whenever he wanted, but now things had rushed forward on their own, there was no use in even arguing. The worst thing was that he didn't even want to argue—not when he was with her. It was so clear, then, that they loved each other and should go on loving each other. It was only when she wasn't there that he could think up all sorts of reasons against it. Right now, for instance, it struck him as all too likely that he'd been played for a fool in a deeper game with her true love, Timmy Sun. She'd pulled the wool over Zhenbao's eyes by saying that it was because of him that she wanted a divorce, and now if there was a scandal, *his* future would be ruined.

He walked a long way without caring where. At a little

restaurant, he had a few drinks and a bite to eat. When he came out, his stomach hurt. He got into a rickshaw, thinking he would visit Dubao in his dormitory, but in the rickshaw his stomach felt worse still. He lost control of himself—the tiniest tremor of pain was more than he could bear—and he panicked. Imagining he had cholera, he told the rickshaw driver to take him to the nearest hospital. Once he'd been admitted, he informed his mother; she rushed to the hospital right away. The next day she came bearing lotus-root powder and grape juice that she'd bought for him. Jiaorui showed up as well. His mother suspected that something was going on between them, and she made sure to scold him in front of Jiaorui.

"Getting sick to your stomach, that's nothing in itself, but I tossed and turned all night, worrying about you—a grown man and you still don't know how to take care of yourself! How on earth am I supposed to look after you all the time? And if I just let you do as you please, I'll be constantly worrying. But if you had a wife, I wouldn't have to. Mrs. Wang, please tell him—he'll listen to what his friends say, even if he won't listen to me. Oh, dear! Here I've been waiting so long till you'd finished your schooling and begun your career. Now that you're finally getting somewhere, don't think you can just let go, let everything fall apart! You have to earn the respect you receive. Mrs. Wang, please, you tell him for me."

Jiaorui pretended not to understand Chinese; she just stood there smiling. Zhenbao's thoughts were in fact very similar to his mother's, but when he heard her, he felt that the way she put things was somehow humiliating. He was embarrassed, and found an excuse to send her away.

That left him with Jiaorui. She walked over to the bed and leaned over the white metal railing, her whole body a painful question mark. Zhenbao rolled away impatiently; he couldn't explain and he couldn't escape his mother's logic. Jiaorui closed the curtain, and the sunlight on his pillow turned to cool shadow. She didn't leave, but stayed to nurse him, bringing tea, water, the bedpan. The enamel basin was ice-cold against his skin; her hands were just as cold. When he happened to glance her way, she seized the chance to speak: "Don't be afraid..." He hated her saying that he was afraid; his expression changed, and she stopped. More time passed. "I have really changed..." she said. Again he shifted uncomfortably, to keep her from speaking. "I won't bring you any trouble, I promise..." And then, "You can't leave me, Zhenbao..." Her broken sentences hung in midair like the pendulums of several clocks, each ticking along at a different speed, each following its own logic and reaching its own conclusions, each rising up at a different moment, each hammering its bell at a different time... to Zhenbao it seemed that the room was filled with Jiaorui's voice, even though she had long since fallen silent.

Evening came, and with the lamps still unlit she threw herself on him and wept. Even in her humiliation she had strength. Through the blanket and the sheet he could feel the firmness of her arms. But he didn't want her strength; he already had his own.

She threw herself across his waist and legs and she wailed. Her hair, a mess of soft, loose curls, exuded heat like a brazier. She was like a child who's been wronged, who cries so much that she can't stop, doesn't know how to, hoarsely crying on and on, having forgotten why she started to cry in the first place. For Zhenbao it was the same. "No, no, no...Don't go on like this, it won't do..." The words required an enormous struggle; he was fighting hard to subdue the surging waves of longing. He spent all his strength in saying "No, no, no" even though he'd forgotten what it was he meant to refuse.

But finally he found something suitable to say. With great effort, he raised his knees, making her get up. "Jiaorui," he said, "if you love me, then you have to consider my situation. I can't cause my mother pain. Her way of thinking is different from ours, but we have to think about her, since she has only me to depend on. The world would never forgive me. And Shihong is, after all, my friend. Our love can only be love between friends. What happened before is my mistake, and I'm very sorry. But now you've written and told him without letting me know—that's your mistake. Jiaorui, what do you say? When he comes, tell him you were only fooling, that you just wanted him to come back early. He'll believe you—if he wants to."

Jiaorui lifted a red, swollen face and stared. In a flash, she stood straight up, apparently astonished to find herself in such a state. She took a small mirror out of her purse, glanced into it while tilting her head this way and that, tossed her hair back loosely, wiped her eyes with a handkerchief, blew her nose, and, without looking at him once, walked out.

Zhenbao didn't sleep well that night, and with dawn came new awareness; it seemed as if someone had come during the night and fallen across him, weeping. At first he thought it was a dream, but then he realized that it was Jiaorui: probably she'd been there for a long time now crying. The warmth of the woman's body lay over him like an eiderdown quilt on satin sheets. He luxuriated in the moment, breaking out in a gentle sweat.

When he was fully awake, Jiaorui left without a word. He didn't say anything either. Later he heard that she and Wang Shihong had decided to divorce, but it all seemed very remote. His mother cried in front of him a few times, urging him to marry, and he put it off for a while, then finally agreed. His mother arranged the introductions. "She's the one then," he said to himself, when he met Miss Meng Yanli.

They met first in someone's living room. Yanli was standing by a glass door wearing a silk shift with ruddy orange stripes on a gray background. Zhenbao's immediate impression, however, was of a vague, enveloping whiteness. Yanli was tall and slender, like a single straight line; the only hint of a twist or turn came at the tips of her girlish breasts and the jutting bones of her hips. When a breeze stirred, and her dress swept out behind her, it made her look thin and frail. Her face was soft and very pretty, and yet the main effect was of whiteness. Yanli's father had died, and her family's fortunes had gone into decline, but at one time they had been a wealthy merchant family, so the two of them had similar family backgrounds. The young lady was twenty-two years old and would soon be graduating from college. Her college wasn't a very good one, just the best she could get into, but Yanli was a good student in a mediocre place; she studied hard and didn't associate much with her classmates. Her whiteness, like a portable hospital screen, separated her from the bad things in her environment. It also separated her from the things in her books. For ten years now Yanli had gone to school, diligently looking up new words, memorizing charts, copying from the blackboard, but between her and everything else there always seemed to be a white membrane. In middle school, she'd received letters from some boys—the elder brothers of her classmates, for the most part. When her family found out about it, they told her not to get involved with people like that. Yanli had never written back.

Zhenbao planned to marry her in two months, after her graduation. During this time, he took her out to the movies a few times. Yanli rarely spoke or raised her head and always walked a little behind him. She knew very well that according to modern etiquette she should walk in front, let him help her put on her coat and wait on her, but she was uncomfortable exercising her new rights. She hesitated, and this made her seem even slower and more awkward. Zhenbao himself wasn't a natural-born gentleman, but he had worked hard to learn the part: he took the matter seriously and thought Yanli quite remiss in this regard. Fortunately, a shy shrinking manner in a young girl is not too unpleasant.

The engagement was short, and secretly Yanli was very disappointed; she'd always heard that these were the best days of one's life. Even so, she was very happy when the wedding day arrived. That morning, combing her hair while still half asleep, she lifted her arms up, looked in the mirror, and felt a strange sense of invigoration—as if she'd been crammed into a glass test tube and was now pushing her head up to pop the lid off, ready to leap from the present into future. The present was good, but the future would be better. Yanli stretched her arms out of the window of the future, and a vast wind blew through her hair.

The wedding was at Yi Pin Xiang Restaurant, with the banquet at Dongxing Restaurant. Zhenbao liked to make a good impression, but he was also careful with money—good enough was good enough for him. He rented a new house not far from his office and had his mother come from Jiangwan to live with them. He spent most of his earnings on work-related socializing, so the household budget was very tight. His mother and Yanli got along fairly well, but Zhenbao had many complaints about Yanli and no one to tell them to. Yanli didn't like exercise; even "the best sort of indoor exercise" had no appeal for her. Zhenbao made a real effort to be a good husband and help her like it, but he didn't feel much physical attraction. At first she'd seemed cute, one undeveloped breast nestling in his hand like a sleeping bird with its own lightly beating heart, its sharp beak pecking at his palm, firm yet without strength—but then his hand had also lost its strength. Later on even this little bit of girlish beauty was gone. Gradually Yanli settled into her new environment, and as she did, she turned into a very dull wife.

Zhenbao started going to prostitutes. Once every three weeks —his life was, in every respect, well regulated. He and some friends would take rooms in a hotel and call in the women; they'd tell their families they'd gone to Suzhou and Hangzhou on business. He wasn't particular about faces, but he liked girls who were dark and a little bit plump. He wanted them fleshy and ashamed, which was his way of taking revenge on Rose and Wang Jiaorui, though he wouldn't let himself view it that way. If such a thing did enter his mind, he immediately reproached himself for desecrating treasured memories. For these two lovers, he reserved a sensitive spot, a sacred corner of his heart. Wang Jiaorui and Rose gradually became so mixed up in his mind that they became one: a naïve, passionate girl who had doted on him, a girl with no brains, or anything to cause him any trouble, though he—with his self-denying logic and steely, superhuman will—had left her.

Yanli had no idea about the prostitutes. She loved him simply because he, among so many others, happened to be her man. She was always saying things like "Wait and ask Zhenbao about it" or "Better take an umbrella, Zhenbao said it's going to rain." Zhenbao was her God, and assuming that role was no problem for him. When Yanli made a mistake, he'd reprimand her in front of other people, and if something escaped his attention, it never failed to escape his mother's. Each time she was scolded in front of the maidservant, Yanli could feel her authority crumbling away beneath her. When her orders weren't carried out, she was again to blame. She hated the disdain in the servants' eyes, and in dealing with them she protected herself by knitting her brows and pouting before she even spoke, her whole face a study in childish chagrin. When she threw a tantrum, she always seemed to be talking back, like a maid or a concubine who has grown used to occupying the bottom rung.

The only time Yanli managed to be mistress of the house— for a few days at least—was when the servants were new, so she liked getting new servants as often as she could. Zhenbao's mother told everyone that her daughter-in-law was useless: "Poor Zhenbao, working so hard at his job to support the family, but when he comes home he's pestered with all sort of domestic details. He can't get a moment's peace." Her words got around to Yanli, and the anger built up in her heart. She grew angrier and angrier, and then she had a child. The delivery was difficult. Yanli felt she'd earned the right to throw a fit. But the child was a girl, and Yanli's mother-in-law had no intention of humoring her. Soon they were irritated with each other all the time. Fortunately, Zhenbao played peacemaker and the embarrassment of a direct confrontation was avoided, but his mother sullenly insisted on moving back to Jiangwan. Zhenbao was very disappointed in his wife: having married her for her tractability, he felt cheated. He was also unhappy with his mother—moving out like that and letting people say he wasn't a good son. He was still busy-busy, but gradually he succumbed to fatigue. Even the smiling wrinkles of his suit looked tired.

When Dubao graduated, Zhenbao, in his role as talent scout, found his brother a job at the factory. But Dubao didn't live up to his potential. Overshadowed by his older brother, he became a loafer, without ambition. He was still single, and quite content to live in a dormitory.

One morning Dubao showed up at Zhenbao's place with a question. The assistant manager of the factory would soon be returning to his home country, and everyone had contributed toward a gift which it was Dubao's job to purchase. Zhenbao advised him to go to a department store and see what sort of silver items they had. The two brothers left the house together and caught the same bus. Zhenbao sat down next to a woman who, without a glance, picked up the child beside her and put him on her lap. Zhenbao didn't pay any attention, but Dubao, sitting across the aisle, gasped in surprise. Lifting himself in his seat, he signaled to Zhenbao with his head. Only then did Zhenbao recognize Jiaorui. She was plumper than before, though certainly not paunchy, as she'd once feared would happen to her. She looked tired, but she was carefully made up, and the pendants of her earrings were gold-colored Burmese Buddha heads. Jiaorui was middle-aged now, and her beauty had turned to plain good looks.

"Mrs. Zhu," said Dubao, smiling, "it's been a long time!"

Zhenbao remembered hearing that she had remarried—that she was now Mrs. Zhu. Jiaorui smiled back. "Yes, it really has been a long time!" she said.

Zhenbao nodded. "How have you been?" he asked.

"Just fine, thank you."

"Have you been in Shanghai all this time?" Dubao asked.

Jiaorui nodded.

"It seems a bit early in the morning for running errands," he continued.

"It certainly is!" Jiaorui said. She put her hand on the child's shoulder. "I'm taking him to the dentist. He got a toothache yesterday, kept me up all night with his fussing, and now I've got to take him in early."

"Which is your stop?" asked Dubao.

"The dentist's office is on the Bund. Are you two going to the office?"

"He is," said Dubao, "but I've got to do some shopping."

"Is everything still the same at the factory?" asked Jiaorui. "No big changes?"

"Hilton is going back. Now Zhenbao will be the assistant manager."

"Oh, my! That's wonderful!"

Dubao never talked this much when his older brother was present; Zhenbao could tell that Dubao felt it incumbent on him, under the circumstances, to do the talking. Which meant he must know all about their affair.

Dubao got off at the next stop. Zhenbao was silent for a while. He didn't look at Jiaorui. "Well, and how are you?" he asked the empty air.

Jiaorui was silent, but after a pause she said, "Just fine." The same question and same answer as before, but now they had an entirely different meaning.

"This Mr. Zhu—do you love him?"

Jiaorui nodded. When she answered, her words were interrupted by pauses. "Starting with you...I learned...how to love...to really love. Love is good. Even though I have suffered, I still want to love, and so..."

Zhenbao rolled up the square collar of her son's sailor outfit. "You're very happy," he said in a low voice.

Jiaorui laughed. "I had to forge ahead somehow. When I ran into something, well, that was it."

"What you run into is always a man," Zhenbao said with a cold smile.

Jiaorui wasn't angry. She tilted her head to one side and thought about it. "True," she said. "When I was young and pretty, I always ran into men. That probably would have happened no matter what I did, once my social life started. But now, there are other things besides men, always other things..."

Zhenbao stared at her, unaware that his heart, at that moment, was aching with jealousy.

"And you?" asked Jiaorui. "How are you?"

Zhenbao wanted to sum up his perfectly happy life in a few simple words, but as he was trying to find them, he looked up and saw his face in the small mirror on the bus driver's right. He knew his face was steady and calm, and yet the vibration of the bus made his face vibrate too, a strange, calm, regular vibration, almost as if his face was being gently massaged. All at once, Zhenbao's face really did begin to quiver; in the mirror he saw tears streaming down...he didn't know why. Shouldn't she have been the one to weep? It was all wrong, and yet he couldn't stop. She should be weeping, he should be comforting her. But Jiaorui didn't comfort him. She sat silently for a long time. Then she asked, "Is this your stop?"

He got off the bus and went to work as usual. It was Saturday, so they had the afternoon off. He went home at half past twelve. He had a small Western-style house with a big, imposing wall out front, but then all the houses in the area, row after row of them, looked exactly the same: gray cement walls, as smooth, shiny, and rectangular as coffins, with flowering oleanders sticking up over the top. The courtyard inside was small, but it counted as a garden. Everything a home should have, his had. Small white clouds floated in the blue sky above, and on the street a flute vendor was playing the flute—a sharp, soft, sinuous, Oriental tune that twisted and turned in the ear like embroidery, like a picture of a dream in a novel, a trail of white mist coming out from under the bed curtain and unfurling all sorts of images, slowly uncoiling like a lazy snake, till finally the drowsiness is just too great, and even the dream falls asleep.

The house was perfectly quiet when Zhenbao walked in. His seven-year-old daughter, Huiying, was still at school; the maidservant had gone to fetch her. Zhenbao didn't want to wait; he told Yanli to go ahead and put the food on the table. He wolfed it down, as if to fill the emptiness in his heart with food.

After eating, he phoned Dubao to ask him how the shopping had gone. Dubao explained that he'd looked at several pieces of silver but none had been suitable. "I have a pair of silver vases here," said Zhenbao. "Someone gave them to us as wedding gifts. Take them to a shop and have them re-engraved. That should take care of it. You can return the money you've collected. It'll be my contribution." Dubao agreed, and Zhenbao said, "Perhaps you should come and get them now." He was anxious to see Dubao and to find out his reaction to seeing Jiaorui that morning. The whole scene had been so nonsensical —and his own response so absurd—that Zhenbao almost wondered if it had really happened.

Dubao came, and Zhenbao casually brought the conversation round to Jiaorui. Dubao tapped his cigarette like a man of experience: "She's gotten old, really old." Which apparently meant, for a woman, that she was finished.

Zhenbao reviewed the scene that morning: yes, she had grown old. But even this he envied. He looked at his wife. Eight years of marriage and still no trace of experience. She was hollow and spotless. She always would be.

He told Yanli to wrap up the two silver vases on the mantelpiece and give them to Dubao. She scrambled around to find a chair, removed the cushion, stood on the chair, got some newspaper from the top of the cupboard, went back to the drawer for some string, found a string that was too short, wrapped up the vases and made a complete mess of it, even ripping the paper into pieces. Zhenbao watched the whole thing with growing irritation. All at once he strode over and grabbed the vases from her. He groaned loudly. "When a person's stupid, everything's a trial!"

Yanli's face flushed with resentment, like a slave girl's. But then she smiled and laughed, glancing quickly at Dubao to see if he was laughing too, afraid he might not have caught her husband's joke. She stood to one side with her arms folded while Zhenbao wrapped up the silver vases. Her features were strangely clouded, as if a white membrane had been stretched across her face.

Dubao was getting fidgety. At their house friends and relatives often got fidgety. He wanted to leave. Anxious to make up for the faux pas, Yanli rallied. She pressed him warmly to stay— "If you aren't busy." She fawned and smiled, her eyes narrowing, her nose wrinkling flirtatiously. She often surprised people with such an unexpected intimacy. If Dubao had been a woman, she would have taken his hand in her own moist palm and held on desperately—imposing herself in a way that was sure to prove distasteful.

Dubao said he really must go. At the door, he ran into the old maidservant bringing Huiying back. Dubao took some gum from his trousers pocket and gave it to the girl. "Say 'Thank you, Uncle,'" Yanli chimed in. Huiying dodged away.

"Ah! So you're embarrassed!" Dubao laughed.

Huiying flipped up her Western-style skirt to hide her face, showing her underwear. "Now you should be really embarrassed!" Yanli cried out.

Huiying grabbed the gum, flipped the skirt over her face again, and ran away laughing.

Zhenbao sat watching his daughter, with her thin, yellow, prancing hands and feet. Before, this child had not existed. He had summoned her out of thin air.

Zhenbao went upstairs to wash his face; downstairs, Yanli turned on the radio to listen to the news. Zhenbao thought it was a good idea for Yanli to listen to the news—part of a modern woman's education. Perhaps she'd even pick up a phrase or two of Mandarin. He didn't know that Yanli listened to the radio just to hear a human voice.

Zhenbao looked out of the window. The sky was blue and the clouds were white, the oleander was blooming in the courtyard, and the flute was still playing in the street—as sharp and wheedling as the voice of a low-class woman. It wasn't a very good flute. The notes were shrill and hurt his ears.

Here on this lovely spring afternoon, Zhenbao looked around at the world he had made. There was no way to destroy it.

The quiet house was filled with sunlight. Downstairs, a man's confident voice came over the radio, droning on and on.

From the moment Zhenbao got married, he'd been convinced that everyone around him, starting with his mother, should be patting him on the back and offering him encouragement. His mother knew how much he'd sacrificed, but he felt that even those who didn't know all the details owed him respect, owed him a little sympathy in compensation.

As a result, people often did make a point of praising him, though never enough, while Zhenbao devoted himself to doing all sorts of good deeds—things he'd take upon himself, without even being asked. He paid off some debts for Dubao, found him a wife, set him up in a house with his family. His sister was a particular problem, and this made him especially considerate toward unmarried or widowed friends. He got them jobs, money—there was nothing he wouldn't do. He spent a lot of time and effort obtaining a position for his sister at a school in the interior, because he'd heard that the male teachers there were all recent university graduates, every one of them unmarried. But his sister wasn't cut out for hardship; she threw a fit and came running back to Shanghai, not even finishing out her half-year contract. His mother sympathized with her daughter, and criticized Zhenbao for being hasty.

Yanli watched all this from the sidelines. It made her very angry on Zhenbao's behalf, and she complained to others whenever she could. But Yanli rarely saw anyone. Lacking a lively, sociable lady of the house, Zhenbao felt it was better to take people out, even if it did cost more. He never brought people home. But on those rare occasions when a friend came looking for Zhenbao and found that he wasn't in, Yanli proved an attentive hostess. She'd treat the guest like the closest of friends, freely discussing Zhenbao.

"Zhenbao always gets the short end of the stick—he's so good to people, so sincere, and then he's the one who suffers! Ah—but that's how it is, isn't it, Mr. Zhang? Sincerity doesn't get you anywhere nowadays! Even his own sister and brother are ungrateful, not to mention the friends who come around only when they want something—and they're all like that! I've seen it all, and Zhenbao won't change his ways, not one bit, even though he's the one who suffers, each and every time. A good man has no place in our world today! That's how it is, isn't it, Mr. Zhang?"

The friend would feel that soon he too would be numbered among the ungrateful, and a chill would creep into his heart. None of Zhenbao's friends liked Yanli, even though she was pretty, quiet, and refined, just the wife for someone else, a perfect backdrop for men busily engaged in vigorous, free-wheeling conversation.

Yanli had no women friends of her own, so she had no chance to compare her life with others' and find out how low she'd fallen in her own household. Zhenbao didn't encourage her to interact with other married women because he knew that she wasn't up to it. Placed in an unfamiliar situation, she would just reveal all her weaknesses and encourage gossip. He forgave her for telling people he was unappreciated, because a woman's perspective is always limited. Anyway, she was protecting him; she hated to see him exploited. But when she made similar comments to the old maidservant, Zhenbao's temper got the better of him and he intervened. Then there was the time he heard Yanli complaining to eight-year-old Huiying. He didn't say anything about it, but not long after he sent Huiying off to boarding school. The house grew even quieter.

Yanli began to suffer from constipation. She sat in the bathroom for several hours each day. That was the only place where it was all right to do nothing, say nothing, think nothing. The rest of the time she also did nothing, said nothing, and thought nothing, but she always felt a little uneasy about it. Only in the day-lit bathroom could she settle down and feel rooted. Yanli bent her head and stared at her own snow-white stomach, that stretch of pure gleaming white. Sometimes she stuck it out; sometimes she sucked it in. Her navel also changed its appearance: now it was the eye of a Greek statue—sweet, clean, expressionless—while the next instant it protruded angrily, like the eye of a pagan god, an eye with an evil little smile but adorable even so, with crow's-feet tucked away in the corners.

Zhenbao took Yanli to the doctor and bought her medicine as recommended by newspaper advertisements. Eventually, however, he decided that she wasn't all that concerned—she seemed to want to hang on to her little ailment as if it contributed to her importance. He stopped worrying about it.

One day, he had a business lunch. It was the plum-rain season, and before he'd left the office the rain started. He hailed a rickshaw and went around to his house to fetch his raincoat. On the way he couldn't help remembering that other time, when he was living at Jiaorui's place, when the weather had changed and he'd dashed back in the rain to get his raincoat— that very memorable day. He climbed out of the rickshaw and went in the front door, wrapped in the faint melancholy of his memories, but when he looked he saw that the raincoat wasn't in the closet. His heart thumped hard, and it seemed that events of a decade ago had come to life again. He walked toward the living room, his heart still pounding. He had a strange sense of destiny. His hand was on the doorknob to the living room, he opened it, and Yanli was in the room, along with a tailor who was standing at the end of the sofa. Everything was as usual, and Zhenbao relaxed. Then suddenly he grew tense again. He felt nervous—no doubt because the two other people in the room were nervous too.

"Are you having lunch at home?" Yanli asked.

"No, I came back for my raincoat."

He looked at the tailor's bundle on the chair, not a trace of moisture on it. It had been raining steadily for at least an hour. The tailor wasn't wearing galoshes. The tailor, when Zhenbao looked at him, seemed a little shaken; he went over to his bundle, pulled out a measuring tape, and started to take Yanli's measurements.

Yanli's hand gestured weakly at Zhenbao. She said, "Your raincoat's hanging in the kitchen hallway to dry." She looked as if she meant to push the tailor away and fetch the raincoat herself, but she didn't move. She just stood there while the tailor busied himself about her measurements.

Zhenbao knew that when you touch a woman in front of others after sleeping with her, there's a change in your manner —no mistaking it. He looked at them both with a cold, clear eye. The great white mouth of the rainy day sucked at the window. Outside was nothing but cold disarray; inside everything was sealed off. There was an intense intimacy between those three people enclosed in that single room.

Zhenbao stood high above it all, distantly observing the two inexperienced adulterers. He couldn't understand. How could she choose such a person? Although the tailor was young, his back was already a bit bent. His face was sallow and there were ringworm scars on his scalp. He looked like what he was: a tailor.

Zhenbao went to get his raincoat and put it on, buttoning it up as he walked back to the living room. The tailor was gone.

"Don't know when I'll be back," Zhenbao said to Yanli. "Don't wait supper."

Yanli approached him deferentially and nodded. She seemed to be upset. Her hands wandered around, finding no place to rest but anxious to be doing something. She flipped on the radio. Time for the Mandarin news broadcast again—the voice of another man filled the room. Zhenbao felt there was no need for him to speak, so he turned and left, still buttoning his coat. He had no idea that his coat had so many buttons.

The door to the living room was wide open, and the candid, straightforward man on the radio went on talking confidently: he was always right. Zhenbao thought: "I've been pretty good to her! I don't love her, but there's nothing I owe her an apology for. I haven't treated her badly. Such a lowly little thing! Probably she knows she's nothing—she wants to find someone even lower than she is if only for comfort's sake. But I've been so good to her, so good!"

Back in the room, Yanli must have felt less than sure of herself: she turned off the radio with a pop. Standing in the entryway, Zhenbao suddenly felt himself choking up. If the man in the radio station, who went on discoursing so fluently, had sensed that his entire audience had all at once shut him off, he would have known what Zhenbao felt—an abrupt blockage, emptiness petrifying the gut. Zhenbao stood on the front steps of his house, facing the rainy street, until a rickshaw came by looking for customers. He got in without bothering to haggle over the fare and was pulled away.

When he came home that evening, the steps were under a foot of water. In the dark and the wet the house looked very different—appropriately enough, he felt. But when he went indoors the hot stifling smell and the line of yellow lamps leading upstairs were as before: the house was still the house; nothing had changed.

At the front door, he removed his shoes and socks, which were soaked through, gave them to the maidservant, and climbed barefoot to the bedroom upstairs. He reached out to flip the switch and saw that the bathroom light was on. When he looked through the half-opened door, the bathroom resembled a narrow hanging scroll in faded yellow-white. The light made Yanli her own faded yellow color. But never in dynastic history has a painting of a pretty woman taken up such an awkward subject: Yanli was pulling up her pants. She was bent over, about to stand up, and her hair hung down over her face. She had already changed into her flowered white pajama top, which was bunched high up on her chest, half caught under her chin. The pajama pants lay piled around her feet, and her long body wavered over them like a white silkworm. In America, the scene would have made an excellent toilet-paper advertisement, but to Zhenbao's hasty glance it was household filth, like a matted wad of hair on a rainy day—damp and giving off a stagnant, stifling, human scent.

He turned the light on in the bedroom. When Yanli saw that he had returned, she hurriedly asked, "Did you get your feet wet?"

"I'm going to soak them right away," Zhenbao responded.

"I'll be right out," said Yanli. "I'll tell Amah Yu to go heat some water."

"She's doing it now."

Yanli washed her hands and came out, and Amah Yu brought the kettle up. Zhenbao sneezed. "You've caught a cold!" said Amah Yu. "Don't you want to close the door?"

Zhenbao closed the door and was alone in the bathroom, the rain still falling hard, clattering on the windowpanes.

There was some sort of potted plant in the bathtub. It had flowers of a tender yellow, and even though it hadn't been out in the rain, it smelled as if it had been. The foot basin was next to the flowerpot, and Zhenbao sat on the edge of the bathtub, bending over to wash his feet, careful not to splash hot water on the flowers. When he bent his head, he caught a whiff of a light, clean scent. He put one leg over the other knee, carefully wiped each toe dry with a towel, and suddenly was overcome with tenderness for himself. He looked at his own flesh, and it was if someone else was doing the looking—a lover, full of grief because Zhenbao was throwing himself away for nothing.

He shuffled on some slippers and stood at the window looking out. The rain had already tapered off and was gradually coming to a stop. The street was now a river; mirrored in the waves, the streetlamps were like a string of silver arrowheads that shot by, then disappeared. Vehicles thumped past, and behind each one a brilliant white wake unfurled like a peacock's tail, washing across the reflections of the streetlamps. Slowly the white peacock's tail sent out golden stars, then lengthened and faded away. When the vehicle was gone, the white-gold arrowheads returned, shooting across the turbid yellow river and disappearing, shooting by, then gone.

Pressing his hand against the windowpane, Zhenbao was keenly aware of his own hand, his own breath, deeply grieving. He thought of the bottle of brandy in the cabinet. He got it down, poured himself a full glass, and stood looking out the window as he sipped.

Yanli walked up behind him and said, "That's a good idea—

having a glass of brandy to warm your stomach. Otherwise, you'll catch a cold."

The warm brandy went straight to his head; his eyes grew hard and hot. He turned and looked at her with loathing. He hated that kind of tedious, polite small talk, and what he especially hated was this: that she seemed to be peering at him behind his back, trying to find out how much he knew.

In the following two weeks Yanli kept peering. Apparently she felt that he hadn't changed in any way—that he wasn't suspicious of her—and in time she relaxed and forgot that she'd had something to hide. Zhenbao was befuddled: now it seemed that she didn't have a secret after all. It was like two white doors, tightly shut, flanked by a pair of flickering lamps on a wild plain at night: you pound at them with all your might, absolutely convinced that a murder is taking place inside. But when the doors open to admit you, there's no such thing. There's not even a building. All you can see, under a few stars, is empty mist and tangled weeds. Now that was truly frightening.

Zhenbao started drinking a lot, openly consorting with women outside the house. It was not at all like before, when he retained some scruples. He came home reeking of drink, or he didn't come home at all, but Yanli always had an excuse, saying that he had a lot of new social obligations for his company that he couldn't refuse. She would never admit that it had anything to do with her. She kept on explaining it away to herself, and when his dissipation gradually got to the point where it couldn't be concealed, she explained it away to others too, smiling slightly, loyally covering up for him. Zhenbao was running wild—almost to the point of bringing prostitutes home with him—but everyone still thought of him as a fine upstanding man, a good man.

For a month it rained constantly. One day, the old maidservant said that Zhenbao's woven silk shirt had shrunk in the wash and needed to be let out. Sitting on the bed with his shoes off, Zhenbao casually remarked, "Get the tailor to come and fix it."

"The tailor hasn't come in a long time," said Amah Yu. "I wonder if he's gone back to his hometown."

"Eh?" said Zhenbao, to himself. "Broken off as easily as that? Not a bit of real feeling—how dirty, how petty!"

"Really?" he asked. "Didn't he come to collect his bill at Dragonboat Festival?"

"His apprentice came," said Amah Yu.

This Amah Yu had been with them for three years. She folded up some underpants and put them on the edge of the bed, with a light pat. She didn't look at him, but the smile on her gentle old face was meant to be comforting. Zhenbao was filled with anger.

That afternoon he took a woman out for a good time, and purposely went around to his house for some money. The woman sat waiting for him in the pedicab. The sky had just cleared and the water on the street had not yet receded; great clumps of parasol trees shone in the yellow river. Across the street, there was a bluish haze on the green trees around the little red houses; damp yellow smoke came out of the chimneys and flew off at a low angle. Zhenbao returned with the money, smacked his umbrella down, and splashed water all over the girl. She cried out sharply. Zhenbao climbed into the pedicab laughing, full of wet, muddy happiness. He looked at the upstairs window. It must have been Yanli standing there, but what he saw was a tea-tray lace doily, yellowing with age, stuck on the bathroom wall—or maybe it was a little white saucer with a tea-stain splotch in the center. Zhenbao smacked his umbrella into the water again. Break it to bits! Break it to bits!

He couldn't smash up the home he'd made, or his wife, or his daughter, but he could smash himself up, the umbrella whacking the water and the cold, rank mud flying into his face. Again he was filled with tender sorrow for himself, a lover's sorrow, but at the same time a strong-willed self stood opposite the lover, pulling and pushing and fighting with her. He had to be smashed to bits! Smash him to bits!

The pedicab drove through the rippling water, and the water splashed the woman's clothes and her leather shoes and leather handbag. She complained, wanting him to pay for the damage. Zhenbao laughed, threw one arm around her, and kept on splashing the water.

After this, even Yanli ran out of excuses. Zhenbao didn't bring back money for the family, his daughter's tuition went unpaid, and the daily groceries were a problem too. At that point, Yanli became a brave little wife. Suddenly, at the age of nearly thirty, she had grown up. She spoke fluently and compellingly, in tearful, eloquent complaints: "How ever can we go on like this? It's enough to kill me—the whole family depends on him! At this rate he'll lose his job at the factory...It's as if he's gone mad, he doesn't come home, and when he does he hits people and smashes things up. He wasn't like this before! Oh, Mr. Liu, can you imagine? Can you tell me what I should do? How am I supposed to cope with this?"

All at once Yanli gained self-confidence. She had social status. She had sympathy. She had friends. One night Zhenbao came back home to find her sitting in the living room talking with Dubao. Of course they were discussing him, and when he appeared, she fell silent. She was dressed all in black, and though the wrinkles on her worried face were visible in the lamplight, she still had an aura of hidden beauty. Zhenbao didn't rush around smashing tables and lamps. He walked in, nodded to Dubao, and said a few words about the weather. He lit a cigarette and sat down casually to discuss current events and the stock market. Finally he said he was tired and would go to bed early. He took his leave of them and headed up the stairs. Yanli simply couldn't understand what was happening— it looked as if she'd been lying. It was all very hard to explain.

After Dubao left, Zhenbao heard Yanli entering the bedroom. Right when she came in the door, he swept the lamp and the hot-water thermos off the little cabinet; they fell to the floor and cracked wide open, smashed to bits. He bent down and picked up the metal base of the lamp, hurling it at her, electrical cord and all. Turning, she fled from the room. Zhenbao felt that she had been completely defeated. He was extremely pleased with himself. He stood there laughing silently, the quiet laughter flowing out of his eyes and spilling over his face like tears.

The old maidservant stood in the doorway gaping, broom and dustpan in hand. Zhenbao turned the light off. She didn't dare enter the room. Zhenbao fell asleep on the bed, slept through to the middle of the night, when mosquito bites woke him. He rose and turned on the light. A pair of Yanli's embroidered slippers were lying in the middle of the floor at cross angles, one a bit ahead, the other a bit behind, like a ghost that was afraid to materialize, walking fearfully, pleadingly toward him. Zhenbao sat on the edge of the bed and stared for a long time. When he lay down again, he sighed. He could feel his old benevolent mood stealing over him bit by bit, wrapping itself around him. Countless worries and duties and mosquitoes buzzed around him, stinging him and sucking at him.

The next day Zhenbao rose and reformed his ways. He made a fresh start and went back to being a good man.

NOTES

PREFACE TO THE SECOND PRINTING OF *ROMANCES*

In September 1944, Eileen Chang collected ten stories that she
had published in various magazines over the previous seventeen
months, made a few revisions, and published them in a volume
entitled *Chuanqi* (usually rendered as "Romances," though
"Legends," especially with the connotation of "urban legends"
would perhaps convey more of the subtly ironic flavor). The
first printing of *Romances* sold out in just a few days. Chang
wrote this preface for the second printing, which was otherwise
unchanged. Five of the six stories in the present collection come
from that edition. The sixth, "Red Rose, White Rose," was
published, in magazine form, in the summer of 1944, but Chang
revised the story quite extensively before she included it in the
1947 revised and expanded edition of *Romances*.

1 *"Hop-Hop" opera*: An operatic style that originated in the
rough rural regions of Hebei Province and eventually merged
with other styles to form Ping Opera, a popular, middlebrow
style enjoyed by many city dwellers. In keeping with her de-
liberate emphasis on the genre's earthy origins, Chang chose
(she had several options) the term *bengbengxi*, i.e., "Hop-Hop"
opera.

2 *Zhu Baoxia*: A Ping Opera actress of some renown in the
1930s.

2 *huqin*: The general name for a class of traditional string instruments which are held upright, played with a bow and fingers, and widely used for folk music and theatrical accompaniment. The tone ranges from twangy to haunting.

2 *Third Daughter Li*: A legendary heroine who (like Third Sister Wang) perseveres through the hard times that ensue when a marriage that has been ordained by fate nonetheless incurs the wrath of family members; the scene in which Li is reunited with her son after many years of hardship is particularly famous.

4 *the painted-lady type*: One of the various role types in traditional Chinese drama; the *huadan*, or painted lady, is a charming and seductive coquette (as opposed to the elegant and morally upright woman, the martial arts heroine, the wicked maidservant, the old woman, etc.).

ALOESWOOD INCENSE: THE FIRST BRAZIER

The title of this story refers to the fragrant shavings or dust of *Aquilarai agalloca*. The Chinese term, *chenxiang*, shares a character with the place-name "Hong Kong" (the English name for the city is derived from Cantonese; in Mandarin Chinese, the city is called Xianggang). This story is one of two broadly parallel tales, both set in Hong Kong, that Chang framed with this incense-burning device. "Aloeswood Incense: The Second Burning" tells of a hapless middle-aged Englishman, a university professor in Hong Kong, who is taken down the garden path by some fellow expatriates—a mother-daughter pair.

8 *Boxer-era courtesans*: The particular courtesan mentioned here is the legendary Sai Jinhua (1874–1936), whose patrons included a Chinese ambassador (with whom she went to Europe) and then, back in Beijing, a German commander who helped to put down the Boxer Rebellion. She was credited with persuading her foreign lover not to sack the Forbidden City, and so became a national heroine. Photographs of Sai Jinhua show her and her courtesan colleagues in long, heavy tunics over trousers, a style of dress that fashion-conscious girls in the 1930s and 1940s—especially those who simply followed trends— would have found ponderously old and unstylish. (Chang herself designed and wore, to great acclaim, an outfit that was loosely inspired by the old Qing tunic-and-trousers combination. Unlike Weilong, she of course integrated the modern touches into the overall design.)

13 *playing the nurse*: In traditional Chinese dramas like *The Peony Pavilion* it is the nursemaid (much like Nurse in *Romeo and Juliet*) who aids and abets secret lovers' trysts.

23 *Pu Songling's old ghost stories*: The eighteenth-century collection known as *Liaozhai zhiyi* (*Strange Tales from the Liao Studio*). Many of the stories feature fox fairies, ghostly creatures who disguise themselves as beautiful women and prey on men (in Pu's morally complex universe, the ghosts may make stronger claims on our sympathy than the humans do). Another common motif, as indicated here, is the grand home which in fact is a tomb. Many of the dupes are young traveling students—male of course. Chang shared Pu Songling's inclination toward depicting humans as morally weak or indecisive and, especially in her earliest stories, there are glimmers of the fox fairy in many of her strong female characters.

23 *Empress Cixi*: The last matriarch of the Qing imperial family, famous for suppressing all attempts at modernization and reform, and for lavish spending on useless adornments.

27 *"Dream of the Red Chamber"*: The eighteenth-century classic novel (*Honglou meng*, also known as *The Story of the Stone*) that is one of the most important influences on Chang, and on Chinese literature in general. It describes the life of a large, wealthy family and their servants, and the central plot is a love story whose purposes include the exploration of subtle emotions and a survey of the effects of experience on young, impressionable minds. The relations between masters and servants in Madame Liang's household (and in the Cao household, in "The Golden Cangue") are clearly modeled on the semifeudal social order that is detailed in this massive (120-chapter) and much-loved novel.

37 *"Secrets of the Qing Palace"*: Probably an invented title, insofar as it refers to a Hollywood production. (The Chinese phrase that Chang uses here, *Qinggong mishi*, has appeared, in recent decades, as a Chinese film title.)

45 *"Burmese Nights"*: Apparently an invented song title, though it may refer to "I'm on My Way to Mandalay," a popular song written in 1913 by Alfred Bryan and Fred Fisher. The concluding verse runs thus: "I'm on my way to Mandalay / Beneath the shelt'ring palms I want to stray / Oh, let me live and love for aye / On that Island far away / I'm sentimental for my Oriental love, so sweet and gentle / That's why I'm on my way to Mandalay / I've come to say 'Good-bye.'"

JASMINE TEA

88   *"Early Tide" magazine*: The title suggests a progressive literary-intellectual magazine of the type that flourished during the New Culture Movement (May Fourth Movement) of the 1920s. The tutor's seemingly offhand inscription would in fact be understood as quite daring, given the magazine's association with progressive ferment of all kinds, including the notion of freely chosen romantic partners.

89   *the faint shapes of tiny bats*: Bats are a traditional good-luck symbol, based on a punning association between the words for "bat" and "good fortune."

LOVE IN A FALLEN CITY

111   *huqin*: See third note to "Preface to the Second Printing of *Romances*," above.

166   *Facing life, death, distance*: A line from the third stanza of the thirty-first poem in *The Book of Songs* (composed between the fifth and tenth centuries BC); the poem's fourth stanza implies that the lovers' vow to remain faithful across time and distance was not kept.

167   *Those legendary beauties who felled cities and kingdoms*: A city-toppling woman, in ancient military strategy, is a beautiful woman who is sent to a rival in order to distract him from his city's defense. It later became a poetic compliment, roughly equivalent to "a devastating beauty."

THE GOLDEN CANGUE

The footnotes in the text of this story are reproduced from *Modern Chinese Stories and Novellas: 1919–1949* (Columbia University Press, 1981), from which Chang's translation is here reprinted.

195 *At least our Master Pai's studies could bear checking into*: Chang's Chinese text makes it clearer that Ch'i-ch'iao is not so much inviting scrutiny of her son's studies as taking comfort in the notion (her notion, anyway) that he will be subjected only to cursory examination, due to his recent bereavement. In other words, his studies can "bear checking into" because the checking won't be very rigorous.

225 *where should the mother and brother look*: Chang's Chinese text makes it clearer that the mother and son would be embarrassed (eyes casting about, at a loss for where to look), though they'd no doubt be looking for someone to blame as well.

SEALED OFF

235 The military situation that creates this interlude is presented very obliquely; all that we know is that the authorities have shut down, or cordoned off, all or part of the city. The authorities, in this case, are probably the Japanese occupiers or (more likely) the Chinese puppet government that answered to them. Chang made a point of never directly referring to the political or military situation in Shanghai prior to the defeat of the Japanese, and thus she usually escaped censorship and was never thrown in prison (as did befall those of her associates who took a more aggressive stance).

240 *the Cosmo*: *Da shijie* (a more literal translation would be "Great World"); a six-story entertainment palace filled with performance venues, food shops, and cinemas.

RED ROSE, WHITE ROSE

255 *"moonlight in front of my bed"*: The first line of a Li Po poem known to every schoolchild in China; the moonlight makes the poet think of his distant, beloved home.

256 *peach blossom fan*: The title of and central device in an eighteenth-century (Qing dynasty) play by Kong Shangran; in the play, a patriotic beauty remains faithful to her missing husband—thought by some to be dead, so that she is in some sense a widow—even when she is attacked by evildoers who want her to marry a traitorous official. As a result of the struggle, she sustains a serious head injury, and bleeds onto a white fan on which her beloved had written a wedding poem. A friend later paints some stems and leaves onto the fan, converting the bloodstains into peach blossoms.

262 *Liu Xiahui*: a sage of the Spring and Autumn Period (roughly the same era as Confucius), famous for his calm indifference to sexual provocation by a beautiful woman.

278 *the Cosmo*: See second note to "Sealed Off," above.

HALF A LIFELONG ROMANCE

Eileen Chang

'They were, he felt, like children who had made a terrible mistake'

When shy young engineer Shijun meets factory worker Manzhen, he is captivated by her hopeful nature and gentle beauty, and a relationship between them quickly blossoms. But family pressures and events beyond their power soon destroy the possibility of their future together. Can the pair find their way back to each other? Or will the trauma of their past obscure the way? Set in 1930s Shanghai, *Half a Lifelong Romance* is a rich and moving tale of love, hopefulness and the malign forces that – despite our greatest efforts – can overwhelm us.

'A dazzling and distinctive writer' *The New York Times Book Review*

OUT OF AFRICA

Karen Blixen

In 1914 Karen Blixen arrived in Kenya with her husband to run a coffee farm. Instantly drawn to the land, she spent her happiest years there until the plantation failed. Karen Blixen was forced to return to Denmark in 1931 and it was there that she wrote this classic account of her experiences. A poignant farewell to her beloved farm, *Out of Africa* describes her strong friendships with the people of her area, her affection for the landscape and animals, and great love for the adventurer Denys Finch-Hatton.

Written with astonishing clarity and an unsentimental intelligence, *Out of Africa* portrays a way of life that has disappeared for ever.

'Compelling . . . a story of passion . . . and a movingly poetic tribute to a lost land' *The Times*

THE GARDEN OF THE FINZI-CONTINIS

Giorgio Bassani

Aristocratic, rich and seemingly aloof, the Finzi-Contini family fascinate the narrator of this tale, a young Jew in the Italian city of Ferrara. But it is not until he is a student in 1938, when anti-semitic legislation is enforced on the eve of the Second World War, that he is invited onto their luxurious estate. As their gardens become a haven for persecuted Jews, the narrator becomes entwined in the lives of the family, and grows particularly close to Micòl, their daughter. Many years after the war has ended, he reflects on his memories of the Finzi-Continis, his experiences of love and loss, and the fate of the family and community in the horrors of war.

'One of the great novelists of the last century' *Guardian*

ULYSSES

James Joyce

A modernist novel of supreme stylistic innovation, James Joyce's *Ulysses* is the towering achievement of twentieth-century literature.

For Joyce, literature 'is the eternal affirmation of the spirit of man'. Written between 1914 and 1921, *Ulysses* has survived bowdlerization, legal action and bitter controversy. An undisputed modernist classic, its ceaseless verbal inventiveness and astonishing wide-ranging allusions confirms its standing as an imperishable monument to the human condition. Declan Kiberd says in his introduction that *Ulysses* is 'an endlessly open book of utopian epiphanies. It holds a mirror up to the colonial capital that was Dublin on 16 June 1904, but it also offers redemptive glimpses of a future world which might be made over in terms of those utopian moments.'

'Everybody knows now that *Ulysses* is the greatest novel of the twentieth century' Anthony Burgess

DUBLINERS

James Joyce

James Joyce's *Dubliners* is an enthralling collection of modernist short stories which create a vivid picture of the day-to-day experience of Dublin life. This Penguin Classics edition includes notes and an introduction by Terence Brown.

Joyce's first major work, written when he was only twenty-five, brought his city to the world for the first time. His stories are rooted in the rich detail of Dublin life, portraying ordinary, often defeated lives with unflinching realism. From 'The Sisters', a vivid portrait of childhood faith and guilt, to 'Araby', a timeless evocation of the inexplicable yearnings of adolescence, to 'The Dead', in which Gabriel Conroy is gradually brought to a painful epiphany regarding the nature of his existence, Joyce draws a realistic and memorable cast of Dubliners together in an powerful exploration of overarching themes. Writing of social decline, sexual desire and exploitation, corruption and personal failure, he creates a brilliantly compelling, unique vision of the world and of human experience.

'Joyce celebrates the lives of ordinary men and women' Anthony Burgess, *Observer*

FINNEGANS WAKE

James Joyce

'riverrun, past Eve and Adam's, from swerve of shore to bend of
bay, brings us by a commodius vicus of recirculation back to Howth
Castle and Environs'

A daring work of experimental, Modernist genius, *Finnegans Wake*
is one of the greatest literary achievements of the twentieth
century, and the crowning glory of Joyce's life. The Penguin
Modern Classics edition includes an introduction by Seamus Deane.

Joyce's final work, *Finnegans Wake* is his masterpiece of the night
as *Ulysses* is of the day. Supreme linguistic virtuosity conjures up the
dark underground worlds of sexuality and dreams. Joyce undermines
traditional storytelling and all official forms of English and confronts
the different kinds of betrayal – cultural, political and sexual – that he
saw at the heart of Irish history. Dazzlingly inventive, with passages
of great lyrical beauty and humour, *Finnegans Wake* remains one of
the most remarkable works of the twentieth century.

'An extraordinary performance, a transcription into a miniaturized
form of the whole western literary tradition' Seamus Deane

OTHER VOICES, OTHER ROOMS

Truman Capote

After the death of his mother, thirteen-year-old Joel Knox is summoned to live with a father he has never met in a vast decaying mansion in rural Alabama, its baroque splendour now faded and tarnished. But when he arrives, his father is nowhere to be seen and Joel is greeted instead by his prim, sullen new stepmother Miss Amy and his debauched Cousin Randolph – living like spirits in the fragile decadence of a house full of secrets.

Truman Capote's first novel, *Other Voices, Other Rooms* is a story of a hallucinatory power vividly conjuring up the Gothic landscape of the Deep South and a boy's first glimpse into a mysterious adult world.

'Exuberant, brilliant, daring, and unabashedly ostentatious' John Berednt

MUSIC FOR CHAMELEONS

Truman Capote

At the centre of *Music for Chameleons* is Handcarved Coffins, a 'non-fiction novel' based on the brutal crimes of a real-life murderer. Taking place in a small Mid-western town in America, it offers chilling insights into the mind of a killer and the obsession of the man bringing him to justice. Also in this volume are six short stories and seven 'conversational portraits', including a touching one of Marilyn Monroe, the 'beautiful child', and a hilarious one of a dope-smoking cleaning lady doing her rounds in New York.

'The superb final achievement by one of the more seriously under-valued American literary careers' *Observer*

SILENT SPRING

Rachel Carson

Now recognized as one of the most influential books of the twentieth century, *Silent Spring* exposed the destruction of wildlife through the widespread use of pesticides. Despite condemnation in the press and heavy-handed attempts by the chemical industry to ban the book, Rachel Carson succeeded in creating a new public awareness of the environment which led to changes in government policy and inspired the modern ecological movement.

'Carson's books brought ecology into popular consciousness'
Daily Telegraph

MOON TIGER

Penelope Lively

Claudia Hampton, a beautiful, famous writer, lies dying in hospital. But, as the nurses tend to her with quiet condescension, she is plotting her greatest work: 'a history of the world ... and in the process, my own.' Gradually she recreates the rich mosaic of her life and times, conjuring up those she has known. There is Gordon, her adored brother, and Jasper, her charming, untrustworthy lover and father of Lisa, her cool, conventional daughter. Then there is Tom, her one great love, both found and lost in wartime Egypt. Penelope Lively's Booker Prize-winning novel weaves an exquisite mesh of memories, flashbacks and shifting voices, in a haunting story of loss and desire.

'Leaves its traces in the air long after you've put it away' Anne Tyler

BABETTE'S FEAST AND OTHER STORIES

Isak Dinesen (Karen Blixen)

These five rich, witty and magical stories from the author of *Out of Africa* include one of her most well-known tales, 'Babette's Feast', which was made into the classic film. It tells the story of a French cook working in a puritanical Norweigan community, who treats her employers to the decadent feast of a lifetime. There is also a real-life Prospero and his Ariel in 'Tempests', a mysterious pearl-fisher in 'The Diver', and a brief, tragic encounter in 'The Ring'. All the stories have a mystic, fairy-tale quality, linked by themes of angels, the sea, dreams and fate. They were among the last to be written by Isak Dinesen, and show her as a master of short fiction. .

'Acutely perceptive, often mysterious stories' *Sunday Telegraph*

ATLAS SHRUGGED

Ayn Rand

Opening with the enigmatic question 'Who is John Galt?', *Atlas Shrugged* envisions a world where 'men of talent' – the great innovators, producers and creators – have mysteriously disappeared. With the US economy now faltering, business-woman Dagny Taggart is struggling to get the transcontinental railroad up and running. For her, John Galt is the enemy but, as she will learn, nothing in this situation is quite as it seems.

Hugely influential and grand in scope, this story of a man who stopped the motor of the world expounds Rand's controversial philosophy of Objectivism, which champions competition, creativity and human greatness.

'A writer of great power ... she writes brilliantly, beautifully, bitterly'
The New York Times